THE
CARNIVAL
AND OTHER STORIES

THE CARNIVAL

AND OTHER STORIES

CHARLES BEAUMONT

SUBTERRANEAN PRESS
2022

First Edition

ISBN
978-1-64524-091-4

Subterranean Press
PO Box 190106
Burton, MI 48519

subterraneanpress.com

Manufactured in the United States of America

TABLE OF CONTENTS

INTRODUCTION:
THE RETURN OF THE MAGIC MAN
by David J. Schow

hen Charles Beaumont died in 1967, I was eleven years old. I never enjoyed the opportunity to shake his hand, or dine with him, or exchange stories. Soon enough, I grew to know him exclusively via his work.

The Twilight Zone was culturally omnipresent, of course, and Beaumont's imprint upon it was indelible and unavoidable. Consider poor Edward Simms, aged far beyond his calendar years in the short story "You Can't Have Them All"—a presagement, not only of Beaumont's premature fate but that of his *Twilight Zone* avatar, Walter Jameson. It was first published in 1954.

Never having enough time was the ostinato of Chuck Beaumont's symphony.

I'm not a Beaumont biographer. Fortunately, known data is fairly available: his childhood meningitis, the five widowed aunts, "Nutt" becomes "McNutt" becomes "Beaumont", odd jobs, false starts, gradual traction, a burgeoning family to support, the $500 *Playboy* retainer fee, race cars, "imported" peanut butter, all his deliriously multidirectional talents and interests.

I hasten to add that my special qualifications for ruminating about Chuck Beaumont amount to exactly zero. I am not Richard Matheson,

nor Chris Beaumont, nor Roger Anker,* all of whom have been diligently drained of recollect in the service of many preceding Beaumont
assemblies—more new collections, in fact, than were published when
Beaumont was alive. Their persistence is another testament to his
longevity.

Tell us more, we beseech the survivors, the intimates. *Tell us again.*
Ultimately the work has to command the podium.

I always saw Beaumont's prose as fitting comfortably into the
realm of John Collier or Gerald Kersh—in fact, almost a bridge
between the two—and a complimentary though polar opposite to the
output of one of his closest intimates, who was also the third member of the *Twilight Zone* trifecta after Beaumont and series creator
Rod Serling: Richard Matheson. In turn, Ray Bradbury, whom they
all admired, cited Roald Dahl or Nigel Kneale, but always came back
to Collier—all spokes of the same creative wheel, very much akin to
the later groupings dubbed the Green Hand, or the Group, or the
California Sorcerers (essentially the loose treehouse of fifteen or so
writers whom critic Robert Kirsch of the *Los Angeles Times* dubbed
"the Southern California school"). Bradbury in fact cited Collier and
Dahl directly in his introduction to the posthumous Beaumont collection, *Best of Beaumont* (Bantam 1982). Seventeen years earlier, while
Beaumont was still alive, Bradbury had written another encomium for
The Magic Man (Fawcett 1965):

> *Some writers are one-idea people. Other writers, far rarer, far*
> *wilder, are pomegranates. They burst with seed. Charles has*
> *always been a pomegranate writer. You simply never know where*
> *his love and high excitement will take him next.*

---

* However, Roger Anker is presently completing a massive and comprehen-
sive Beaumont biography—*Trapped in the Twilight Zone: The Life and Times
of Charles Beaumont*—that extends to nearly 300,000 words, which may be
available shortly after you read this. And it is *wonderful*.

There's a *Twilight Zone* episode called "A Penny for Your Thoughts," written by Beaumont confederate George Clayton Johnson (as his first original submission to the series—two prior story sales had been scripted by Rod Serling). It is the stressful tale of Hector Poole, a milquetoast bank teller who flips a coin into the change box of a newsvendor only to see the coin land perfectly in its edge—after which Poole discovers he has gained the ability to read other peoples' thoughts!

To me, Chuck Beaumont and Richard Matheson were the opposite sides of that coin, and Serling's *Twilight Zone* was the edge they landed upon. A precarious, impossible, complimentary balancing act, consistently renewed, consistently surprising, and utterly in tune with the environs of Serling's new neighborhood, almost as if the Zone had been constructed as their playground. They were fast friends and committed allies, but one was just slightly *darker* than the other.

Matheson was a homebody and family man who enjoyed explorations of "ordinary people in extraordinary circumstances." Beaumont did this as well, but his characters and themes seemed to hew toward the nightside of the alley—grimmer, more nihilistic, with more unforgiving fates in store. *Darker.* By and large the Matheson narratives for *Twilight Zone* concluded with a comfy restoration of order; Beaumont's, by contrast, often lead to death, madness, or worse things waiting.

As Lee Prosser once wrote, "Pursuit of a dream, loneliness, and death were three of his major themes."

Bradbury, Kersh, and Collier were all in the front lines of the war to make fantasists more respectable in literature by transcending their pulp origins. Publication in slicks such as *Collier's* or *The Saturday Evening Post* was hard-won. Ray Russell made no secret of the fact that he found "traditional" sci-fi bottomlesssly dull, but when he became the fiction editor of the still-new *Playboy* in 1954, he serialized Bradbury's *The Martian Chronicles* and championed Chuck Beaumont, whose sale of "Perchance to Dream" to the October 1958 issue became his very first *Twilight Zone* episode the very next year.

9

It was also the first produced episode of the series to be scripted by somebody other than Rod Serling.

Serling's concomitant urge to qualify fantasy as legit is an important insight into an era when science fictional or horror themes were automatically sidelined as juvenilia. During this period the Beats started to gain the notice and sponsorship of major New York publishers with real book deals. Genre writers were classed with downscale sensationalism and penny-per word hackery. This was a strait-jacket that needed shucking, and *Twilight Zone* proved that regular, ordinary folks, once led to the well of fantasy, would eagerly drink of their own accord.

Russell—who had published Jack Kerouac by 1957—later contended that the lure of television and feature films diluted Beaumont's public profile as a serious author. I would add to that, as culprit, a lack of *novels.* This was a period when big, dense, serious books were all the rage—everything from beach behemoths like *Exodus* (Leon Uris) and *Hawaii* (James Michener) to William Burroughs' *Naked Lunch* and Vladimir Nabokov's *Lolita.*

Beaumont only published two novels in his lifetime: a pellmell suspenser co-written with John Tomerlin (collectively as "Keith Grantland"), *Run from the Hunter* (Fawcett 1957), and a crackling, timely drama about bigotry and racism, *The Intruder* (Putnam's 1959) (later to become the only Roger Corman film that ever lost money, according to Corman; in a word, a "message picture"). Meanwhile, Richard Matheson had already published two of his most impactful books, *I Am Legend* (Gold Medal 1954) and *The Shrinking Man* (Gold Medal 1956). Beaumont's long-in-work novel, *Where No Man Walks* (begun in 1957), was never completed beyond a smatter of endlessly-rewritten chapters. His fourth short story collection, *A Touch of the Creature*, suffered a similar death-by-delay as he began to succumb to the malady that would destroy the remainder of his too-short life. *

---

* *A Touch of the Creature* was the original title of the collection ultimately issued as *Night Ride and Other Journeys* (Bantam 1960) after undergoing many changes in the content lineup. A new collection of oddities and rarities titled *A Touch of the Creature* was published by Subterranean Press in 2000.

Alzheimer's Disease and associated degenerative dementias were not commonly known or discussed until the mid-1970s. Like Serling (who died at age 50), Beaumont was a workaholic and heavy smoker.

During Beaumont's heyday, the prejudice or preference of editors was that short stories could only lead to novels…or lead writers astray from publishing with film or TV deals. Bradbury had certainly become a household name with few novels to show for it, and others attempted or preferred the gem-like polish and perfection of a good story to the time-suck and sprawl of a novel. I'd class both Beaumont and Matheson in this company, as well as Fritz Leiber, Theodore Sturgeon, Harlan Ellison, Jane Rice and yes, even John Collier. Gerald Kersh produced plenty of novels but is little-read today.

Two sides of the same coin: Beaumont mostly adapted his published fiction, while Matheson tended to write originals for Serling. Mostly. Beaumont favored often-extravagant character names ("Sherman Boetticher," "Gavin McCreigh," "Pearl Jacobean," etc.)* while Matheson often repurposed the names of his own family members—Richard, Dick, Ruth, Chris and so on.

Both Beaumont and Matheson wrote roughly a hundred short stories each, many variously repurposed into other media. The two friends also collaborated on the screenplay for *Night of the Eagle* (1962), aka *Burn Witch Burn*, an adaptation of Fritz Leiber's novel *Conjure Wife*. Beaumont wrote a great deal of nonfiction but Matheson, to my knowledge, did only a single piece (outside of appreciations, intros, afterwords and the like): "SF Unlimited," for the April 1956 issue of *Writer's Digest*. By contrast, anyone seeking insight into Beaumont's passions would do well to hunt up *Remember? Remember?* (Macmillan 1963), his collected essays for *Playboy*,

---

* "Boetticher" from director Bud Boetticher, obviously. "Gershenson" in "The Man with the Crooked Nose" most likely references Joseph Gershenson, a music supervisor Beaumont would have met while working at Universal Studios, where Boetticher also toiled on the B-unit. "Korngold," in "The Trigger"? Oscar-winning composer Erich Korngold.

et al, on everything from the heyday of pulp magazines to the loss of cinema palaces. When Beaumont rhapsodizes about the nostalgia of classic radio or movie serials (each of which he breaks down into distinct, almost scholarly periods), he makes Bradbury sound saccharine, or Ellison, bombastic—to the discredit of neither writer, of course. Beaumont's focus is sharper and more on the mark as a documentarian, while not beyond the wistful, he doesn't let the tendency fog his lens, either.

You should seek out that book and read it, as soon as you finish this one. It's akin to a *Twilight Zone* chapter-play about revisiting lost loves and watching them live again, if only for one final, scintillant moment. Beaumont's entry on how Charlie Chaplin was rejected by America is heartbreaking because it's true, perhaps even forgotten, now:

> *Film doesn't last forever, and memory fades. And though we speak of a wonder that held the world enchanted for three generations, the wonder has demonstrably begun to dim. The young in America do not know Chaplin at all, except as the monster the press has built, and that is sad...and tragic. For the artist and his art, separable as they may and must be, are of vital importance to the cultural and moral development of America. If we allow ourselves to forget what we had, then we shall never understand what we lost, and that will make us poor indeed.*

It's rather what I imagine having a conversation with Chuck himself might have been like.

Tell us more, Chuck. Tell us again.

CHUCK BEAUMONT died at age 38. Had he achieved the longevity of Bradbury (91), Matheson (87) or Ellison (83), we might not have seen many of the stories in this volume—ever. At least, they might have "appeared differently," for in the 1960s specialty publishers had fewer professional resources and were much more (ahem) subterranean. But for the singular exception of the mass-market *Best of Beaumont* in '82 (yes, *four decades* ago), most of our earnest resurrections have been as much a matter of archeology as bibliography; dusting off, reconstructing fragments, reconsidering stray manuscripts. Thanks to the small press—and what it grew into, starting in the 1990s—Beaumont lives.

Following *The Hunger and Other Stories* (Bantam 1957), *Yonder* (Bantam 1958) and *Night Ride and Other Journeys* (Bantam 1960), those contents were redistributed into *The Magic Man* (Gold Medal 1965) and *The Edge* (Panther [UK only] 1966). *Best of Beaumont* featured four newly-published tales. Further file finds—some never published, some unpolished, some never collected—appeared in *Charles Beaumont: Selected Stories* (Dark Harvest, 1988), which was reprinted in paperback as *The Howling Man* (Tor, 1992). The previously-cited *A Touch of the Creature* (Subterranean 2000) added fourteen more tales to the brew (with three *additional* stories in a special lettered edition) and the beautiful-but-pricey *Mass for Mixed Voices* (Centipede, 2013) revisited the contents of *Selected Stories* and added two more, both offered here as well. These latter collections were showcased as limited editions which quickly sold out, making their contents fair game for regrouping.

In 2015 Penguin Classics presented *Perchance to Dream*, a Beaumont "greatest hits" sampler to demonstrate what readers had been missing, nearly a half-century after his death. That same year, they also offered a trade paper reprint of *A Touch of the Creature*, with all stories accounted for. Valencourt's approach was very similar to that of Penguin Classics, which around the same time began to produce very welcome (and affordable) collections of work by Shirley Jackson and Richard Matheson.

It just so happens that Beaumont's first-ever published story, **"The Devil, You Say?"** (1951), formed the basis for one of my very favorite *Twilight Zones*, "Printer's Devil," featuring Burgess Meredith as the diabolical Mr. Jones ("Mr. Smith" in the TV version). Most of the stories from this early period reflect Beaumont's safe landing in an assortment of popular digest-sized sci-fi magazines; this debut occurred in *Amazing Stories*.

"Elegy" (1953) published in *Imagination*, was also fated to become a *Twilight Zone* episode, with very strong reverberations of Bradbury's "Mars is Heaven" (first published in 1948). Mr. Greypoole becomes the show's "Jeremy Wickwire," who serves the men Liebfraumilch. (In the story it's apricot [not dandelion!] wine).

The worst of pulp sci-fi meets the worst of pulp hardboiled crime in **"The Last Caper"** (1954), a quick jape written for *The Magazine of Fantasy & Science Fiction*. By 1954, *everybody* was aware of Mickey Spillane's million-selling thug, Mike Hammer, hence this story's "Mike Mallet." This tale functions best on the level of snappy patter, almost stream-of-consciousness writing—a fast grind to fill a hole, or snatch a paycheck.

Johnmartin simply does not wish to die, *ever*, in **"Mass for Mixed Voices"** (1954) published in *Science Fiction Quarterly*. Whereas most stories about immortality emphasize the longing, regret and ennui of endless years, Johnmartin embraces the exact opposite, for the best reasons, in this early glimpse of "modern" Beaumont writing—a bittersweet, heartfelt character doomed by a relentless system.

Similarly, Lorenzo Gissing becomes a death obsessive in **"Hair of the Dog"** (1954) from *Orbit* #3. The character is pointedly named after the famous author of *New Grub Street* (1891), an evergreen go-to novel for any writer compelled to hack for a living. And like nearly all those writers, Beaumont more than once visited the devil's-deal-gone-wrong story, as here.

In the current madhouse of streaming, "immersive" entertainment in 4K, 6K and 8K, **"The Quadropticon"** (from *The Magazine of Fantasy & Science Fiction*, 1954) could have been written this afternoon. In all the ensuing years, no other conceit in the story has changed by a particle. The rocket jockey foolishness at center stage here can easily be read as a foretaste of what Beaumont would have to endure during production of *Queen of Outer Space* in 1956—his first feature screenplay gig. (See how much the Death Ray from this story reminds you of the Beta Disintegrator from the movie.)

With one foot in the genre mags and the other planted firmly in the slicks via seven story sales to *Playboy* (through 1954-56), Beaumont made his debut appearance in a competing "girlie mag," *Rogue*, with **"The Love Master"** (1957) under the pseudonym "S.M. Tenneshaw," which had been used by a number of writers who needed to diversify into alternate identities for the sake of sales, notably Frank M. Robinson, the editor who bought the story! (Other "Tenneshaws" included Robert Silverberg, John Jakes, and Edmond Hamilton.) "The Love Master" is a direct lineal descendant of John Collier's "The Chaser" (1940, later adapted as a *Twilight Zone* episode.)

By the time **"A World of Differents"** debuted in the collection *Yonder* in 1958, *The Hunger and Other Stories* had appeared in hardcover under the subtitle *A Collection of Violent Entertainments*, and more printed Beaumont short stories were available than ever before. Also new to *Yonder* were **"Anthem"** and **"Mother's Day."** (I would not wish to be the person tasked with proofreading "Differents.")

Beaumont's love for fast cars and auto racing informs **"The Trigger,"** from *Mystery Digest* (1958). You can find further intel about hot wheels and high revs in his only other book-length work, *Omnibus of Speed* (G.P. Putnam's 1958), co-edited with William F. Nolan.

By 1959, Harlan Ellison had become the fiction editor at *Rogue*, and concocted the "C.B. Lovehill" pseudonym for Beaumont's contribution "The Howling Man." As Ellison wrote in *Selected Stories*: "The C and B are obvious; *beau* I twisted out of the French to get *love*, though idiomatically it was a stretch, and *mont* became *hill*." On the contributor's page the photo of "Lovehill" was actually fellow editor Frank Robinson. The pen-name was deployed for other Beaumont stories in *Rogue*, including **"Genevieve, My Genevieve."**

Original to *Night Ride* (1960) was **"Buck Fever,"** an achingly beautiful horror about sighting life through a rifle scope and deciding whether to take it...or not.

C.B. Lovehill returned to *Rogue* with **"Dead You Know"** (December 1960), in which Diggory Sprool attempts to work out the tried-and-true voodoo plot against Emma Hurlbut—oh, those *names* again!—but with a *life-sized* effigy. Then the story hangs left into an ending so abrupt that it's a separate shock.

"Mourning Song," featured in *Gamma* #1 (1963), was the last completed short story Beaumont would ever write, according to William F. Nolan, who related to Darrell Schweitzer in *Speaking of Horror: Interviews with Writers of the Supernatural* (Borgo Press 1994): "*Gamma* was a West Coast magazine created by Charles E. Fritch, who was to become a long-time editor of *Mike Shayne's Mystery Magazine* in later years. He got together with another writer named Jack Matcha, and myself, and the three of us launched *Gamma*. We used the *The Magazine of Fantasy & Science Fiction* as our model. We put out five issues over a two-and-a-half year period. Terrible distribution problems finally killed it."

"Mourning Song" illustrates the prose mastery Beaumont had achieved, once he stopped trying to please the pulps or service the digests. Gentler—like an Earl Hamner *Twilight Zone*—yet darker, evoking Manly Wade Wellman's John the Balladeer (also note the writer's modernist abandonment of formal quotation marks, here).

"Something in the Earth" was a much older trunk story that appeared in *Gamma* #2 (1963).

Beaumont's final original script—that is, not farmed out or ghostwritten—was "An Ordinary Town," which he pitched and sold to *The Outer Limits* in December, 1963, shortly after the publication of *Remember? Remember?* Beaumont's revision of his first draft teleplay was dated January 3rd, 1964. The episode was never produced. That same month, CBS definitively canceled *The Twilight Zone* after five seasons.

Charles Beaumont died February 21st, 1967, in Woodland Hills, California.

Eighteen years later, **"Insomnia Vobiscum"** would debut in *Best of Beaumont* (Bantam 1982). It is almost literally a one-liner, inadequate to the long absence of Beaumont from the printed page.

Now dead, Beaumont speaks to us quite frankly of death and its portents in **"My Grandmother's Japonicas,"** a semi-autobiographical turn about the death of his mother written sometime in 1954. Its tone is a bit more what we want from "resurrected" Beaumont—the voice of a long-absent friend returned, whether from vacation or recuperation, different yet the same, identifiable but with its fidelity mysteriously adjusted. Death in one form or another shadows every paragraph, especially "lingering" death, in very conscious evocations of Poe. It was finally published in the 1984 small press anthology *Masques*, edited by J.N. Williamson.

The remainder of the newly-presented tales fell to the stewardship of Roger Anker, who slotte: **"Appointment with Eddie," "The Carnival,"** and **"The Crime of Willie Washington"** into *Selected Stories*, which also featured introductory reminiscences by everyone from Matheson, Ellison and Bradbury to Ray Russell, Frank Robinson, and Robert Bloch.

Almost immediately thereafter, "The Carnival" became the center-piece of a special feature in *Rod Serling's The Twilight Zone Magazine* (June 1989), focusing on Beaumont's life and career. Ironically it was the final issue of the magazine; its swan song.

"The Wages of Cynicism" came as a very brief Beaumont con-tribution to *California Sorcery* (Cemetery Dance, 1999) via co-editor William Schafer, whose own Subterranean Press would publish *A Touch of the Creature* the very next year. Apparently "Cynicism" failed to make the cut, but was a good fit as an "original" to an anthology showcasing the Group with all new, original stories, except for three reprints; two of these due to the deaths of Group members Chad Oliver (died 1993) and Robert Bloch (died 1994). Bill Nolan was co-editor of the project.

Technically, the first appearance of **"The Child"** was as a 552-copy chapbook designed as a bonus to accompany the publication of *The Twilight Zone Scripts of Charles Beaumont* (Gauntlet Press, 2004), edited by Roger Anker, who later incorporated the story into *Mass for Mixed Voices*, along with "The Life of the Party."

Completely new to this present volume, previously uncollected, and never before published anywhere is **"Beast of the Glacier,"** which reads unavoidably like a movie treatment thanks to the present tense and the way it presents plot beats. Regardless, it's an interesting yarn (as they called 'em in those days) just a tiny bit reminiscent of Karl Edward Wagner's subsequent medical horror story "The Fourth Seal."

BY NOW you may have perceived that the contents of this book represent samples from practically *every single one* of Beaumont's published collections (absent the reprint books and *A Touch of the Creature*)—a double album, if you will, hinged on cusp between his life and death.

A few more points of connection:

Roger Anker described Beaumont's meeting with John Tomerlin: "(W)hile working as a tracing clerk for California Motor Express in 1949...the two discovered they shared a passion for words (as well as a skill for getting out of work)."

Now *that* I can relate to. The feeling that every moment spent not writing is a tiny death, that even eating and sleeping and—Zeus forbid—earning a living to feed the home fires might be writing time squandered, another idea lost, another story evaporated. It's the obsession that turns the muse into a near-sadistic lover, demanding and punitive.

Which is why Chris Beaumont has heartbreakingly bittersweet memories of his father as absent, yet present—in the way of those rare people who, when you speak to them, have the uncanny knack of making you feel like you're the only person in the room. You have their full attention and engagement, but only for that brief window of time until they fly away to slay some other dragon or chase a shooting star of inspiration, which objective then commands equally full notice.

Success, to an extent, had made Charles Beaumont a husband and father in absentia. My own father was mostly gone, working his ass off in the Arctic Circle, from the time I was in fourth grade until I was a junior in high school, by which time I was very definitely a self-made lost soul. (In my case as well, a 16-year-old became the "man of the house"—my older brother, Leo.)

A codicil to this ability mentioned above—call it the magic of deep focus—is the power to juggle a dozen projects at once, yet make everyone feel you are working for them alone. I can relate to that, too. It's not a personality flaw (I hope) so much as a survival mechanism biased toward *getting the job done and segueing on to the next job*. Focus and large swaths of concentration are often going to be taken personally as slights by people you love. They may not comprehend or have experienced the ability to think inside the netherzone, the workplace where five hours can vanish like five minutes.

Something that rebounded cruelly on Chuck as he began to age in fast-forward.

As for juggling assignments, I've done that, too, with a number of TV tie-in paperbacks, on behalf of a couple of friends who didn't mind being walked into their first (and frequently *only*) book credit, albeit pseudonymously. I'd secure the deal and sometimes write the first chapter or three, hand them a deadline and some cash, and *abracadabra*! Sometimes it actually worked out. Other times it turned into a rescue operation. I felt a little bit like Beaumont must have felt, parceling out magazine and *Twilight Zone* assignments to fellow members of the Green Hand or the Group. Why, again? Because after breaking the ice with a studio licensing department and delivering the goods to their satisfaction, they were offering me multi-book deals, sometimes for four books at once.

I have also experienced lucid dreaming and the ability Beaumont once described as "dreaming in chapters"—that is, the dreams are progressive and episodic. But to my certain recollect, I've never had a nightmare...at least not while dreaming.

Mind you, I am in no way trying to set myself up as some sort of analogue to Charles Beaumont, neither as peer nor fellow traveler. I would not claim to come close to the staggering level of his talent, which prompts my admiration. I know the man solely and completely through his work. But thanks to many of the same experiences, I feel a sense of distant kinship with his life, which has impacted me in many terrific ways, and continues to enrich my existence. I have no idea *what* might lie in wait on the flipside of my own magic coin.

My favorite photo of Chuck Beaumont is from that October 1958 issue of *Playboy*, which as a bonus features a pictorial on Mara Corday (of *Tarantula*, *The Giant Claw* and *The Black Scorpion*). The candid snap is of Chuck on the set of *Queen of Outer Space* with Zsa Zsa Gabor. As noted, it's also the issue that first published "Perchance to Dream."

Prefacing that selfsame story as editor for the anthology *The Fiend in You* (Ballantine 1962), Beaumont observed:

> *A train thunders by late at night, you gaze idly at the dark rushing mass, you see a patch of light and within that patch of light, a face; in a wink of time it is gone—but, having seen it, you know it will never be gone, you know you will see that face in your dreams perhaps forever. Such is the insubstantial stuff of which fiction—or madness—is made.*

That's also what reading a Beaumont story at its very best can feel like. So here are a passel of them, for your reading pleasure.

The coin is impossibly standing on its edge and we have literally gained the ability to read the thoughts of Charles Beaumont!

Diligently, do we come back to the Beaumont wellspring. *Tell us more, Chuck. Tell us again.*

— David J. Schow

Many thanks to Roger Anker and John Scoleri for helping out with all the whys and wherefores — DJS.

THE DEVIL, YOU SAY?

(1951)

It was two o'clock in the morning when I decided that my attendance at a meeting of the International Newspapermen's Society for the Prevention of Thirst was a matter of moral necessity. This noble Brotherhood, steeped in tradition and by now as immortal as the institution of the public press, has always been a haven, a refuge, and an inspiration to weary souls in the newspaper profession. Its gatherings at Ada's Bar & Grill—Open 24 Hours A Day—have made more than a few dismiss their woes for a while.

I had just covered a terrifically drab story which depended nine tenths upon the typewriter for its effect, and both brain and throat had grown quite dry in consequence. The extra block and a half over to Ada's was a completely natural detour.

As usual at this time of day, the only customers were newspapermen.

Joe Barnes of the *Herald* was there, also Mary Kepner and Frank Monteverdi of the *Express*. Warren Jackson, the *Globe's* drama critic, sat musing over a cigar, and Mack Sargent, who got paid for being the *News's* sports man, seemed to be fascinated by improvising multiple beer rings on the tablecloth.

The only one I was surprised to see was Dick Lewis, a featured columnist for the *Express* who'd lately hit the syndicates. He usually didn't drop in to Ada's more than two or three times a month, and then he never added much to the conversation.

Not that he wasn't likable. As a matter of fact, Dick always put a certain color into the get-togethers, by reason of being such a clam. It gave him a secretive or "Mystery Man" appearance, and that's always stimulating to gabfests which occasionally verge towards the monotonous.

He sat in one of the corner booths, looking as though he didn't give a damn about anything. A little different this time, a little lower at the mouth. Having looked into mirrors many times myself, I'd come to recognize the old half-closed eyelids that didn't result from mere tiredness. Dick sat there considering his half-empty stein and stifling only a small percentage of burps. Clearly he had been there some time and had considered a great many such half-empty steins.

I drew up a chair, tossed off an all-inclusive nod of greeting and listened for a few seconds to Frank's story of how he had scooped everybody in the city on the *Lusitania* disaster, only to get knocked senseless by an automobile ten seconds before he could get to a phone. The story died in the midsection, and we all sat for a half hour or so quaffing cool ones, hiccoughing and apologizing.

One of the wonderful things about beer is that a little bit, sipped with the proper speed, can give one the courage to do and say things one would ordinarily not have the courage to even dream of doing and saying. I had absorbed, *presto*, sufficient of the miracle drug by the time the clock got to three am, to do something I guess I'd wanted to do in the back of my mind for a long time. My voice was loud and clear and charged with insinuation. Everybody looked up.

"Damnit, Lewis," I said, pointing directly at him, "in order to be a member in good standing of this Society, you've just got to say something interesting. A guy simply doesn't look as inscrutable as you do without having something on his mind. You've listened to our stories. Now how about one of your own?"

"Yeah," joined Monteverdi, "Ed's right. You might call it your dues."

Jackson looked pleased and put in: "See here, Lewis, you're a newsman, aren't you? Surely you have *one* halfway diverting story."

"If it's personal," I said, "so much the better. I mean, after all, we're a Brotherhood here."

And that started it. Pretty soon we were all glaring at poor Dick, looking resentful and defiant.

He then surprised us. He threw down the last of his drink, ordered three more, stared us each in the face one by one and said:

"Okay. All right. You're all just drunk enough to listen without calling for the boys in white, though you'll still think I'm the damndest liar in the state. All right, I admit it. I do have something on my mind. Something you won't believe worth beans. And let me tell you something else. I'm quitting this screwball racket, so I don't care what you think."

He drained another steinful.

"I'm going to tell you why as of tomorrow I start looking for some nice quiet job in a boiler factory. Or maybe as a missionary."

And this is the story Dick Lewis told that night. He was either mightily drunk or crazy as a coot, because you could tell he believed every word he said.

I'm not sure about any of it, myself. All I know for certain is that he actually did quit the game just as he said he would, and since that night I haven't even heard his name.

WHEN MY father died he left me a hundred and twenty-two dollars, his collection of plastic-coated insects, and complete ownership of the *Danville Daily Courier*. He'd owned and edited the *Courier* for fifty-five years and although it never made any money for him, he loved it with all his heart. I sometimes used to think that it was the most precious thing in life to him. For whenever there wasn't any news—which was all the time—he'd pour out his inner thoughts, his history, his whole soul into the columns. It was a lot more than just a small-town newspaper to Dad: it was his life.

I cut my first teeth on the old handpress and spent most of my time in the office and back room. Pop used to say to me, "You weren't born, lad, you appeared one day out of a bottle of printer's ink." Corny, but I must have believed him, because I grew up loving it all.

What we lived on those days was a mystery to me. Not enough issues of the *Courier* were sold even to pay for the paper stock. Nobody bought it because there was never anything to read of any inter-est — aside from Dad's personal column, which was understandably limited in its appeal. For similar reasons, no one ever advertised. He couldn't afford any of the press services or syndicates, and Danville wasn't homebody enough a town to give much of a darn how Mrs Piddle's milk cows were coming along.

I don't even know how he managed to pay the few hands around the place. But Dad didn't seem to worry, so I never gave the low circulation figures a great deal of thought.

That is, I didn't until it was my turn to take over.

After the first month I began to think about it a lot. I remember sitting in the office alone one night, wondering just how the hell Dad ever did it. And I don't mind saying, I cussed his hide for not ever tell-ing me. He was a queer old duck and maybe this was meant as a test or something.

If so, I had flunked out on the first round.

I sat there staring dumbly at the expense account and wondering, in a half-stupid way, how such a pretty color as red ever got mixed up with so black a thing as being broke.

I wondered what earthly good a newspaper was to Danville. It was a town unusual only because of its concentrated monotony: nothing ever happened. Which is news just once, not once a day. Everybody was happy, nobody was starving; everlasting duties were tended to with a complete lack of reluctance. If everyplace in the world had been like Danville, old Heraclitus wouldn't have been given a second thought. It hadn't had so much as a drunken brawl since 1800.

So I figured it all out that night. I'd take the sheets of paper in front of me and pitch them into the wastebasket. Within an hour I'd call up everyone who worked with me, including the delivery boys, and tell them that the *Danville Daily Courier* had seen its day. Those people with subscriptions, I thought, would have to try to find me. I had about ten dollars left and owed twenty times that in rent and credit.

I suppose you just don't decide to close up business and actually close it up—right down to firing all the help—in an hour's time. But that's what I was going to do. I didn't take anything into consideration except the fact that I had to go somewhere and get a job quick, or I'd end being the first person in Danville's history to die of starvation. So I figured to lock up the office, go home and get my things together, and leave the next afternoon for some nearby city.

I knew that if I didn't act that fast, if I stayed and tried to sell the office and the house, I'd never get out of Danville. You don't carry out flash decisions if you wait around to weigh their consequences. You've got to act. So that's what I started to do.

But I didn't get far. About the time I had it all nicely resolved and justified, I was scared out of my shoes by a polite sort of cough, right next to me. It was after midnight and subconsciously I realized that this was neither the time nor the place for polite coughs—at least ones I didn't make. Especially since I hadn't heard anyone come in.

An old boy who must have been crowding ninety stood in front of the desk, staring at me. And I stared right back. He was dressed in the sporty style of the 1890s, with whiskers all over his face and a little black derby which canted jauntily over his left eye.

"Mr Lewis?" he said, hopping on the side of the desk and taking off his white gloves, finger by finger. "Mr Richard Lewis?"

"Yes, that's right," is what I said.

"The son of Elmer Lewis?"

I nodded, and I'll bet my mouth was wide open. He took out a big cigar and lit it.

"If I may be so rude," I finally managed to get out, "who the hell are you and how did you get in here?"

His eyes twinkled and immediately I was sorry for having been so abrupt. I don't know why, but I added, "After all, y'know, it's pretty late."

The old geezer just sat there smiling and puffing smoke into the air.

"Did you want to see me about something, Mr—"

"Call me Jones, my boy, call me Jones. Yes, as a matter of fact, I do have some business with you. Y'see, I knew your father quite well once upon a time — might say he and I were very close friends. Business partners too, you might say. Yes. Business partners. Tell me, Richard, did you ever know your father to be unhappy?"

It was an odd conversation, but Mr Jones was far too friendly and ingratiating to get anything but courtesy out of me. I answered him honestly.

"No, Dad was always about the happiest person I've ever seen. Except when Mother died, of course."

Jones shifted and waved his cane in the air.

"Of course, of course. But aside from that. Did he have any grievances about life, any particular concern over the fact that his newspaper was never very, shall we say, successful? In a word, Richard, was your father content to the day he died?"

"Yes, I'd say he was. At least I never heard him complain. Dad never wanted anything but a chance to putter around the office, write his column, and collect bugs."

At this he whacked the desk and grinned until all I could see was teeth. "Ah, that's very good, m'boy, very good. Times haven't been like they were in the old days. I'd begun to wonder if I was as good as I made out to be. Why, do you know that Elmer was my first customer since that time Dan'l Webster made such a fool of me! Oh, that was rich. You've got to hand it to those New Hampshire lawyers, you've just got to hand it to them."

He sat chuckling and puffing out smoke, and, looking squarely at the situation, I began to get a very uncomfortable sensation along the back of my spine.

"Your dad wasn't any slouch, though, let me tell you, Dick. That part of the deal is over. He got what he wanted out of his life on Earth and now he's—what's that wonderful little expression somebody started a few centuries ago?—oh yes, he's paying the fiddler. But things were almost as bad then as they are now, I mean as far as signed, paid-up contracts go. Oh, I tell you, you humans are getting altogether too shrewd for your own good. What with wars and crime and politicians and the like, I scarcely have anything to do these days. No fun in merely shoveling 'em in."

A long, gassy sigh.

"Yes sir, Elmer was on to me all right. He played his cards mighty clever. Included you, Dick m'boy. So all I have to do is make you happy and, well then, the deal's closed."

By this time I felt pretty much like jumping out the window, but shot nerves or not, I was able to say:

"Look, Grandpa, I don't know what in hell you're talking about. I'm in no mood for this sort of thing and don't particularly care to be. If you were a friend of Pop's I'm glad to see you and all that, but if you came here for hospitality I'm afraid you're out of luck. I'm leaving town tomorrow. If you'd like, I'll walk you to a nice clean hotel."

"Ah," he said, pushing me back into my chair with his cane, "you don't understand. Lad, I've not had much practice lately and may be a trifle on the rusty side, but you must give me my dues. Let me see—if I remember correctly, the monthly cash stipend was not included and therefore was not passed on to you."

"Look—"

"The hundred and fifty a month your father got, I mean. I see you know nothing of it. Cautious one, Elmer. Take it easy, son, take it easy. Your troubles are over."

This was too much. I got up and almost shouted at him.

"I've got enough troubles already, without a loony old bird like you busting in on me. Do we take you to a hotel, or do you start traveling?"

He just sat there and laughed like a jackass, poking me with his cane and flicking cigar ashes all over the floor.

"Dick m'boy, it's a pity you don't want out of life what your father did. In a way, that would have simplified things. As it is, I'm going to have to get out the old bag of tricks and go to work. Answer one more question and you may go your way."

I said, "All right, make it snappy, Pop. I'm getting tired of this game."

"Am I right in assuming that your principal unhappiness lies in the fact that your newspaper is not selling as you would like it to, and that this is due to the categorical fact that nothing newsworthy ever takes place in this town?"

"Yeah, that's right on the button. Now—"

"Very well, Dick. That's what I wanted to know. I advise you to go home now and get a good night's sleep."

"Exactly what I plan to do. It's been charming, Mr Jones. I don't mind saying I think you're a nosy galoot with squirrels in the head. Anyway, do you want to go to a hotel?"

He jumped down off the desk and started to walk with me toward the front door.

"No thank you, Richard lad; I have much work to do. I tell you, stop worrying. Things are going to be rosy for you and, if you watch your step, *you'll* have no fiddler to pay. And now, good night."

Jones then dug me in the ribs with his cane and strode off, whistling "There'll Be a Hot Time in the Old Town Tonight."

He was headed straight for the Little Creek bridge, which gradually opened off into flat pastures and a few farm houses. Nothing lay beyond that except the graveyard.

I suppose he didn't know where he was going, but I was too confused and tired to care much. When I looked again there wasn't hide nor hair of Mr Jones.

He was promptly forgotten. Almost, anyway. When you're broke and owe everybody in town, you're able to forget just about anything. Except, of course, that you're broke and owe everybody in town.

I locked up the office and started for home. The fire and fury were gone: I couldn't get up the gall to phone everyone and do all the things I'd planned to do.

So, miserable as a wet dog, I trudged a few blocks to the house, smoked a half dozen cigarettes and went to bed, hoping I'd have the guts to get on the train the next day.

I WOKE up early feeling like a fish left out in the sun too long. It was six o'clock and, like always at this time, I wished that I had a wife or a mistress to get me a big breakfast. Instead I hobbled downstairs and knew exactly what Mother Hubbard felt like. I fixed a lousy cup of coffee and sat down to a glorious dish of cornflakes. I knew that train was mighty far away and that in a little while I'd go to the office, reach in the filler box, and help set up another stinking issue of the *Daily Courier*. Then would come the creditors and the long line of bushwa. Even the cornflakes tasted rancid.

Then I heard a distinct thud against the front door. It struck me as being odd, because there had never before been any thuds at that particular front door which made precisely that sound.

I opened it, looked around and finally at my feet. There, folded magnificently and encircled with a piece of string, was a newspaper.

Since the *Courier* was the only paper Danville had ever known, and since I never read the thing anyway, it all looked very peculiar. Besides, none of my delivery boys ever folded in such a neat, professional manner.

There wasn't anybody in sight, but I noticed, before I picked it up, that there was a paper on the doorstep of every house and store around. Then people started coming out and noticing the bundles, so I gathered it up and went back inside. Maybe I scratched my head. I know I felt like it.

There was a little card attached to the string. It read:

Complimentary Issue

If You Desire to Begin or Rebegin Your Subscription, Send Check or Cash to the Office of The Danville Daily Courier. Rates Are Listed Conveniently Within.

That was a laugh, but I didn't. Something was screwy somewhere. In the first place, there weren't supposed to be any morning deliveries. I, Ernie Meyer, and Fred Scarborough (my staff) started the edition around eight o'clock, and it didn't get delivered until six that night. Also, since no one was in the office after I left and nothing whatsoever had been done on the next day's issue — let alone the fancy printing on that card, which could have been done only on a large press — well, I got an awfully queer feeling in the pit of my stomach.

When I opened up the paper I about yelled out loud. It looked like the biggest, most expensive, highfalutin' city paper ever put together. The legend still read *Danville Daily Courier*, but I'd have felt better if it had said the *Tribune*.

Immediately upon reading the double-inch headlines, I sat down and started to sweat. There, in black, bold letters were the words:

Mayor's Wife Gives Birth
to Baby Hippopotamus

And underneath:

At three am this morning, Mayor and Mrs Fletcher Lindquist were very much startled to find themselves the parents of a healthy, 15-pound baby hippo. Most surprising is the fact that nowhere in the lineage of either the Mayor or his wife is there record of a hippopotamus strain. Mrs Lindquist's great-grandfather, reports show, was a raving lunatic from the age of twenty-three to the time of his death, fifty years later, but it is biologically unsound to assume that such ancestral proclivities would necessarily introduce into later generations so unusual a result. Therefore, Danville's enterprising,

*precedent-setting Mayor Lindquist may be said to have proved his
first campaign promise, to wit, "I will make many changes!"*

Continued on page 15

I don't have to recount what I did or thought at all this. I merely sat
there and numbly turned to page fifteen.

*Displaying his usual cool and well-studied philosophy, the
Mayor announced that, in view of the fact that the Lindquists'
expected baby was to have been called either Edgar Bernhardt
or Louisa Ann, and inasmuch as the hippopotamus was male in
sex, the name Edgar Bernhardt would be employed as planned.*

When queried, the Mayor said simply, "I do not propose that our
son be victim to unjudicious slander and stigmatic probings. Edgar will
lead a healthy, normal life." He added brusquely: "I have great plans for
the boy!"

Both Mrs Lindquist and the attending physician, Dr Forrest
Peterson, refrained from comment, although Dr Peterson was observed
in a corner from time to time, mumbling and striking his forehead.

I turned back to the front page, feeling not at all well. There, 3 inches
by 5 inches, was a photograph of Mrs Fletcher Lindquist, holding in her
arms (honest to God!) a pint-sized hippopotamus.

I flipped feverishly to the second sheet, and saw:

FARMER BURL ILLING COMPLAINS
OF MYSTERIOUS APPEARANCE
OF DRAGONS IN BACKYARD.

And then I threw the damn paper as far as I could and began pinch-
ing myself. It only hurt; I didn't wake up. I closed my eyes and looked
again, but there it was, right where I'd heaved it.

I suppose I should have, but I didn't for a moment get the idea I was
nuts. A real live newspaper had been delivered at my door. I owned the

only newspaper in town and called it the *Danville Daily Courier*. This paper was also called the *Danville Daily Courier*. I hadn't put together an issue since the day before. This one was dated today. The only worthwhile news *my* paper had ever turned out was a weather report. This one had stuff that would cause the Associated Press to drop its teeth.

Somebody, I concluded, was nuts.

And then I slowly remembered Mr Jones. That screwy Mr Jones, that loony old birdbrain.

He'd broken into the office after I'd left and somehow put together this fantastic issue. Where he got the photograph I didn't know, but that didn't bother me. It was the only answer. Sure — who else would have done such a thing? Thought he'd help me by making up a lot of tall tales and peddling them to everyone in town.

I got sore as hell. So this was how he was going to "help" me! If he'd been there at the moment I would have broken every bone in his scrawny old body. My God, I thought, how'll I get out of this? What would I say when the Mayor and Illing and Lord knows how many others got wind of it?

Dark thoughts of me, connected to a long rail, coated from head to toe with a lot of tar and a lot of feathers, floated clearly before my eyes. Or me at the stake, with hungry flames lapping up... Who could blame them? *Some* big-time magazine or tabloid would get a copy—they'd never miss a story like this. And then Danville would be the laughing stock of the nation, maybe of the world. At the very best, I'd be sued blue.

I took one last look at that paper on the floor and lit out for the office. I was going to tear that old jerk limb from limb—I was going to make some *real* news.

HALFWAY THERE the figure of Fred Scarborough rushed by me a mile a minute. He didn't even turn around. I started to call, but then Ernie

Meyer came vaulting down the street. I tried to dodge, but the next thing I knew Ernie and I were sitting on top of each other. In his eyes was an insane look of fear and confusion.

"Ernie," I said, "what the devil's the matter with you? Has this town gone crazy or have I?"

"Don't know about that, Mr Lewis," he panted, "but I'm headin' for the hills."

He got up and started to take off again. I grabbed him and shook him till his teeth rattled.

"What *is* the matter with you? Where's everybody running? Is there a fire?"

"Look, Mr Lewis, I worked for your dad. It was a quiet life and I got paid regular. Elmer was a little odd, but that didn't bother me none, because I got paid regular, see. But things is happening at the office now that I don't have to put up with. 'Cause, Mr Lewis, I don't get paid at all. And when an old man dressed like my grandfather starts a lot of brand-new presses running all by himself and, on top of that, chases me and Fred out with a pitchfork, well, Mr Lewis, I'm quittin'. I resign. Goodbye, Mr Lewis. Things like this just ain't ever happened in Danville before."

Ernie departed in a hurry, and I got madder at Mr Jones.

When I opened the door to the office, I wished I was either in bed or had a drink. All the old handsetters and presses were gone. Instead there was a huge, funny-looking machine, popping and smoking and depositing freshly folded newspapers into a big bin. Mr Jones, with his derby still on his head, sat at my desk pounding furiously at the typewriter and chuckling like a lunatic. He ripped a sheet out and started to insert another, when he saw me.

"Ah, Dick m'boy! How are you this morning? I must say, you don't look very well. Sit down, won't you. I'll be finished in a second."

Back he went to his writing. All I could do was sit down and open and close my mouth.

"Well," he said, taking the sheets and poking them through a little slot in the machine. "Well, there's tomorrow's edition, all—how does it go?—all put to bed. They'll go wild over that. Just think, Reverend Piltzer's daughter was found tonight with a smoking pistol in her hand, still standing over the body of her—"

I woke up.

"Jones!"

"Of course, it's not front-page stuff. Makes nice filler for page eight, though."

"Jones!"

"Yes, m'boy?"

"I'm going to kill you. So help me, I'm going to murder you right now! Do you realize what you've done? Oh Lord, don't you know that half the people in Danville are going to shoot me, burn me, sue me, and ride me out on a rail? Don't you—but they won't. No sir. I'll tell them everything. And you're going to stick right here to back me up. All of the—"

"Why, what's the matter, Dick? Aren't you happy? Look at all the news your paper is getting."

"Hap-Happy? You completely ruin me and ask if I'm happy! Go bar the door, Jones; they'll be here any second."

He looked hurt and scratched the end of his nose with his cane.

"I don't quite understand, Richard. *Who* will be here? Out-of-town reporters?"

I nodded weakly, too sick to talk.

"Oh no, they won't arrive until tomorrow. You see, they're just getting this morning's issue. Why are you so distraught? Ah, I know what will cheer you up. Take a look at the mailbox."

I don't know why, but that's what I did. I knew the mail wasn't supposed to arrive until later, and vaguely I wanted to ask what had happened to all the old equipment. But I just went over and looked at the mailbox, like Mr Jones suggested. I opened the first letter. Three dollars dropped out. Letter number two, another three bucks. Automatically

I opened letter after letter, until the floor was covered with currency. Then I imagined I looked up piteously at Mr J.

"Subscriptions, m'boy, subscriptions. I hurried the delivery a bit, so you'd be pleased. But that's just a start. Wait'll tomorrow, Dick. This office will be knee-deep in money!"

At this point I finally did begin to think I was crazy.

"What is all this about, Jones? *Please* tell me, or call the little white wagon. Am I going soggy in the brain?"

"Come, come! Not a bit of it! I've merely fulfilled my promise. Last night you told me that you were unhappy because the *Courier* wasn't selling. Now, as you can see, it *is* selling. And not only in Danville. No sir, the whole world will want subscriptions to your paper, Richard, before I'm through."

"But you don't understand, Jones. You just can't make up a lot of news and expect to get by with it. It's been tried a hundred different times. People are going to catch on. And you and me, we're going to be jailed sure as the devil. Do you see now what you've done?"

He looked at me quizzically and burst out laughing.

"Why, Dick, you *don't* understand yet, do you! Come now, surely you're not such a dunce. Tell me, exactly what do you think?"

"Merely that an old man stepped into my life last night and that my life has been a nightmare ever since."

"But beyond that. Who am I and why am I here?"

"Oh, I don't know, Mr Jones. You're probably just a friend of Dad's and thought you could help me out by this crazy scheme. I can't even get angry with you anymore. Things were going to hell without you— maybe I can get a job on the prison newspaper."

"Just a queer old friend of Elmer's, eh? And you think I did no more than 'make up' those headlines. You don't wonder about this press—" he waved his cane toward the large machine which had supplanted the roll-your-own—"or how the papers got delivered or why they look so professional? Is that press your imagination?"

I looked over at the machine. It was nothing I'd ever seen before. Certainly it was not an ordinary press. But it was real enough. Actual papers were popping out of it at the rate of two or three a second. And then I thought of that photograph.

"My God, Jones, do you mean to tell me that you're—"

"Precisely, my lad, precisely. A bit rusty, as I said, but with many a unique kick left."

He kicked his heels together and smiled broadly.

"Now, you can be of no help whatever. So, since you look a bit peaked around the face, it is my suggestion that you go home and rest for a few days."

"That news...those things in the paper, you mean they were—"

"Absolutely factual. Everything that is printed in the *Danville Daily Courier*," he said gaily, "is the, er, the gospel truth. Go home, Dick: I'll attend to the reporters and editors and the like. When you're feeling better, come back and we'll work together. Perhaps you'll have a few ideas."

He put another sheet in the typewriter, rested his bushy chin on the head of the cane for a moment, twinkled his eyes and then began typing like mad.

I staggered out of the office and headed straight for Barney's Grill. All they had was beer, but that would have to do. I had to get drunk: I knew that.

When I got to Barney's, the place was crowded. I ordered a beer and then almost dropped it when the waiter said to me:

"You certainly were right on the ball, Mr Lewis, you and your paper. Who'd a'ever thought the Mayor's wife would have a hippopotamus? Yes sir, right on the ball. I sent in my subscription an hour ago!"

Then Mrs Olaf Jaspers, a quiet old lady who always had her coffee and doughnut at Barney's before going to work at the hospital, said:

"Oh, it was certainly a sight to see. Miz Lindquist is just as proud. Fancy, a hippopotamus!"

I quickly gulped the beer.

"You mean you actually saw it, Mrs Jaspers?"

"Oh my yes," she answered. "I was there all the time. We can't any of us figure it out, but it was the cutest thing you ever did see. Who was that old fellow that took the picture, Richard? A new man?"

Everyone began talking to me then, and my head swam around and around.

"Mighty quick of you, Lewis! You've got *my* subscription for two years!"

"Poor Burl never did catch those pesky dragons. Ate up every one of his turnips, too."

"You're a real editor, Mr Lewis. We're all going to take the *Courier* from now on. Imagine; all these funny things happen and you're right there to get all the news!"

I bought a case of beer, excused myself, went home, and got blind drunk.

IT WAS nice to wake up the next morning, because even though my head split I felt sure this was every bit a dream. The hope sank fast when I saw all the beer bottles lying on the floor. With an empty feeling down below, I crawled to the front door and opened it.

No dream.

The paper lay there, folded beautifully. I saw people running down the streets, lickety-split, toward Main Street.

Thinking was an impossibility. I made for the boy's room, changed clothes, fixed some breakfast, and only then had the courage to unfold the issue. The headlines cried: EXTRA!! Underneath, almost as large:

S.S. QUEEN MARY DISCOVERED
ON MAIN STREET

An unusual discovery today made Danville, U.S.A., a center of world-wide attention. The renowned steam ship, the S.S. Queen Mary, thought previously to be headed for Italy enroute from Southampton, appeared suddenly in the middle of Main Street in Danville, between Geary and Orchard Ave.

Embedded deep in the cement so that it remains upright, the monstrous vessel is proving a dangerous traffic hazard, causing many motorists to go an entire mile out of their way.

Citizens of Danville view the phenomenon with jaundiced eyes, generally considering it a great nuisance.

Empty whiskey bottles were found strewn about the various decks, and all of the crew and passengers remain under the influence of heavy intoxication.

In the words of the Captain, J.E. Cromerline:

"I din' have a thing to do with it. It was that damned navigator, all his fault."

Officials of the steamship line are coming from London and New York to investigate the situation.

Continued on page 20

That's what it said, and, so help me, there was another photograph, big and clear as life.

I ran outside, and headed for Main Street. But the minute I turned the corner, I saw it.

There, exactly as the paper had said, was the *Queen Mary*, as quiescent and natural as though she'd been in dock. People were gathered all around the giant ship, jabbering and yelling.

In a dazed sort of way, I got interested and joined them.

Lydia Murphy, a school teacher, was describing the nautical terms to her class, a gang of kids who seemed happy to get out of school.

Arley Taylor, a fellow who used to play checkers with Dad, walked over to me.

"Now, ain't that something, Dick! I ask ya, ain't that something!"

"That, Arley," I agreed, "is something."

I saw Mr Jones standing on the corner, swinging his cane and puffing his cigar. I galloped over to him.

"Look, Jones, I believe you. Okay, you're the devil. But you just can't do this. First a hippopotamus, now the world's biggest ocean liner in the middle of the street — You're driving me nuts!"

"Why, hello Dick. Say, you ought to see those subscriptions now! I'd say we have five thousand dollars' worth. They're beginning to come in from the cities now. Just you wait, boy, you'll have a newspaper that'll beat 'em all!"

Arguing didn't faze him. I saw then and there that Mr Jones wouldn't be stopped. So I cussed a few times and started off. Only I was stopped short by an expensive-looking blonde, with horn-rimmed glasses and a notebook.

"Mr Richard Lewis, editor of the *Danville Courier?*" she said.

"That's me."

"My name is Elissa Traskers. I represent the *New York Mirror.* May we go somewhere to talk?"

I mumbled, "Okay," and took one more look at the ship.

Far up on the deck I could see a guy in a uniform chasing what couldn't have been anything else but a young lady without much clothes on.

When two big rats jumped out of the lowest porthole and scampered down the street, I turned around sharply and almost dragged the blonde the entire way to my house.

Once inside, I closed the door and locked it. My nerves were on the way out.

"Mr Lewis, why did you do that?" asked the blonde.

"Because I like to lock doors, I *love* to lock doors. They fascinate me."

"I see. Now then, Mr Lewis, we'd like a full account, in your own words, of all these strange happenings."

She crossed a tan leg and that didn't help much to calm me down.

"Miss Traskers," I said, "I'll tell you just once, and then I want you to go away. I'm not a well man.

"My father, Elmer Lewis, was a drifter and a floater all his life, until he met the devil. Then he decided what would really make him happy.

So he asked the devil to set him up in a small town with a small-town newspaper. He asked for a monthly cash stipend. He got all this, so for fifty-five years he sat around happy as a fool, editing a paper which didn't sell and collecting lousy bugs — "

The blonde baby looked worried, because I must have sounded somewhat unnatural. But maybe the business with the boat had convinced her that unusual things do, occasionally, happen.

"Mr Lewis," she said sweetly, "before you go on, may I offer you a drink?"

And she produced from her purse a small, silver flask. It had scotch in it. With the élan of the damned, I got a couple of glasses and divided the contents of the flask into each.

"Thanks."

"Quite all right. Now, enough kidding, Mr Lewis. I must turn in a report to my paper."

"I'm *not* kidding, honey. For fifty-five years my dad did this, and my mother stuck right by him. The only thing out of the ordinary they ever had was me."

The scotch tasted wonderful. I began to like Miss Traskers a lot.

"All this cost Pop his soul, but he was philosophic and I guess that didn't matter much to him. Anyway, he tricked the devil into including me into the bargain. So after he died and left the paper to me, and I started to go broke, Mr Jones appeared and decided to help me out."

"To help you out?"

"Yeah. All this news is his work. Before he's done he'll send the whole world off its rocker, just so I can get subscriptions."

She'd stopped taking it down a long time ago.

"I'd think you were a damned liar, Mr Lewis—"

"Call me Dick."

"—if I hadn't seen the *Queen Mary* sitting out there. Frankly, Mr Lew—Dick, if you're telling the truth, something's got to be done."

"You're darn right it does, Elissa. But *what?* The old boy is having too much fun now to be stopped. He told me himself that he hasn't had anything to do like this for centuries."

"Besides," she said, "how did I get here so quickly? The ship was discovered only this morning, yet I can't remember—"

"Oh, don't worry about it, kid. From now on *anything* is likely to happen."

Something did. I went over and kissed her, for no apparent reason except that she was a pretty girl and I was feeling rotten. She didn't seem to mind.

Right on cue, the doorbell rang.

"Who is it?" I shouted.

"We're from the Associated Press. We want to see Mr Richard Lewis," came a couple of voices. I could hear more footsteps coming up the front porch.

"I'm sorry," I called, "he's just come down with Yellow Fever. He can't see anybody."

But it wasn't any use. More and more steps and voices, and I could see the door being pushed inward. I grabbed Elissa's hand and we ran out the back way, ran all the way to the office.

Strangely, there weren't many people around. We walked in, and there, of course, was Mr Jones at the typewriter. He looked up, saw Elissa and winked at me.

"Listen to this, boy. BANK PRESIDENT'S WIFE CLAIMS DIVORCE— EXPLAINS CAUGHT HUSBAND TRIFLING WITH THREE MERMAIDS IN BATHTUB. 'Course, it's rather long, but I think we can squeeze it in. Well, well, who have you there?"

I couldn't think of anything else, so I introduced Elissa.

"Ah, from the *Mirror!* I got you down here this morning, didn't I?"

Elissa looked at me and I could tell she didn't think I had been trying to fool her.

"Have you turned in your report yet, Miss?"

She shook her head.

"Well, do so immediately! Why do you think I took the trouble of sending you in the first place? Never mind, I'll attend to it. Oh, we're terribly busy here. But a shapely lass like you shouldn't have to work for a living, now should she, Dick?"

And with this, Jones nudged Elissa with his cane, in a spot which caused me to say:

"Now see here Jones—this is going too far! Do that again and I'll punch you in the snoot."

"I must say, Richard, you're just like your father. Don't lose a minute, do you!" I reached out to grab him, but the second afterwards he was over on the other side of the room.

"Tut tut, m'boy, not a very nice way to treat your benefactor! Look at that basket there."

I looked and so did Elissa. She looked long and hard. The room was full of money and checks, and Mr Jones danced over with a mischievous glint in his eyes.

"Bet a couple could take just what's there and live comfortably for a year on it. That is, if they were sure there would be more to come."

He sidled over to Elissa and nudged her again, and I started swinging. Before I landed on my face, a thought came to me. It was a desperate, long-odds, crazy thought, but it seemed the answer to everything.

"Tell you what, Jones," I said, picking myself up off the floor and placing Elissa behind me. "This is a little silly after all. I think you're right. I think I've acted in a very ungrateful fashion and I want to apologize. The *Courier* is really selling now, and it appears that it'll make me a lot of money. All thanks to you. I'm really sorry."

He put the chair down and seemed pleased.

"Now then, that's more like it, Dick. And, er, I apologize, young lady. I was only being devilish."

Elissa was a sophisticated girl: she didn't open her mouth.

"I can see that you're busy, Mr Jones, so if you don't mind, Elissa and I will take a little walk."

I gave him a broad wicked wink, which delighted him.

"That's *fine*, m'boy. I want to get this evening's edition ready. Now let's see, where was I…"

BY THIS time it was getting dark. Without saying a word, I pushed Elissa into the alley behind the shop. You could hear the press chugging away inside, so I began to talk fast.

"I like you," I said, "and maybe after all this is over, we can get together somewhere. But right now the important thing is to stop that bird."

She looked beautiful there in the shadows, but I couldn't take the time to tell her so. Vaguely I sensed that I'd somehow fallen in love with this girl whom I'd met that same day. She looked in all ways cooperative.

I did manage to ask: "You got a boyfriend?"

Again she shook that pretty blonde head, so I got right back to the business at hand.

"Jones *has* to be stopped. What he's done so far is fantastic, all right, but comparatively harmless. However, we've got to remember that he's the devil after all, and for sure he's up to something. Things won't stay harmless, you can count on that. Already he's forgotten about the original idea. Look at him in there, having the time of his life. This was all he needed to cut loose. Dad made the mistake of leaving the *idea* of my happiness up to Mr Jones's imagination."

"All right, Dick, but what do we do?"

"Did you notice that he read aloud what's *going* to happen tonight, Elissa?"

"You mean about the mermaids in the bathtub?"

"Yes. Don't you get it? That hasn't happened yet. He thinks up these crazy ideas, types 'em out, gets 'em all printed, and *then* they take place.

He goes over, takes a few pictures, and in some way gets the papers delivered a few minutes later, complete with the news. Don't ask me why he doesn't just snap his fingers—maybe he enjoys it this way more."

"I suppose that's, uh, sensible. What do you want me to do, Dick?"

"It's asking a lot, I suppose, but we can't let him wreck the whole world. Elissa, do you think you could divert the devil for about a half hour?"

Looking at her, I knew she could.

"I get it now. Okay, if you think it'll work. First, do me a favor?"

"Anything."

"Kiss me again, would you?"

I complied, and let me tell you, there was nothing crazy about that kiss. I was honestly grateful to Mr Jones for one thing at least.

Elissa opened the front door of the office, threw back her hair, and crooked a finger at the devil.

"Oh Mr Jones!"

From the alley I could see him stop typing abruptly. More than abruptly. So would I.

"Why, my dear! Back from your walk so soon? Where is Richard?"

"I don't know — he just walked off and didn't say anything. Now I'm all alone."

The devil's eyes looked like tiny red-hot coals, and he bit clean through his cigar. "Well," he said. "Well, well, *well!*"

"You wouldn't like to take me out for a few drinks, would you, Mr Jones?"

The way she moved her hips would have me bite through my cigar, if I'd had a cigar. She was doing beautifully.

"Well, I had planned to — no, it can wait. Certainly, Miss Traskers, I'd be pleased, more than pleased, oh, *very* pleased to accompany you somewhere for a spot. Richard has probably gone home to talk to other reporters."

With this he hopped over the desk and took Elissa's arm.

"Oh, my dear girl, it has been so long, so very long. Voluntarily, I mean."

She smiled at the old goat and in a few minutes they were headed straight for Barney's Grill. I almost chased them when I heard him say, "And afterwards, perhaps we could take a stroll through the woods, eh?"

As soon as they were out of sight, I ran into the office, took his material out of the typewriter and inserted a new sheet.

I thought for a few minutes, and then hurriedly typed:

Devil Returns Home

The devil, known also as Mr Jones, cut short his latest visit to Earth because of altercations in Gehenna. Mr Elmer Lewis, for some years a resident of the lower regions, successfully made his escape and entry into heaven, where he joined his wife, Elizabeth. The devil can do nothing to alter this, but has decided to institute a more rigorous discipline among his subjects still remaining.

And then, on another sheet I wrote:

Office of Danville Daily Courier Disappears

The citizens of Danville were somewhat relieved this morning as they noticed the disappearance of the office of the town's only newspaper, the Courier. All the news reported in the pages of this tabloid since April 11, furthermore, was found to be totally false and misrepresentational, except the information printed in this edition. Those who paid for subscriptions have all received their money in full.

Richard Lewis, the editor, is rumored to be in New York, working for one of the large metropolitan newspapers.

The community of Danville continues a normal, happy existence, despite the lack of a news organ.

I walked over to the machine, which still ejected papers, and quickly inserted the two sheets into the slot, exactly as I'd observed Jones do.

At which point the universe blew up in my face. The entire office did a jig and then settled gently, but firmly, on top of my head.

WHEN THINGS unfuzzed and I could begin to see straight, I found myself sitting at a typewriter in a very large and very strange office.

A fellow in shirt sleeves and tortoise shells ambled over and thumped me on the back.

"Great work, Dick," he said. "Great job on that city hall fire. C'mon, break down, you set it yourself?"

Of course, as was becoming a habit, I stared dumbly.

"Always the deadpan—wotta joker! So now you're in the syndicates. Some guys are just plain old lucky, I guess. Do *I* ever happen to be around when things like that bust out? Huh!"

He walked away, and by degrees, very carefully, I learned that I'd just scooped everybody on a big fire that had broken out in the city hall.

I was working for the *Mirror*, making $75.00 per week. I'd been with them only a few days, but everyone seemed very chummy.

It had worked. I'd outsmarted the devil! I'd gotten rid of him and the paper and everything. And then I remembered.

I remembered Elissa. So, come quitting time, I asked the first guy I saw:

"Where does Miss Elissa Traskers work, you know?"

The fellow's eyes lit up and he looked melancholy.

"You mean the Blonde Bomber? Whatta gal, whatta gal! Those legs, those—"

"Yeah—where does she work?"

"Second floor. Flunks for Davidson, that lucky—"

I got down to the second floor quick. There she was, as pretty as I remembered her. I walked up and said:

"Hello, honey. It worked!"

"I beg your pardon?"

She didn't have to say any more. I realized with a cold heartless feeling what it was I'd forgotten. I'd forgotten Elissa. Didn't even mention her on either of those sheets, didn't ever mention her!

"Don't you remember, honey? You were doing me a favor, coaxing the devil to buy you a few drinks…"

It was there in her eyes. She could have been staring at an escaped orangutan.

"Excuse me," she said, picked up her coat, and trotted out of the office. And out of my life.

I tried to get in touch with her any number of times after that, but she didn't know me each time. Finally I saw it was no good. I used to sit by the window and watch her leave the building with some guy or another, sit there and wish I'd just left things like they were while Mr Jones was having fun. It wasn't very peaceful, but so what. I ask you, so what?

DICK SAT in his corner, looking serious as a lawyer. We'd all stopped laughing quite a while back, and he was actually so convincing that I piped up:

"Okay, what happened then? That why you want to quit newspaper work—because of her?"

He snickered out the side of his mouth and lit another cigarette.

"Yeah, that's why. Because of her. But that isn't all. You guys remember what happened to the Governor's wife last week?"

We remembered. Governor Parker's spouse had gone berserk and run down Fifth Avenue without a stitch on.

"You know who covered that story, who was right there again?"

It had been Lewis. That story was what had entrenched him solidly with the biggest syndicate in the country.

"All right. Can any of you add two and two?"

We were all silent.

"What are you talking about?" Jackson asked.

Dick threw down a beer and laughed out loud, though he didn't seem particularly amused.

"I wasn't so smart. I didn't stop the devil; I just stalled him awhile. He's back, y'understand, he's back! And this time he's going to get mad. That's why I'm quitting the newspapers. I don't know what I'll do, but whatever it is Mr Jones is going to do his damndest to make me successful."

I was about to start the laughter, when I saw something that cut it off sharp. I saw a very old gentleman, with derby, spats, and cane, leaning against the bar and winking at me.

It didn't take me long to get home.

ELEGY
(1953)

Port: Asteroid K7

The fiery metal leg fell into the cool air, heating it; burnt into the green grass and licked a craterous hole. There were fire flags and fire sparks, hisses and explosions and the weary groaning sound of a great beast.

The rocket grumbled and muttered for a while on its finny tripod, then was silent; soon the heat vanished also.

"Are you all right, sir?"

"Yes. The rest?"

"Fine, sir."

Captain Webber swung himself erect and tested his limbs. "Well, then, Lieutenant, has the atmosphere been checked?"

"The air is pure and fit to breathe, sir."

"Instruct the others to drop the ladder." A door in the side of the rocket opened and men began climbing out.

"Look!" said crewman Milton, pointing. "Trees and grass and little wooden bridges going over the water."

Beyond the trees a brick lodge extended over a rivulet which foamed and bubbled. Fishing poles protruded from the lodge windows.

"And there, to the right!"

A steel building thirty stories high with a pink cloud near the top. And, separated by a hedge, a brown tent with a barbecue pit before it, smoke rising in a rigid ribbon from the chimney.

Crewman Chitterwick blinked and squinted his eyes. "Where are we?"

Distant and near, houses of stone and brick and wood, painted all colors, small, large; and further, golden fields of wheat, each blown by a different breeze in a different direction.

"I don't believe it," said Captain Webber. "It's a *park*—millions of miles away from where a park could possibly be."

"Damned strange," said Lieutenant Peterson, picking up a rock. "We're on an asteroid not shown on *any* chart, in the middle of a place that belongs in history records."

A little man with thin hair stepped briskly from a tree clump. "Well, well, I hadn't been expecting you gentlemen, to be perfectly honest," the little man chuckled, then, "Oh dear, see what you've done to the property of Mr Bellefont. I do hope you haven't hurt *him*—no, I see that he is all right."

An old man with red hair was seated at the base of a tree, apparently reading a book.

"We are from Earth," said Captain Webber.

"Yes, yes."

"My name is Webber, these are my men."

"Of course," said the little man.

"Who are you?" asked Webber.

"Who—Greypoole, Mr Greypoole. Didn't *they* tell you?"

"Then you are *also* from Earth?"

"Heavens, yes! But let us go where we can chat more comfortably. Follow me." Mr Greypoole struck out down a small path past scorched trees and underbrush.

They walked onto a wooden porch and through a door with a wire screen; Lieutenant Peterson first, then Captain Webber, Mr Friden, and the rest of the crew. Greypoole followed.

"You must forgive me—it's been a while. Take chairs, there—there. Please be comfortable."

Captain Webber glanced around the room at the lace curtains, the needlepoint tapestries and the lavender wallpaper.

"Mr Greypoole, I'd like to ask some questions."

"Certainly, certainly. But first, this being an occasion—" the little man stared at each of them, then shook his head, "ah, do you all like wine? Good wine? I shall be back soon. Forgive me, gentlemen."

He ducked through a small door.

Captain Webber exhaled. "Friden, you stay here; you others see what you can find. Scout around. We'll wait." The men left the room.

Crewman Chitterwick made his way along a hedgerow, feeling cautiously, maintaining a delicate balance. When he came to a doorway he stopped, looked about, then entered.

The room was dark and quiet and odorous. Mr Chitterwick groped a few steps, put out his hand and encountered what seemed to be raw flesh; he swiftly withdrew his hand. "Excuse," he said, then "Uh!" as his face came against a slab of moist red meat.

Mr Chitterwick began to tremble and he blinked furiously, reaching out and finding flesh, cold and hard.

When he stepped upon the toe of a large man with a walrus mustache, he wheeled, located the sunlight, and ran from the butcher shop...

The door of the temple opened with difficulty, which caused crewman Milton to breathe unnaturally. Once inside, he gasped.

Row upon row of people, their fingers outstretched, lips open but immobile and silent, their bodies prostrate on the floor. And upon a strange black altar, a tiny woman with silver hair and a long thyrsus in her right hand.

Nothing stirred but the mosaic squares in the walls. The colors danced here; otherwise, everything was frozen, everything was solid.

Even the air hung suspended, stationary.

Mr Milton left the temple...

There was a table and a woman on the table and people all around the woman on the table. Crewman Goeblin rubbed his eyes and stared.

It was an operating room. There were masked men and women with shining scissors and glistening saws in their hands. And up above, the students' aperture: filled seats, filled aisles.

A large man stood over the recumbent figure, his lusterless eyes regarding the crimson-puce incision, but he did not move. The nurses did not move, nor the students. No one moved, especially the smiling middle-aged woman on the table.

Mr Goeblin moved…

"Hello!" said Lieutenant Peterson, after he had searched through eight long aisles of books. "Hello!"

He pointed his gun menacingly.

There were many books with many titles and they all had a fine gray dust about them. Lieutenant Peterson paused to examine a bulky volume, when he happened to look upward.

"Who are *you?*" he demanded.

The mottled, angular man perched atop the ladder did not respond. He clutched a book and looked at the book and not at Lieutenant Peterson.

Peterson climbed up the ladder, scowling; he reached the man and drew in a breath. He looked into the eyes of the reading man and descended hastily…

Mr Greypoole reentered the living room with a tray of glasses. "This is apricot wine," he announced, distributing the glasses. "But—where are the others? Out for a walk? Ah well, they can drink theirs later. Incidentally, Captain, how many Guests did you bring? Last time it was only twelve. Not an extraordinary shipment either; they all preferred ordinary things. All but Mrs Dominguez—dear me, she was worth the carload herself. Wanted a zoo, can you imagine?—a regular zoo, with her put right in the birdhouse. Oh, they had a time putting that one up!"

Mr Greypoole chuckled and sipped at his drink. He leaned back in his chair and crossed a leg. "Ah," he continued, "you have no idea how good this is. Once in a while it does get lonely for me here—why, I can remember when Mr Waldmeyer first told me of this idea. 'A grave responsibility,' he said, 'a *grave* responsibility.' Mr Waldmeyer has a keen sense of humor, needless to say."

Captain Webber put down his glass. Outside, a small child on roller skates stood unmoving on the sidewalk.

"Finished your wine? Good. Perhaps you'd care to join me in a brief turn about the premises?"

Webber sighed, stood up. "Friden, you stay here and wait for the men." He followed Greypoole out onto the porch and down the steps.

Crewman Friden drummed his fingers upon the arm of a chair, surveyed his empty glass, and hiccoughed softly.

"I *do* wish you had landed your ship elsewhere, Captain. Mr Bellefont was quite particular and, as you can see, his park is hopelessly disfigured."

"We were given no choice. Our fuel was running out."

"Indeed? Well, then, that explains everything. A beautiful day, don't you find, sir? Fortunately, with the exception of Professor Carling, all the Guests preferred good weather. Plenty of sunshine, they said. It helps."

When they passed a statue-still woman on a bicycle, Captain Webber stopped walking.

"Mr Greypoole, we've *got* to have a talk."

The little man shrugged and pointed and they went into an office building which was crowded with motionless men, women and children.

"Since I'm so mixed up myself," Webber said, "maybe I'd better ask—just who do you think *we* are?"

"The men from the Glades, of course."

"I don't know what you're talking about. We're from Earth. They were on the verge of another war—the 'Last War'—and we escaped and started off for Mars. But something went wrong—crewman named Appleton pulled a gun, others just didn't like the Martians—we needn't go into it; Mars didn't work out. We were forced to leave.

Then, more trouble. We ended up lost with only a little store of fuel and supplies. Friden noticed this city or whatever it is and we had just enough fuel to land."

Mr Greypoole nodded his head slowly. "I see… You say there was a war on Earth?"

"They were going to set off the X-Bomb."

"What dreadful news! May I inquire, Captain, as to what you intend to do now?"

"Why, live here, of course!"

"No, no—that's quite impossible."

Captain Webber glanced at the motionless people. "Why not? What *is* this place? Where *are* we?"

Mr Greypoole smiled.

"Captain, we are in a cemetery."

At that moment, Friden and the other crewmen arrived. Chitterwick blinked.

"I heard what he said, sir. The man's insane."

"What about *this?*" Friden asked. "Take a look, Captain."

He handed Webber a pamphlet.

In the center of the first page was a photograph, untinted and solemn; it depicted a white cherub delicately poised on a granite slab. Beneath the photograph were the words: *Happy Glades.*

"It's one of those old-level cemeteries!" said Webber. "I remember seeing pictures of them."

He began to read the pamphlet:

> *For fifty years an outstanding cultural and spiritual asset to this community, Happy Glades is proud to announce yet another innovation in its program of post-benefits. Now you can enjoy the afterlife in surroundings which suggest the here and now. For those who prefer that their late departed have really permanent eternal happiness, for those who are dismayed by the fragility of all things mortal, we of Happy Glades are proud to offer:*

1. The duplication of physical conditions identical to those enjoyed by the departed on Earth. Park, playground, lodge, office building, hotel, house, etc., may be secured at varying prices. All workmanship and materials attuned to conditions on Asteroid K, and guaranteed for permanence.

2. Permanent conditioning of late beloved so that, in the midst of surroundings he favored, a genuine Eternity may be assured.

Webber swung toward Greypoole. "You mean *all* these people are dead?"

The little fellow proceeded to straighten the coat of a middle-aged man with a cigar.

"No, no," laughed Mr Greypoole, "only the main Guests. The others are imitations. Mr Conklin upstairs was head of a large firm; absolutely in love with his work, you know—that kind of thing. So we had to duplicate not only the office, but the building—and even provide replicas of all the people *in* the building. Mr Conklin himself is in an easy chair on the twentieth story."

"And?"

"Well, gentlemen, what with the constant exploration of planets and moons, our Mr Waldmeyer hit upon this scheme: seeking to extend the ideal hereafter to our Guests, he bought this little asteroid. With the vast volume and the tremendous turnover, as it were, *Happy Glades* offered this plan—to duplicate the exact surroundings which the Guest most enjoyed in Life, assure him privacy, permanence."

"But why here? Why cart bodies off a million miles or more when the same thing could have been done on Earth?"

"My communications system went bad, I fear, so I haven't heard from the offices in some while—but you tell me there *is* a war beginning? That is the idea, Captain; one could never really be sure of one's self down there, what with all the new bombs and things being discovered."

"And where do you fit in, Mr Greypoole?"

The little man lowered his eyes. "I was head caretaker, you see. But I wasn't well—gastric complaints, liver, heart palpitations, this and that, so I decided to allow them to change me. By the time I got here, why, I was almost, you might say, a machine. Now, whenever the film is punctured, I wake to do my prescribed duties."

"The film?"

"The asteroid covering that seals in the conditioning. Nothing can get out, nothing get in—except rockets. Then, it's self-sealing. They threw up the film and coated us with their preservative, or Eternifier, and—well, with the exception of my communications system, everything's worked perfectly. Until now..."

Captain Webber spoke slowly. "We're tired men, Mr Greypoole. There are lakes and farms here, all we need to make a new start—more than we'd hoped for... Will you help us?"

Mr Greypoole clucked his tongue. Then he smiled. "Yes, Captain, I will. But first, let us go back to your rocket. You'll need supplies."

Captain Webber nodded. They left the building.

They passed a garden with little spotted trees and flowers, a brown desert of shifting sands and a striped tent. They walked by strawberry fields and airplane hangars and coal mines; past tiny yellow cottages, cramped apartments, fluted houses; past rock pools and a great zoo full of animals that stared out of vacant eyes; and everywhere, the seasons changing gently: crisp autumn, cottony summer, windy spring, and winters cool and white...

The six men in uniform followed the little man with thin hair. They did not speak as they walked, but looked, stared, craned, wondered...

And the old, young, middle-aged, white, brown, yellow people around them did not move.

"You can see, Captain, the success of Mr Waldmeyer's plan, the perfection here, the quality of Eternal Happiness. Here we have brotherhood; no wars or hatreds or prejudices. And now you who left Earth to escape war and hatred, you want to begin life here?"

Cross-breezes ruffled the men's hair.

As they neared the rocket, Greypoole turned to them. "By your own admission, from the moment of your departure, you had personal wars of your own, and killed, and hurled prejudice against a race of people not like you, a race who rejected and cast you out into space again! From your *own* account! Gentlemen, I am truly sorry. You may mean well, after all—I *am* sorry." Mr Greypoole sighed.

"What do you mean, you're sorry?" demanded Webber.

"Well..."

"Captain—" cried Chitterwick, blinking.

"Yes, yes?"

"I feel terrible."

Mr Goeblin clutched at his stomach.

"So do I!"

"And me!"

Captain Webber looked at Greypoole. His mouth twitched in sudden pain. "I'm sorry, gentlemen. Into your ship, quickly." Mr Greypoole motioned them forward. Crewman Milton staggered, groping for balance. "We—we shouldn't have drunk that wine. It was—poisoned!" Greypoole produced a weapon. "*Tell* them, Captain, tell them to climb the ladder. Or they'll die here and now."

"Go on. Up!"

The crew climbed into the ship.

Captain Webber ascended jerkily. When he reached the open lock, he coughed and pulled himself into the rocket. Greypoole followed. "You don't dislike this ship, do you—that is, the surroundings are not offensive? If only I had been allowed more latitude! But everything functions automatically here; no real choice in the matter, actually. The men mustn't writhe about on the floor like that. Get them to their stations—the stations they would most prefer. And hurry!"

Dully, Captain Webber ordered Mr Chitterwick to the galley, Mr Goeblin to the engineering chair, Mr Friden to the navigator's room...

"Sir, what's going to happen?"

Mr Milton to the pilot's chair.

"The pain will last only another moment or so—it's unfortunately part of the Eternifier," said Mr Greypoole. "There, all in order? Good, good. Now, Captain, I see understanding in your face; that pleases me more than I can say. My position is so difficult! But a machine is geared to its job—which, in this case, is to retain permanence."

Captain Webber leaned on the arm of the little man. He tried to speak, then slumped into his control seat.

"You do understand?" asked Mr Greypoole, putting away the weapon.

Captain Webber's head nodded halfway down, then stopped, and his eyes froze forever.

"Fine. Fine."

The little man with the thin hair walked about the cabins and rooms, straightening, arranging; he climbed down the ladder and returned to the wooden house, humming to himself.

When he had washed all the empty wineglasses and replaced them, he sat down in the large leather chair and adjusted himself into the most comfortable position.

His eyes stared in waxen contentment at the homely interior, with its lavender wallpaper, needlepoint tapestries…

He did not move.

THE LAST CAPER

(1954)

o you're Mike Mallet," I said, feeding him some knuckles. He went down—fast—and began to whimper. When he came back up I got my knee under his chin and teeth flew out like the popcorn they used to pop on those drowsy October porches when I was a kid and Mom and Dad used to say "Ah! Ah!" and we'd drink the lemonade and eat the popcorn and breathe the Illinois air which was like old wine.

"Spill it. Mallet," I snarled, but I guess he thought I meant blood. It wasn't pretty. What is?

I tapped him on the forehead with the chromalloy butt of my blaster, just for kicks, and started through his pockets.

There wasn't much. A ray pistol disguised as a ball point pen, a shiv, a sap, a set of knuckles, a paralyzer, a Monopoly score card, eight candy bars, a bottle of Bromo-Seltzer, a picture of an old dame with a funny look (with *For Mikey, with love, Mommy* scrawled suspiciously underneath in crayon), a paint brush, a ticket to Mars (outdated), a copy of *Sonnets from the Portuguese*, a can of Sterno and a card marked: HONORARY MEMBER—EAST ORANGE CHAPTER LADIES LEAGUE FOR PRESERVATION OF THE AMERICAN BEAUTY ROSE. And that was all!

If he had it, if Mallet really did have what I was after—the Chocolate Maltese Falcon—it wasn't on him. I toed at his face and jammed the candy bars into my mouth: they tasted real fine, mostly because I'd had nothing in my stomach except straight rye for over seventeen days. The rest of the junk I tossed out the window.

"Come on, friend," I said, but he just laid there bleeding. It made me a little mad, and I'm kind of ugly when I get mad. I went through the door into his outer office. His secretary was there.

"Next time *open* the door before you come through it, big boy," she spat.

I didn't answer. My eyes were riveted to her body. She was wearing a slinky gold gown that looked like it had been painted on and she was laying on a big leather couch, writhing. I still felt pretty mean, so I moved in—fast.

I've got to admit I was plenty surprised when I found out that the gown really *was* painted on; but it made things easier.

"Get much hot weather around here?" I snapped, my eyes traveling up and down her body like ball-bearings over a washboard.

"Sometimes yes," she said evasively, "sometimes no. It comes and it goes."

"Oh yeah?" She was all right; a little wildcat, and I like wildcats just fine. She threw a vicious kick at my groin but I dodged and grabbed her leg. Then I grabbed her other leg. Then I grabbed her other leg. Oh, she was different, all right. But good!

After I finished with her I jammed her into the typewriter cabinet and let the door slam shut. Dames!

I was feeling a lot better by now, though. Kind of like spring in the air and the first time you carried the books home for that freckle-faced girl next door and goodbye and hello and the dead years of your childhood. I knew I could find that Chocolate Maltese Falcon now, no matter how cleverly Mallet had hidden it.

I stormed back into his office. He was coming to, getting to his knees. This time I used a poker on his head. It cracked. The poker, that is.

I went to work, thinking, it's got to be here, it's *got* to be here! I kicked over the book case, took an ax to the desk, piled the chairs into the fireplace, pushed the safe out the window, cut the carpet into Band-Aids, ripped out the light fixtures, flooded the restroom and wrote a couple things on the walls with some charcoal. Mallet was starting to groan a little so I dropped the bathtub on him: he stopped groaning.

Still no Chocolate Maltese Falcon!

The place was getting pretty untidy by now. I decided I'd better ease up or somebody'd figure there'd been trouble.

Just then a movement caught my eye. I jerked around. A tall blonde was walking by the window. I knew she was tall— Mallet's office was on the ninth floor. She looked all February, silos in the rain, clear lakes full of trout. I started after her and was halfway out when there was a knock at the door.

Rat-tat! Rat-tat!

I jumped to answer it but my foot skidded on some blood and I went down for the ten count, hitting my head on one of the Brancusi statuettes Mallet kept around for laughs. Right away an inky black pool came at me: it splashed over my brain and pretty soon it was like lying on your back high on a hill somewheres on a black night where the stars are coruscating and dancing their cosmic rigadoon. Before I blacked out completely, though, I felt the butt of a blaster hit the side of my face. Then it was curtains...

The voice cut through the brain-fog like a knife going through butter. There was a million firecrackers going off inside my head. Pow! Pow! Pow!

"You Gunther Awl?" a voice said.

I spit out a couple teeth. "Yeah," I choked, "I'm Gunther Awl." It was a lie. I wasn't Gunther Awl at all. But I figured I'd better play it safe.

"C'mon, snap out of it," the voice ordered. I got up, slow-like, and staggered to a chair.

"All right," the voice said, "let's have it."

I focused my eyes. It was a fat guy, with curly hair and jowls and a tattoo of Botticelli's *Venus on the Half-Shell* on his forehead. A fink. A patsy.

"Anything particular in mind, badman?" I drawled. The gun butt came down again with savage force and I found myself spiraling into that inky black pool again. Only this time it was like being inside a kaleidoscope and the kaleidoscope is turning like the Giant Barrel over at Coney and you're trying to stand up but the Barrel keeps turning too fast and you keep falling down and every time you fall you slide a little closer to the sparkling fragments of color at the top of the kaleidoscope and the bright white light filters through like it's a big pool with hundreds of jeweled fishes with bright white teeth swimming around in it. Then suddenly you're at the top...and you come to again.

"Where's the Falcon, Awl?" the fat man said. "And don't get funny this time."

"No spikka da Heenglish," I faked, but it wasn't any good—I could see that. It didn't stop him for more than two minutes, three at the outside.

He hawked convulsively and I thought he was going to heave, then I saw that he was laughing. What at? I wondered. He stopped laughing before I could dope it out.

"Don't push it, rocket-jockey," he said. I could tell he wasn't joking. This monkey was playing for keeps.

"Look," I said, "you got the wrong boy. I ain't Gunther Awl. My name's Bartholomew Cornblossom."

"Yeah," he said, grinning, "I know." He shifted the blaster to his left hand and let me have a backsided right across the puss.

When his hand came off and dropped to the floor, I knew I was in for some surprises myself.

He started to change form—fast—and in less time than it takes to skin a jackrabbit, like the hick says, I was staring at a lousy Venusian. I hated him right away because I didn't understand him and I always hate what I don't understand. Sometimes I hate what I *do* understand.

I had to stall. "What's your angle, cousin?" I asked. "What good's the Chocolate Maltese Falcon to a Venusian?"

There was that laugh again, coming from one of his ears. I did a quick mental flashback as that green blob of jelly came at me.

How had it all started...

I'D BEEN sitting in my office that day playing euchre with 1742-A, my secretary. She was beating me—bad—and that made me plenty sore, because I don't dig getting beat; not by a robot, anyway. 1742-A was a robot. Who can afford real secretaries at fifty credits a caper? Besides, business had kind of slacked off.

Well, I was reaching over to turn her off, when this redhead walks in like she owned the place, which she didn't: I rented from a Mrs. Murfreesboro over in Jersey—a bigmouth dame that liked me okay.

"Hello, Bart," the redhead said. She had on a fur coat. It was dead—murdered. I told her to sit down and she said thanks I will and sat down. So far it figured.

She got out a flask from her purse and gave it to me before I could say boo. I shot her a look and let the rye trickle down my craw. It was good rye, fine rye.

"What's the caper?" I snapped.

Then she told me about this thing, the Chocolate Maltese Falcon. She said it was a family heirloom that her old man left to her when he kicked off. She said not only was it worth plenty scratch on the open market, but it had great sentimental value to boot. She said she hired Mike Mallet as a guard, and that's when the trouble started. Next morning: no Mallet, no Falcon.

My job: Find Mallet, get the Falcon, bring it back.

"I suppose," she said, pulling out some vitamin capsules, "that you're in business for your health." She did big things with her eyes. I was impressed.

"No," I told her, "I ain't in business for my health."

She pouted a little. "All right," she said then, "how'd you like a nice new C-note, Handsome?"

"I'd like it fine, ma'am," I said.

"And if you're successful," she cooed, "maybe—who knows?—maybe there'll be a little bonus…"

"You mean?" I pulled her onto my lap and grabbed some lip. It was plenty great. It made me think of oceans crashing against lonely rocks and cotton candy and the carnival where the man in the bright vest says "Hurry! Hurry!"

Then she scrammed. Without leaving a deposit.

"ARE YOU going to turn over the Falcon peacefully?" the green snake guy was saying, "or must we resort to measures best described as strong?"

I laughed in his faces. The butt flashed out and I was sinking, sinking into that old inky black pool…

When I woke up, my arms were tied. My legs were tied. I was sitting in a straight-back chair. It wouldn't have been so bad, maybe—except I was hanging upside down.

"We shall see now how bravely the Earthling struts!" The Venusian slithered over toward the radio. I wondered: What's his pitch? How come he's so interested in a family heirloom?

"You'll never get nothing out of me," I snarled.

The radio hummed into life.

"What the—" I began, lamely.

The Venusian crammed a gag into my mouth. "Listen!" he said.

I listened…

"MONDAY... MONDAY... *Monday!"*

"No, David, please—don't touch me. I came to see you tonight to say...goodbye."

"Goodbye?!"

"Yes! For a few blind, crazy—wonderful—hours, you made me forget that I'm over thirty-five, a married woman and mother of six. But now—"

"Now?"

"—Lord Henri is back. He's—brought the children. I—oh David! Don't touch me! Hold me close!

"Monday!"

"David!"

THEN I got it. Leave it to a stinking wet-belly Venusian to think up the *real* tortures. A soap opera!

I listened to the electric organ's moo. Maybe I shouldn't admit it, but I can't stand soap operas. Oh, I know, *One Man's Cosmos* is mainly what's kept the planets from all-out war, but...well, they give me a pain in the gut.

I tried to shut my ears, but it was no dice...

"...WILL MONDAY be able to make David understand? *How* can she explain to him that she remains loyal to her husband, Lord Henri Winthrop, *not* because she loves him but because he has come back from the Erosian uprising a hopeless paralytic? And what of David? How can he tell Monday that her husband is really dead—murdered—and that his, Lord Henri's, neurotic twin brother, Hugo Winthrop, is playing the part of the invalid husband? How can David let her know that the portals to their happiness lie open—when Hugo threatens to expose David's lurid past as a privateer and *tsi-tso* frond smuggler for the Martians?...And the children! Will the operation actually restore little Tuesday's eyesight? Will Wednesday be able to exorcise the Uranian bandit who has inhabited her body? Will Friday regain her memory in time to stop Nick Branzetti's evil plan?... Tune in tomorrow at this time to see what Fate has in store for—OUR GAL MONDAY: *The Real Life Story that Asks the Question: Can a Girl from a Little Lunar Rocketport Find Happiness with Jupiter's Richest, Most Handsome Queek?...* And now, a word from—"

"**WOULD YOU** care to tell me the location of the Falcon *now*, Mr. Cornblossom?" asked the Venusian, removing the gag.

"I don't know where it is," I snapped. "I don't know. I don't know!"

"Very well..."

He turned the radio higher. And I thought: My God—it might have been television...

"**...YOUR DISHES** and thurpets sparkling bright, dazzling white, with the new washday miracle that requires no rinsing, in fact, requires no water: STAR-FLAKES!... Just open the cage, let out a few flakes, turn them loose on those greasy pots and torgums and—just watch 'em eat up that grime! PRESTO! The job is finished. Then all you have to do is drop the dead flakes into a handy container and bury them somewhere. Remember! STAR-FLAKES are 99.44 per cent ALIVE!..."

"**WHERE IS** the Falcon?"

"I don't know! I don't know!"

"**...AND NOW** stay tuned for the program that follows: The best loved, most respected program in the world: ONE MAN'S COSMOS: *The Story of Just Plain Gratch, the Friendly Tendril-Tender of Betelgeuseville—*"

"**ALL RIGHT,** you damned fiend!" I screamed. "All right! I'll tell you!"

"Ah." The Venusian turned the program off just as my mind was beginning to go. He let me down.

"Before I give it to you," I said, "would you mind letting me know why you're so interested? After all, even if the statue's worth money, you don't need—"

"Statue!" The snake guy chortled and choked. "Statue!" I thought he'd break up; then he sobered—fast. "The bird with the whimsical cognomen," he hissed, "happens to contain enough D-plus-4-over-X grains to blow up a planet!"

Well, that was a kick in the pants, all right.

The government had been going ape trying to figure out who'd stolen the secret D-plus-4-over-X grains. Now I had the picture. Redhead. My beautiful employer. A lousy spy. She'd lifted the bomb from the government and then somebody'd lifted it from her.

Real sweet. Where did it leave me, Bart Cornblossom, Private Orb? At the short end of the stick, that's where.

"The planet I refer to," the Venusian was saying, "is, needless to remark, your own."

"Not," somebody said, "if I can help it!" It was Mike Mallet—groggy, but still plenty tough. He got a half-nelson around the Venusian, grabbed the blaster and in a second Mr. Venus-man was out of the story.

"Hiya, Bart—" Mallet said, then he seemed to remember. "You son of a—"

"Drop the gun. Mallet," a voice said. Mallet whirled around in time to catch three good blasts in the belly. I could smell it clear across the room.

"Hello, baby," I snarled.

"Hello, Bart," she said. "Now be a good boy and play ball. I know you've got the Falcon."

"Come and get it."

She ripped off her clothes and sat in my lap. I started to think of July when I saw that she was wavering, changing. She wasn't no redhead—she was a Martian!

"Mallet was going to turn the Falcon back over to your government," she said, nibbling at my schnoz. "I had to do it. You can see that, can't you?"

"Sure," I said. "I can see that."

"But you're not like that, Bart. You're smart—I can tell. Look"—She twiddled her antennae like a couple castanets—"you've always made a mess out of me inside. Ever since that first kiss. Miscegenation be damned, that kiss was for real! So listen—with the money my government'll pay me for the D-plus-4-over-X grains, we could really live it up."

"Sure, baby," I said, "but I ain't going nowhere all tied up in this chair."

She planted one on my kisser and I felt all May and golden fields of ripe wheat and barefoot in soft river mud. She undid the ropes.

"We've got to hurry, though," she whispered. "The grains explode—or, I should say, implode—every 36 hours: we have barely enough time to ship them away. But first—oh darling, squirrel, my own Bart—we're going to be so very happy..."

She was beautiful, green hair or no green hair, and I held her body—close—and felt her breathing and thought about her next to me at night and the dough and—

I hated it. It made me sick, deep down where it hurts.

"Darling—"

I let her have it in the gut. She sprawled. I grabbed the blaster and pretty soon there was some jam on the floor instead of a dame.

"I'm sorry, baby," I whispered to the sticky heap, "really sorry..."

I don't know—maybe I cried, maybe I laughed. I only know I went crazy mad for a few seconds.

Then I straightened up and thought: so, it's all over. End of the caper. Back to the office and a few straight shots and a couple lousy credits.

But wait. Good gravy, I thought: The Falcon! If she was telling the truth and those D-plus-4-over-X grains really were inside—and getting ready to explode, I mean implode...

I could hear them coming. Lots of them. I ran to the window—big ones, armed, none of them smiling. Venusians, Martians, Jovians—

There was a wild chuckling then. "Heh heh heh!" I took the lunky out of my mug and snapped it away and went through the door.

The chuckling was coming from the typewriter cabinet. I opened it. I should've known better than to be nice to any chick with three legs. They're poison with two—but with three! "What's the gag?" I snarled.

She told me. I couldn't believe it—I made her go through it four times. Then fear started to tear up my stomach muscles.

Mallet had had the Chocolate Maltese Falcon, all right. But he'd been smart. Yeah, smart.

He'd had it melted down into candy bars!

And I'd been hungry, so—

It wasn't easy to take. All the bums in the Galaxy were after the Chocolate Maltese Falcon. Which meant that all the bums in the Galaxy were after me. Because—

Now I *was* the Chocolate Maltese Falcon!

Sweat Niagaraed down my face. The D-plus-4-over-X grains had been missing for—how long? No, no, I thought. Jeez!

I belted the nutty dame a good one on the smeller and listened to her yell until it got boring. Then the door burst open. The big Jovian started to ankle over, hate in his five little pig eyes.

71

I squeezed the trigger and turned the Jovian into a blood pudding like they used to serve in those English places with names like Seven Oaks and Ukridge.

Then the Venusians came in and I figured the better part of valor was to blow. A couple squeezes of the trigger and I blew.

I got behind Mallet's desk and loosened my tie and pushed my hat back on my head, thinking, this is it, Bart boy, this is it.

They were getting ready. That door would fly open in a second—

All of a sudden I felt something happening inside my gut, rumbling like you get after a slug of rye. It started to ache—bad—and the second the scum of the universe spilled in, came up.

Fast.

And then I wasn't Bart Comblossom anymore. I was Christmas and the smell of afternoon turkey and playgrounds here you fall down and scab up your knees and have to run home to Mom and Dad and hello how are you and a piece of the sky just fell Chicken Little and now it's falling falling and how long is eternity Gramp? and Gramp saying it's a right mart piece o' time boy and don't cry son because worse things than blowing up can happen to a man lots worse things and you're floating floating out there with the whole world for a teeter-totter for ever and ever and ever...

MASS FOR MIXED VOICES

(1954)

The garden suddenly hushed and Johnmartin looked up, puzzled, shears in hand. He listened. "What is it?" he asked of the mandrake, which wept; the mongrel mimosa hunched and began to tremble. Johnmartin frowned. "What do you sense, my friends? What disturbs you so?"

The door burst open, and uniformed men came into the garden; they were not careful of the flowers and their boots were smelly with polish.

"What do you want?" asked Johnmartin. A man stepped forward.

"I am the District Coordinator," the man said, in a voice that shook the hybrid orchids and made them fade. "Why did you not answer the letters?"

"I saw no letters."

"You were issued eight; they were delivered to this Level and not returned. Why did you not answer them?"

"Because I didn't read them. I never read letters: they upset me."

"A bad and felonious practice," said the Coordinator. "There are laws governing false receipt of State mail. Under other circumstances I've no doubt you would be properly disciplined; however, I for one, am inclined to leniency. It is a failing. Come now, we must go."

Johnmartin looked at the men and his brows furrowed. "What are you talking about?" he demanded. "What is the meaning of your entering my Level uninvited, damaging my plants, polluting the air? My taxes are paid, the rent is up to date. Leave me alone."

The Coordinator smiled. "But on the most glorious of all days... surely you haven't forgotten!"

Johnmartin dropped his shears. "What? No, no! Still, I haven't been keeping track very carefully; perhaps you are right, you probably are. Well then, in that case, gentlemen, I owe you an apology. I'd meant to speak to the Supervisor about this a long time ago, but what with one thing and another—" he gestured about the glassed multi-floral garden "—as you can see, my time has been quite full. Now, if you'll be good enough to wait one moment..." He picked up the shears and delicately clipped a fungus from a Venusian agranosia blossom. "Nasty things; got to watch them. So, we'll straighten out this matter."

Johnmartin went into a small room and placed a heavier tunic about his shoulders; he returned and frowned briefly at the trailing vestalion which lay crushed beneath the men's feet, then he smiled. "Gentlemen, shall we leave? I can't be too long or there'll be no stopping the creepers."

The Coordinator glanced at his men, shrugged very slightly and led the way out of the garden. And when the last had gone, a gentle questioning susurrus ran through the million growing things...

"Ah," said the Supervisor, waving Johnmartin to a chair, "very glad to see you. After that mixup with the mails, we were afraid that you'd become impatient—tried to 'jump the gun,' as it were. An awful business: happened last Time—though, of course, the information is not widely known. Chap shredded himself in a machine. The very devil to piece together, as you can imagine, since he'd arranged for a fan to blow him all over. However, we soon had him as good as new and in top shape. But there's nothing of the sort here, eh? Everything in order, I take it, all ready?"

Johnmartin shook his head.

He stated his request. "Preposterous!" said the Supervisor. "Unheard of! Entirely without precedent! Perhaps you are mad?"

"No," said Johnmartin.

"No? Then you are joking? A mistake, yes, it must be a mistake." The Supervisor riffled swiftly through the pages of a fat brochure. "You are Johnmartin, XIX, Level IV, City?"

"Oh, yes."

"And you *are* in Golden Time?"

"Yes."

"Plus four months, twenty-two days?"

"I suppose so; I think your records are correct."

"Then I don't understand."

"It's very simple," said Johnmartin, though he began to feel uneasy somehow, and tired. "You see, sir, I should prefer not to die."

"But that's—ridiculous!"

"I hadn't thought of it quite that way, sir."

The Supervisor snapped his finger-joints and fumbled in a box for a cigar. He lit the cigar. "Well, it is. Everyone wants to die."

"I don't."

"You surely cannot mean that. Good heavens, you want to go on living—forever?"

"Yes."

"I must think about this." The Supervisor slumped in his chair and pulled at his joints; he read the brochure carefully. "It's really the most extraordinary thing I ever heard," he mumbled.

Johnmartin became confused. He looked down at his hands and saw the way the sun fell upon them, turning the soft hairs to white over the rough grey gristle of flesh, shadowing the myriad wrinkles and embossing the dark blue veins; then he looked at the Supervisor, and hid his hands beneath his tunic. He wished to be back in his garden. But the wish was faint and was being rapidly replaced by memories long forgotten. Memories of wars and cities, jobs, philosophies. Reasons. He hadn't bothered with reasons for years: he had been content. Now he was being reminded, and it all seemed wearisome.

"Explain yourself," said the Supervisor abruptly.

"That isn't so easy," said Johnmartin; "I hadn't thought explanations would be necessary."

"You hadn't thought—See here, did you think that you could become the first immortal man in the history of the world, simply by walking into my office and requesting it?"

"Not exactly that, sir. I just didn't think there would be any objection. *Is* there an objection?"

"We will come to that presently. First, it would be of immense interest to me to hear the motives behind what you ask. It is the first time anybody has seriously asked it, you must know." Johnmartin thought hard, trying to identify in order to convey. He opened his mouth several times.

"Come, come! Look at your record, man! It isn't, after all, as if you've not lived a full life. Exemplary action in seven major wars; creditable Service in State functions for fifty years; a fine Level; hundreds of descendents—none mutants...Why, it was you who averted, by dint of extreme patriotism, the uprising on Mars in '76!" The Supervisor rose from his chair and proceeded to pace the floor with his hands behind him. Incredulity retarded his speech. "Been everywhere, seen everything—life has been routine and colorless for you since the beginning of the fourth cell decomposition. What reason, then, could you have for wishing to continue a humdrum existence—an existence without benefit to you and of detriment to the System?"

Furiously and determinedly, Johnmartin tried to clear his head of the placid acceptance that had filled him for so long. He tried to locate words which could express what he so strongly felt.

"The sun rising every morning," he began, "does it thrill you?"

"I beg your pardon?"

No, no. It couldn't be done that way. Why hadn't he thought of these things before? Why had he permitted himself isolation to such luxurious extent? But, of course, there had been so much to do, so very much.

"Are you not exhausted? Do you not yearn for the peace, the rest of oblivion? In short, what does life offer you?"

The memories swirled over him now, and the quiescence dispelled somewhat. He had had reasons clearly defined once, he recalled: there was the day he'd made the decision. But there had been no need to tell anyone of it then, so he had allowed it to become lost in its fulfillment.

The Supervisor said, "Wait a moment," and pressed a switch on his desk. A metallic voice answered: "Your honor."

"Find Dr Guvney," said the Supervisor, "and send him to my office immediately;" then: "I must be sure."

Presently a man in a white uniform entered the office, saluted and pulled a small machine on wheels over to Johnmartin's chair.

"Examine him. Let's get to the bottom of this." Johnmartin submitted to the coils and handles and sparks. "He is ready; the cells are in Four Stage and all but gone, sir."

"And he is not mad?"

"Why, no sir."

"Very good. You may leave, Doctor."

The man left with his machine.

"Well?" asked the Supervisor, puffing his cigar.

"It's like this," said Johnmartin, for the reasons were seeping back in again. "If death is what any of the religions say it is, then I don't want it, because all the heavens sound dull and the hells worse. And if death is nothingness, I want it no more, because there is neither rest nor peace in nothingness. Oh, there was a time—long ago—when I wanted death, but I discovered the reason for that: it was because it seemed natural. But it isn't natural."

He was approaching it; this was part anyway.

"I fought the wars, as you say, and married and had the allotted number of children—and when my wife had her Time, I was sad, but she wasn't. And I've loved, too, and served—all the things you say. For all the Time Stages. Then, I discovered something."

"Yes?"

"I discovered Johnmartin, XIX. Try to understand—"

"Get on with it!"

"The Tapes gave us a picture, which I believed, of two Goliaths: Science and Nature: and the picture shows a mighty struggle between the two. And since it seemed natural, I accepted the triumph of Science and rejoiced. But then, after an assignment on Mercury, I came upon the relics left to me by my mother, Mary, III. The relics were books, held in rot by plastic, but the pages were clear; and soon I learned to read—"

"What, books!" said the Supervisor, frowning. "I didn't know any existed... But you say you read these?"

"Yes. I was clever, then; don't ask how I managed this. Perhaps in my Transformation something was done to my brain. At any rate, I found another story of the two Goliaths: one I'd suspected but had never been able to pluck out. The story showed them not warring; instead, they walked together. I wonder what happened..."

"I fail to see—"

"And in the other times, do you know what destroyed men?"

The Supervisor pulled at his tunic impatiently.

"This: when the wisest of them discovered what I had, they were faced with death. So their tragedy was not mine, do you see? I was then only in Stage Two: I had life. There was a line in one of the books and it is my answer, sir. The line is, '*There is an eternity of wonder In a single rose petal.*' From that time, I've been doing just that."

"*Doing just what?*" The Supervisor lost control of his voice.

"Why, studying rose petals!" said Johnmartin. "A whole garden for a Stage of years; and, do you know, I'm only beginning to understand the simplest plants. How marvelously long before I understand Johnmartin, XIX!"

"You mustn't talk like that! Have you spoken of these things to anyone else?" The larger, handsome man applied a handkerchief to his forehead.

"I thought of it. Never have, however. Somehow, I imagine, I felt that sooner or later everyone would find out for himself. Better that way."

After a long pause, the Supervisor said: "My dear fellow, I wonder if you've any idea of what you're saying."

The Supervisor was talking and parading nervously about the room, wringing his hands. "Consider only this one point," he was saying. "If it were possible, and we were at all inclined to grant your request, and you were to speak to others and convince them—why, soon everybody might want to become immortal!"

Johnmartin smiled. "Well, wasn't that the original idea?"

"What do you mean?"

"Wasn't that why science was urged and pleaded with and pushed to perfect more and more ways of defeating man's cripplers and killers—first cancer, then heart disease, then all the other ills? Wasn't the idea to immortalize the species? Why else was a method perfected whereby naturally-deteriorated body cells could be replaced?"

"No! I'm sure that couldn't have been it. The idea is nonsense. Why, overnight the Earth would be glutted; soon all the other planets it's possible to reach. We'd have to stop multiplying!"

"Yes, that's true," said Johnmartin, not wistfully. "We'd have to sit down and study ourselves, and know ourselves, and start to receive life. Is there something wrong with that?"

"Standstill. Dead stop. No progress; nothing to build for—"

"—but ourselves."

"Selfish. Unspiritual."

Johnmartin walked to the window and looked out over the aseptic steel city. Placing an arm across his shoulder, the Supervisor spoke in a voice suddenly almost kindly.

"I think you are acting on a whim. Too much time alone, those foolish book-relics... You needn't be reminded of these facts, but in our system a death occurs but once every fifty years, on the average: the Time Stages were so arranged, as the Tapes tell us, by wiser men than

79

we. Are we to disavow the divine, immutable law: Life-Death? And in doing so, eliminate the World Festival? Not to mention the Military Delegation's ceremonies—one of the greatest assets to peace."

"I'm sorry," said Johnmartin.

"Think! Think of the tourist trade that would be lost, *lost!* The shop-keepers would set up an unbearable howl. And I tremble to think of the reaction of the Universal Council of Churches, when they learn they must put off their World Wake for another half-century. The whole structure of the system would, in fact, be seriously impaired."

Johnmartin was silent. He thought of his garden and of his friends in the garden, his needy little friends who were even now withering, some of them, and falling...

The Supervisor went on more quickly, after consulting his wrist timepiece. "To disappoint these millions would be immoral and shame-ful; it would put an end to Unity. So look at it this way. In submitting gracefully, you serve all mankind!"

He doesn't understand, Johnmartin thought, *he doesn't understand at all. He doesn't see all his reasons melting before one small blade of grass. He doesn't understand.*

"At 17:00 tomorrow the Festival begins. Delegates from all twelve planets plus adjoining satellites will be the first to greet you, personally. There will follow entertainment such as you've never dreamed of, such as a man enjoys only once in his lifetime! Wined, dined, showered with the plaudits and bon voyages of a happily envious world, until your heart is fit to burst with pride. Then, everyone gathers at the Square and there are appropriate, though short speeches from the 4H Clubs, the Church Council, etc., etc., while you recline in state amidst rare furs and silks. The Moment of Silent Prayer as you are administered a tasty liquid, to speed up cell decomposition; you slip, quietly into a subtle languor of heavenly forecasts, the world cheers 'Farewell, Johnmartin!' and you are subsequently dismembered. Now then, old man, how does *that* sound?"

"Terrible," said Johnmartin, a tear in his eye.

The Supervisor pressed numerous buttons on his desk.

Two metal robots with metal tentacles rolled into the room, their sound-boxes crackling.

"Do not let this man out of your sight. He is to talk with no one other than myself. Escort him to his Level, give him ten minutes in his—garden!—and bring him back here." The Supervisor's eyes narrowed. He spoke to Johnmartin. "I regret that this has been necessary; but you have forced me to it. Your relatives have all been notified: they will be present in the Square tomorrow. They are proud and happy, Johnmartin; do not disappoint them as you have disappointed me."

The robots whisked Johnmartin out of the room and down the long grey hall.

Within the glass cage which flew beneath the city, he tried to think of what had happened. But instead he thought of a man named Alexander, who had lived when the dust was mountains. Great Alexander, whose rage at Death for taking his friend Hephaestion was so profound that it caused him to enter a thousand homes and sacrifice a thousand lives. And there was the thin bearded man of dead years ago, whose assassination had filled the Earth with mourning for countless generations…

He wanted to fight, to run away and wander alone through green fields and mountains and return to days of shrines and cemeteries, when death was despised. But he knew he could not. For where were the fields and mountains, now? You could not fight a world.

A voice. "Have we, changed our mind?" There was genuine concern in the voice.

Johnmartin glanced at the soundbox of one of the robots. "No."

"I advise you to think, oh, very hard. It will be so much more pleasant if you see things our way."

A rebellious oath tore to Johnmartin's throat; then, calmly but immediately, and fully formed, it became a thought, which made him smile and say: "I will try," and after a pause: "Do you suppose one small favor might be granted me?"

The voice tingled. "Of course."

"May I have the ten minutes...alone? There is but one exit to my garden, and perhaps with the time to myself, to consider in a new light what you have said—"

"I will issue the instructions." The bulbs on the robots glowed briefly. "Your request will be carried out."

"Thank you."

You could not fight a world, but you might cheat it—with tricks it no longer remembered...

The cage stopped, then entered a different tube; soon they were at the Level. The robots opened the door and wheeled through rooms, finally they came to the garden entrance. Tentacles disengaged hissingly.

Johnmartin hurriedly closed the door. His breath was coming with difficulty now and the sensation of excitement pulsed through his body. For a moment he stood looking at the flowers and listening to his heart.

"My friends," he said, "is this the way you greet me?" He crooked his finger and lifted a yellow rose. "But no, no! You mustn't all be so sad!"

The flowers answered in many ways.

The violet ombala pods huddled together; the Martian sandweed drooped; the Mandragoras sighed with nearly human voices; the crystal-sage, the tulips, all exfloreating sadness in soft ways...

Sunlight came upon Johnmartin and he smiled. Then he began to walk, from plant to plant, to all the plants in the garden, gathering a pinch of golden pollen from one, from another a bit of leaf or a small seed; but from each, something. Mostly seeds he gathered, and when his hands were full, he walked to a table and leaned there, pulling air into his lungs.

The flowers had quieted and the garden was still, almost, it seemed, expectant, waiting.

Johnmartin stood looking about, drinking into his mind the many growing reasons he'd been unable to express. Then he pushed the small scraps into a mound and put them into his mouth and swallowed them. And soon they were all gone.

The robots came into the garden.

"Goodbye," Johnmartin said, but he smiled.

"I am delighted," the Supervisor was saying, "delighted." He was dressed entirely in black. From time to time he removed tears from his eyes with a handkerchief, which was also black. "Yes, yes, yes. It would have been so distasteful otherwise—we'd have had to cut out your tongue and all sorts of ugly things like that, together with appropriate excuses. I should never have forgotten it. As it is, why, the whole thing has gone beautifully. Most successful, orderly Death in my experience, I'd say! Tell me, what changed your mind?"

Johnmartin looked away. The crowd was deafening and the big three-dimensional screen hurt his eyes. "I couldn't shirk my duty to humanity."

"Well spoken!" The Supervisor beamed. "Ah—it couldn't have been the dancing girls and the parties, eh?" He digged slyly at Johnmartin's ribs.

A siren suddenly began to whine and the crowd fell silent: there was only the sound of the cameras, and of shuffling feet.

The Supervisor's voice boomed into a microphone. "Dear Friends, we are gathered here today in great sadness. Oh, dark the skies with mourning and bleak the..."

The voice droned on and on and soon sobbing was heard; then uncontrolled lachrymose cries, blowings of noses and grief-stricken coughs. A hidden organ played a melody in the minor key, and robots rolled noiselessly down aisles, distributing tissues.

In the elevated, transparent coffin, Johnmartin fidgeted and wished it were all over. He could not feel tired, for they had done strange restorative things to his body: he could only feel impatient, and a little ashamed.

"...in a better world, where we shall all, one day, come face to face with..." The voice went on.

And then, after endless minutes, abruptly the Services concluded. A solemn procession of men moved up to the platform, filing slowly past the coffin; occasionally someone would run fingers across Johnmartin's face: the Taram priest from Venus left an oily glob on his forehead. Johnmartin tossed restlessly.

The Supervisor approached, hands folded tightly together. His countenance reflected humility in the face of the unknown, unsubdued thought tempered by stoic, resolute recognition of his unhappy duty. He asked, sonorously: "In conclusion, if there is anything, any small service we can perform, you have but to ask."

"There *is* something."

"Only name it!"

"I would be very grateful if...afterwards...you would bury the— remains—in my garden."

The Supervisor frowned, then shrugged. "It is done."

"And one other thing. Could you manage to keep my plants, all of them, in perpetual care? Water them and feed them, but otherwise leave them in peace? Could you do that for me?"

The Supervisor turned to the multitude and spoke into the microphone. "By all let this be heard! That Johnmartin, XIX, deceased, shall be taken to his...garden...and that the garden shall forever from this day be kept as he himself kept it!"

A great cheer.

Johnmartin relaxed. "Thank you."

"Very well!" The Supervisor took Johnmartin's hand and shook it vigorously. "And now, farewell!"

A beautiful woman came onto the platform with a silver tray, upon which rested a single flask of finest translucent alloy. Within, the liquid was amber and it shone in the artificial suns.

The crowd was now mute and immobile. The organ music had stopped. The woman moved toward the casket respectfully; once she smiled, and then handed the flask to Johnmartin. "Farewell! Farewell!"

Holding the sweet liquid in his mouth, he looked over the eager, silent people, the tired, bored, satiated people, whose eyes glistened with curiosity and envy and anticipation.

He swallowed.

His brain began quickly to swirl, but pleasantly, and the scene before him dissolved into a colored wash. Inchoate, unwilled images took vague form and he yielded to their development.

Until there was only the kaleidoscopic progression of the images.

Sad faces he saw, and heard sighs of monotony in a gleaming cold world. Rusted metal-men and tarnished grey machines, standing skeletally on open empty plains...

Beautiful people, all yawning, plummeting through a Space of stars and blackness...

And, sharper, clearer than the rest, the final image. Johnmartin clung to it, smiling, a long time before the final darkness came.

It was a garden he saw, his garden, alive with plants from every corner of the Earth and from every planet in the world. It was warm and familiar. But there was something which was not familiar.

In the garden, where the sun could get to it, standing young and small among the others, was a flower. And though still moist with the earth from which it had sprung, the flower stood proudly and stretched out peculiar little buds and tendrils and drank the sunlight. And there was something in it of every other blossom.

Johnmartin welcomed the darkness.

HAIR OF THE DOG

(1954)

rterio—what was that you said?"

"—sclerosis."

"Bunky?"

"Yes."

"Our Bunky?"

"Yes."

"God!"

"Sic transit gloria mundi. A rare case. Poor chap—went out like a light. Just like a light."

"But I mean—Bunky, of all people! Up in his studies, young, well-off, good-looking, everything to live for!"

"Ave atque vale, old boy."

"I can't believe it."

"Here today, gone tomorrow."

"God!"

Up until now, Lorenzo Gissing had thought about death, when he thought about it at all, which was practically never, as one of those things one didn't think about. The frequency of its occurrence among the lower classes especially made it impossible. None of his relatives had ever died, to his knowledge. Nor had any of his good chums. In fact, he had never once looked upon a human corpse. The entire subject, therefore, was dismissed as pointless, morbid, and not a little scatological, no more to be worried over than the other diseases that came as direct sequels to unclean living habits.

So the news of Bunky Frith's rather pell-mell departure from this world affected Lorenzo as few things had. His reaction was one of total disbelief, followed by an angry sense of betrayal. He took to his rooms. He refused to eat. He slept little, and then fitfully, leaping to the floor from time to time and cursing, knocking the blue china about and gazing at his image in the mirror.

"God!" he exclaimed every so often.

The funeral was the usual sort of thing, though perhaps a shade more elaborate than most. Lorenzo sat dazed throughout. The flowers made him ill at the stomach. The music was unbearable. And Rev. Bottomly's oration struck a new low. Presently, however, services ended and it was time to line up for a last look at old Bunky.

"Dear old pal!" cried Lorenzo, when his turn had come to stand before the dead man. *"What has happened here?"*

They had to carry him away. His eyes had rolled up in his head, his skin had paled and, all things considered, he looked not quite as good as the late Frith.

His studies immediately took a dip; such had been his scholastic standing at the university that this was fatal. He left the ivied walls and took up residence in the city. He became a changed person. From a happy-go-lucky Pierrot to a fog-bound Raskolnikov. Overnight. He lost touch with his parents, with his friends, and even with his tailor. He thought of only one thing: Death. His money went for any literature connected with the subject, and when he was not thinking about it he was reading about it. The books were without exception humorless and dispiriting, though the medical publications were the worst of all. They had pictures. In color.

He bought every manner of medicine imaginable. He was inoculated against, or given reason to believe he would not contract, diphtheria, smallpox, chicken pox, elephantiasis, polio, jungle rot, cirrhosis of the liver, Bright's disease, hoof and mouth disease, and the common cold. He avoided drafts and stuffy rooms. He checked daily with four doctors to make sure he did not have cancer, heart trouble, or perforated ulcers.

Then he read a book on the statistics of death. It floored him. He gave up all thought of travel, almost of movement of any kind. It nearly drove him insane. With disease one could fight back, take precautions, guard oneself—but what chance did one have against accidents? If you went into the streets a safe might fall on your head, if you stayed at home a thief might murder you and then set the house afire.

Lorenzo was thinking these things one night when he found that he had wandered far from home. The gurgle of the Thames could be heard beyond a fogbank. It was late. He remembered poor old Bunky and how frightful he had looked—like dried paste there in the coffin, and dead, dead, dead. He ran a pale hand through his thick, bushy hair.

Why not? Do it yourself and at least you won't have to go on waiting for it. There were worse things than drowning. Arteriosclerosis, for one.

He took a step. A finger tapped his shoulder. He let loose a strangulated cry.

"Mr. Gissing?" The man was dressed in execrable taste: jaunty bowler, plus fours, a dun jacket of reprehensible fit. "Mr. Lorenzo Gissing?"

"Yes. Who are you? What are you going about prodding people for? I might have had a heart attack!"

"I'm sorry—I didn't mean to startle you. But you were about to jump into the river."

Mr. Gissing said "Coo" or something that sounded like coo.

"I represent a firm," the man said, "whose services you may find attractive. Shall we talk?"

Lorenzo nodded dumbly. His armpits discharged cold pellets of perspiration as he became aware of what he had been about to do.

"Very well," the man said. "Now then. Does the thought of death keep you up nights, plague you, torture you, prevent you from full enjoyment of life's rich bounty? Does it?"

"In a manner of speaking."

"And do you wish to be rid of this nagging worry?"

"Good heavens, yes! But how?"

"I'll tell you how, sir. I represent the Eternal Life Insurance Company and—"

"What was that?"

"—and we are in a position to help you. Our plan is roughly this: We offer Eternal Life to our clients. Now, we've been established since—"

"Oh dear, is this some sort of quiz program? Because, if it is—"

"Of course, we'll have to sit down and discuss this in more detail. Get your signature on some contracts and the like. But a run-down of our services may be stated in this way: For a very nominal fee—very nominal indeed, sir—to be paid to us monthly, we give you immortality."

"You're not the de—"

"Oh no. I merely work for the company. Mr. Asmodeus, our president, has given up canvassing. It's a very old firm."

"Well…"

"Think of it, Mr. Gissing! No more worry about death! But life—happy, content, healthy, eternal, free to do what you choose without thought to consequences."

"Hmm."

"And all for a very low monthly payment."

"What sort of payment?"

"There will be, of course, the usual waiting period. Then— by the way, which do you prefer, the first or the fifteenth?"

"Oh, I don't know—the first, I guess."

"Then on the first of the month and every subsequent month, you will just slip your payment in the mails to us, and, why Mr. Gissing, you'll just go on living, that's all!"

"What *sort* of payment?"

"One hair. Plucked from your head on exactly the day the payment comes due—never before."

"Did you say one hair?" Lorenzo started calculating and remembering his wild heavy brown bush.

"One hair. No more, no less." The man dug in his briefcase for some papers. "Each shall represent a month of life to you."

Lorenzo gulped. "Well now," he said, "that's not exactly eternity."

"Rather close though," the man smiled, "wouldn't you say?"

"Yes," Lorenzo agreed, remembering approximately how many hundreds of thousands of hairs one is supposed to have on one's dome.

"Are you interested?"

"I'm interested. But tell me this—what happens when they're all gone?"

"Then you die."

"Oh."

"It's the best we can do. You won't get a better offer."

"Well, I mean, is that all? I just—die? Where's *your* profit?"

"Ah, Mr. Gissing, I wouldn't have suspected such business acumen in one so young. But you're quite right. There is one other little matter."

"I supposed as much. My soul, eh?"

"You won't miss it. They're sort of like an appendix, nowadays."

"Well…"

"Shall we talk business? I do have other calls to make."

"All right."

The man spoke for almost an hour. Then he gave Lorenzo the contract to read. It seemed in order. Lorenzo signed all copies in a peculiar reddish ink provided by the man. Then he was given a brochure, a number of self-addressed envelopes, a carbon of the contract, and a payment book.

"It will be renewed every hundred years or so," the man said, beginning to put things away. "Well!" he said. "That seems to take care of about everything. We're all fixed up now. I think you'll be quite happy with the arrangement—our firm does quite a volume business. You'd be amazed. Good evening, Mr. Gissing. Remember now, the first payment falls due on the first, which is forty-five days from now."

"Good evening," Lorenzo said. But the man was already gone.

"LORENZO, YOU'RE looking peculiar."

"Peculiar, Mama?"

"So healthy! That *savoir vivre,* that smile, that twinkle in the eye! Is this my boy?"

"It is, Mama. In the flesh. Quick now, what has happened? Father ill?"

"No—worse luck. Dead."

"What? Dad? Dad dead?"

"Quite."

"Oh."

"Last week. Fell off his horse whilst hunting a fox. Cracked his skull, poor thing."

"Well, that's the way it goes. *Sic transit gloria mundi.*"

"You're taking it remarkably well, Lorenzo."

"Here today, gone tomorrow, Mama, I always say. Part of the game, what? Well, at least we shan't have to suffer. I imagine poor old Dad's estate is tidied up. That is—"

"Oh Lorenzo!"

"Yes, Mama?"

"Your father, bless his departed soul, has kept something from us."

"And what might that be, Mama?"

"He—I mean to say, your father—well, he—"

"Yes? Yes? Yes?"

"Stony."

"Oh no!"

"Yes. Not a sou. How he ever managed to keep us in such luxury, why, it must have taken everything! Such a good man, not to worry us."

"Yes, quite so, quite so. Mama, when you say 'not a sou' I assume you're indulging in a slight overstatement of the situation. That is to say, surely—"

"Nothing. Except debts. Whatever shall we do? There's scarcely enough for the funeral expenses."

"Good heavens!"

"What is it, Lorenzo?"

"I've just remembered something. An appointment in the city—business; you know. I must leave at once!"

"But my son, you've just arrived!"

"I know. Well, chin up! I'm off!"

Back in the city, Lorenzo Gissing thrashed a good bit at this blow. How ludicrous, after all. Here one is offered eternal life, or very nearly that, and the next thing one knows, one has no money with which to enjoy it. He took to brooding, and might have continued to do so indefinitely, had not a happy thought occurred. He smiled. He visited his tailor.

"My dearest!" he said not long afterwards to the Lady Moseby, formerly of Tunbridge Wells now of London, rich, widowed and lonely. "My very dearest only one!"

Anastasia Moseby had heretofore been spared the attentions of bachelors both eligible and ineligible owing to the genuineness of her despair at the death by his own hand of her husband. Sir Malcolm Peterhenshaw Moseby, Bart. This despair was transmitted by the pallor in her face and the quietness of her speech, which qualities actually made her more attractive and generally desirable. She was known as a woman who had loved and would not love again.

Lorenzo Gissing demonstrated the fallacy of this notion by walking down the old aisle with the now beamingly radiant lady, to the incipient dismay of certain other parties in attendance.

She was a woman transformed.

"Lorenzo, duck," she enthused later, at the proper time and place. "I do love you."

"And I love you," Lorenzo responded.

"I love you more than anyone or anything else on Earth!"

"And I love you more than anyone or anything else in the entire galaxy."

"We shall be so very happy."

"Fantastically, deliriously, I'm sure."

"And will you love me all your life?"

"I resent the question's implication."

"Sweet, we are such a pair, we two. I know and understand you so well, Lorenzo. The others—"

"Yes, what about the others?"

"They are saying—no, I cannot even repeat it!"

"What, what? Is this to be a marriage of secrecy and deception?"

"They're saying, Lorenzo my dearest plum, that you married me only for my money."

"The swine! Who said it? Who? I'll beat him to within an inch—"

"Hush, my duck! You and I know differently, don't we."

"Indeed we do. By the bye, what *does* the bally old bank book come to?"

"Oh, I don't know. A few hundred thousand, I should imagine. What does it matter?"

"Matter? Not at all. Only, well, you see—I've had some baddish luck."

"Not really."

"Yes. Wiped out. Utterly."

"I see."

"Yes. Well, never mind; I've my application in at the terminal for a clerk's position. It won't be much, but by the Almighty, we'll make it, and without your having to dip—"

"Lorenzo! Kiss me!"

"There!"

"You'll never have to worry about money, so long as you kiss me like that and are faithful to me. This one must go right."

"I beg pardon?"

"Nothing. Only that just before Sir Malcolm's tragic death, the details of which you must have read, I—well, I discovered he had been faithless to me."

"The fool. Darling, oh my darling!"

It did not consume a great deal of time for Lorenzo to arrange for the account to be put in both their names. As soon as this was accomplished, and he had withdrawn the greater portion of it, there was a marked change in the relationship. Anastasia's fey charm was all well and good for a while, downright pleasant once or twice, but as Lorenzo put it to her one evening, there were other fish to fry.

The day before he left for Cannes, he received an unstamped letter in the mails, which read:

A FRIENDLY REMINDER!

Your first payment falls due in exactly two (2) days.

Thank you.

> Asmodeus, Pres.
> ETERNAL LIFE INS. CO.
> Gehenna

It made him feel good somehow, in a creepy kind of way, and he left whistling. He did not kiss his wife goodbye.

HAVING PLUCKED one hair from his head, placed it into an envelope and included a covering letter, Mr. Gissing set forth to enjoy himself. He learned rapidly the extent to which this was going to be possible.

Having made certain improper overtures to a bronzed and altogether statuesque beauty sunning herself in the Riviera warmth, he was annoyed at the approach of said beauty's husband: tall, angry, and, Lorenzo felt sure, a circus giant. There followed an embarrassing scene. The husband actually hit him. In the mouth.

But he didn't feel a thing. And though he had never previously been athletically inclined, Lorenzo's amazing staying power—this extra dividend—eventually tired the irate husband to a point whereat it was possible to kick him senseless. It made quite an impression on the bronzed statuesque beauty, and they subsequently enjoyed a relationship which, though brief, was nothing if not satisfactory.

Mr. Gissing proceeded to cut what may be described as a wide swath. He became increasingly mindless of consequences. He traveled from point to point with the unconcerned purpose of a bluebottle fly, leaving untold damaged reputations and memorable evenings in his wake. Each month, on the first exactly, he mailed away the hair, praised his good fortune, and went on to newer conquests. He set records for derring-do, performing publicly such feats as diving three hundred feet into a bathtub, and wrestling a giant ape to the death.

At length, however, as is often the case with the most adventuresome of hearts, he tired of the gaiety, the lights and the tinsel, and began to long for the comforts of hearth, dog-at-the-feet, and wife. He therefore gave up his apartment in Tangier, composed an effusive letter of apology to Anastasia—explaining that the death of his father had sent him temporarily barmy—and returned home.

Nothing had changed. Anastasia was as lovely as ever: forgiving, understanding, loving. She tended to his wants as though he had not been gone for the better part of five years. There was not one word of recrimination at his having spent most of the money. They settled in their cozy little cottage and, aside from noticing a slightly peculiar look in his wife's eyes once in a great while, Lorenzo Gissing partook of the pleasures of domesticity, content until the old urges should again assail him.

✦ ✦ ✦

IT WAS during dinner, with Heine the spaniel lying on his feet and roast beef lying on his plate, that Mr. Gissing dropped his coffee cup to the floor.

"What did you say?" he demanded.

"I merely remarked, dear," answered his wife, "that it's a pity you should be losing your hair so rapidly."

"It's a lie!" Mr. Gissing raced for the mirror and stood transfixed before it, running his hands over his head. "It's a lie!"

"Well, you needn't get so broken up about it. Lots of people lose their hair. I shall still love you."

"No, no, no, that isn't the point. Do you really think that I am?"

"No question about it."

"God!"

It was quite true. It was going fast. How strange that he hadn't noticed before—

He noticed now. It was as if it were all rotting off, so to speak. "My God!" cried Mr. Gissing. "I'm shedding!"

It thinned first at the front of his head: the hairline receding some ten or fifteen inches. In short order it was reduced to a definite tonsure, giving him the curious appearance of a profane monk. He became frantic, finally to the point of spilling the beans to Anastasia.

"But how dreadful!" Anastasia said, "Oughtn't you to complain to the Better Business Bureau? I'm sure it must be some terrible fraud."

"What shall I do? I'm going bald, don't you understand?"

"Now I wonder," Anastasia said, "if that's what's happening to all the men that go bald? I mean, are they clients of Mr.—what's his name—Asmodeus—too?"

"You don't believe me!"

"Now, dear, you've always had a vivid imagination. But if you insist. I'll believe you. Why not see a scalp specialist?"

"Of course! Yes, I will!"

He did. The specialist, a Dr. Fatt, shook his head sadly. "Sorry, old man. One of those rare things. Nothing we can do."

He went to other specialists. They also shook their heads. He thought of saving the hairs as they fell. But no. In the contract it was clearly put forth:

"—that this hair shall be plucked from the head on the exact day payment falls due; never before, otherwise client risks forfeiture of his security..."

"The fiends!" he groaned. "They're responsible for this! Why didn't somebody warn me I'd go bald?"

Mr. Gissing lived the life of a tortured man, running from scalp specialist to scalp specialist, inundating his almost totally unhirsute head with a great variety of oils, herbs, juices and powders. He submitted to treatments by diet, magnet, X-ray, vibrator, and once tried hanging a dead toad from the lattice at midnight. Nothing helped. He grew balder and balder and—

At last, down to no more than twenty single hairs, he waited for the first of the month to roll 'round, and then carefully sliced the plucked hair into two sections, and mailed one of the sections off. He received a letter the same day.

Dear Mr. Gissing:
In Hades, we do not split hairs.
Very truly yours,
Asmodeus

He got off the remaining section hurriedly.

Finally, when only one solitary tendril protruded from his pate, one tiny hair flourishing like a lone palm tree in a gigantic desert, Mr. Cissing, nearly speechless with anxiety, contacted the newly founded Binkley Clinic.

"You've come to the right place," said Dr. Binkley, saturnine of expression and comfortingly beshocked and tressed with carrot-colored filaments.

"Thank God," said Mr. Gissing.

"Not a bit of it," said the doctor. "Thank me."

"Can you really keep me from going bald?"

"My dear sir, the Binkley method will grow hair on a billiard ball." He pointed to a green-felt-covered table, on which rested three billiard balls, each covered with a thick hairy matting.

"That's all quite nice," Mr. Gissing said, "but will it grow hair on *me?*"

"I guarantee that in one month you will begin to feel the effects."

"Feel the effects—be specific, man. In one month's time, will there be any growth?"

"My method is expensive, but rightly so. Yes, Mr. Gissing: though slight, there will definitely be hairs upon your head in one month's time."

"You *promise?* That is, you've done it before?"

"With scalp conditions such as yours, which are uncommon, yes, I can say unequivocally, I have."

"Let's begin immediately."

It was necessary for Mr. Gissing to stand on his head for several hours and then submit to having his dome raked with a strange electrical device rather like a combination cotton gin and sewing machine.

"Be careful," he reminded the doctor every few minutes, "do not on your life disturb that last hair. Don't even go near it."

Upon leaving the Binkley Clinic, Mr. Gissing put a Band-Aid over the hair and returned to his cottage, tired but happy

"It's all right now," he said with jubilance to his wife. "I've this month's payment. And by next month I am guaranteed a new growth. Isn't that *wonderful?*"

"Yes, dear. Supper is ready now."

After stowing away his first undyspeptic meal in some time, Mr. Gissing turned to his wife and was shocked to observe how wan and beautiful she looked in the firelight. He felt a surge of sorts.

"Anastasia," he said. "You're looking fit."

"Thank you, Lorenzo."

"Very fit indeed."

"Thank you, Lorenzo."

"In fact, if I may remark, you're looking positively pretty, somehow."

"You are very gallant."

"Nonsense. See here, you're not angry about what happened as a direct result of poor old Dad's death, I mean my skipping off and all that—"

"Not angry, no."

"Good girl. Good *girl*. It's the way a man's constructed, one supposes. Well, it's all over now. I mean, we were barely getting to know one another."

"Yes..."

"Say, pretty sage of the old boy—meaning me—outsmarting the devil himself, what?"

"Very sage indeed, Lorenzo. I'm tired. Do you mind if I go to bed?"

Mr. Gissing smiled archly and delivered a pinch to his wife's backside. "Oh," he exclaimed, "I can feel it growing already. The hair. I can make the payment tomorrow—it *is* the first, isn't it?—and by next month I'll be able to start all over again without any fears. Dr. Binkley says *his* hair won't shed. Think of it!"

They retired and after a certain amount of wrestling and one thing and another, Mr. Gissing dropped off to a very sound sleep. He dreamed.

"ANATASIA! OH my Lord!"

"Yes dear, yes, what is it?"

"You mean *where* is it! It's gone, that's where. *Gone*, you understand?"

"I don't know what you're talking about."

'The hair, you idiot. It fell off. Lost. You must help me look for it."

They looked. Frantically. In the bedroom. In the bed. In the bedclothes. The mattress. The sheets. The pillows. Nothing. No hair.

"Again, we must look again. Carefully this time. Oh, *carefully!*"

They covered every inch of the room, then every other room, on hands and knees.

"Are you sure you had it when you came in?"

"Yes. I checked."

"Well, have you looked in all your pockets?"

"Yes. No—wait. No. Not there."

"Then where did you lose it?"

Mr. Gissing gave his wife a withering look, and continued his prayerful search. He inspected his clothes minutely. His shoes, his socks. The bathroom drain. The combs. Everything, everywhere.

"We must find it. It's getting near midnight."

"But dear, we've looked all day and all night. Can't you just sort of forget about it?"

"Anastasia, from the way you talk one would think you *wanted* to see me sizzle!"

"Lorenzo, what a discourteous and utterly unattractive thing to say!"

"Just keep looking."

At last, exhausted, breathless, hungry, his mind a kaleidoscope of fear, Mr. Gissing hurled himself onto the bed and lay there trembling.

"Would this be it?"

He leapt to his feet. He took the hair from his wife's hand. "Yes! Yes, it is! I'm sure of it—see, how brown it is. It isn't yours, yours is all black. Oh Anastasia, we're saved! I'll get it in the mails right away."

He started back from the post office still shaken by the experience and was almost to the door. A finger tapped his shoulder.

"Mr. Gissing?"

"Yes, yes?" He turned. It was the man he'd encountered by the Thames, so long ago. Still badly dressed.

"Well, what is it? Almost had me, didn't you?"

"Come with me," the man said.

"In a pig's eye I will. The payment's already in, old boy, and on time too. According to the con—"

The man's clothes suddenly burst into flame and in a moment Mr. Gissing found himself confronted by a creature unlike any in his experience. He quailed somewhat.

"*Come—with—me.*"

A hand of hot steel clutched Mr. Gissing's arm, and they began to walk down an alley where no alley had ever seemed to be before. It was quite dark.

"What," Mr. Gissing shrieked, "is the meaning of this, may I inquire? The contract clearly states that as long as I get a hair off to you on the first of every month everything's in order."

"That is not quite correct," said the creature, exuding the kind of aroma one smells at barbeques. "One of *your* hairs."

"But—but that *was* my hair. I saw it. No one else was in the house. Certainly not in the bedroom. Except my wife—and she's brunette."

The creature laughed. "It was not yours."

"Then what—oh surely not! Anastasia, unfaithful? I can hardly believe it."

They walked in silence. The creature said nothing.

"My heart is broken!" Mr. Gissing wailed. "Another man in *our* bedroom! What sort of world is this where such iniquity is permitted to exist! Surely it can be no worse where we are going."

They disappeared into the blackness.

Anastasia Gissing never saw her husband again. She was left to seek solace from her thoughts and a small brown-haired spaniel named Heine. She bore up well.

THE QUADRIOPTICON

(1954)

I t was a dark musty place, bigger than it had to be and faintly reminiscent of a family crypt. The asbestos-and-cork walls were peeling like the bark of a dead tree, the proscenium drapes were holey rags, the ceiling was covered with a million plastered cracks. But Projection Room #7 had a nice carpet: rich, thick, crimson.

Like Sherman Boetticher's face. Of course he tried to fake it by putting on his informal smile, but this failed because the smile looked as if it had been drawn on with a burnt match by a small boy. To the assembled crowd stationed in regiments in the tan leather studio chairs, the truth was evident: Sherman Boetticher was coming loose at the hinges.

Finally he looked at his watch, giggled once and trembled forward. "All right," he said, "I guess we'll just have to proceed. I'm sure Rock was unavoidably detained; however, in deference to Mr. Mendel, who is, as we all know, a very busy man—Jimmy! Let's go."

The lights dimmed down to almost absolute blackness. Then a thin blue spot came on and picked around the room for a few seconds before lighting on the mole-faced producer. Boetticher opened his mouth and began: "Ladies and gentlemen, what you are about to witness will take its place as the most unusual, the most startling, the most precedent-smashing advancement in the history of the motion picture. Thanks to a revolutionary—"

"Hands up, everybody!" A tall well-built man in a trench coat stepped suddenly into the spotlight and gave Sherman Boetticher a quick hard push. The man held something in his hand that glinted silver. "This is the vice squad! You're all under arrest for violating the Mann Act, the Woman Act, and what is that couple doing in the third-row balcony?" Marcus Mendel, the studio manager, smiled the quickest, smallest, most obligatory of smiles and swiveled his head back toward the screen.

Boetticher's little fists unballed and he took the tall man's arm. "You're just in time, Rock. Now if you'll take a seat..."

"Rock, please," Boetticher whined.

The man whose real name was Leroy Guinness O'Shea winked and brought his hand down on a bare and exceedingly freckled back. "Bless me, if it isn't the tail well calculated to keep you in suspense!"

Sheila Tyler smiled gaily. "Hello, doll."

"Darling!"

Rock Jason stumbled across legs to his chair. He sat down next to the corpulent-hipped queen of the columnists, Dolly Dixon, whose sudden kewpie smile gave her face the look of a crumpled balloon. "Rock, you naughty boy—I swear, I mean, you'd be late for your own funeral! Aren't you knocked out?"

"In a sense," Jason said, removing the flask and shaking it disappointedly. Then he leapt up: "I *refuse* to sit next to this woman!"

Dolly Dixon's face reddened and then exploded in a germ-laden laugh. "Stop, oh stop!"

Boetticher's eyes were now his only mobile feature. "Why?" he asked dutifully.

"Because," Jason said, planting a kiss on the powder-caked cheek, "she gets grabby."

"Stop, Rock, you old rogue, you old liar!"

Jason smiled. He hiccupped. "Well, all right—but no kneesies."

"Ha ha. That's just so deliriously funny!"

He jerked his head around. Only one person in the world would dare to be so openly sarcastic to him: Robbie. Dear Robbie, his co-star, the face that launched a thousand fan magazines.

"Ah," Jason cooed, "America's *other* sweetheart. How are you, love?"

Robin Summers wasn't smiling at all. "Just dandy," she said. "Now does Mr. Box Office think he might shut up long enough for us to see the picture?"

She was indecently beautiful today. Golden-brown skin lustrous against the white no-sleeved blouse, wild black hair set off by simple silver earrings...and that thin black ribbon around her throat...

"Don't fret, darling," Jason said. "If you miss it now you can catch it at your nearest bagnio."

Dolly dissolved. Her jellyfolds of fat quivered and exuded the powerful aroma of musk. The combination, the perfume and the flask of whisky, made Jason's head float uncomfortably.

Robin Summers threw herself back in her chair. Her round full lips were pulled down in inexpressible anger.

Jason hiccupped again. "On with the production!" he hollered. "I yield the floor."

The lights got dim again and the spot picked up Boetticher's faulty and helpless figure.

"As I was saying," he intoned, "this is an historic occasion. What you are about to watch is the newest innovation, and the greatest, since 3-D—since sound, even! Through a secret process, which we have spent ten years in developing—"

Jason fingered his mustache and snorted lowly. He leaned toward Dolly's ear. "Poor Sherm is a dear sweet thing," he whispered. "Lies so convincingly, don't you agree? I mean, is there *anyone,* who doesn't know that this little fellow—what's his name, Gottfried, Gottschalk—invented it, by accident..."

"—and from now on, all of Galactic's pictures will employ the use of this startling invention, the Quadriopticon. Now, I'm not going to bore you with a lot of technical language at this present instant. But basically, what we have here is a machine that literally puts *you* inside the picture! That's what I said. No glasses are required for this process, no discomfort, no eyestrain. The use of the revolutionary Prismascopic screen not only gives the illusion of third dimension, but makes this illusion stick! Ladies and gentlemen, the 3-D 'flatties' are a thing of the past. No more throwing things at the audience to suggest realism—folks, it's there, all the time! And why? you ask. Because the image is broken up for you by the Quadriopticon, which works exactly like the human eyes. The Prismascopic screen is actually many screens, each overlay representing the effect of each frame of depth on the naked eye." Boetticher tapped his glasses for effect. "Ever try looking through a screen door? What do you see? Wait now —two things, each completely different. If you concentrate on the screen, then you can't see anything else outside; if you 'adjust' your human telescopes, see, then the screen disappears —right? Well, this amazing machine permits us to do just that with our image, in exactly the same identical way."

Boetticher looked proudly disdainful over the blank pond of faces.

"But let's save some surprises. Believe me, please, take my word for it, it's revolutionary. It'll put Galactic Pictures right back into position as the foremost production unit in the world!" Boetticher was warming up; the embarrassment flushed out of him: it was his baby. He began to sound like a bad carny barker, the words most frequently used being *revolutionary* and *tremendous.*

"And so," he said, "it was only natural that the world's first picture in 4-D—"

Ears perked up: these were the magic words. 4-D!

"—should star the inimitable team, Rock 'n' Robbie, those grand troupers and America's Sweethearts. Ladies and gentlemen, we give you the most thrilling story ever written, a tremendous follow-through on the current science fiction trend—" Herman Mancini, the writer, sank down in his seat "—*The Conquest of Jupiter!* Starring Rock Jason and Robin Summers! Filmed in fabulous color with the fabulous 4-Dimensional Quadriopticon camera!"

The spot flicked out and the room was dark. Rock Jason smiled: he'd seen the rushes. They were pretty fair. It involved some hocus-pocus with a prismed screen—which he could hear being lowered in the blackness—and some junk sprayed out through a bellows, "to bring not only sight and sound but also *smell* to motion pictures." It was all right. It would kick up some excitement and that would net him more dollars— but it would die out, just as everything had since the big 3-D craze. Then Galactic would be back riding on his shoulders. Which was all right, too.

He could hear Robbie breathing in back of him. The little moron—of them all, he thought, she detests me most. Well, such is Fame's Cross. Great men have ever had their enemies. Didn't she know he could kill it for her, like *that!* Just refuse to play in a picture with her. Then where would the independent Miss Summers be? The independent, beautiful, lovely, desirable Miss Summers...

"I'm so excited," Dolly was whispering, "I could just flip. Couldn't you just flip, Rock?"

"Like a trained dog, sweet."

"Well, they're certainly keeping us on edge. Leave it to Sherm. Sherm's a live wire. Sherm's going places."

"Sherm," Jason said truthfully, "stinks."

The lights came on again. Billy Zelmo, the comic, got up and did a Bronx cheer. There were rustlings.

"A little difficulty getting the sync right," Boetticher called nervously from the booth.

Jason swam across the legs and tumbled out into the aisle, stopping only to stick out his tongue at Mendel.

"Fear not!" he hooted. "Fortunately, among my variegated talents, I am a highly skilled projectionist." Still carrying along the flask, he careened up the aisle.

Robbie was furious. He could tell. Why should she get so furious? Her eyes were flashing embarrassedly, those black black eyes.

"Here now boys, let me at it!"

"It's all right, Rock," Boetticher rattled, "it's all right. We got it fixed okay now. Why don't you just—"

"Nonsense. Permit a trained man to make it official."

He didn't exactly know why he was doing it. He could see the agony outside on the faces of the others in the film: Guy Randolph, the old regular, the scared-to-death ex-Shakespearean who once went three years without a picture job; Burton Mitchell, on his last legs, hungry for the break this seemed to be; the rest, the frightened people who all knew that this roll of celluloid could make or break them, depending upon its outcome. And now Rock Jason was doing his damndest to louse it up for them.

"Rock, this is important. We've got to snag Mendel. *Please* sit down."

The lights had been killed. The Quadriopticon, a weird box that didn't even look like a projector, had begun to hum and warm.

"Don't tell me what to do, you—sycophant! I said I'd fix it and that's what by God I intend to do!"

Jason pushed Boetticher's limpid form away and advanced on the machine.

There was a small door on the back. He opened this.

"Don't touch!" someone said, trying to grab his hands. "You shouldn't touch!" It was little Mr. Gottschalk.

"Avaunt!" he yelled at the bald-headed old man, and gave him a push, too.

Mr. Gottschalk stumbled out of his way.

Behind the tiny door was a pair of electrodes. The ball-pointed shafts of metal crackled and danced white hot light. Beyond the field was an indented knob. Jason started to reach.

"Nein, nein! Wait. I will turn it off—"

His right hand, which held the metal flask, was draped across the bare metal control cabinet; with his left hand, Jason reached far in and felt the sparks tickle and fry his flesh. The whisky container touched metal at the exact moment he grabbed the flying knob.

Rock Jason felt a giant hand pick him up and toss him away, far away, where it was all dark and quiet...

"Commander Carlyle, sir, I—" The man stuttered helplessly, "Sir, how do you keep it up? Sizzling jets, you haven't slept for five nights."

One by one Rock Jason opened his eyes. He shook his head vigorously and said, "Ohhh." He tried to, but somehow could not quite, put things together; he was overcome with the greatest drowsiness he had known since that memorable do in Malibu. Sleep crudded his eyes and brain.

"You're perfectly right, Ronnie. Can't account for it. So tired..."

"Beg pardon, sir?"

Jason looked at the young man. Let's see—of course: a binge. Probably with Doris Dulane, the bitch. She'd tanked him up, or let him get tanked up, and now they were pulling one of their idiotic gags. Like Eddie Fritz's famous upside-down room.

"Ronnie, be a dear child and take the ridiculous Mason jar off your head. And steer me to a bed. Quickly."

Ronald Curtis, a fairly typical Sunset Boulevardier and an incurable whiner, stood at strict attention. Pretty cocky, all considered. If it hadn't been for Jason's big heart, the kid would still be perched on a stool at Schwab's dreaming of the movies.

Jason pinched the flesh of his arm. Sleep. Great Oliver, what had he been drinking! "Darling," he said with immense control, "I'm in no mood for jokes. Tomorrow perhaps. A bed is what I'm in the mood for now. A soft bed. Do you understand?"

The young man looked hopelessly bewildered. "But, Commander Carlyle, sir—that is—"

Very well. Tend to the ignoramus later. "Never mind. I'm sure I will be convulsed with the hilarity of this situation by next morning. I am not now amused. So go away, and leave me alone."

Jason's head nodded toward the desk. There was a ringing reverberating clang. He reached up and felt the glass helmet. "And *what*," he moaned, "this is I'd like to know. Goddam it, help me off with it—this minute!" He began to search for clamps, sensing a fuzzy blackness clouding his mind.

"Sir, be careful! The rips haven't been repaired yet."

"Ronnie, I love you like a son, genuinely I do. But if you don't get this thing off me and stop this nonsense immediately, I'm afraid I'll have to discuss your future with Mendel. I'm a sick man. What the devil are you talking about—rips?"

"The Mercutians, sir. Their armada surprised us. We were hit."

"Stop that!" *We were hit...* Of course. That horrible science fiction thing. These were lines from the movie. They'd rigged up the room to look like the first scene set. INT. ROCKET SHIP—COMMANDER'S CABIN—MED. SHOT. And this was the bit where Jason as Commander Derek Carlyle was supposed to be working day and night because only he knew how to repair the damage to the complex machinery.

"Benson and Carstairs are dead, sir. Their air ran out."

Charming. Now what was the next line? Oh yes. *Very well, Lieutenant. Fix me some black coffee. I'm going out there and finish the job.*

"Yes, sir."

"Oh, shut up."

"Sir?"

"I said—darling, whose captivating idea was this? Doris'?"

The young man kept looking confused, standing there quietly looking confused. Well—damn good acting. Give him that. Maybe too good.

Strange, Jason thought, that he couldn't remember *anything* about last night. He knew he was supposed to have appeared for Boetticher's party with the Quadriopticon. But—oh yes—he'd stopped by the Inferno first, for a very short one. Then...*then?*

"We got the last one, sir."

"*Last* what?"

"Mercutian. Johnson beamed his forward jets. That wipes them all out. Sir—if we get the damage repaired in time, we're Venus bound!"

"Ronnie, *please*—my head!"

"I'll get the coffee, sir."

The young man saluted smartly, did an about face and marched out of the room.

Must be Doris. Who else would have the money to build such a duplication of the set? The cabin was perfect. To the last detail. They'd even put him in that monstrous spacesuit dear Carpenter had dreamed up, the swine. How unchic can you get? Next thing they'd be putting him in Indian blankets. Spacesuits. Whither thou, Thespis?

Ohhh. One's head. Well, figure it out later. Get some sleep is the thing now.

He tore viciously at the clamps that secured the helmet. They slipped loose. He lifted off the glass bubble.

He found he could not breathe; the blackness fuzzed up entirely and he fainted promptly.

Very dark...very quiet...

"Commander Carlyle, sir, I—" The man stuttered helplessly. "Sir, how do you keep it up? Sizzling jets, you haven't slept for five nights."

Jason pulled himself into consciousness. *Now* what was it? The whole idiotic bit again? He tapped upward with tentative fingers. The Mason jar, right back on his head. And he'd taken the thing off. Hadn't he?

"You shall pay for this, Ronnie Curtis. In full."

"Benson and Carstairs are—"

Well, maybe it's part of the gag. Let him pass out and then wake him up and start it again, ad nauseum.

"I know, I know—dead. Wonderful. Fine. At least Benson and Carstairs have got some peace and quiet now. Stop looking so foolish! And *do* for heaven's sake stop saying 'sizzling jets!' What a line!"

"Yes, sir. About the damage, Commander—"

"Fix it yourself. What am I talking about? Say, weren't you just in here a minute ago?"

"No, sir."

"And stop saying 'sir'!" Jason rapped at the helmet perched on his shoulders. "I am dying," he said. "Here, help me up. Get me a Bromo. I'm going to have a word with Doris."

The young man assisted Jason to his feet. They walked out of the cabin.

"For Pete—" Jason stopped and stared. "Just how far does a gag go?"

It was the rocket ship, perfectly done. Except the bars under his hands didn't feel like silver-painted plaster. They felt very real.

The young man thrust some odd-looking things into his hands. "Good luck, sir."

Suddenly, he was being helped up a ladder. Below, a number of extras he'd never seen stared in unbelieving admiration. "There goes a *man*," someone whispered. "You couldn't drag *me* out there," commented another.

"Now wait a minute!" Jason cried. Above, the alloy roof was gashed and instruments hung lose. The night looked very black.

A powerful aroma suddenly seemed to permeate the helmet, cutting up through his nostrils. The smell of dryness and deserts, cooked up by Pa Franklin to simulate the odors of far space. If there *were* odors in far space.

He began to feel peculiar. What was all this, after all? Was he actually on the set again, for a remake? He looked for the crew, James the director, Bolana the cameraman—but there was only the ship and these crazy people and the stars.

Then a horrible thought occurred to him: So this is the DT's! Dr. Morris had warned him. Plenty of times.

Delirium tremens. Oh no. No. But what else?

Jason found himself on the outer hull of the rocket. Exactly as in the first scene of *The Conquest of Jupiter.* In fact, everything followed the scene. Now he was supposed to start fixing the airlock or some sort of gimmick and a Mercurian—beg pardon, *Mercutian,* and where did these "science" fiction writers think the planet Mercutio was located?—a Mercutian devil-man was supposed to creep up on him and—

"Look out, sir!"

Jason glanced up dazedly from the twisted machinery and faced a gigantic orange creature with scales and eyes of an alarming protuberance.

"Pinkie, for God's sake don't *do* that!"

The creature came closer, slowly, leering with the pride of the special effects department, three mouths where the eyes should have been but weren't. It said something that sounded like: "Umbawa unbawa, figgg-ouf!"

"What was that, Pinkie? I can't hear a word with this imbecile thing on. Repeat?"

"Umbawa unbawa, figgg-ouf!"

"Stop growling. And take off that moldy left-over from *John Carter on Mars* and tell me when the hell this bit is going to end."

The creature was almost upon him, liquid fire oozing from the giant pores between scales. Its body odor suggested that of the Inside Man at the Putrefaction Works.

"Shoot, sir! Oh, sir!"

"He's a cool one, Commander Carlyle. Knows what he's about."

"Pinkie. That is, I wish—Pinkie?"

"UMBAWA UNBAWA, FIGGG-OUF MAGOFU!"

"Good God!"

Jason tried to turn and run but his magnetic shoes held him fast to the hull. He whipped around and permitted his jaw to drop as the creature's arms began to encircle him.

"Please! I've told you a dozen times, I'm not that way. Especially here in front of—Pinkie? I'll have you fired. I will."

Automatically Jason wrenched loose one hand from the steaming tentacles and squeezed the trigger of the gun he'd forgotten about. A beam of light sprang out into the monster's face. "Umbawa unb-a-wa figg—" The monster fell and proceeded to float away in the darkness of space, its stench floating after it, if too slowly for comfort.

"Magnificent! Carlyle knew his gun wouldn't have been any use except at close range. What *guts.*"

Jason's fingers seemed to move of their own accord about the broken machinery. He watched with fascination. Then his legs took over and brought him back down the ladder.

"She'll be all right now, men," his voice said.

"Hurrah! Hurrah!"

"Now," said Jason's voice, "Denton, you and Marchelli do the patchwork. I'm going to catch a few winks. Wake me at 0700 promptly."

His legs propelled him along the catwalk and took him back into the cabin.

He lay down on the bunk. "DT's," he said, aloud. "They're murderous."

Sleep came to the courageous commander of the spaceship *Starfire;* sleep well earned by a man who had toiled five days and five nights to bring his craft safely through the greatest space battle of all time.

Jason started to remember something just before unconsciousness set in. "Murderous," he mumbled and closed his eyes.

"Aldridge, you traitorous cur. Court-martialing is too good for you!"

"You mean...?"

"Exactly."

Jason scratched his head. How long, he wondered, does this kind of thing go on? After all, DT's are supposed to wear off, aren't they? Or are they—?

"What do you propose to do about it, earthling?" the uniformed navigator spat. It was the ex-Shakespearean, Guy Randolph. A small part, but plenty dramatic. Well, play along. Scene two, isn't it? You've discovered that the navigator, Aldridge, is really a Venusian in disguise and is the one who alerted the Mercutians and caused—oh Mancini, from the Pulitzer Prize to *this?*—caused the Mercutians to attack and ambush. Now he, Aldridge, had misrouted the *Starfire* and they were headed for Jupiter—the Death Planet. Great. Great little plot. Academy Award.

"What do you propose to do about it, earthling?"

Fight scene. Big fight. Well, delirium tremens only means that you're dreaming. Jacket off. Sleeves up. Sneer. "Get ready, Aldridge—unless you're too yellow."

"You would overrun our world and bring the pestilence of war that ruined your own?" Randolph declaimed in a bad imitation of Maurice Evans. "Never!"

"Take," Jason said, hauling off, *"that,* Venusian filth!"

He carefully missed Randolph's jaw. The man grinned savagely and lunged, his hands snaking up around Jason's neck.

Jason pulled loose the fingers and caught his breath. "What's the big idea, darling?" He started to walk away, massaging the bruised flesh. Very real, he thought, for a dream.

The navigator flung himself upon Jason's back and they fell to the floor. Randolph pounded away, changing form the while: presently, he was a sticky green ameba-like blob.

"Never again," Jason resolved, wishing he had one drink nonetheless. He tore himself free and ran out the door and slammed the door shut. He hurt all over. "Enough," he panted, "is enough!" He went to the airlock and began to pull it open.

Blackness. Inside his head.

Very dark... Very quiet...

"Aldridge, you traitorous cur! Court mar—"

Like the rushes of a film turned back for editing. Right back to the same damn line. And Randolph wheeling around in his chair.

"You mean?"

Jason remembered how the first scene had gone back. What had done it? Of course. Changing the script. Everything went fine until he did something that Commander Derek Carlyle wouldn't do, something that was impossible to the structure of the story. Then, *zip!* All over again. The dim realization came to him that if he was ever to get out of this he would have to follow the script to the end. But how the hell could that be? No. No no. Not with what was coming up!

"Exactly."

Scene 3: Having beaten Aldridge to death, Commander Carlyle discovers stowaway on board. Beautiful chick. Sweet-smelling, too. Robin Summers. Usual mad-then-glad bit. Robbie is in love with him. Kiss. Headed for peril. Jupiter unknown planet. Maybe hostile. Phew!

"What do you propose to do about it, earthling?"

Bless little Herman. What was this lousy picture about anyway? Earth is being fried by strange ray from space. Authorities send ship to Venus to investigate. Ship has spy. Fight with Mercutians. Land on Jupiter. Turns out Jupiter the real menace. Jovians have Death Ray. Knock it out. Return home. Earth saved. Hotcha.

"You would overrun—"

Well, anyway they cut out those opening scenes. Space battles cost money, be praised. That would have been jolly.

Scene 4: The landing on Jupiter. Jovians appear and my oh my what a fight. Two days to film it. Murder.

Scene 5: They take Robbie hostage.

Scene 6: Commander Carlyle slips inside their temple and is captured.

Scene 7: The *Rakana!*

"Take *that*, Venusian filth!"

Jason fought hard. After all, Randolph was getting along. Sixty if he was a day.

He stomped the greenish blob to a jelly—for the matinee kiddies—and kicked it triumphantly into a corner.

His nostrils filled with the odor of charred flesh. Now, why charred flesh? Oh well. It made him gag. Smells. All the time these smells!

"Commander, we're off our course!"

"Ronnie, you sweet thing. How observant. I mean, how very observant. That is: Very well, Lieutenant—I know all about it. Aldridge was a spy. We're going to have to try for a forced landing on Jupiter."

"*Jupiter!* Screaming asteroids, sir, that planet looks dangerous!"

"Danger is our business, Lieutenant."

"Yes sir. Jupiter it is."

That's it. Just reroute and land on Jupiter. Mancini, you brain, even the schoolboys know better than that. Forget it. The young man stuck his head in the doorway.

"Stowaway on board, sir."

"All right, I'll have a look."

Wearily, Jason rubbed his head and went with the Lieutenant.

"Robbie, dear!" he said, when they brought the prisoner forward. "How nice to see *some* one human. I'm having a dream, you know." Jason giggled. "You're looking splendid. Smelling splendid, too."

"I told you I'd be with you always, Derek," Robbie said, eyes glistening. "And I meant it."

"Why did you do this foolish thing?"

"Because I love you."

Jason grinned. Little liar. Oh, what a lie. "Say that again, darling."

"I love you, Derek."

"I should be angry, furious—but I'm not. We're in trouble, I suppose you know that."

"I know."

"And I suppose they told you we may not get out of this alive."

"It doesn't matter. Not as long as I'm with you."

Jason felt an impulse. Would Commander Derek Carlyle or would Commander Derek Carlyle not sweep the girl into his arms? It wasn't in the script. But—it was beginning to appear—it was all right if you didn't change it altogether. Revisions didn't hurt. Scripts are always being revised.

He swept her in his arms and kissed her and waited for the old fuzzy blackness to come. It didn't.

"Sweetheart!"

She *was* looking splendid. Carpenter did much better by her costume, such as it was. Some absolutely essential impedimenta, three or four sequined disks of varying shapes and all about the size of fig leaves.

The diaphanous gown served only to heighten the effect of the deep cherry-nut tan skin and the slender curves. And the scent...how could even Galactic's labs come up with a perfume that was so purely the odor of clean fresh woman? The look in her eyes, her black dancing eyes, was of an alarming sincerity.

He was going to suggest that they go elsewhere to chat, say to his cabin, where he could show her his navigational charts, but—Mancini had taken care of that. Commander Carlyle. Good egg. A nonagenarian in a harem. Duty first!

But as he looked at her, Jason felt strangely sad. It was the way she had pronounced the word *love.* Not brittle and lifeless, but—well, as if she really meant it. This part of the dream was not so bad, he decided. Maybe even worth the whole thing.

Nonsense, Jason!

Nonsense, your Aunt Hermione. Why kid yourself? You love the girl, don't you? Admit it in a dream, at least. After you wake up, you can hide in that gin-soaked shell if you want to and keep her from ever knowing...

"Jupiter ahead, sir!"

"Tell Michaels to prepare the brakes." Jason put a protective arm around Robbie. Her shoulder trembled. He could not bear to look into her eyes. "We'll make it, men, if we keep our heads!"

"I DON'T care. You stay here if you want to, Jeff. I'm going in."

"But it's sheer suicide! You don't stand a chance in a million of getting out with your skin—"

"It's a chance I'll have to take."

"Derek, listen to me. There's a thousand of those ugly devils and everyone spoiling for a fight. They'd pick you up and—well, you know what happened to Fontaine."

"Yes. I—know."

"Well then, make *sense,* Derek! We can still clear out while there's time."

"Sorry, Jeff. No dice. I've made up my mind."

"You crazy fool. I wonder if that girl knows how much you love her..."

"It isn't just for Cynthia, Jeff. Don't you understand—it's our only chance to get at that Death Ray."

"Then I'm going to go with you."

"No. One might make it, not two. You go back to the ship, Jeff— that's an order."

"Yes, sir."

"Shake?"

"I—good luck, Derek. Good luck. We'll be waiting."

Jason watched the figure of Jeff Manning, the engineer, walk off toward the *Starfire.* Burton Mitchell, of course, looking as if he'd never spent a day at the phone praying for a call from Central Casting. Maybe he wasn't such a bad sort. They were all behaving well.

Stop it, you ass. This is a fit of some kind you're having. Burton Mitchell is a pitiful and extremely annoying has-been and if he hadn't pestered you to death—still—What's the story, are you letting these Perils-of-Pauline heroics warp your better judgment?

Twice in the picture Mitchell—Manning—had saved his life. Minor episodes. But he was touched. Couldn't help it. Everybody seemed so damned sincere about their corn. This flea-bitten space opera, running the gamut of emotions, the most basic emotions, simplified down to absurdity. But maybe it was the first time Rock Jason had ever been exposed, or permitted himself to be exposed, to real emotions of any kind. In Hollywood, he guessed, you've *got* to rely on dreams for lasting values. Dreams were the only things with value.

Look at him now. The climax of the picture. The big scene. Hero stuff. And yet he was feeling less like Rock Jason every moment and more like Commander Derek Carlyle, Herman Mancini's brainchild. Or was he merely feeling like Leroy Guinness O'Shea in days long ago, when the stage was a magic world and such things as love and honesty existed...

Jason felt the anger surge and he didn't try to check it. Trick-suits or not, pimple-faced extras or no pimple-faced extras, he hated the Jovians for what they had done. They had Robbie, the bastards. Well, they wouldn't have her long, by the holies!

He vaulted with great bounding leaps over the rough terrain and crouched at the marble wall of the temple. A guard slithered toward him, hissing. He let him have it. The guard fell. He wrapped the scarlet cloak about his shoulders and faked his entrance into the hall.

The animal smell almost asphyxiated Jason. Direct from the reptile house—he remembered. Together, for effect, with essence du stable.

The Emperor of Jupiter sat upon his throne, clucking gleefully.

"I thought our little ruse would work, Commander. Ah, don't attempt to shoot me. I am covered by a force field. And fifty *Kranek* pistols are aimed at your heart." It was Toby Bowles. Old Toby, who'd made a fortune playing villains because of his impossible face. Even with the weird makeup there could be no mistaking the kindly character actor. Or could there?

"You scum!" Commander Carlyle raged.

"Scum, eh? We'll see how the heroic commander's song changes after he sees—this!"

The emperor motioned with his hand and two slaves pulled aside a thick purple curtain.

"Cynthia! Robbie!"

"Derek!"

"Ah, a most touching reunion." The emperor laughed gutturally.

Robbie was spread-eagled and chained to the wall. The diaphanous gown was gone: she was as naked as the production code would allow. Bright thin red stripes crisscrossed her shoulders and other inoffensive regions.

Commander Carlyle spluttered out an oath and raced forward. The force field knocked him to his feet.

"Cynthia, what have they done to you?"

"Nothing," the emperor laughed; then he sobered, "…yet."

"I'll kill you, you Jovian filth!" Commander Carlyle hurled. "Then I'll have you fired, do you hear me? Blackballed by every studio from here to—"

"Strange talk, earthling. Bold talk. But we have more to show you. Come."

Two burly slaves, both looking alike, both resembling great lizards, pinioned Jason's arms and pushed him along roughly. They went through many halls and finally entered an immense rotunda.

An oversized machine something like a searchlight hummed and droned madly in the center of the room.

"The Death Ray!" Commander Carlyle exclaimed. The next lines of dialogue were lost in his fury.

"I see you recognize our little weapon. I thought perhaps you might be interested. Its effects are slow. But they are lasting. The warmth your Earth feels now will be increased in a very short time to a heat so unbearable no life can exist."

"Then you move in. Right?"

"As you say, right. We're becoming rather overpopulous here."

"You cold-hearted—Toby, listen to me. Turn that thing off. And then turn Robbie loose. Immediately. Is that clear?"

"Prepare the prisoner for the *Rakana*!"

"Oh, let's not go through that miserable thing." Jason felt unwell. He had turned green just watching the stuntman. The late stuntman it was now.

"We will test your courage, brave soldier." Right straight out of *Gunga Din*.

"Let's talk it over, shall we?"

The blackness began to fuzz up. Stop it. You're too close to the end now. Keep this up and you'll land smack back at the beginning of reel nine!

"Do your worst to me. But release the girl."

"Ah!" the emperor said. "In accordance with the rules, I make you a promise. It is a fair one. In the event that you are victorious in the arena, both you and the girl will be free to leave unharmed."

There were soft, hissing, laughing sounds.

Commander Carlyle grinned wildly. "You've made yourself a deal, snakeface."

"Take him away."

Jason left happily. The *snakeface* had been his own.

Then he thought of what was to come and he stopped being happy.

THE DARKNESS of the cell was oppressive. It pushed in. The smell department had gone crazy here. A whiff from a local dairy, froufrou of abattoir, the gentle aromas of cattle barns, stables, cod-liver oil—every repulsive smell in the world. Jason alternately trembled and squared his jaw. It took thought.

On the one hand, this was a fit of the DT's and so, one way or another, he would wake up by and by and everything would be jim-dandy. Plus the fact that according to the script Carlyle is victorious. But there was the other hand. Which was that the great stuntman, Ralph Laurie, who had in his career flown through fiery hoops, leaped into ravines and braved death in every conceivable manner, had been killed in this scene. The gorilla had killed Laurie. Stupid to use a gorilla anyway. Who ever heard of gorillas on Jupiter? Who ever heard of *anything* on Jupiter!

Jason thought about the big ape Bobo, painted a sickening bedroom pink, and he began to tremble more often than he squared his jaw.

He had about decided to give the whole thing up when the wooden gate was pulled open and light cascaded in. Two Jovian lizard men also cascaded in. They dragged Jason into the center of the vast circular arena. The crowd cheered madly.

The Jovians slithered away.

Then Jason remembered. Whirling, he saw Robbie. Tied to a stake in the exact center of the sandy circle. She was breathtakingly beautiful now. He went over to her.

She looked very frightened. The ropes had been carefully placed— Lila, from props, had spent almost an hour getting the rough thick loops just right. One above the breasts. One below them. One around the tummy. One—below.

"Robbie, darling!"

"Derek. Whatever happens, I love you, I love you, I—"

Jason put a hand over her lips. "You mustn't say it," he whispered. "Not after the way I've treated you. But Robbie, if we get out of this—I'll make it up. I swear I'll—"

"Derek, look out!"

The crowd's scream whipped him around. Jason swallowed.

It was Bobo. The gorilla. With that look in his eye.

"Nice Bobo. You remember me. Rocky? *Jungle Goddess*— remember?"

The ape walked on all fours twice around Jason. The crowd hushed.

Bobo stopped and scratched. Jason sighed. His heart was thumping. He noticed the flimsy spear the guard had put in his hand just before abandoning him to this dirty creature.

"Bobo, get back. Get back now. Don't do anything foolish."

Someone threw a heavy rock. It hit the ape's behind. "Aarrrgh!" The ape roared disapproval and began to lope straight for Jason.

They sprinted around the arena a few times, the ape hot on his opponent's heels. Jason started to climb the wall. The black fuzziness. He dropped down. The giant creature was thundering toward him.

He closed his eyes. Nothing happened.

He opened his eyes.

Bobo was beating his villainous old chest and hooting at Robbie.

Jason ran over and delivered a well-aimed kick to the gorilla's hindquarters, which were already tender from the rock. Bobo turned, scratched and leapt, saying "Aarrrgh! Aarrrgh!" They fell thuddingly on the sand. The gorilla's arms were crushing his chest.

"For heaven's sake," Jason managed to gurgle, "you're squashing me, you idiot!" They rolled over. And over. The crowd roared. The gorilla roared. Jason roared.

Then Bobo screamed an unearthly unjovian scream in the suddenly quiet arena.

Jason watched the ape clutching and flailing at the spear shaft, which was buried in soft chest flesh. He heard the thunder of over a ton of life hitting the sand. Then, when Bobo twitched no longer, he walked over, bowed in the direction of the emperor's box and pulled out the spear. As he did so, he wondered briefly what had happened.

The throng went crazy. Guards came galloping into the circle, hissing threats, and the emperor's voice could be heard screeching, "KILL the earthling! Kill him!"

"So," Commander Carlyle cried, *"this* is how the ruler of all Jupiter rewards bravery and keeps his promises!"

"Kill him!"

A *Kranek* gun crackled and Commander Carlyle grabbed at his shoulder. He dropped on one knee, tried to shake the pain from his mind.

Then he saw why the crowd had gone so crazy. The crew of the *Starfire,* stationed at crucial posts, were letting loose the fury of zam guns; the Jovians were falling like ants under a spyglass; the stink and sizzle of death on Jupiter filled the heavy air.

Of course! At this point in the scene they come to rescue him!

Commander Carlyle rose to his feet and raced along to the Royal Box. He reached up and pulled the fatty emperor down into the sand.

Toby fumbled with a pistol.

"Oh no you don't!" Commander Carlyle plunged the already bloodied spear into Toby's quivering throat. Then he ran back to the stake and cut loose Robbie's bonds. She collapsed into his arms; he winced at the pain in his shoulder and lifted her to the waiting, loyal Jeff.

"Thanks, boy."

"Okay, skipper!"

He grabbed a *Kranek* and blasted his way through the disorganized Jovians to the rotunda.

The lizard guard whirled, hissed disdainfully and brought his blaster into play. Commander Carlyle dodged the lethal ray and leapt upon the enraged Jovian.

This part, he recalled vaguely, was played by a particularly scrawny extra, so he directed his blows toward the Adam's apple, together with a few good ones to the belly. The Jovian dropped, hissing and moaning.

Commander Derek Carlyle took careful aim with his *Kranek* pistol. Then he fired. The ray hit the machine dead center. He fired again and again. Soon the Death Ray apparatus was a melted pile of steaming junk.

He smiled inscrutably and turned in time to blast the guards out of the doorway. Then he clutched a conveniently placed velvet cord and swung the length of the hall over the heads of the lizard horde, high over them, in a long, graceful arc—then, in the sunlight, he ran, blasting his way to freedom.

There were Jovians waiting at the ship. Loyal, good and true Jeff lay dying on the volcanic soil and a slimy snake on legs was slithering away with Robbie in his stunted arms. "Wait a second, friend."

The Jovian turned. The blast caught him directly in the face. He screamed.

Commander Carlyle helped Cynthia into the ship. Then he limbed back down.

"Jeff," he said. "Come on, let's—Jeff!"

"Sorry, Derek. This is one hand I'll have to sit out on. You'll—have to—go on without me. This is curtains."

"Jeff!"

More Jovians came barreling for the ship. *Kranek* rays cut through the air. One caught Jason's shoulder. Wait a minute—didn't the script girl catch that? For Pete's sake, that shoulder was supposed to be already hit. Never mind that now. Just get in the ship. Hurry!

The lizard men were battering at the door, slicing the alloy with their pistols.

"Let 'er rip!"

The jets thundered to life.

Commander Carlyle chuckled. "That ought to warm 'em up."

He could smile now.

The *Starfire* rose slowly like a gigantic phoenix; then it flashed off, a silver wink in the black-velvet sky.

Commander Carlyle stood at the starboard port. His eyes were sad. His arm was around the girl. She snuggled closer.

"Goodbye," he said, "Jeff, Harry, Don—all of you down there who didn't make it. You died, but your lives were not given in vain. Earth will never forget your sacrifice!"

"And Earth will never forget," said the young lieutenant, "a man named Carlyle. God bless you, sir. We all love you."

"Yes," Cynthia said, snuggling still closer as the stars whisked by, "we all love you, Commander Derek Carlyle!"

"Robbie," Jason said, holding her, pressing her nearer. "Robbie. Robbie, darling."

This time the blackness came and Jason didn't fight it. He only tried to hold onto that golden tan arm a little longer...

WHISTLING. APPLAUSE. Cheers. Jason blinked, half expecting to find himself back in the *Rakana* field.

He tensed his body.

He opened his eyes, expecting to see Bobo the gorilla. Instead he saw Sherman Boetticher.

He closed his eyes again. It was almost as bad.

"Rock—you all right? Speak to us. Say something."

"Breeng on de dancing gorls," Jason said. The dream was over. He remembered it all now. Or most of it, anyway.

"That's our Rock. Say, you had us worried, boy!"

"What'd I do, faint?"

"I wouldn't know—you just sort of stood here, watching the picture."

He looked puzzled—

"Is that so unusual?"

"Well, what I mean is, you pulled your hand out before Hymie could switch off the Quad and just—well, you didn't say boo. Just watched the picture."

"Is—is it over now?"

"Is it over? Listen to the man! It's a goddam sensation. It was the smells that did it. Oh, *what* a brainstorm those smells were!" Boetticher was smiling broadly. "Excuse me now. Got to go meet our public."

He went outside, burbling happily. The voices were loud.

"How is your hand, Mr. Jason?" Little Mr. Gottschalk looked anxious.

"Beautiful, an artist's," Jason said, thinking of other things.

"I was afraid did you hurt it. Bad type business. Nobody, not even me, knows all about this machine. But so? Maybe all great inwentions get borned like me, isn't it?" The little man looked quite sad. "I tell you tzegret: what I am working on is not for movie camera. No! At first, I sink I got tzegret to forse dimansion! Is beautiful! But—it wouldn't work. T'ousand times I tried: nossing, wouldn't work." He sighed. "So, I turn it into movie camera. All right?"

Jason nodded slowly, wondering about several things all at once.

The door opened. Dolly Dixon stood puffing. *"Daaar*ling!" she ululated, "but it was the most! I mean, the end! I mean, what'll you just do with all your money?"

"Excuse me." Jason brushed past the confused sphere of columnists and looked around the room and then walked quickly out the doorway, tearing loose from the adoring crowd.

She was walking fast.

"Robbie. Wait."

Robin Summers turned around. "For what?" she said. "It's your show, isn't it?" Her black eyes didn't seem so angry. Why didn't they seem so angry? Jason thought for a moment they looked almost as they did on Jupiter.

"Robbie, I want to say some things to you. Will you listen?"

"If I have to," she said, but not harshly; and her skin was even more shining gold in the lights.

THE LOVE-MASTER

(1957)

y wife is frigid," said the young man, getting directly to the point. "That's the long and the short of it."

"Nonsense!" Salvadori raised a desiccated finger to his fine Roman nose. "Women," he declared, "are creatures of milk and blood and fire; they are cradles of delight, ships of spices, doorways leading to lands of wonder!"

"That may be," responded the young man. "But my wife Beatrice—"

"—is no different." Candlelight shot the rapids of the Love-Master's brook-gray hair as he nodded impatiently. "I assure you of that."

"You don't know her."

"She is a woman? Young? Healthy?"

"Yes."

"Then I do not need to know her." Salvadori rolled the wheelchair up close to his visitor and studied the lean, pale features. There was something vaguely disturbing here, something a bit off-center, but he could not place it. Perhaps the hat, a large and incongruous Stetson. "Mr. Cubbison, I trust that you, yourself, are not—ah—"

The young man flushed. "There is nothing wrong with me," he said. "Physically."

"Then," Salvadori said, "you have little to worry about. Only remember this: There is no such thing as a frigid woman. They are all as alike as locks, and want but the proper key."

"Nice simile," Cubbison granted, "but not very believable. I've tried everything."

At that the Love-Master grinned, crookedly, like an ancient tiger. He was incredibly old, that much one could see in the parchmented flesh, the veined and white-whiskered arms, the woolen shawl tucked under tremulous knees; but there was power of a kind in that creaking hull of skin, and from those dark olive eyes there shone a light that told of other years, better days.

"*Everything*, Mr. Cubbison?"

Once again the visitor flushed. His glance traveled uncomfortably over the dusty room, returning at last to the old man in the wheelchair. "I think perhaps we ought to get down to business," he said nervously. "But I warn you, I haven't much faith in love potions or spells or any of that sort of thing."

"Nor do I," replied Salvadori. "They are buncombe."

Cubbison's eyes flickered. "I'm afraid I don't understand," he said. "I'd heard that you were some kind of a wizard."

"And so I am," the old man laughed. "In a way. But I am no thief. I offer no magical formulae for success: merely the benefit of personal experience. This disappoints you?"

"It surprises me."

"Then you are typical. I cannot count the number of young frustrates who have come to me expecting miracles, hoping for pentagrams or, at the very least, genii. They all felt quite cheated when I offered them, instead, conversation. But that attitude changed soon enough."

"Indeed?"

"Oh, yes. For, you see, I have never had an unsuccessful case."

"Never?"

Salvadori adjusted his white silk scarf. "Never," he said, humbly. His eyes momentarily gathered the distance of years. "There is actually nothing complex or sinister about it," he said. "Had I been a great matador in my youth, I would today be dispensing advice to neophyte *toreros;* similarly, if I had been a great race driver, or hunter, or soldier. As it happens, I was a great lover." He sighed. "Alas, the rewards for my endeavors were not tangible. They could not be carried in the pocket, like a bull's ear, or mounted on the mantel, like a gold cup; yet they were real enough, and I have them all—*here.*" Salvadori tapped his forehead.

Cubbison coughed, and the old man's mind surfaced. "Well, young fellow, do you want to avail yourself of my services, or not?"

"I can't see that it would do any harm."

"Very well, then. Pull up a chair."

The thin, hatted man dusted the seat of a harp-back with a handkerchief of fine linen, and moved forward. "About the price—" he began.

"Afterward," Salvadori chuckled. He settled his iron-maned head against the pillow, closed his eyes and murmured: "Describe the subject. High points only, please."

"Well, she's...fairly attractive. Twenty-seven years of age. Hundred and ten pounds, I imagine. Good shape. May I smoke?"

"Describe the subject, Mr. Cubbison."

The young man took a long puff on the cigarette, then blurted, "Dammit, she's a fish, that's all. When we married, I understood that she'd been everywhere, done everything; you know, woman of the world. But I can't believe it. No matter what one tries, Beatrice simply shakes her head and treats the whole thing as if it were a pathetic joke. Of course, she *claims* to want to love—don't they all?—and she *pretends* to cooperate, but the end is always the same. Sometimes she cries, or laughs, or sits awake all night smoking; mostly she just says, 'Sorry, no good.'"

Salvadori listened carefully. Occasionally he would open one eye, then close it again. At length, when the visitor had concluded, he put his hands together and said, "Mr. Cubbison, I am glad to report that yours is one of the more basic dilemmas. I anticipate no difficulty whatever."

The young man's eyes widened. "You can say that?" he asked. "After all I've told you?"

"Of course." Salvadori leaned forward in the wheelchair. The guttering candle brought his handsome profile into sharp relief. "In fact, I shall prescribe a comparatively mild, but highly effective, remedy. Cubbison, have you ever heard of 'The Chinese Flip' method?"

"No, I can't say that I have."

"Then listen. Performed with anything approaching accuracy, this should put an end to your problem." Upon which remark, Salvadori went on to describe in minute detail Method 12 which he'd learned a half-century before in Bechuanaland. He observed the shocked expression on his visitor's face and went through it all a second time.

"Good Lord," said the young man.

"Nothing, really, once you get the hang of it. But a word of caution—don't overdo. And now, good evening. I will see you tomorrow at midnight."

The Love-Master watched the gaunt young client walk dazedly from the room; then, when the door was closed, he fell into a sleep of dreams.

Next evening at twelve the soft knock came, and Salvadori wheeled his ageing body to the door. It was Mr. Cubbison, looking frailer and paler than ever before.

"No saccharine displays of gratitude," the Love-Master murmured, "and, please, no lurid descriptions. A simple check for one hundred dollars will suffice."

But the young man did not smile or make a move toward his checkbook.

"What's the trouble; are you ill?" Salvadori inquired, frowning. "It went well, needless to say?"

"No," the visitor said. "It didn't."

"Not at all?"

"No."

"Hmm." Salvadori looked startled for an instant, then regained his composure. "Well," he smiled, "it appears I underestimated the subject. Score one for her!"

"I'm afraid it isn't any use," Cubbison said, sighing deeply. "Of course, if you could meet her—that is—"

"Sorry! I no longer make house calls. It's a cardinal policy I've had to adopt, for reasons that should be manifest. For almost twenty years, Cubbison, women have tried to seduce me out of retirement; they have come by the hundreds and employed every low trick known to the female mind, but always they have failed. In the School for Scandal I am a professor *emeritus,* and so it must and shall remain. Besides, we're in no trouble yet. Merely a call for stronger medicine..."

The old man tented his fingers and thought for a long time.

"Cubbison, I think we are going to try a little something called *'The Australian Hop'*—a facetious-sounding but nonetheless lethal technique, originally developed for a certain recalcitrant maiden in the brush country, who—but never mind that. Tell me, how are your muscles?"

"All right, I suppose."

"Then pay strict attention. The first step..."

In a way, Salvadori felt ashamed, for Method 18 was nominally for advanced students. It was a lot of technique for an amateur to handle. Still, there was one's reputation to consider; and though one might become old and jaded, one had to eat...

WHEN THE gloved knock sounded again the following night, Salvadori chuckled, imagining the beatific expression of his client.

"Well?"

Cubbison shook his head sadly: there was a look of ineffable weariness—and defeat—about his eyes. "No go," he said.

Salvadori blinked. "This," he hawked, "is difficult to believe. You followed my instructions?"

"To the letter."

"And the subject…did not respond?"

"Oh, she responded, all right. Like a dead eel. Like a frozen trout— See here, Mr. Salvadori, I'm very much afraid that Beatrice is beyond even your powers. I think we ought to give up. She and I will just go on living like sister and brother."

"What?" The Love-Master reached out a trembling hand and laid it across his client's face. "Mr. Cubbison, don't be obscene. You have not, I hope, orally capitulated with your wife?"

"Beg pardon?"

"Let it go. Be quiet a moment; I must think." Salvadori made fists and put them to his temples. "In the summer of '04," he said slowly, "in Florence, I made the acquaintance of a certain princess, an altogether ravishing vessel but, alas, caught up like a fly in the web of virtue. It was perhaps my second most trying case, hard fought and won at no small expense. However, *won.* As I recall, it was Method 26—*'The Drunken Reptile'*—that turned the trick."

Mr. Cubbison, looking thin and wan beneath the Stetson, shrugged.

"My boy, my boy," Salvadori said gently, in a voice thick with confidence, "you mustn't despair. Remember: 'No tree so tall/it cannot fall.' Now listen. .."

As the Love-Master spoke, seated there like a time-lost fragment of Roman sculpture, Cubbison's eyes grew large and frightened and occasionally he gasped.

Then he grinned. "Salvadori," he said, "what you have just described is without doubt the most shocking thing I've ever heard. But," he rose, "it might work!"

"Might? It will," the old man said. "You can count on that. Beatrice will love you forever!"

But when the visitor left Salvadori did not find sleep so easy. It had been a long time since he'd heard of a woman whose defenses could withstand both *The Chinese Flip* and *The Australian Hop*. He could not even imagine a woman in *this* age upon whom Method 26 would not work its fiendish spell.

And yet...

"SHE LAUGHED at me," the hatted Cubbison said, hotly. "Called me a damned acrobat!"

"You are surely exaggerating!"

"Not a bit. Laughed, I tell you. Said, 'Bunny, that's a scream!'"

"At what point?"

"The penultimate point. Where, according to your thesis, she ought to have been undulating in helpless frenzies."

"Gad." Salvadori bit his lip. "In this case, I fear it's time we brought out The Big Guns. Mr. Cubbison, yours has turned out, I must confess, to be a rare case; most rare, indeed. But the battle is not lost."

At which time the Love-Master, throwing caution to the winds, explained the workings of Method 34. '*The Tasmanian Trounce, Double Switchback and Rebound!*' It shocked even *his* hardened sensibilities; but it was fool-proof. No female could resist its insidious puissance; not possibly!

"She fell asleep," Cubbison said, one night later.

Salvadori got a wild, frantic look in his eyes. He outlined the dreadful Method 37—'*The Creeping Terror*—which, he recalled, had driven the Marquis de Silva Ramos's wife mad as a March hare thirty summers previous.

"She yawned," said Cubbison.

And Salvadori thought. *What a woman! She must indeed have been everywhere and done everything!* Carefully, he went through his entire repertoire, not excluding the nerve-shattering *Belgian Carousel*' (Method 51) nor even '*Roman Times*' (Method 60), held in reserve since its first use on the adamant Lady Titterington, long gone to her reward.

But always it was the same. Always Cubbison would return with his report of failure. "She giggled," he would say; or, "She just looked at me."

Until at last, Salvadori saw clearly that there was but one thing to do.

"Mr. Cubbison, I have reached a decision. It violates my strictest rule of business, but, under the circumstances, there is, unhappily, no choice."

"Yes?" said Mr. Cubbison.

"There is one technique," Salvadori whispered, "which I have not mentioned. Method 100. It bears no name. It is absolutely guaranteed: on that, sir, I would stake my life." His countenance reddened with fierce pride. "However—to describe it to you would (and I mean no offense) be tantamount to handing a jar of nitroglycerin to a three-year-old baboon. I shudder to think of the consequences of even one small error... Only two men have ever mastered Method 100. The first, or so the rumor goes, was Don Giovanni. The second, myself. Therefore—"

The young client leaned forward, breathing heavily. "Therefore, I shall make my first house call in fifteen years!"

Cubbison leaped to his feet; he seemed on the edge of tears. "Salvadori, can you mean it?" he quavered. "Would you?"

The old man raised a claw. "I dislike emotional excess," he said with distaste. "Please sit down and pay attention. Now: you will make very certain that the room is in darkness. Understood?"

"Yes, of course."

"And do not call me until the subject is nearly asleep. That is quite important. Should my identity be discovered"—Salvadori gave way to a paroxysm—"I'd have no peace for the rest of my days. The subject would be at my door constantly, entreating, imploring, threatening... It would be horrible."

"But," said Cubbison, "here is something. If *I* cannot repeat Method 100—"

"Once," Salvadori said, "is enough. She will, of course, go on hoping, but meanwhile (the ice having been broken, as it were) the other techniques will suffice."

The young man took the Love-Master's bony shoulders. "I—I hardly know what to say."

"Say good night, Mr. Cubbison. I do this only because it is necessary, and do not wish to dwell on it. I shall see you later."

HAVING BRAVED the strumpet winds, Salvadori sat panting wearily in the darkened alcove, ruminating with displeasure on the ordeal before him. When a knight is old, he mused, heavy lie the cudgels. Heavy the mace and heavy the dirk, and hard the battle.

He began to nod sleepily.

Then a voice whispered, "Now!" and the Love-Master straightened, senses alert. He rolled the chair in rubbery silence to the black room and entered.

"Cubbison?" he hissed softly.

No answer.

Well enough. Instinct brought him to the panoplied bed. Reflex put him into it.

He lay still for a time, going over Method 100 in his mind; then, listening to the steady breathing, absorbing the feral warmth, reluctantly he struck.

It went perfectly.

At the precise moment planned, he hurled his wizened frame back into the chair, exited the room, whispered "Cubbison, hop to it!" and caromed clattering out of the house, into the dark and wind-swept streets.

All over. He rumbled loose a mighty sigh. Reputation or no reputation, he told himself, rolling up the concrete ramp to his quarters, he would never again break the rule.

Sleep for the Love-Master was immediate.

Promptly at midnight the next evening, there came again the gloved knock. Salvadori set aside his dish of smoked oysters. He was weak and racked with bamboo shoots of pain, but no longer disturbed.

"Come in, Mr. Cubbison."

The young man entered; he was smiling peculiarly.

"The charge," Salvadori said crisply, "is one thousand dollars. Cash, if you don't mind."

The visitor laid ten one-hundred-dollar bills on the scarred table.

"I trust it went well?"

"Oh, yes!"

"Everything satisfactory?"

"Yes!"

"Then, Cubbison, good-by to you."

The visitor, however, made no indication that he was prepared to leave. His smile grew broader. Then, suddenly, he rushed forward and planted a kiss on Salvadori's forehead.

"Damn it, boy," the old man spluttered, "get away!" Then Salvadori, the Love-Master, touched his assailant and gasped. His eyeballs threatened to roll from their sockets.

For the visitor, still smiling, had stepped back and, for the first time, removed the large Stetson; and golden locks of hair had cascaded forth.

"Cubbison, in the name of decency!"

"I hope that you'll forgive me, darling," the visitor said, taking off coat, trousers, shirt and other encumbrances, "but it was the only way I could have you. And I couldn't take less!"

Salvadori's knuckles bleached against the chair arms. Within moments, to his profound dismay, he was staring at a woman of immense beauty—full-rounded, soft, and white as an elephant's tusk.

"Cubbison!" Salvadori croaked, refusing to believe the trick that had been played. *"Cubbison!"*

The woman paused. "Call me Beatrice," she said.

And then she sprang.

A WORLD OF DIFFERENTS

(1958)

A-B-C-D-E-F-G-H-I-J-K-L-M-N-O-P-Q-R-S-T-U-V-W-X-Y-Z.

ow these are the symbolkeys to what I am saying. What is Earthword TELEPATHY doesn't work because I think out and nobody hears me. All the time I think. It is maybe that I am alone of the livers, if that's the story then I send this message by my last cone that wasn't shot to hell (and it was a farrago hiding it from them). *Figure out the language, figure it out.* Of course, it isn't easy but you can try, *I* tried and I ain't no scientist. To make help I am (*Earthword*) deatomizing (?) a book which contents all words and send this with message. Study the book it is FINNEGANS WAKE by James Joyce. It is where I learned Earth language also from when I listen to the Earthman who captured me talk.

The reason that it is I don't send this message with our ciphers is this: that, What has happened to my body, for crying out loud? O gig goggle of gigguels. I can't tell you how! It is too screaming to rizo, rabbit it all! Why I can't walk or hold a writing stick to make our symbols or any- thing else already. *Helpless!* I can't hardly work this machine but that I watched the Guard (he calls it a *tripewriter)* who uses it when it is late and dark. You stare at it for hours and then you hit key and say damn-goddamn-it and when it is a long time the *words* come out on paper. But there are only Earthwords on tripewriter. So you work hard to understand me, you get the drift? It is no good if they catch me, then it is pain, I know. Thats what happens they are so cruel.

Now listen I'm no scientist. All I know is we were traveling out of formation to study more on atmosphere and I was damn pilot, we were going to rejoin the group later on in the day. Atmosphere near water which you call LAKE. But when we are nearly through, What is it? Something has gone wrongo with the ship. I can't control it and we fall into the drink only it is that I get the door opened and while the ship is sinking I crawl out. But there is no time for suiting!

What a luckyness I don't die you bet your sweet ars.

Well its blacking up in my head. I crawl out of the LAKE and the ship is gone. I remember what I thought it was I AM THE FIRST OF OUR RACE TO BE ON EARTH BY THE GREAT HORNED TOAD! Then I see I have only got one cone left.

When I am awake finally I try to walk, but, What's up with my legs? Different something. WHAMBO! I am a pratfall. So it was late and no sun and hard to see. No more any of my clothes are left: then, mother-naked, I sampood myself with galawater and fraguant pistania mud, wupper and lauar, from crown to sole. So it is not so cold but to breathe is a horse of another color. O Mother that took the cake to breathe. What will I: die? All alone, thinks me, and theres nobody nothin nohow and I'm alone on Earth…

I thought if a planet inhabitant will come along maybe I can explain our mission its friendly see and we ain't a-aimin to cause no trouble, that we are just looking for a new place into which to live. *But maybe he will be afraid of me,* I thought, *or I will be afraid of him!*

Well when I figgered that the (*Earthword*) jig is up I saw this Earth man. Great God Amighty I said what a strange basteed! Four legs this creature and a long tail with the horns on the head. Describe it? Hustle along, why can't you? Spitz on the iern while it's hot. I wouldn't have missed it for irthing on nerthe. Not for the lucre of lomba strait.

Oceans of Gaud, I mosel hear that! Ogowe presta! Ishekarry and wash-meskad, the carishy caratimaney? Sez I crawling up near it and told him my name saying, Heres what happened old podnuh. But I can't talk very good and the Earthman is eating and only one word very hard to spell, Moooooooo.

Then I saw other Earthman and some were like this big sonuvabitch but others were smaller with four legs and some by (*Earthword*) MAGIC were flying in the atmosphere like ships and no machines in them. Wings! With so many different.

I ain't no scientist. All I could do is drive my craft before nobody told me about Earthmen being all different. Or that you could live without suits, thats why you have to understand this: no suits. You can breathe the air only no fun pops.

Well nobody pays attention to me and I am going to starve to death or something. So I cry out for help, me alone, the first and with only one cone. "Somebody help me!" I think, "My name is—" (*Earthword*) etc. (?)

Thats when the giants came. Holy Scamander, I sar it! Ocis on us! Seints of light! Zezere! They are in a machine the machine going stop and here are the giants getting out and givin us a looksee. I'm making sounds and afraid what if they're not friendly! And I can't stop throat sounds: Subdue your noise, you hamble creature! Deataceas!

O am I so afraid when I see them close. Big just ain't the word. Ah, but one was the queer old skeowsha anyhow, trinkettoes! And sure he was the quare old buntz too, foostherfather of fingalls and dotthergills. But here is the funny part they are horrible but not like the way we are taught, like completely different. No. Thats the scorcher. Hair, tendrils, on their heads and they are (Earthword) anthropomorphic (?) and built like brick outhouses, no less. Stretch me, pull me out of shape, make it six times as long, and ugly? Ouch!

Well I'm pretty brave. So I clambered right up to them and telepathed hello there, my name is etc. I am part of a patrol from Zaras, we have to move and we were sort of lookin her over. My ship crashed and I thought maybe you'd take care of me until I can get word through to my buddy-buddies.

They didn't scream. They just looked at me that layed on the wet grass and I knew they didn't dig my conception. Of course I couldn't understand them either then, but of nature I remember what they said, they said:

—*Hank, it's a miracle!*

—*Now for God's sake, don't go jumping the gun! We'll have to look into this.*

—*It's a miracle, I tell you! Just as I'd prayed, Hank!*

—*Just got lost, or abandoned, or...*

I thought: Our civilization is a thousand years more advanced nor yours, folkses, and we want to be friends, if poss, we'll share and share alike, kay, keeds?

No intelligible response: to make the Gripes hear how coy they are (though he was much too schystimatically auricular about *his ens* to heed her). Giant Hank reaches down and picks up me and the other, also Giant but two fat-hills in front, long hair on head, bigger buttinsky, says:

—*Owww-poor-ittle-feller-izums'al-wosted?*

No sense here! (They got them two languages, one I figured out, this; but another that they talk most of the time to me just do not come through. Nemmine.)

Well brother am I gullible. Scared and hungry I figured to let them take over me. I let them pick up me—practically there is no (*Earthword*) gravity—and I trusted. Tired, get what I mean and hungry wow. And pains all over so that what it was I did I went to sleep before I could be finding out even wha's wha.

Did somebody say Earth people friendly? Let me at him is all because I am just one single Zarasan and heres what happened to *me*.

Incredible! Semperexcommunicambiambisumers. (Poor little sowsieved subsquashed me! Already I begin to feel contemption for them!)

Its got me beat how much time there went by right then. But always they're saying, He's sick, he's sick, and the black kept getting in my head hard to get used to. Natural? When I'm conscious in moments I begin TELEPATHY (no answer) and I look to see how the land lays. With another one Giant all the time its:

—*Hes gotta blong tuh somebody, for Cry Eye.*

And:

—*We've checked everywhere. I can't lose him!*

Well they put me in a cage first. Yes in a prison. I wake up and where am I? Behind bars. No clothes still but a white clothy thing I don't know what the hell. The ground in the cage is soft BWAAANG! but then I see there is something in the cage there with me. With the arms and the legs. And furry. I thought wow whats this!

Well I'm pretty brave. So when this liver wouldn't talk I challenged him in custom and we fought very hard, yes. Whatta fight! While that Mooksius with preprocession and proprecession, duplicitly and displussedly, was promulgating ipsofacts and sadcontras this raskolly Zarasan he had allbust seceded in monophysicking his illsobordunates...and his babskissed nepogreasymost got the hoof from my philioquus right in the snoot! Its insides came out dry and it was still. We'll see now, is what I thought, then whos bossman. We'll see now.

Then the Giant Earthman with the fat-hills and long hair came in and stood by my cage.

—*Iz-tzums-aw-wet?* the Earthman said and picked up me and did unspeakable things so bad I can't talk about them. Back home you do what he did to me thats all, you get the bis in the gretch. Humiliation? Jing.

I tried to fight but it wasn't no dice on because Earthman like the Giants are superstrength. I said, See here, is this how you treat visitors? Is this how a Guest is treated by Earth-dwellers in the name of Pete?

—*Him'th-talkin'* he said. Such tongue!

Then you don't know, you just don't know. Great things they put in my mouth and tubes places if I told you you would say I'm lying, it's so doity, and tried to smother me. Tortures like this all the time. When I sleep its wake up and when I try to talk what is it? Go to sleep.

And worse. Well Lord knows how long this rebop went oi No communication, *Quas primas*—but 'tis bitter to compot my knowledge's fructos of. Tomes. They pretend they do not understand me or maybe they are so jerkhead they cannot translate even now. And every day I talk to them and sa who I am and why are they torturing me, what have I ever done to them?

I have surprise they didn't take away my cone, they found it finally, then where would I be? Once they tried but screamed threats and they said,—*Iddumswiddah-pwaysing.* (Meaning?) And let me have it back.

I was thonthorstrok that time.

Well this Earthman who is my Guard and maintorturer is what they call WRITER. When it is light and I am too tired to walk—impossible! Whooth!—he will leave alone me. Maybe come in and say,—*Quite a set of lungs boy givin em a rest?* But the other Earthman who is what they call a chick or doll-type housewife, never. Always it is that this one hits and ounches me and holds me up in her giant hands and does these unspeakable things. Always she says,—*So glad he can be ours, so glad, Hank, I knew we didn't do wrong, we asked around, we watched the papers didn't we?* (—*We're kidnapers,* says another one Giant.)

Well I tried to make a message to home but my hands have trouble to work. A writing stick they gave me but it would not god-damn. Halfway through my dispatch, what did they do? They took it away and said,—*See the widduh wabbit him him dwawed?* But all right you couldn't have read it anyway.

Then what I saw is Writer working this machine. I stopped to fight and was quiet for long and watching. The language I learned, then when I watched, I can see what to operate. Writer now he is very cool,—*Here,* he says *this is how the tripewriter works, baby.* And when he caught me with his books, he says,—*Here, try some Joyce, kid maybe you can make some sense out of it.*

My captors have beat it for a short while. Writer is at what is called a Library doing research for novel, but I can hear the voice of Giant Shewife at near place: Nextdoor-neighbors. I escaped my cage and am finishing now hurry-up in case they see: that would be bad. Then they hit you. But pretty clever of me for being no scientist?

I will get free tonight (snakes in clover, picked and scotched, and a vaticanned viper). After they torture me with what they call (*Earthword*) BOTTLE and go asleep then I will climb out of this cage that Shewife calls CRIB and, fast, because I learned how. Fool them. Then I will make a twist on what they never let me touch, a device thing they always say,—*Don't ever play with that, that's the gas-heater, don't ever touch that its dangerous.*

So you come pronto but forget all that jazz about being friendships for these are vicious warlike creatures.

Try friendships and you know what they'll give you? They'll give you prison and torture like the kind O

I can't even start to tell you.

Bring weapons—Perkodhuskurunbarggruauyagokgorlayorgrom-gremmitghundhurthrumathunaradidillifaititiliibumullunukkunun!—the big ones. But watch out for me. I'll be in a field away from the falling buildings, you know what I mean. And Amen brothers, you bet.

ANTHEM

(1958)

I

TITLES

FADE IN

1   CLOSE SHOT—PAINTING—COVERS SCREEN

This is Brueghel's THE FALL OF ICARUS.

> VOICE O.S.:
> > (Fake Mountain Ballad style,
> > with guitar)

When Ick saw the birds And how they flew,
And said to himself,
"I'll do it, too!"
And got out his feathers
And got out his glue—
The Dream wasn't new.

> SECOND VOICE O.S.:

Not even then?

> FIRST VOICE O.S.:

Not even then.

Camera moves leisurely over painting, pausing at the Flemish plowman and the shepherd.

> SECOND VOICE O.S.:
>
> Wait a minute! Where is he?

> FIRST VOICE O.S.:
>
> Who?

> SECOND VOICE O.S.:
>
> Icarus! The guy who wanted to fly to the stars— the guy with the old dream.

Camera moves into picture for EXTREME C. U. of a pair of legs sticking out of the water.

> FIRST VOICE O.S.:
>
> Well, something went wrong. You see, the sun got too hot, and—

> SECOND VOICE O.S.:
>
> He never made it.

> FIRST VOICE O.S.:
>
> That's right. He never made it.

> FADE OUT

II

FADE IN

2	PAN SHOT—THE UNIVERSE:

In all its starry magnificence. (Process; or footage from INTOLER-ANCE—come on, Mr. Lamberger, you can do it, if you try!)

VOICE O.S.:

(Ook it up a la Corwin;
March-of-Timsey)

This is what we're talking about. Look! Look!

SECOND VOICE O.S.:

Hey, is it true that they twinkle? I mean really.

FIRST VOICE O.S.:

Sure, they twinkle, And don't let anybody tell you different, little guy!

We diddle around Orion, getting good comp. This drives the kids wild, Mr. Lamberger, see—*science fiction!* We sneak the message in right under their noses. You idiotic poop.

Okay: strings up; *schmaltzissimo!*

VOICE O.S.:

(Get Presley for this)

Ever since Man crawled
Out of the slime
And looked at the time
And said, "It's late!"
He started to dream;
He started to hate...

SECOND VOICE O.S.:

What'd he dream about? What'd he hate about?

FIRST VOICE O.S.:

This! Don't you get it, Mac? Man wanted *out!*

SECOND VOICE O.S.:

How come?

FIRST VOICE O.S.:

Now you're talking like my boss Lamberger who thinks I am working on INVASION FROM THE STARS.

SECOND VOICE O.S.:

You're drunk. You've been writing movies for five years now, and you still think they're gonna do a *good* s.f.'er. You're drunk.

FIRST VOICE O.S.:

On with the script!

SECOND VOICE O.S.:

Some script. You'll get fired. Well, okay: *How come?*

FIRST VOICE O.S.:

(What the hell does O.S. mean?)

How come we flopped out of the water and died and did it again and wouldn't rest until we could walk in dust up to our derrieres? How come we don't just sit down and drop the whole thing? Life, I mean.

SECOND VOICE O.S.:

I dunno.

The planets and the stars are on fire now; they're like the dust from an immense diamond suddenly struck by a great hammer; and their dust is alive on a field of dark velvet. (Got that, Mr. Set Designer?)

FIRST VOICE O.S.:

But it takes more than dreaming. Look: We're locked in a closet. It's filling up with garbage.

The air's going out of it. It's on fire. But we won't reach out and turn the key.

CHORUS OF ONE THOUSAND BRUNETTES O.S.:

Why?

FIRST VOICE O.S.:

Because our fingers are frozen in prayer and our heads are filled with fear; because we're covered with the crust of burial grounds and our hands are dripping wine.

SECOND VOICE O.S.:

We ever gonna make it? We ever gonna get to the stars?

FIRST VOICE O.S.:

A good question!

FADE OUT

III

FADE IN

3   RICHMOND BLAST-OFF AREA—EXT.—DAY—MED. SHOT
Professor Isaac Gold, fortyish, and Professor Fred Inman, somewhat
younger, are standing together, bareheaded, on the rim of a platform.
The dawn is steel-gray and damp. They are in heavy coats.

> PROF. GOLD
>> (looking O. S.)
>
> …y'know, Fred, twenty years from now they'll be calling her
> a pig. Put her in a museum along with *The Spirit of St. Louis,*
> and all the snot-nosed brats will laugh at her.

> PROF. INMAN
>
> It's taken a long time.

> PROF. GOLD
>
> They'll forget. We'll be paragraphs in text-books, Freddie—
> us and Myerson and Scott and…all of us. Historical data.
> They'll never write about—well, about *this* morning. Look,
> Freddie, goddamnit, look at her!

They look upward and CAMERA ASSUMES THEIR POINT OF VIEW.
The rocket gleams dully, a smooth metal giant pointing straight toward
the stars.

> PROF. GOLD
>
> I wish we could be aboard.

PROF. INMAN

Yeah.

They circle the platform, hands in pockets.

PROF. GOLD

I was afraid we wouldn't make it, you know?

PROF. INMAN

Well, we did make it, sir. Next week she'll go to the Moon; then we'll see Mars. Venus, maybe. After that—O hell, the sky *isn't* the limit. There'll be no limit. We'll go everywhere!

PROF. GOLD

(thoughtfully)

Everywhere...

PROF. INMAN

I was walking by the barracks last night. I passed your window. Thought I saw something... Professor Gold, you were praying.

PROF. GOLD

(turning to his friend)

Was I?

They look a long while at the rocket. Then they turn and walk back across the empty field, on past the guards and sentries. The CAMERA SWINGS BACK TO THE ROCKET, BACK TO THE STARS.

FADE OUT

IV

FADE IN

4   INSERT—NEWSPAPER

The headline, dated 1980, reads:

WAR DECLARED!

CAMERA MOVES THROUGH to paragraph at end of paper. C.U.

...due to the declaration of a national emergency, the scheduled experimental flight of the moon rocket AD ASTRA has been indefinitely postponed. It will be weather-treated and will remain under constant guard at Richmond Arena, until such time...

FADE OUT

V

FADE IN

5   BATTLE MONTAGE—(Stock; any old World War II stuff)

Bombs exploding in N.Y.C.; planes strafing boy scout picnics; etc., etc.

6   EXT SHOT—RICHMOND ARENA—MED

A bomb has demolished the shed housing the AD ASTRA. There is movement nowhere. Guards have been dismissed. The rocket stands nakedly alone in the middle of the battered field, her weather-covering blowing in rubbery shreds in the cold wind.

FADE OUT

VI

FADE IN

7   (Production Note: Conceive quick method of getting across passage of fifteen years without resorting to calendar bit. Also, through montages, blend in gradual deterioration of rocket—it's stripped by adventurers and kids, it rusts, it begins to fall apart.)

8   MED SHOT—EXT RICHMOND ARENA—TWILIGHT

(Possibly delete scene of Prof. Gold and Prof. Inman standing at ravaged rocket, discussing futility of persuading gov't to resume Moon Project. War is over now; work that in, too.)

9   MED CLOSE—EXT RICHMOND ARENA—DAY

The rocket is being loaded into a number of big trucks. Make truck drivers beautiful dames in flesh tights. (Got to work in sex *somehow.*)

QUICK CUT TO

10   BIG CLOSE UP—HARRY LAMBERGER

He is a weasel-faced, sharp-eyed, heartless, soulless huckster who doesn't give a damn whether we ever get to the moon. He's just out for the doller-oos. (Your big chance, Lamberger; now you can make like Hitchcock and play in your own film. Or is it type-casting?)

He grins widely as he watches loading procedure.

11   MONTAGE

Showing trucks taking rocket from town to town, setting up of tents, crowds gathering to gawk as, OVER-SCENE, we hear:

VOICE:

(barker type)

Built in 1980 at a cost of several million dollars, this here space ship could have flown to the moon! But fuel cost money and the war...

QUICK CUT TO

12   MED CLOSE SHOT—INT CIRCUS WAGON— HARRY & WIFE

Harry is drooling into a tankard of suds.

HARRY

O brother! And you din't think th' idea would work! 'Rocket ships, who wants to see rocket ships?' Ha-haaa-aa-a!

EMMA

What wife, I'm asking, likes any idea that includes shelling out five hundred G's?

HARRY

Sweetheart, baby, if you will kindly make another count of today's take? Every bum in this whole country is dyin' to pay his $2.50 for a guided tour through th' only rocket ship in the world. Hey, hoo-boy, now, I'm tellin' ya—leave it to ol' Lamberger...

FADE OUT

VII

FADE IN

13   (Production Note: More years pass. Make Lamberger older.)

14   CLOSE SHOT—SIGN READING "STARBURGERS—DINE IN THE STARS!"

CAMERA PULLS OUT and wanders through the rocket ship, now an exclusive, though somewhat down-at-the-heels, restaurant. All portholes are painted with phony stars. Place is jammed. Old Lamberger beams.

FADE OUT

VIII

15   (Production Note: Attn: Special Effects Dept.: This has got to be short but clear. One, another war— super bomb. Two, Passage of time— use *clever* gimmick. Maybe shoot back for L.S. universe, from time to time. You figure it out, you're getting paid more than I am.)

IX

FADE IN

16   LONG SHOT—FOREST

It is the forest primeval. Trees bigger and uglier than any trees we know today; vines a la Tarzan hanging around. It's green and wet and quiet, except for the chatter of monkeys or something slithering through the underbrush. Real atmospheric: feeling of doom everywhere. (Production Note: It had better be damn clear what has happened to Earth.)

In the midst of this, we DOLLY IN on the AD ASTRA, upright once again. Pretty miserable condition, but still majestic, still suggestive of her appearance when Professors Gold and Inman were slobbering over her. This could have been our solution.

It's a good day. The sun is out and picks up the few unrusted spots on the ship's hull, making it glint and shine. We see all sorts of animals clambering around her. When we TRUCK INSIDE, we can't even recognize the restaurant—it's a shambles. Piles of junk. CAMERA MOVES slowly, picking up signs that this was once a mighty spaceship. Control panel— left intact by shrewd old Lamberger—is acrawl with spiders. CAMERA MOVES IN for close shot large porthole, the painted stars twinkling...

FADE OUT

X

FADE IN

17   MED SHOT—INT CAVE

A fire blazes in the center of the cave. Neanderthal-type men and women, and a couple mutants, plus maybe a panther-girl, are seated around a fire, tearing at a slab of raw meat. Over in a corner, others are tearing at themselves—stylistic, bloody fight. (Shoot up their nostrils.) CAMERA DOLLIES IN for MED C.U. lone cave-man. He's standing at mouth of cave.

18   DIFFERENT ANGLE

This particular caveman is not so toothy and dirty and repulsive as the others in the cave, but he is not Robert Taylor, either. In the b.g., shadowed by immense trees, the ruins of cities, coming suddenly to view out of the phantasmagoric aspect(!) is the AD ASTRA—almost fallen to pieces now.

The caveman looks at his fellow creatures eating and fighting inside. Then, slowly, he lifts his head and—CAMERA FOLLOWING—stares at the clear night sky, black-velvet black and filled with all the stars and all the planets that one universe can hold.

They seem to be on fire now, these stars and planets: vibrant and alive, shimmering, dancing holes of brightness.

(Production Note: If possible, Sid, this constellation should be given a *mocking* and at the same time *beckoning* appearance. Can do?)

FADE OUT

XI

FADE IN

19   MED SHOT—INT HOLLYWOOD STUDIO—WRITER'S OFFICE

Writer, resembling caveman at mouth of cave, hangs himself with thirty-five-dollar hand-painted tie.

FADE OUT

THE END

Mother's Day

(1958)

His hair was red, but his face was redder, and I never saw such sadness in the eyes of a man before. Not a new sadness, either, but something old and strong and buried deep inside. He sat down at my table.

"Good evening to you," I said, smiling.

He looked up, wrenched off his helmet, and rubbed his sweaty face into an even brighter red brightness.

"Good evening," I said again, but without the smile.

"Beer!" he said to the little Venusian who had rolled up. "Earth beer. American beer—understand?" The waiter shook his tendrils angrily and made motions in the air: *"Please use Accepted Signs, wise-fellow."*

The sad red man did so, following a gigantic shrug. He sat quiet as death until the beer arrived, and the waiter had rolled away. He swigged loudly and belched louder still. He looked at me. "Cop?" he said.

"No."

"It would be my luck. I practically live with these over- grown spiders, and the first Earthman I see, what is he: a goddam cop." He snorted disgustedly.

"You're wrong," I said, and offered him a cigarette. He examined it carefully, saw it was a Terran make. He lit up, sighing.

I extended my hand. "Looks like we're going to be together a while," I said. "The *Ginger* isn't due for three more hours. I suppose you're headed for Earth? My name is—"

"Stop play-acting, sonny! You know who I am and you're about to wet your pants over it. Well, I don't care, understand? Not one little bit. Go ahead and laugh your fool head off!"

"I'm sorry. I've not been in touch with Earth for quite a while. Why *should* I laugh at you?"

He examined me with a beady eye; then he sank back in the booth. "Reasons," he said.

"Care to talk about them?" I poured him another beer.

"I only thank the Lord my dear sweet mother—bless her bones— was spared the shame," he murmured. "It would have killed her dead."

"Tell me about it," I said.

"I will, by God!" he said, and he began to talk.

THEY NEVER would have found out I killed that jasper *(the man with the red hair said)* if it hadn't been my black Irish luck to leave fingerprints all over the house. Of course, there was the fact that it was well known that this here particular fella had announced his intention to marry my youngest sister, Amarantha, which made it look pretty suspicious, I suppose, considering my public sentiments. Besides which, three people seen me do it. But otherwise, who would have known? Nobody, that's who.

So they caught me—not without the best kind of fight, I want you to know—and in less time than it takes, Mrs. McCreigh's favorite son was thrown in the pokey.

Now there is no worse place on the face of the Earth, nor elsewhere for that matter, than these new-fangled jails. Used to be they had bars made of steel and so you was spared temptation: Nowadays it looks just exactly like you're in a swell apartment with the windows wide open. Course, you *touch* them windows and you get enough charge to knock you back to yesterday. I know. I tried.

Well, sir: "Gavin McCreigh," the judge says to me, "for the willful murder of Edgar Johnson, we hereby sentence you to spend the rest of your natural life in exile upon the asteroid *Spartanburg.*"

Sent a chill right through my stummick. Spartanburg! On that mess of mud, a man's 'natural life' couldn't be expected to exceed a day and a half at the outside!

But being Irish-American and a human being of the White race, I took her on the chin. Says I: That's how the cards fall! That's how the big ball bounces!

Spartanburg, as you well know, or ought to if you've ever looked inside a micronews, is crawling with giant bugs and disease of the absolute worst kind. A body would be dead before he started.

So, I mean to say, me loving life and brooking no desire to perish out in the middle of space any more than the next one, maybe you can see why I give her some thought when they come to me with their proposition.

"Gavin McCreigh," says they, "choose. Life or death—which'll you have?"

"Life," says I enthusiastically.

"Come with us."

It almost shook the teeth out of my head when they told me what it was all about—me, of all people, me: Gavin McCreigh: American!

(Give me some more to drink. Get that hoppin' toad over here with some beer!)

"For the advancement of science," they said. I truly thought they was joking, swear I did, but it was no joke.

I, Gavin Patrick Quentin McCreigh, was to be the first Earthman to marry a Martian!

Needless to say, I told them where they could put *that* noise. "Let's go," says I. "Let's go to Spartanburg. I'll walk if need be, or you can tie me with a rope at the jet-end and *drag* me—anything, my buckos, anything; but not this."

Some choice they give me, wouldn't you say? Die of a lingering disease a million miles from home, or take the holy vows with an outsize cockroach!

"If it's such an honor," says I, "then why don't you do it yourself?"

They shoveled me back into my hole, and I set there ticking off the days. You ever hear stories about Spartanburg? Man don't have a chance. Longest *anybody* was known to last in that slime was two weeks. They watch you on the screens—everybody does—sitting at home with their TVs. All over the world. Watch you take sick and die.

They put a TV in my room so as I could watch old films of that ax murderer—what was his name—Buechner?—going stark raving crazy mad. Poor fella run around nutty as a squirrel until finally the bugs got him. Took the varmints two minutes by the clock, and poor old Buechner was just parched ones.

Well, that did her. I swallowed my fierce Irish pride and give them a buzz and told them all right, by God, I'd marry their Martian beetle and would they please get the thing over with in a hurry.

What a change! You'd think I was the King of England the way they puttered and spit over me, getting me this, getting me that—never letting me out of the cell, you understand, but treating me to cocktails and squab under glass and—it was okay. That part of it was all right.

'Course the papers was coming out with their headlines all about it, like and similar with TV and ekcetra. All the high mucky-mucks from Mars was here and twice as happy about the whole thing as we was, mainly because they had been angling to move in on us before their country went plumb dry. Dis*gust*ing the way them creechures sucked around!

For myself, I always figured we had enough race problem as it was, but I guess you know what happened. It had started even when I was there: They flooded in like crickets, took over, and set up their housing projects, messing up the land with big old glass bubbles.

Ha! Guess maybe they was sorry they used glass, hey? Imagine some of our boys threw a couple of stones that just accidentally landed somewheres.

But then, I warned them. Said, Looky: It ain't as if we don't have enough trouble trying to live on the same planet with all the yellow ones and black ones and the rest, we got to 'adjust' to people who ain't even people in the first place, but more like common roaches. I asked, ain't we got enough of a burden as it is?

They wouldn't listen. Deef and dumb. Now look what they got on their hands. Earth ain't even Earth no more. Swear, I'm glad I didn't stick around to see what happened *afterwards...*

I mean, referring to after the day when it all really begun.

They got me out and decked me in finery from my neck to my toes and, keeping guard, waltzed me into the Prison Hospital. It was crowded to the living rafters with folks: reporters, newsboys, diplomats and ekcetra.

And then—I fainted. Swear I did—fainted. Or like to. I was introduced to my future wife!

"This is Jane of Mars," the warden says to me. "Shake hands," says he with a frown.

Ever shake hands with a Martian? It's like taking holt of a wet sponge. But I thought of Buechner and grabbed on.

This Jane—she wasn't no different from any of the others.

Big as I was, standing there on four legs, twittering them aunt-emmies. "How do you do," says she with her thumbs.

By a stroke of good fortune, I managed not to throw up right then and there, you may be sure.

Well, the officials come and told me as how Jane was elected by unanimous decision—Miss Mars!—and what we was supposed to do, why we was gathered together and the rest of the malarkey.

Then they got a Martian and one of our own men and, next thing I knew they was saying (one aloud, the other in this sign language):

"Blahblahblah and ekcetra: Do you, Jane of Mars, take this Earthman to be your lawful wedded husband?"

"I do," says the cockroach.

"Do you, Gavin Patrick McCreigh, take this girl, Jane of Mars, for your lawful wedded wife?"

My intruls was boiling with the shame and the humiliation. "I do," says I.

"I now pronounce you man and wife."

"Well?" says the warden.

"Well?" says I.

"Aren't you going to kiss the bride?"

I'll make a long story short right about here, because it's a matter of considerable pain for me to go into the details of what followed then.

We was given a house, a regular house, but specially treated so we could both live in it—which must have cost a pretty penny. Half of it was hers, though, and this here part was full of rocks and stuff and all that stuff the Martians live around like lizards.

They kept a strict watch. Guess because maybe they knew I'd hightail it the minute I could. Particularly at night, we was kept tabs on. I don't know what they expected—but I just kept my mouth shut and talked civil as I could to this Jane and stayed out of her way.

She stayed out of mine too. Always looking sad and forlorn like, always telling me how we had to make a go of it for the sake of this and the sake of that. But when I let her know I had hid the meat cleaver, well, she just says: "I don't understand, I don't understand." But she steered clear after that.

After a week of this misery and hell, with me halfway wishing I *had* of gone to Spartanburg to begin with and upheld to the limit my honor and dignity as a white man, the boys trouped in.

Says: "Gavin McCreigh." Says: "Jane of Mars. We must talk to you."

And when they told me what it was they wanted to talk *about*, what they demanded and insisted on, for the "interests of science"—well, this was one healthy red-blooded American male who wished he'd of been borned a eunuch.

What could I do? What chance did I have?

It was essential, we was told, to find out what would happen. No other way of telling. And since these here Martians looked like cockroaches only to *me* (due no doubt to the manner in which I was brought up)—aside from all them legs and aunt-emmies they pretty well resembled human beings—and there'd be a lot of mixing going on—well, this was really, says they, the whole point of marrying me off to one!

I let 'em all know what I thought about it, you can bet your bottom credit on that. I let 'em know they was going against every natural law and that they'd be punished sure as there's a hell below.

But they told me: "We'll be watching, Gavin McCreigh!"—which any way you look at it is downright obscene—"and unless you want a vacation on a certain asteroid, we suggest you follow through."

So—because an Irishman can do anything he's got to do, and do it well—I followed through.

Next week afterwards a peculiar thing happened.

They sent me back to jail.

Talk about your reliefs! I lazed around watching the TV and reading newspapers and wondering in a sort of vague way about it all. What was next? Would I get to stay here smarting from my shame, or would they toss me back with that Martian? But I figured, well. I've done my bit, the good Lord knows, so maybe they'll leave me alone.

Everything went jimdandy until about, oh, I'd say about two-three weeks had gone by. Then I woke up one morning feeling like the last rose of summer pulled up by the roots and stomped on. Got out of bed and fell flat on my face just exactly like I was Lord High. Dizzy I was, and fuzzheaded. When they brought in the breakfast, damn if I didn't heave all over the floor!

Now I want you to understand that for Gavin McCreigh, who'd never seen a sick day in his whole life, this here was mighty peculiar indeed. I didn't say nothing, and it passed and I felt fine for a while—until the next morning.

'Twas the same thing, only twice as bad. Couldn't even keep boiled eggs down.

Then the pains begun.

I set there cramped up, the pains shooting through me like lightning bugs for quite a spell. Finally I got to the visiscreen and hollered for help.

The doctors all come on the double, almost like as if they was waiting for just such a thing to happen. I wouldn't know. Anyway, they rolled me over, and punched and poked and shook their heads and give me some slimy stuff to take, and the pains stopped so I said: "Leave go of me. I'm all right!" But they wouldn't. They made X-ray pictures, and drew up charts, and I didn't spend fifteen minutes to myself all that day.

And that's the way it went. They took away my TV. They took away my reading newspapers. The tapes—everything, every touch with the outside. Put me to bed, too, they did and said, "Now don't you get alarmed, now don't you get alarmed."

Alarmed!

By damn, I near like to fell out of the bed when I seen the weight I was putting on. When you're sick, thought I, you're supposed to get all thin and piney; and here I was pooching out like a fed hog.

"Amazing!" says they. "Fantastic!" Then: "The gestation period seems to be the same as with the ordinary Martian." Fortunately, I didn't know the meaning of that word then, or I would probably of killed myself, since there were numerous sharp things still left laying around.

But I see the word ain't new to you. You're wondering, are you?

All right. Come about five weeks, with me looking like the blue ribbon sow—only sicker'n a dog—and *still* not understanding it all, they come in, their old lips drawn back in Chessy smiles a yard wide—but worried too.

"Gavin," says the warden, "we got a little news for you." Then they told me.

I, Gavin Patrick Quentin McCreigh, son of Mrs. Samuel Denis McCreigh, Irish-American from Atlanta, Georgia, forty-two years of age, male and in my right senses—was about to have a baby.

✤ ✤ ✤

YOU DON'T remember none of this? Well then, maybe you just don't believe, is that it? All right, by Neddie Jingo, you see this here scar? I didn't get it in no duel, sonny.

I got it when three days later they rushed me to the hospital—and me in agony—for what is known as a see-sarian section.

Don't ask me how it happened. I ain't no damn doctor. They went on about 'backwash' or something and talked about a lad named Gene, but it didn't make no sense to me at all, at all.

All I knew was, I was under that ether a long old time, and when I got out I had this scar and I was normal size again.

"This puts a new shading on our relations with Mars," says the warden.

"Puts a new shading," says I, "on a whole hell of a lot of things."

Says he: "Well, my bucko, that's the way she goes."

Says I quick as a wink: "That may be the way she goes now, but that sure ain't the way she used to go."

Then they brought it in.

Now understand. I don't and never did hold with the common notion that any newborn young'n is necessarily the prettiest sight on this here Earth. But when they toted *this* thing in, thought I: Gavin, you should have been borned a bald-headed Englishman. Because it was—and I don't color the facts—far and away the ugliest piece of meat ever beholden on the face of the globe.

All red it was and bellering to the top of its lungs—if it had lungs.

Didn't have no aunt-emmies, and right down to the waist it could have been a healthy normal child. Except for the fact it had twice the healthy normal number of legs: four, to be exact. Four little cockroachy legs, and them kicking and flailing in my face till I had to scream to get the crawly thing off of me.

It was an experience.

Well, I thought, anyway this'll sure as the devil put a crimp into the idea of intermarriage if the whole shooting match don't come to nothing else. But you know what? They claimed it was *cute.* You hear me?

"As beautiful a child as anyone could wish" was the way I heard it put.

IT TAKES a lot to sour an Irishman on his own home soil, that it does, but this did the trick, you may bet your spaceboots. I had to do something and do it mighty quick, or it'd be curtains for Gavin McCreigh.

Do you know what they had planned? Planned to put us back in the house and see if it worked out! Just like that: one-man's-family style!

Says I: "You can't make me do it."

Says they: "Spartanburg is reached in two weeks by the direct route."

Says I: "If I may call your gentlemen's kind attention to one fact: According to law, and tradition, only women have babies— correct?"

"Well..."

"And according to lawful records, one Gavin Patrick Quentin McCreigh, *male,* was found guilty of murder and sentenced to The Rock. Correct?"

"Well..."

"All right. Inasmuch as *I* have just given birth to a bairn, and inasmuch and notwithstanding as men can't have children, that makes me a mother. Correct?"

"Hmmm," says they.

"And being as how I'm a mother and therefore no longer the same person, and the thought of sending a *mother* to Spartanburg is unconstitutional on the grounds of being against God and law—"

Thanks be for my golden Irish tongue, is all I can say. For when I was finished, they was so screwjeed they didn't know whether to shoot me or send me a Mother's Day card.

Anyway, they dropped the charges against me and—legally anyway—I was a free man.

Free to endure my shame. They came after me like buzzards: Sign this; sign that; would I make a testimonial? Would I endorse two dozen and fifty things, from highchairs (with an extra footrest) to oatmeal. You wouldn't believe it! I had half the diaper laundries in town after me.

Well, I saw it was financially to my good to stay a spell in the same house with this Martian woman Jane. Wasn't easy, but the big hurt had been done, and so I acted out the part of the changed man: pretended I was right in love with my little family. Phew! Some family—three people and ten legs!

Finally, though, I had enough money from these testimonials and digest articles and lectures in Denmark and ekcetra to make my move. Junior never did have a name: they was having a contest at the time—he was exactly one year old, and according to the rest of the damfool world the cutest tyke that ever was, but according to me a blooming four-legged monsterosity.

The Irish don't forget. And this Irishman had endured more pain and torment than St. Patrick with the snakes— though on the whole I'd say they was more agreeable creechures. I waited until I knew for fair we weren't being watched in any of the secret ways they'd cooked up. Then I got me a good stout shillelagh and went into the bedroom and woke up that Martian shrew that was palming herself off as my wife and working it through me and my unfortunate situation that her whole damn race of bugs could infest our world.

"Get up!" says I.

"I'm not asleep," says she.

I told her what I aimed to do, but it didn't seem to scare her none: these Martians don't know fear nor any other decent emotion. Just stared at me with them crocus-eyes full of confusion and sorrow, all calculated to make me drop my shillelagh and leave her be.

Made me so dingdong mad I let out a cuss that turned the air blue and hove to. But she wouldn't yell, damn her! Just—took it. If she'd yelled or asked me to quit—anything *human*—maybe it wouldn't of happened.

When I seen what I'd done, I looked around and there was this other little brute, little four-legs, standing up in his crib, wiggling all over and glaring out at me with the fires of Hades in his eyes. Then he begun to bawl fit to wake the whole block. So I left, pretty fast.

It didn't take long for me to grab a ride on a space scow headed far away.

I escaped some things. But some things I didn't. I been give scars I'll never get over, never if I live to be a hundred years. I can't go back. And even if I could, I wouldn't. Not back to my shame—not to a world that ain't my world any more, crawling with the filth of the universe.

They got no room for me there now. They gave me eternal shame and cast me out and Gavin McCreigh will never have a home again...

✦ ✦ ✦

THE MAN whose name was Gavin McCreigh got to his feet. "Forget what I told you, sonny," he said. "It was stoppered up; now it's out, and I'm better for it. But you forget. And if you want my advice, stay away from Earth—just remember it the way it was before they all went crazy with this brotherhood business."

He started to leave, putting on his helmet, pressing the restaurant's inner air-lock button. I called to him: "Wait."

He turned around.

"I'm sorry, Gavin," I said, "but you're right. An Irishman *can't* forget, not even if he wants to. You're a dead thing now, the last of your kind in all the Galaxy; but I've looked for you a long time. A very long time... Mother."

He started to run, but it wasn't difficult to overtake him. After all, four legs are better than two.

THE TRIGGER

(1959)

It was a warm room; one, Ives decided, that had been lived in, despite its enormity. Real logs lay in a real fireplace. Originals by Wyeth and Benton and Hopper studded the walls. In a corner, near the concert grand piano, stood a fine mahogany bar, with a tasteful assortment of bottles—most of them half-full—on the shelves behind.

Not at all the sort of room a man would choose to commit suicide in.

Ives tapped the gleaming hardwood floor with his toe. Lieutenant Bracker, a four-square giant of a man, turned and smiled. "Rug's out getting cleaned, I imagine," he said. "He used a .45. They make quite a mess."

"Yes." Phillip Ives brushed away the quick image that had sprung into his mind. He walked over to the mantel and inspected, for the tenth time, one of the numerous model racing cars that decorated the house. This was a bright red roadster, shark-snouted and, somehow, vicious.

"That's called a Ferrari," Bracker said. "Around twenty thousand bucks. Lawrence has a garage full of them."

"Had," Ives corrected, replacing the model. "Had."

Bracker shrugged. "Miserable word," he said. "But I don't hear much else lately."

A door opened and a woman entered the room. She might have been attractive; you couldn't tell. Now she looked lost and afraid.

"I'm sorry to have kept you waiting," she said. "I—wasn't dressed."

"That's perfectly all right, Mrs. Lawrence," Bracker said, in a surprisingly tender voice. "We won't stay long." He nodded his head toward the lean, short man in the corner, the man whose painfully plain suit and drugstore tie gave him a meek, apologetic air. "This," Bracker said, "is Mr. Phillip Ives. He's connected with the Homicide Division in San Francisco. I hope you won't mind if he asks you a few questions."

The woman studied Ives, then went to the bar; she made three scotch-and-waters before replying. "Do you think Oscar was murdered?" she asked.

"No," Ives said, taking the drink. "The department has definitely ascertained that your husband took his own life."

"But—"

"Now that you've had some time to think, perhaps you can help us find a motive." There was something hard and metallic, expressionless, about the lean man's voice. It told you that he was more than just a policeman, more than a man with a job. A specialist called in to perform a delicate operation on a patient he'd never seen before would speak this way. Upon the patient's death, he would express sorrow; but only because he had failed in his duty—not because a life had been lost. He wouldn't be interested in life.

"There was no motive," the woman said, a bit angrily. "Oscar was a happy man."

"It has been my experience, Mrs. Lawrence," Ives commented, "that people who commit suicide are seldom happy. And they always have a reason. In your husband's case, can you recall any differences in his behavior prior to the…incident?"

"No."

"Are you quite sure?"

The woman walked to a window, then turned. "For the past year and a half," she said, "my husband was happier and more content than he'd ever been. Sports cars, as Mr. Bracker knows, were his hobby. He'd always wanted to be a sort of impresario, but business obligations never gave him the time. Then he retired, suddenly, and devoted himself completely to the thing he loved most. He was like a child—like a child who'd finally gotten the toys he had always dreamed about. Anyone can tell you!" She took a swallow of the scotch and shuddered. "He was the happiest man I've ever known!"

Ives set his drink aside. His eyes were cold. "Then you can say, *for certain,* that he was not behaving at all oddly toward the last?"

"For Christ's sake, man," Bracker said, taking a step.

"Well?" Ives demanded.

The woman stood very still; then, slowly, as if in defeat, she nodded. "He was—I don't know—moody the last week, you might say. Not a lot, actually. But—"

"But he was withdrawn, quiet, thoughtful?"

"Yes."

"Thank you, Mrs. Lawrence." Ives put on his sweat-stained Stetson, turned, and walked out of the room, out the door, into the damp and rain-flecked air. Bracker followed, an annoyed expression on his face.

"You don't care much for my tactics, do you, Lieutenant?" Ives asked.

"To be frank, no."

"Neither do I. Unfortunately, it is the only way I can get results."

"What results?"

"I'm not too sure. For one thing, we know that the pattern is unbroken. I spoke earlier with Mrs. Addison and Mrs. Vaile. They said essentially the same things. No reason for their husbands to commit suicide; yet each man had grown moody the week before. 'Thoughtful'..." The two policemen paused for a light to change. "May I have a look at that note again, Lieutenant? Lawrence's."

Bracker fished a photostat from his wallet. The words on it read, "Dearest Louise: I'm sorry. I know how unhappy this will make you, but it's the only way out."

"Out of what?" Ives murmured.

"You tell me," Bracker said. "That's why you're here."

The lean man smiled. "Of course." In eight months there had been four suicides. In each instance, the man had been a celebrated figure, or had been wealthy, all had achieved much in life. The local police had suspected murder, but that was out of the question.

So they had called in Phillip Ives, who possessed a reputation in his field. He was known as a fanatic. To him, there were Open Files, but never, never Unsolved Cases. The thwarting of criminals (not the undoing of crime) was his life. He had no special hours. No special home. No special office. Except in name: he was "with" the San Francisco Division of Homicide. A loner, they said, remembering vaguely that he was supposed to have had a wife, once. Just the man.

"I suppose you've observed that all four men belonged to the same club, Lieutenant?"

"Of course," Bracker said, exasperatedly. "The Sportsman's Haven. We're not stupid, Mr. Ives. We're just tired."

"I can understand that. I was merely thinking out loud." They stopped at a 1938 Chrysler sedan; it was faded gray, covered with forgotten dents and bruises; it sat, askew, as if victim to some horrible accident. "The answer," Ives said, clambering into the car, "is, nevertheless, at that place."

Bracker removed a handkerchief and wiped his face. "Mr. Ives," he said, "I hate to argue with you, because the chief thinks you're pretty hot. But after the second time we saw the coincidence, and I personally covered every member of the club. And there's nothing there; I mean, inside. But look—four guys are supposed to've knocked themselves off. First was Fred Addison. He got at least five hundred grand a year out of his lumber business. Nice wife, plenty of stuff on the side; and I checked 'em all out, too. No problems. Suddenly he decides to swallow half a can of lye. Lye! I mean, he knew what it'd do to his stomach, he was smart enough to know that! Okay. Next we have that young Parker kid. Millions, from his old man. Broads to burn. He shoves a letter opener into his chest, that's what they say. Just like that. And Vaile—you know, it's real easy to believe that a guy who's two steps from being governor of the state all of a sudden decides to jump out of a window. Real easy."

"What are you getting at, Lieutenant?" Ives asked, something of a smile at the corners of his mouth.

"Well," the big man said, "I know what the doc says; he says there wasn't any foul play. And I went over the whole business with a comb, and I couldn't find anything out of line, either. But, four suicides in eight months—all connected—it just doesn't happen."

"Yes, go on."

"I'll tell you the truth, Ives. I think it's murder. I think somebody, somewhere, has figured out a way to bump these guys so it won't show. The Cap thinks I'm in the bag, but—" Bracker gave a final swipe at his face with the handkerchief and flipped away the cigarette he'd been smoking. "I suppose that's what you think, too."

"To the contrary," the lean detective said. "There is no doubt whatever that the men were murdered. I'll talk to you later. Lieutenant."

Ives slammed the door and drove off, tires spinning on the wet cement.

THE SPORTSMAN'S Haven was a squat, rather ugly building, constructed of tan bricks and hung with nautical symbols. In place of a doorknob was a small ship's wheel. A rusted bell, marked *Thistledown,* supplanted a buzzer. Ives rang the bell.

The door was opened by a sumptuously clad Negro. He said, "Yes?" after a good look up and down.

Ives removed a bulging plastic wallet from his hip pocket, plucked out his identification.

"Yes, sir," the Negro said.

The interior of the club was dimly lit; it resembled a high-class cocktail lounge. Fish netting covered the walls. There were etchings of whalers and ancient four-masters, and photographs of yachts, mostly white. In the corners, tiny fires wriggled in chafing dishes. Exactly eighteen men occupied the room.

Ives put a cigarette in his mouth and ambled over to the far wall. Here a picture window gave a splendid view of the Sound; of the two immense yet graceful yachts sitting solidly, as though buried in cement, and of the numerous smaller craft, bobbing and rolling with the swells. And beyond, the mist-grayed water, rippling endlessly out of sight.

"May I be of some assistance to you?"

A large man in a flannel suit, topped with the inevitable cap, stood unsmiling. Clearly, he was displeased. And, perhaps, nervous.

"It might be," Ives said. "Who are you?"

"The owner. Eric Korngold."

"Mr. Korngold, I'm with the police. We're troubled at the number of incidents that have taken place among the members of this club."

The large man nodded. "Terrible," he said. "Simply awful. I've thought a good deal about it; but it makes no sense whatever. When I heard about Mr. Lawrence I nearly fainted. Yes."

An inch-long ash fell, trailing gray down Ives's suit. "I'm going to speak frankly with you, Mr. Korngold. I know you've been bothered quite a bit with questions and snooping, but that can't be helped."

"Of course. I understand completely."

Ives nodded. "People kill themselves for a lot of reasons," he said. "Money is number one. Number two, however, is women. Now I've been informed that women are not allowed in the Sportsman's Haven. Is that correct?"

"Absolutely," Korngold said. "Without exception."

"Formally speaking, you mean."

"How's that?"

"Mr. Korngold, do you provide call girls for your club members?"

The man's face hardened into tight lines. For a moment he seemed unable to speak. Then he said, "No."

Ives shrugged. "Well," he said, "it was a thought. Thanks for your cooperation."

Korngold wheeled and strode angrily away.

He wouldn't lie, Ives thought. It would be too easy to check. Besides, Bracker has probably done it already. A smart cop. Damn!

He glanced over at the bar, which was dark and quiet. A tall, angular man in a white jacket stood wiping pony glasses. Another man sat over a drink, talking softly. That would be Carter Sexton, of the Sexton paper mills. Forty-three, married, father of two boys, rich.

Ives was suddenly overcome by a feeling of frustration. He had gone into the case with his usual sure-footed, imperious calm. And why not? Hadn't it been he who'd cracked the eight-year-old Yedor mystery, sending the benevolent Horton directly to the gas chamber? And who but Ives had hounded unhappy Mrs. Gottlieb into a full confession of her various poisonings? "It's the difficult cases that are easy," he'd often said. "The more complicated you get, the more likely you are to leave clues. Really *simple* murders are much, much harder to solve."

Well, there was nothing simple about this. It was a murder case without a murderer.

He sat down on the bar stool.

"Yes, sir?"

"Something strong," Ives said, his eyes closed. "Something that will warm my insides."

As he tried to sort out the pieces and fit them together, he heard, vaguely, the drone of voices. Mr. Sexton was whispering now. And the bartender was whispering, too, as he put various liquids into a short, thick glass.

"It is called a Black Russian," the angular man in the white jacket said. "I think you'll be pleased."

Ives threw it down recklessly. It did the job. "Another," he said. He noticed and did not notice that Sexton had gone out the door. "What's your name?" he asked when the bartender returned.

"Morrow," the man said. "Harold Morrow."

"Do *you* have any ideas?"

"About what, sir?"

"About the deaths."

"Of course, Mr. Ives." The bartender smiled. "Oh, you're famous, sir—that is, to anyone who dabbles in true crime. I recognized you at once."

"Flattered." Ives took another swallow of the drink, which was a rum concoction. "Also, baffled. Are you?"

The bartender retained his smile, which exuded small delight. "Baffled, sir, and fascinated. I knew the gentlemen well, and I can't imagine any reason for them to have done what they did. It's not my business to pry; still, they seemed such, well, such *happy* men!"

Ives murmured something indistinct. For three days he had been investigating, examining, thinking; now his brain was tired, as he was tired. Perhaps it was coming home, after so many years. No; Seattle wasn't home. It was just a place.

"It's certainly a pity, sir, that you'll finally have to admit to an unsolved case. Rodney Brown mentioned in his study of California murders that you would never recognize the existence of such a thing—an unsolved case, that is. But here you are."

"Yes. Here I am. Morrow, how is it that you know so much about me?"

"As I said, sir, true crime is a hobby of mine. I'm no expert or anything, but I read the books—Boucher, Roughead, Pearson, Brown. And you figure quite prominently in most of them."

Ives hiccupped. He found that he liked this fellow, wanted to stay and hear more. The voice had a soothing, melodious quality to it; Morrow seemed to understand, the way bartenders are supposed to.

"...but think they're unfair," he was saying. "Picturing you as such an inhuman machine. That's what Sherlock Holmes was, but he was an imaginary character. Boucher mentions that you had a wife, sir. Is that true?"

"Yes," Ives said.

The voice went on, and suddenly, his mind loosened by the drinks, and by the memory of familiar landmarks, he began to think of Greta. After such a long time. For a while he dwelled on the happy days; then, as he knew it must, the final picture—the picture of the apartment and its odd smell; of the doctor, leaning over the bed of Greta, still and unmoving— came into focus. God, if he'd only stayed home. If he hadn't gone out on that ridiculous, miserable case...she might have lived. But, alone, with no way to reach the telephone, no way to call out—

"...it must be a lonely life," the bartender said.

"It is," Ives responded, distantly.

"I don't know what I'd do if I were in your shoes," Morrow went on. "Brown hints that it was your ambition that killed your wife, but that seems terribly harsh..."

On and on the man talked, slowly, carefully, in the melodious voice. On. And on.

When the remembering crowded in his head, Ives tossed down the drink, placed two dollars on the bar, and went outside.

The air did no good. He knew that it was true: he had killed Greta, and he was lonely, and that was why he was such a fanatic, such a droll sleuth. And also true he had failed in this case. It made no sense and it would never make sense.

He walked across the slimy boards, up the stairs, to the edge of the street.

When the light turned to green, he stepped out; from another street a bus came groaning, preparing for a left turn. Ives continued, hardly seeing at all. He thought of Greta. And he thought, if this is failure, then what is the usefulness of Phillip Ives?

A part of him whispered, the pain could end. It could end.

All you have to do is wait a second longer, take a step; just one.

The memories exploded. He started forward.

"Hey, buddy—watch it!"

Ives automatically jumped aside; the vast, helpless bulk of the bus swept within inches of him, its horn bleating.

"You okay?" a man asked.

Ives shook his head. "Yes. I—" Suddenly he realized what he had almost done and it chilled him. "Thank you."

The man hurried off.

Ives stood still, while people brushed by him, thinking.

Then he clenched his fists and ran to the parked Chrysler, hoping, praying that he would not be too late.

HE WAS precisely one hour too late. By the time he reached the gray-white mansion on the hill, Carter Sexton was dead. The millionaire lay sprawled across an Oriental rug, a bullet lodged somewhere inside his skull.

"Ives," Lieutenant Bracker barked, "how in the holy hell did you know about this? I just got the call twenty minutes ago myself!"

"There is no time for explanations," Ives said, replacing his hat. "Let's say this. If I'd been a little smarter, Sexton would be alive. If I'd been a little dumber, I'd be dead along with him."

"Hold on, damn it. You can't just toss something off like that. I want to know how you—"

The lean detective whirled around and walked briskly out of the room. He went to a public telephone booth and placed a call. Then he got into his car and drove to Queen Anne Hill.

Two hours and thirty minutes later he reappeared at the Sportsman's Haven.

"Bartender!"

The angular man in the white jacket looked up. A flicker of surprise crossed his face. "Mr. Ives, I thought you'd gone."

Ives stared at the man. "A Black Russian, Harold," he said. "Have one with me. I wish to celebrate."

The drinks were prepared with uncertain haste.

"Mr. Sexton is dead, by the way," Ives said. "Did you know?"

The bartender gasped. "But—are you serious? I was talking to him only a few hours ago! How—did it happen?"

"Oh, shot himself," Ives said, casually.

"That's very bad news. He was one of our finest members."

"Yes." Ives lifted the glass. "Mr. Morrow?"

The bartender frowned. "I honestly can't see what you find to celebrate, in view of this shocking—"

"Why," Ives interrupted, "the conclusion of the case."

Morrow smiled, wryly. "I'm afraid I made those first ones a bit too strong."

"Not at all. Harold, and I hope I may call you Harold—I believe I have figured out this riddle. Would you care to hear my answer?"

"Yes," the bartender said. "I would, very much."

"Well," Ives said, scraping a fleck of egg from his tie, "it's this way. And bear with me, for it does get complicated in parts. Well: four people—I beg your pardon; five people—commit suicide. They are supposedly happy, however, and have no apparent reason for committing suicide. But now, Harold, as any psychologist will tell us, this is a very doubtful sort of a proposition. It takes an awful lot to get a man to conquer his natural instinct for survival. Were they the victims of foul play, we wondered? No. Though the view was held by certain officers, it was merely a desperate reaction, one might say. These deaths were, most definitely, suicides.

"We had only one pattern: the men belonged to this club. Beyond that there was no logic, no thread. Or so we thought. Then I discovered another pattern, and it was damned important. *These were all human beings.* May I have another drink?"

The bartender mixed the fluids hurriedly, served someone else who had appeared, returned. "Please go on, Mr. Ives."

"Well, I dropped the criminological approach, because it wasn't getting us anywhere, and tried to remember what I'd read of human psychology. One thing came back, clearly. I forget the book. 'Within each human heart there is a trigger. When a person destroys himself, we know then that something, or someone, has pulled that trigger.' You wouldn't recall who said that, would you, Harold?"

The angular man was silent.

"Anyway," Ives went on, "it meant that every human being on Earth is a potential suicide. Every person on Earth is capable of it, just as he's capable of murder; and needs only the right combination of circumstances—mental or physical. So: obviously, Harold, something or someone was activating the trigger mechanism on each of our unfortunate club members. I preferred to think, someone. Which is really quite extraordinary. In fact, the first new method of murder I've encountered in ten years!"

"It's certainly an interesting theory. I'll say that," the bartender said; "but it isn't much more than that, is it, Mr. Ives?"

"Oh, I suppose not. Still, let me go on. I did some investigating, some digging around in the pasts of the recently departed. Starting chronologically, I looked up the facts on Fredric Addison, our first case. He had a hundred and sixty-two thousand in the bank, a loving wife, et cetera. But there was something else. I hit upon it in one of the newspapers. In 1943, Mr. Addison got into some trouble with a Marine. The Marine claimed Addison had made 'untoward advances' on him after inviting him up to the apartment for a non-existent party. Of course, Addison paid off, and the episode was blown away. But it's interesting, wouldn't you say?"

The bartender picked up a towel and began, slowly, to wipe a martini glass. The hum of conversation from the main room filtered in. "I don't believe I follow you, sir."

"You will. Next I examined Ray Vaile's record. A clean one, on the surface. But deeper down, do you know what I found? Vaile had once been in love with a certain motion picture actress; they'd been engaged. Then she dumped him, and he married a local girl. But he wrote impassioned letters to the actress for years afterwards. Parker, a draft-dodger, a coward. Oscar Lawrence was a humanitarian sort. A driver had been killed in one of his racing cars. Some columnists put the blame on Lawrence's shoulders. As for Sexton, he'd washed out of college. Plagued with doubts about his intelligence. Felt bad about it. Now do you see, Harold?"

"No," the bartender said, the light from the martini glass reflecting in white slivers on his face.

"Oh, come. Those were the *triggers* of the men! Their Achilles' heels, if you like. Of course, they'd hidden them, even from themselves; but, now, Harold, if someone were to uncover these sore points, bring them out into the open…it's not too difficult to understand their actions then."

"It's quite a theory, Mr. Ives."

"But I'm not finished. I began to think on all cylinders once I'd reached that hypothesis. Very well, very well. I had a method: but what about the other details? How did this fit in with the coincidence of all the men belonging to the same club? It got easier once I'd licked that problem."

"And did you lick it?"

"Yes. Obviously, Harold, there would have to be one person at the club—the murderer—busily engaged in pulling triggers, as it were. One person all the others would instinctively trust, regard almost as a friend—or perhaps as a father confessor. I began to think about him. What was he like? What would his motive be?"

Ives deliberately peeled the cellophane off a package of cigarettes, tore out a folded square of silver foil, removed a cigarette.

"Smoke?"

"No."

"Well, the motive. He'd have to be interested in psychology, needless to say. More than likely, his apartment would be filled with textbooks on the subject. Secondly, he would have to be either a bored millionaire, indulging in the game for the intellectual sport of it, or—"

"Or what?" the bartender asked.

"Or," Ives continued, lighting the cigarette at last, "he'd have to be a frustrated fellow—one who felt he ought to be as successful as those around him, for, of course, he was a good deal brighter than they. Frustrated and vengeful, I thought, and a little batty, too. There are a lot of people like that, you know, Harold: people who can't abide the good fortune of others. Sometimes they feel that Fate has cheated them, and this is good, because then their fury is impotent; they can only blame Fate. Sometimes, though, they blame society or even, in advanced cases, the very persons they envy so. In that event it's nasty, because eventually they go off their heads and start shooting.

"I decided that my man was among this group: a self-styled god, only without worshippers. He'd knocked around for years, hanging to the periphery of the high social world in one capacity or another, letting his hate build up. Then he'd hit upon his truly unique method of murder—perhaps the crudest I've ever heard of—and that was that. Well, what do you think, Harold?"

"Mr. Ives," the bartender said, "they certainly didn't exaggerate when they said you were a man of imagination. But—" He picked up another glass, began polishing it. "But granting the theory, I'd say you were in a bad way."

"Oh?"

"Well, I mean, even if you found this fellow and he admitted—to you—that it was true, there'd be nothing you could do to him. What if he told you that he had every intention of going on with his 'murders,' as you call them? What then? You'd have to spend the rest of your life watching, helplessly, while he killed whoever he cared to."

Ives sucked smoke into his lungs and grinned; it was not a nice thing to see. "You're assuming, Harold, that I'm an honest cop. But I'm just as much of a fanatic in my own way as he is in his. One failure, just *one,* and it will all have been for nothing. So, if I ever find him (and I don't mind admitting this; you'll never get anyone to believe you if you repeated it) I'll simply frame him. It would be my word against him, you see. And—well, I know a couple of doctors who would be glad to do me a favor, make a suicide look exactly like a murder."

The bartender stopped wiping the glass.

"However," Ives said, "since he *is* a fanatic, such measures really won't be necessary."

There was a silence.

THE NEXT suicide occurred on the following morning. It was phoned in by one of two policemen who had been diverted from their usual route and sent to the home.

Bracker sat down. "You were right," he said, in a voice filled with suspicion and awe. "He shot himself through the mouth."

Phillip Ives nodded, somewhat wearily.

"Now would you mind explaining how the devil you knew about it? He hasn't been dead over six hours. No one heard the shot. You've been with me, here, all night—come on, Ives, before I go out of my mind! How did you know Harold Morrow was going to kill himself?"

"He didn't," Ives said. "I killed him. In a way."

Lieutenant Bracker looked on the verge of hysteria. He got up, walked to the tiny window, came back, and slammed his palm down on the table. "Goddamn it! I—"

"Sit back down. Lieutenant. I'll be glad to tell you what happened."

Ives spoke carefully, with his eyes closed, as if dictating the story for later transcription in a memoir.

When he stopped talking, Bracker's jaw had dropped. The big policeman shook his head.

"You see, your theory of murder was correct, after all."

"Just a second," Bracker said. "The framing part I get—I can even see this maybe scaring Morrow into suicide. But you didn't use that?"

"No. Once I'd realized, standing there in front of the bus, ready to stay rooted and be killed, once I knew that he was our boy, I phoned information for his address. Getting into the apartment was simple enough; it was a common lock. There I found several hundred books on psychology and true crime (which, doubtless, one of your men saw, without really seeing); also, in one of the volumes, information on all Sportsman's Haven members. Three more were slated to die, incidentally. Morrow had spent a lot of time finding their weak spots, and he'd found them, all right. Anyway, it was enough to show the extent of his psychosis. It was enough to show that the man considered himself perfect. To such a person, failure was unthinkable."

"So?"

Ives smiled. "So I simply pointed out to him that there would always be *one* failure, one person whose hidden trigger he would never find."

"Yours?"

"No. His. Even God, I told him, did not have it within His power to commit suicide. When Morrow saw that this was true, he became so depressed that he killed himself."

Bracker opened his mouth and closed it again.

"Then again," Ives said, "perhaps he wanted to prove that I was wrong, and that he *was* perfect. In any event, the case is closed. May I buy you a coffee, Lieutenant?"

GENEVIEVE, MY GENEVIEVE

(1959)

ntoinette Burgoyne, like the ancestral mansion in which she lived, was a large, stately, somewhat absurd and altogether impressive monument to the South of song. Like the mansion, she was unreal. But if it was difficult to believe in her, it was impossible to ignore her. When Mrs. Burgoyne spoke, in her honey-and-thunder voice, the world listened. Of course, the world did not extend beyond the limits of her yard. The ancient elms and poplars there were sentinels against the enemy. Barbarians beware!

I walked through sun and shadow timidly. Although I'd met Mrs. Burgoyne and her dark-haired candlewax daughter before, at the various social function to which my mother, a practicing aristocrat, dragged me, I did not suspect that either of them was aware of my existence. I was a Southerner, it's true, but my great-grandfathers had not fought with any particular distinction in The War (indeed, they'd sensibly fled to Europe for the duration); the roots of our family tree could be traced no further back than 1850; and our house, though ornate, was known to have been a bagnio in the halcyon days. Also, most devastatingly, Mother had had the misfortune to be born in Philadelphia. Which, of course, placed us in the distasteful category of *nouveaux riches*—to the genuine Old Families, a status only slightly above that of the carpetbaggers. Mrs. Burgoyne herself, she whose ancestors helped found New Orleans, was supposed to have commented apropos of this: "One cannot have royal blood through transfusion." And perhaps that was right. In any event, she and her palely-beautiful daughter were courteous enough to Mother and me, particularly of late, but cool and distant at all times, like a queen and a princess among coal miners.

No more than six families had ever been allowed to enter the grounds of Heatherly, the Burgoyne estate. And no more signal honor could be imagined. In her wildest fancies, perhaps, my mother saw herself being asked to tea; but she did not take the dream seriously, nor was she frustrated; for to her the inaccessibility of the blooded few accounted in large part for their charm.

Which made Mrs. Burgoyne's call the more mysterious. Having long before permitted myself to sink into the vilest forms of barbarism, I was astounded to find myself being asked to pay a visit. Yet more astounding was the sense of jubilation which swept over me. Almost shamefully, for I was a *modern* Southerner contemptuous of the notion of aristocracy, I realized that nothing could have pleased me more.

Heatherly was as fine as it appeared on the picture post cards. Approaching it from the soldiering trees, across smooth green lawn, I felt the years drop away; the city melted, all but the Vieux Carré; and I was back in the vanished era of grace and manners, of opulence, of propriety.

A snowtopped Negro opened the door. I gave my name, in cathedral tones, and followed the man through a museum of tapestries and flowers and paintings and vases and furniture as old as America, or older.

Mrs. Burgoyne was in the living room. She looked, if anything, larger than before; more regal, more commanding. The butler ceased to be at a glance from her steel-blue eyes.

"Mr. Nelson," she said, regarding me from the opposite side of the room, "I appreciate your coming."

"My pleasure," I said, and blushed. Something was not right with my voice. In these surroundings, it was the voice of a foreign peasant anxious but not quite able to learn the language.

Mrs. Burgoyne nodded. "Will you have tea?"

I said that I would and she pulled a velvet cord and we waited in frosted silence for the butler to reappear. He set the silver service down and vanished again. Mrs. Burgoyne motioned toward the couch, poured two cups of tea, then said: "Mr. Nelson, discretion is one of the most charming and useful of all human attributes. It is particularly becoming to a lady. However, I am aware of the extent to which discretion has disappeared in our present society. Therefore, to spare you confusion, I shall come directly to the point."

I cleared my throat.

"I asked you here for a particular reason. It would be pleasant to say that it was a desire for your company, but that is not the case. As you may have surmised, I feel that the difference in our social levels is unfortunately such that there can be no real communication between us. Do you find that snobbish?"

"Well," I fumbled, "no, not really, I suppose."

"Don't be silly. Of course it's snobbish. That is because I am a snob." Mrs. Burgoyne took a sip of tea. "We're a stubborn breed," she said. "I imagine that the next generation will find it difficult to believe that such anachronisms as we existed. In spite of this, we propose to hang on to our quaint values, Mr. Nelson, for we are convinced that the world we represent is a better one than yours."

"Maybe so."

"Please don't agree with me. There is nothing so tedious as a discussion of an unarguable truth. Besides, I did not call you here for your reactions to our way of life."

It was said pleasantly, but my neck began to burn and I rose from the couch. "Then why *did* you call me here?"

"Frankly, Mr. Nelson," she said, "to put to you a proposition. Sit down."

I sat down. Mrs. Burgoyne walked to the door and closed it securely. Then she closed the wide windows. The scent of lavender grew heavy in the room; it was the scent of years, of age.

"Mr. Nelson, you have met my daughter, Genevieve. I should like to know what you think of her."

"I think," I said, truthfully, "that she is one of the loveliest creatures I've ever seen."

"Of course," said Mrs. Burgoyne. "That much is evident. But have you any other reactions?"

I thought for a moment. "She's very shy," I said. "Snobbish, like yourself. Modest. Proper." I groped for the word. "Different?"

MRS. BURGOYNE smiled for the first time. "Yes," she said. "I'm happy you were able to make that observation She is indeed different. And the difference lies in the truth of your other judgments. Girls today are, by and large, neither modest nor proper nor snobbish. They are concerned wholly with the struggle for equality and for the dissolution of that happy balance now referred to as the 'double standard.' They aspire to the status of men. To achieve success, of course, they must prove themselves capable of assuming the responsibilities of men. But not merely the responsibilities; the attitudes, also. What they do not appear to realize, Mr. Nelson, is that when they become equal to men, they become also indistinguishable from them. The sole difference between sexes then becomes a matter of physiology. Will you take some more tea?"

I shook my head. I could not imagine why Mrs. Burgoyne was telling me these things, nor could I quite believe that I was hearing correctly.

"Civilization," she continued, "consists of persuading ourselves, through artifice, that we are not animals. We celebrate and control certain functions, veil others in mystery, and pretend that others do not exist. Which is to the good. In such a way did the concept of love begin, and love, as I'm afraid I must remind you, is the finest expression of civilization." The ageing lady sighed. "Today, owing to the efforts of the progressive educators, the mystery of love is being dispelled. To be more precise—and I cannot express to you the pain it gives me to say this—sex is being taken from its shadowed arbor and set into the bright light of day. Young girls are being told that there is nothing sinful in sex, nothing bad, nothing particularly good, and certainly nothing special. They are being told that it is a normal function. They are, in short being told the truth. And I cannot imagine anything more tragic."

Mrs. Burgoyne rose and walked the wide window and stood there staring out at the dazzle of roses.

"Sex *in itself*," she said, without turning, "is a disagreeable activity. It is undignified, unpleasant, and bestial. Above all, it is insignificant. Performed as a matter of course, as it increasingly is these days, it must occupy a level of importance rather lower than sneezing." She paused and I could see the creeping red on her flesh. "In my time," she said, "sex was terribly important. It was mysterious and strange and fearful and lovely. It had been made so through deception, and I, for one, realized this. But I applauded the deceivers. For they had given me the key to a fantastic garden, and the garden was exclusively mine..."

Mrs. Burgoyne paused again; then she turned, and she was no longer blushing.

"Mr. Nelson," she said. "I have raised my daughter as I myself was raised—in sweet ignorance. She knows nothing of the outside world. I have not given her 'the facts of life,' but, instead, something of infinitely more value. Poets call it 'that loftier truth.' Her mind, Mr. Nelson, is pure. She is a maiden. Do you have any idea what I'm talking about?"

I said, "I think so. You mean Genevieve is a virgin."

The honey became thunder. "Ugly word! I mean, young man, that she is a *maiden*. There is a distinction. It is possible to be technically virginal and at the same time unmaidenly. Genevieve is...unstained. Innocent. She is *pure*."

I nodded and said that I thought I understood now what she meant.

"Genevieve is eighteen, Mr. Nelson. In the loveliest flower of her womanhood. I have kept her sheltered in this house, under my supervision, since the day of her birth. Soon, however, very soon, it will end. She will have her debut. Men will notice her. She will want to go out with some of them. Almost certainly, one of these men will seduce her. Having made a careful study of available bachelors in New Orleans, I can say with great assurance that the experience will be awful."

I picked up one of the small cakes because I was beginning to feel very conscious of myself. "You can't be sure of that, Mrs. Burgoyne," I said. "If you brought you up as strictly as you say, she might wait until she got married."

"Of no importance whatever," snapped the woman. "While it is doubtful that in this society *any* girl would wait for marriage, the point holds even if Genevieve should go against custom. There is no good hoping that she can have forever what I and so many young ladies had, of course; I realize that. But one thing I *can* give her. And that is the right introduction."

Mrs. Burgoyne levels her gaze upon me.

"THE FIRST time, Mr. Nelson, is of inestimable importance. If it goes well, one remembers it forever, no matter what happens subsequently, and the memory is sweet and warming, as few memories are. If it goes badly, however if it is anything less than perfect, a damage is done which nothing can ever quite repair. I can think of no moment in a woman's life more critical than her first sexual experience."

She paused. I swallowed. "Mrs. Burgoyne," I said, "you told me that you'd get to the point. I'm afraid you're taking the long way around."

She poured another cup of tea, went to the door, checked it, returned, and continued in a near whisper:

"I have already said, Mr. Nelson, that I do not consider you to be of our station. You are therefore ineligible for Genevieve's hand. However, perhaps through desperation, I made a careful study of your activities during this past year."

"You—Now, look, Mrs. Burgoyne, I don't—"

"Please be still. I learned, my boy, that you—ah—indulged yourself with nine different women in this twelve-month period. Ordinarily, of course, this would have deterred me from further investigation. However, I had an instinct. So I continued. I interviewed or had interviewed each of the females with whom you had your affairs. They were hesitant, at first, to reveal the necessary information; but eventually, through various inducements, they cooperated."

"What do you mean, cooperated?" I said, my voice cracking.

"They discussed in detail your manner of love-making."

"Mrs. Burgoyne!"

"*Sit down*, young man! I hope you don't think this is any more fragrant to me than it is to you!"

"And what do you mean by *that?*"

"I mean that in my two years of investigation, I have assembled a record of bestiality, depravity and crudeness, of ineptitude and plain amateurishness, which, if released, would instantly relegate the works of Sade and Kraft-Ebbing to the children's section of any country library. I was shocked, in the beginning, at the state to which the art of love had fallen. Then, as I progressed, the shock became a sort of numbness, and for this I shall never be able to express my gratitude. The new liberation, Mr. Nelson, has given us a race of fumblers and fiends!" She closed her eyes a moment, then opened them. "You," she said, "are different. The reasons are unclear, for you were given the facts—or lies—of life at the age of seven. At thirteen you drew a template of the act of creation with painstaking accuracy. Fourteen saw you succumbing to the charms of a young nymphomaniac named Alice Eliot, and by the time you had passed your seventeenth birthday, you had accumulated a store of experience which, if unknown to the most dissipated Roman, is probably no more than normal in these times. Sex, by all rights, ought to have become a sort of gymnastic exercise meant to add tone to the ego. Peculiarly, this has not happened. Instead, in an altogether freakish way, you have resisted the temptation common to your fellows. You do not take sex for granted."

"How could you possibly know that?" I demanded.

Mrs. Burgoyne smiled again. "The details of your technique," she said. "And a remark you are fond of making. I quote: 'As hard as it is for men and women to sleep together, I can't figure out how come there are so many babies.'"

I reddened.

She patted my hand in a motherly fashion. "That betrays a basically naive outlook, Mr. Nelson. It indicates that in spite of your exposure to the decay of our present society, you have remained innocent. Yet at the same time you are skilled in the arts of love. According to all reports, you are…just a moment." She walked to an ancient desk, unlocked it, withdrew a heavy ledger. "Nelson. Nelson," she murmured, flipping through the pages. "Ah. You are gentle, imaginative, polite but firm, responsive at all times to the moods of your partner, aware of the necessity for at least the deep pretense of love, aggressive, durable, and, most important, satisfying. Physically you leave little to be desired."

My mouth, I know, must have fallen open. I had to say something, but "May I have another cup of tea?" hardly seems, as I think about it, appropriate.

Mrs. Burgoyne said, "Of course," and poured. "Now here's something interesting!" She adjusted her bifocals and leaned close to the page. "I quote—"

"*Who?*"

"Never mind. 'Jimmy always smells so fresh!'" Her eyes came up. "Now where did you discover such an old-fashioned trait?" A quick smile. "Here again: 'He's the greatest, because like he never forces anything. He seems to know just what you want and what you don't want. Thoughtful, I guess you'd say. Like he really wants *you* to have a good time.'" Mrs. Burgoyne removed the spectacles and closed the ledger. "What it adds up to," she said, "is this. You are the closest thing to a gentleman I've been able to find. Your attitude toward sex seems to be in the right direction, unless you've changed in the past week. Have you?"

"No," I said. "That is—"

"Excellent. Mr. Nelson, let me ask you this. Do you find my daughter sexually stimulating?"

"How's that?"

"Are you," Mrs. Burgoyne went on, relentlessly, "attracted to her? Does she excite you emotionally? Mr. Nelson. given the right set of circumstances, would you care to sleep with Genevieve?"

THE ROOM was terribly silent.

"Well?" the aristocratic lady said.

"Well, Mrs. Burgoyne, that's a hell of a question, I mean it really is. I just don't know—I mean, I don't think I know...no. What are you getting at?"

"You'll be told in a moment. First I must have an answer. I repeat: Would you enjoy sleeping with Genevieve, my daughter?"

I looked around the room, at the paintings of stern grandfathers, at the cream spinet, the roses, the chandelier, at the woman who represented one of the best families in the South. I thought of the lovely thin girl with the soft hair and large eyes.

"Yes," I said. "I would."

"You're absolutely sure?"

"Yes," I said, judging from the heat of my body that I had gone from deep red to purple.

"Fine. I can't tell you how pleased I am to hear you say that!"

"You are?"

"Yes, indeed. Now, Mr. Nelson, I want you to know that I have no intention of taking advantage of you. I drew out the admission only to reassure myself of certain points. Owing to the, ah, temporary nature of the relationship—for, as I've said, marriage would be *quite* out of the question—I am prepared to reimburse you. No, no! I knew you'd object. But it's final."

It wasn't that I didn't know. It was that I couldn't allow myself to believe it. "For what?" I asked.

"For allowing my daughter to know the true wonder of sex at least once in her lifetime."

"For—"

"—sleeping with her, Mr. Nelson. The old lady smiled. "Now we must, unfortunately, become a bit specific. She has never so much as been kissed, you see, and—"

"Mrs. Burgoyne!"

"But that is quite important! Even you, Mr. Nelson, could hardly be expected to cope with an unkissed *eighteen-year-old*. It is natural these days to take that for granted, certainly. But nothing...do you understand me?...*nothing* is to be taken for granted with Genevieve. The kiss must in itself be a sort of consummation, worked up to, slowly. As for the element of pain, it is desirable, but should be reserved. It's entirely a matter of pacing. Genevieve is fragile, so very fragile, Mr. Nelson! Clumsy handling could break her. But then, you aren't clumsy, are you? As to the question of disrobing—"

"Mrs. Burgoyne, for God's sake!"

"What's the matter, Mr. Nelson? Do you feel ill?"

"No! But—"

"I was only going to say that the disrobing must be done with discretion. She has never seen a naked man before, and the sight might very well upset the balance of forces. Men are so hairy, you know. Not that I object! But it is a taste one must acquire gradually, as with pickles. I feel therefore that it would be well for you to undress elsewhere than in her sight, and to do so with utmost dispatch. Unnecessary lingering over this aspect of the operation could very well leave you with a great deal of lost ground, if I make myself clear."

A heavy spring propelled me from my seat. "Mrs. Burgoyne." I said, "is it possible that you're serious?"

"I am almost invariably serious," she said. "As a debutante, I tried to learn a group of amusing stories, but I was not adept at them and so abandoned the idea. I don't believe I have made a joke since the winter of 1922."

"You mean," I said, "that you actually want me to sleep with your daughter?"

"That is correct."

I sat down again. If anyone was ever faced with a similar problem before, I hadn't heard about it. "What," I said, "would Genevieve think?"

"Oh, she's been informed," said Mrs. Burgoyne pleasantly. "She likes you. In fact, although she is far too shy to admit it, and too naive to think of it, she is attracted to you. I ascertained that through our 'chance' meetings in the past few months."

"Oh," I said. Then blurted: "It's—crazy! Impossible!"

Mrs. Burgoyne frowned. "Why?"

"*Why?* Because this kind of thing just isn't... Well, I mean, I mean..." My brain slipped down my throat and my head was left empty. "When did you have in mind?"

"Now," said Mrs. Burgoyne.

"Now?"

"Now," she said. "Genevieve is in her room, waiting. Paul Henry will escort you to the correct door. He will then drive me to Biloxi, where I shall attend a floral exhibit and visit friends. The La Tourettes. A fine family. Colonel La Tourette, you know, was an intimate of General Lee's."

"Really?" I said. "I didn't know that. That's very interesting."

"Yes. I'll return in three days. That will allow you Discovery, Development, and Fruition." Her large white arm reached up, her fingers tugged silently at the velvet cord. "Are there any questions?"

"No," I said. "No questions."

"Good. I want you to follow your instincts, of course, and I wouldn't dream of meddling. But I must warn you again—Genevieve is a maiden. She will be terribly frightened at first. Be patient, Mr. Nelson. The fright will pass. And *please*, be gentle. Make it perfect for her."

"I'll do my best," I said.

"That's a good boy; of course you will." She kissed my cheek. The door opened. The white-skulled Negro appeared.

"Paul Henry," said Mrs. Burgoyne, "please show Mr. Nelson to Genevieve's room."

"Yes, ma'am."

"And hurry back. I don't want to be late."

"Yes, ma'am. Mr. Nelson?"

As though in a dream I turned and walked to the door and walked into the hall with the butler.

"Have a good time!" Mrs. Burgoyne called.

"All right," I said.

"This way, sir."

We proceeded through the museum hall to a circular staircase. Its steps were covered by a soft crimson rug. Two cherubs poised at the tip of the bannister I looked back at them as we ascended the stairs. They seemed to be laughing.

The second door to your right, sir," said the butler.

"Thank you," I said.

Expressionlessly he turned and walked away. I stood at the top of the staircase a long time. Finally I heard the front door open and close and heard the soft purr of an old Rolls-Royce and then I heard nothing, except my heart.

I took out a cigarette. I remember doing that. It tasted better than a cigarette had ever tasted before, but then it went bad and I looked for a place to put it out but there was no place, so I pinched off the hot end and scattered it on the rug and put the rest of the cigarette back into my pocket. My body was coated by a cold wet film. Portions of the film were breaking away and making paths down my sides.

I took a step toward the stairs, and stopped.

I turned.

Fourteen very light steps took me to the door the butler had indicated. It was thick, white, old. I raised my hand and looked at the door.

Just as reason was on the point of winning its argument, I reached down and turned the iron knob and walked into the room.

GENEVIEVE BURGOYNE was in bed. It was one of those flowery beds with frilled top and carved posts, all soft and pink and white and feminine. Genevieve lay under a quilt. It outlined her body, and I thought again how fine that body was. Against the polar linen, her black hair blazed. I forced myself to look at her face. It was a beatitude of innocence. Fear lived in it, but there was no blush. Only the pale smooth flesh of a hothouse plant, carefully nurtured.

In a hushed voice the girl said: "Is...is Mother gone?"

I nodded.

"We're...all alone?"

"Yes," I said, "but you needn't be upset, I—"

"For how long?"

"Three days," I said.

"Three whole days?"

Yes," I said, "but—"

"*Wow*!" said Genevieve Burgoyne flinging off the quilt. She wore a faintly-flowered nightgown which buttoned at the throat. She unbuttoned it. "I mean, how lucky can you get?"

"I beg your pardon?"

She leaped out of bed and walked over to me, slowly. "Well, one thing I've got to give the old girl. She can pick 'em. You're downright cute." She then pulled my head down and kissed me. On the mouth. "Mmmm," she said, or something like Mmmm.

"Miss Burgoyne, I think—"

"Honey lamb, that's what you all don't want to *do*! Now, Mama, she thinks all the time. She's so busy thinking she just plain old doesn't see what's going on. You know what I mean?"

"No," I said, "I don't know what you mean. I'm confused."

She giggled and came toward me.

"Well, honey, now, you just relax. Don't get all tensed up like that." She kissed me again, and I could feel her fingers working at my shirt buttons. "Little Jenny gonna get the great big man all unconfused." She drew back. "Dammit, *relax!*"...

The names in this narrative have been changed, to protect the innocent.

BUCK FEVER

(1960)

ive of the seven days had passed, without luck. They had tried normal tracking and then, at Arents' suggestion, the Indian method of still hunting, but the three men could find nothing worth shooting at. The October rain chilled them, and the mountain trails tired them, and the quiet forest kept its secrets.

Now it was the morning of the sixth day, and Nathan Colby was beginning to feel desperate. He had been standing in this clump of huckleberry bushes for almost two hours, absolutely still, afraid to move. The cold had penetrated his heavy clothes, but for some reason, his hands were perspiring, and his throat was dry. He was a big, well-made man with thick, square fingers and a face that would never look wholly clean because of the heavy film of beard, and he had seldom been nervous, but he was nervous now. He held the .300 Savage tightly and prayed for deer. When Arents and Ransome appeared from behind one of the half-growth cedars, he knew at once that they had failed again.

"How is it going?" George Ransome asked. He was a large man also, but his face was soft and white.

"Fine," Nathan said.

"Fine." Paul Arents shook his head. "Colby, haven't you seen *anything?*"

"No, sir."

"God!" The senior partner of Worldwide Mills leaned his carbine against a tree and lit his pipe with a solid silver lighter. "Well," he said, "I don't understand it. The woods are full of deer. That much I know."

"Maybe they're hiding out," Nathan said, once he'd calculated the risk of a joke.

"Maybe."

The three men stood quietly in the rain for a while. Nathan glanced away from his employers. At the beginning, they had both looked virile and important in their Abercrombie & Fitch hunting costumes; now, after almost a week, there was something vaguely foolish about them. The bright red jackets and caps, the scratchy plaid shirts, the thick trousers, the boots, appeared oddly festive and, somehow, out of place. In any case, he was glad that Maureen was not here to see them with their shining rifles.

She'd asked him not to go, he recalled. "I can't picture it, Nat," she'd said. "I really can't. I mean, actually, the thought of being trapped alone for a week in some godforsaken place with those two pompous fools— it's creepy!"

Of course he'd told her to be quiet. Maureen simply didn't understand. Women never did understand the value of office politics; it wasn't in their nature. It seemed so elementary, yet his own wife could not grasp the deep and serious meaning of such a thing as an invitation from the top men to join them in their private hunting trip. It was more than an honor, he'd told her. "For God's sake, Lewis and Peterson have been angling for it for years, can't you get that through your head?" It was practically a symbol, he'd explained. It said, 'Nathan, we've had our eye on you. We think there's a future for you here at Worldwide. But we've got to see whether or not you fit.'

"What do you mean, 'fit'?"

"You know what I mean. Don't be such a damn child. Arents and Ransome move in a select circle, and before they let anyone in—"

"—they've got to make sure he won't start dropping forks. Right?"

"No."

She didn't have any idea of the importance of the thing.

It had gone very well, too, at first. The ride to the mountain was fine. Both Arents and Ransome had unlimbered, and they'd chattered away at him about the pleasures of hunting. It wasn't employee and employers; it was three men on their way to do what men do. The fact that he had never shot a deer (and he'd decided not to fake this) did not, strangely enough, work against him. He'd heard of the initiation rites that followed a tyro's first kill, and he supposed it was this secret that entertained them. Also, it was true that Ransome seemed genuinely anxious to share the experience with him. On the other hand, Arents was not quite so warm. He seemed to have other reasons for going to the forest.

Anyway, damn it, it had been fine, those first few days. They'd risen early in the morning, when the deer come down from the high places, and they'd tracked with great stealth, and Nathan had become filled with the strong fire of envy. These people knew how to live. They did things right, and they accounted to themselves.

But, with the absence of game, a subtle change had come over the camp. The joking ceased, for one thing. Arents, looking imperious again, had begun to clean his rifle incessantly, and he would stare over at Nathan. His glance would say, or suggest: We're having no luck because of this interloper. Somehow, his eyes said, Colby must be scaring the animals away.

For these, and other reasons, Nathan felt panic. Everything now seemed to hinge on their finding a deer. If they returned empty-handed, he knew that a coolness would develop, because Arents and Ransome would be embarrassed. And when a big man becomes embarrassed, he becomes uncomfortable, he starts to hate.

It was as simple as that. If they got a deer, he would be on his way to the top in the business; if they did not, he would soon be finished.

"You have to expect this kind of thing though, actually," Ransome was saying. "I mean, it's the element of chance, you might say, that's the whole point of the sport. Isn't that right, Paul?"

The tall man with the prematurely gray hair and the hard skin that stretched taut across his bones nodded. "Yes, I suppose that's right," he said.

"I mean, see, if you knew in advance, Nathan, if you *knew*—you understand?—that you were going to come home with a trophy, well, then it wouldn't be much of a game, would it?"

Nathan was about to answer, when Arents said, "Be still, can't you, George?"

The two older men were not very similar in temperament. George Ransome had the plodding good sense that holds businesses together; Paul Arents had the spark of genius, the almost inhuman drive that makes a corner grocery store into a chain of supermarkets overnight.

"Let's say to hell with the still hunting," Ransome said, suddenly.

Nathan nodded in relief. It had sounded very complicated, and he never had a clear idea of what he was supposed to do. But the others kept reassuring him. "Nothing to it. You just stand downwind, you're the driver, you see? The deer comes at you. When it sees you, it veers off one of the escape routes. There are only two of them and Paul and I will have them covered. We can't miss."

But no animal had appeared to put the theory to a test. And, being separated, Nathan found that he had entirely too much time to think. He had time to think of the past three years, and what seemed to be happening between himself and Maureen. Why the hell couldn't she grasp this one simple, basic principle? Playing forces against each other, getting in with the bosses, doing little extra things—these were the deciding factors in any business. It was all personality. Sheer talent alone couldn't get you anywhere these days.

Still, her attitude did annoy him; and he resolved, there in the forest, to speak to her about it. This "stupid little hunting trip," as she'd put it, was potentially worth an extra three thousand a year, and—who could say?—perhaps even a junior partnership. And he was sure she wouldn't complain too bitterly about having a little money in the bank for a change.

Besides, when you got right down to it, what was so damned bad about taking a vacation with the people you work for? What was there in that to make a woman cry?

It was ridiculous...

"We have about an hour left," Arents said, in a hopeless voice.

"Maybe something will turn up, you never can tell," Ransome said. "Don't be discouraged, Paul."

"Why not?"

"Because. Look at it this way: we've gotten Nathan here all fired up, all excited. It's his first time, so we've got to find something. You remember your first time?"

"Certainly."

"Remember the kick you got out of it?"

Arents nodded; a half-smile formed on his lips. "It was—an experience," he said.

Ransome chuckled loudly. "His first time out, Nathan, and do you know what? I couldn't believe it. A perfect neck shot. The deer dropped in its tracks, I swear that's true. A fine five-pointer." He winked. "Lucky."

"Not luck," Arents said. "Skill. I aimed for the neck, I hit the neck."

"My first time, Nathan," Ransome said, "I gut-shot a scruffy little doe."

He went on to explain what a gut-shot was. The sky was thick with fat grey clouds, like old balloons, and the rain continued to fall in a silver mist, as he droned.

Arents was the first to see it.

He put out his hand and silenced Ransome.

Nathan followed their gaze. His heart stopped. Up ahead, perhaps fifty yards, the autumn leaves and brown grass had sprung together to form an animal. It was walking slowly, with tentative steps.

"Two-pointer," Arents whispered, reaching for his rifle.

Ransome nodded. The faces of the two men were suddenly very tense. Their eyes were no longer lidded and sleepy. "A beauty."

Paul Arents carefully raised his carbine. His hands were steady.

"No," Ransome whispered. "This ought to be Nathan's."

"What?"

"His .300 is better at this range, Paul. Give it to him. There'll be more."

Arents lowered the gun and looked at Nathan. "All right," he said, softly. "But hurry. He'll have our scent in a minute."

The Savage was loaded and ready. Nathan put the rifle to his should and got the deer in his sights.

"Easy, now," Ransome soothed. "Don't get nervous. Don't get all tight."

He tried to loosen the muscles in his back.

The buck stopped walking and froze. Its head snapped up.

"The neck," Arents said, urgently. *"Now."*

Nathan tried to remember those mornings on the range in '46 when he was able to get inside the small black circle seven times out of ten.

"Now, you idiot. *Shoot!*"

The sight lifted until the gleaming metal barrel pointed at the deer's neck. Nathan's finger curled about the trigger, squeezed.

There was a sharp, echoing report.

The deer turned and ran and vanished.

He lowered the rifle and knew that he had missed. He had missed everything.

Arents was glaring furiously. Ransome stepped between them and said, "Not so good. But let's take a look anyway."

They plunged ahead, across the bands of hemlock, Arents moving with surprising speed—in the forest, as in the office, he seemed to be utterly in command—Ransome jogging along at a somewhat slower pace. Nathan followed. He felt numb.

"Miss," Arents pronounced, straightening.

Ransome did not rise. He was searching the ground, patting it with his hand. "There isn't any blood," he murmured, "but that doesn't mean an awful lot. Sometimes they don't bleed for ten seconds or more."

"I had him in my sights," Nathan said. It sounded weak, and he was ashamed for having said it.

Arents nodded. His face was strained, filled with disappointment. "Yes."

Then Ransome got to his feet. "I'm afraid we've got some work ahead of us," he said slowly. "The deer is wounded."

"How do you know?"

"Look here." In the large man's hands was a scattering of short brown hairs. "The hair is brittle on the back legs. A bullet will knock some of it off," he said.

Arents took a firmer grip on his rifle. "Well," he said, "if the leg is broken, he can't be too far." He studied the trees and the brush, then struck off down the nearest clear path.

After several minutes of silent walking, the three men stopped. Arents turned, and there was an unpleasant smile on his face.

"All right," he said.

Nathan saw the deer crouched, quiet, unmoving, in a cover of huckleberry bushes. A bright wash of blood stained the animal's left rear leg. "Is he dead?" he asked.

Ransome shook his head. "No," he said. "It's a haunch wound, and the leg's busted, okay, but he's alive. If you'd hit one of the front ones, now, it wouldn't even have slowed him up. I once brought down a good four-pointer running at the head of a big herd, and his front leg had been shattered twice. It didn't bother him."

Nathan came closer to the deer. It was surprisingly small, rather like the fauns he had watched years ago at the zoo; no larger, it seemed, than an average collie. The tan coat glistened in the rain, clean and soft as a new glove. The tiny black feet were also clean, and reminded him of a child's ballet slippers.

Then he saw the blood, again, and looked up at Arents. The tall man's attitude seemed to have changed once more. He appeared to be pleased. Perhaps it was that they'd come to the mountain for deer and now they would return with deer and that was all that actually mattered. "Well, he's a nice little buck."

Ransome smiled. "Very nice," he said. Then he turned to Nathan. "You'd better finish him off now. They regain consciousness and I understand the pain is pretty bad."

The deer was still. Nathan Colby nodded his head and brought up the rifle. All I have to do, he thought, is pull the trigger, and I'll be in. I'll be given the initiation rites and Arents will accept me and that will be it.

Just squeeze the trigger, he thought.

"Come on," Arents said. "Let's get it over with…"

The deer remained frozen in the brush. Nathan looked at it, and suddenly it occurred to him that he had never seen anything quite so delicate as this creature. Some animals are beautiful, he thought: I never realized that. This was a buck, but there was a pliant, feminine quality to it. It was like a young girl, sleeping, without fear, and without care.

Nathan rubbed a hand across his bearded cheek. He could not recall ever having been frightened of anything before in his life, although of course he must have been; it was certain that he had never allowed himself to be deflected from a chosen course. In that sense, he was a ruthless man.

But he had never had to kill an animal.

"Come on," Arents said again.

His finger tightened on the trigger. Over the metal sight, he saw only the wounded deer. Even in its agony, it had fallen into a graceful pose. In no way did it seem to be waiting for death to release it; instead, it seemed, trustful and innocent, sure that the big, square man in the hunting jacket would be kind.

Looking at the buck, Nathan's thoughts turned to Maureen. For no reason. Except that she had trusted him, also. She still trusted him.

For a second the deer's eyes came open, and Nathan met their soft, dark gaze; then they closed.

"What the devil's the matter with you, Colby?" Paul Arents put his carbine to his shoulder.

"Wait." Nathan turned and faced his employer, and the pressures built in his mind. The two stared at one another for a long moment. There was eagerness in Arents' eyes, anticipation, and other things.

"Wait for what?" he said.

"I don't want you to shoot, Mr. Arents."

"You don't want me to shoot? What are you talking about?" The tall man squinted down the barrel of the carbine.

"Mr. Arents," Nathan heard himself saying, "if you pull that trigger, I'll tear you apart, so help me God."

The tall man paused.

Ransome looked worried; he drew a long breath. "I'd—put the gun down, Paul," he said, "if I were you."

Arents seemed to examine the situation; then he lowered the rifle. "Very well," he said. Then, in a quiet, firm voice: "You know what this means, I suppose?"

"Yes," Nathan said. He spoke clearly. "I know exactly what it means. And I don't care, for the moment."

"Well," Arents said, "that's fine. That's excellent. I must say that I think this trip has been extremely successful, on the whole; I was worried for a while. George, here, thought you had something, you see. I couldn't agree. I told him that you didn't seem to be a man who could accept responsibilities. We argued, George and I. Now I'm happy to have my doubts justified."

Nathan said nothing. He could only watch it all slip away and know that he would not and could not do anything to stop it.

"Now," Arents went on, "may I ask what you intend to do?"

"I'm not sure."

"You're not sure! I suppose that now you think of yourself as the only one here with any sense of compassion. The deer is small and helpless and you can't bring yourself to allow it to be slaughtered. Am I right? Unfortunately, there is one small flaw. You see, it was neither George nor I who wounded that animal. It was you, Colby. You aimed to kill and missed and broke the animal's leg. Now you don't have the guts to put it out of its suffering."

"All of this jabbering," Ransome said, tapping his forehead with a handkerchief. "My God."

Arents' voice was harsh. "I feel sorry for you," he said. "You're big and tough and ambitious, but you'll never make it, Colby. Why? Because you're yellow."

The words stung. Nathan felt the muscles bunching in his arms, and he knew that in a moment he would drive his fist into that pompous, tight-drawn face.

"Well?" Arents said.

Ransome coughed. "You can't let the animal suffer," he said. "That wouldn't be sportsmanlike."

"What about a veterinary?" Nathan asked precisely, not because he felt that he could talk to Ransome and be understood, but because he felt, now, that Ransome did have a little of the true hunter in him, perhaps, some love for the cool woods and the chase. There was no question why Arents came to the mountain.

"No good," the large man said. "A haunch wound like this is nasty. He'd die before you got him to the nearest town."

"Are you absolutely sure of that?"

"Yes, I'm sure. Nathan—I believe I know how you feel. Really. You'd like to see the deer leap up and be well. But that can't happen now, don't you understand?"

Arents pulled his collar up around his neck. "I'm getting a stomach full of this," he said. "Since you feel the way you do, Colby, at least have the decency to let one of us do it."

Nathan looked at the deer, which was quiet; then at the two men. "Go back to camp," he said. "I'll be along."

"But—" Ransome began.

"I'll be along."

"It's a disgrace," Arents said, turning. "A damn' disgrace."

The two men walked back through the trees, and soon they were out of sight and Nathan Colby was alone with the deer.

He stood there, watching it, and thinking, for a long time. The smell of the rain was good to him and he saw that the sky was deep gray, which meant that it would go on raining. The forest had not changed. It would not change.

He laid his gun aside and knelt by the wounded animal. His thick, square hands reached out and stroked the soft coat, gently.

Then, with great care, he picked the rifle up again, aimed it, and sent a bullet into the deer's neck. The creature twitched violently, but soon the twitching stopped and it lay still.

Nathan Colby did not look back. He grasped the rifle by its barrel and smashed it against the trunk of a tree and then hurled it with all his strength into the dark brush.

Later on, he returned to camp.

DEAD YOU KNOW

(1960)

o sooner had he finished shrinking his grandmother's head than the telephone played Mozart's *Eine Kleine Nachtmusik* and he knew, instantly, that he would not be able to murder his wife that evening.

"Yes, yes," he barked into the violet mouthpiece, "yes?"

"Digg?"

Diggory Sprool's face flushed a warm color and his tone softened considerably. "Yes," he said.

"This," said the voice, "is N. N."

"How are you, N. N.?"

"Hang it all, I hate to disturb you like this. But, well—"

"I'll be right over."

"Good scout. Say, you're sure Emma won't mind? Might mean all night, y'know."

"She won't mind."

"Great little wife! Only wish my Myrt had one half of Emma's consideration and understanding. 'Deed I do. Well then, we'll see you in a little while?"

"Right away, sir."

"And, Digg—"

"Yes, sir?"

"N. N. Fish don't fail to appreciate sort of company spirit. You're a White Man!"

"Oh, sir."

Mr Sprool replaced the telephone in its cradle and made a rude noise with his mouth. Then he opened the five padlocks to the door, stepped outside and, sighing, went upstairs.

"Dear heart!" he said to his wife. "Sweet! I have bad news."

Mr. Sprool's wife, Emma Sprool, a large woman, shifted her weight in the campaign chair. "I hate you," she said expressionlessly.

"Dove, please—no tears. True, I must leave you; but not for long. A little office work to clear up. Back as soon as I can, eh, hon?" He got into his galoshes and macintosh.

"I hate you." she said.

"So long!"

Mr. Sprool walked in the rain, reflecting bitterly upon the evening. And, as the walk was a longish one. and there was no immediate *divertissement*, he began also to reflect upon his life in general.

It had begun with the head.

UP UNTIL his thirteenth birthday, little Diggory had expressed his love for the Arts with simple clay figurines, which he kept hidden from his parents though there was small need to as they were seldom home anyway, being itinerant evangelists.

But then, one day, purely on a whim, he had decided to reproduce as perfectly as possible the head of his best friend, one Willard Ratchet.

How he'd run about gathering materials! Eyeballs from an optometrist's office; teeth from a dental laboratory; hair from puzzled acquaintances—it had taken nearly a month! But when the job was done, even Diggory was impressed.

He'd sent it via post to Willard's mother, whose reaction alone was payment aplenty for his labors.

More heads had followed, each an improvement over the other, until at last his room would contain no more heads at all.

He had therefore moved.

However: "Sprool," he'd cautioned himself one night, "let's be sensible about this." So, regretfully, the majority of the pieces were incinerated, leaving only certain choice items such as his Aunt Nell, Uncle Cecil, and others similarly dear.

Aye, those were the days! Mr. Sprool reflected.

Or were they? *Were* they the days? True enough, the stipend provided by his parents sufficed to accommodate his wants—a bit of bread and cheese from time to time, a few tons of clay monthly—and permitted him the leisure to pursue the Muse. But, oh! The loneliness! The bitter biting loneliness which was his lot then. For of course, being shy, he had never permitted the world to encroach upon his island.

Had it been Fate? Providence? Or was it merely Vagrant Chance that set in his path, at the penultimate moment of his depression, that Spring Flower known then as Emma Hurlbut, now Mrs. Sprool and no longer a Spring Flower?

How had it happened?

What Demonic Force had overseen and meted out to One so Innocent a Portion so Unkind? This double tragedy: the marriage out of loneliness; and then, the cessation of his sinecure with the sudden demise, on the ill-starred weather balloon *U. S. Stars & Stripes*, of his mother and father, who had latterly forsworn religion in favor of meteorology.

"Why?" demanded Mr. Sprool aloud, receiving no answer but the wind.

Emma. A child of sloth—he'd seen that on the first night of their honeymoon when, after the romantic glass of wine by candlelight, she had fallen into a torpor from which it was impossible to rouse her. So soon had disillusion set in!

And it was downhill from then on.

He recalled their myriad battles and how Love lay fallen the victim during each. Until, presently, the Love turned into Hate and the Hate grew like wild grass in a forgotten garden.

And, penniless now, how it had been necessary for him to take a position with a freight forwarding concern— there to rise, in time, to the post of Chief Dispatcher.

And of the Muse? Do it on Sundays! After work! Make it a hobby!

It was at this point that Mr. Sprool had taken to shrinking less heads. It was at this point that he had begun to murder his wife.

A VINEGARY smile spoilt the otherwise symmetrical features of Mr. Sprool's face. He stopped altogether now, at the threshold of the freight office.

The first Emma had been crude. Thrown together hastily from scraps. But—she was sufficient. He'd spent all night on her, and when she was finished, did she not suggest to an almost eerie degree the original model?

Mr. Sprool, though drugged with sleep, had pondered briefly that night. The obvious occurred to him: shoot her, stab her, choke her. But these he quickly rejected, or decided to save for evenings when inspiration might flag.

"Well, Em, you old hog, you old cow, you old wart upon the name of femininity, you old—" His scorn, though delivered *sotto voice*—Mrs. Sprool was quite a large woman and not altogether deaf—had yet a freshness to it, and vocally speaking at any rate, that particular evening was *never* recaptured. Often afterwards, in deeper moods, he would merely glower darkly before getting down to business.

But, that first evening, the first time he'd ever murdered Emma! It had been absolutely delightful. He'd chosen an icepick for the occasion, and it was well upon morning before he had left the little secret den and tip-toed into the bedroom.

And, as his ingenuity improved, so did the effigy. Every night it became more perfect, more true to life, until at last—what with the insertion of mock veins and vessels and organs and whatnot—it was truly difficult to tell the difference. Once, as he was prepared to cleave the skull with a meat-axe, he could have *sworn* the figure recoiled. But, needless to say, it had been only his imagination.

Oh yes, life had taken on a rosier hue since he started killing Emma. Even limiting himself to once a week—it frequently took that long to rebuild the mannequin after each atrocity—it proved a constant challenge to his genius.

Consider, he considered, with what clandestine stealth he conducted himself so that the real Emma remained convinced he spent every night engaged in the pursuit of philately.

Emma had never guessed, too, because the basement was such an arduous journey from the living room. And now since he lacked the proper appetite for a genuine murder, he had only to wait until she passed on from natural causes. Which would be soon, very soon, at the rate of her present growth.

And when that day should arrive, thanks to the insurance company, no longer then the N. N. Fishes, the dreary freight offices, the need to slave all day and frequently all night on Dead Overs from Dubuque...

Considerably heartened by this reverie, Mr. Sprool advanced into the building and greeted his employer and adjusted the green eyeshade about his forehead.

"GOOD WORK, Digg. Go home, catch a little snooze before that wife of yours begins to wonder."

Home.

Late, true; but he wasn't tired. Not tired: the night was nubbinical, there was still time to kill old Em!

He hissed some blithe Mendelssohn between his teeth softly, making way down the stairs and across the floor to his den.

He went inside and mentally reminded himself to be more careful with the locks.

And—there she was!

"Dumpling!" said Mr. Sprool, removing his coat and galoshes and securing the door. "Sunshine!

Last night's finishing touches had been masterworks, he decided. How tired he must have been to allow the genius so to flow, gush, spurt. It was all there. Emma, to a T!

"Dollbaby!" said Mr. Sprool, removing his vest and rolling up his sleeves.

She sat in a campaign chair that reproduced exactly the one upstairs. Her dress: the same: her hair, eyes, ears, nose, throat: identical. With such secret satisfaction did Mr. Sprool ruminate, as he busied himself, upon the facts of this Emma's construction. How even such minutiae as the fingernails, scaly and rinded, were better than carbon copies, and how her hand was attached to the bursting bosom as if to check an incipient "mutter."

Taking from the closet a large mason jar. Mr. Sprool advanced upon the figure of his wife. "Love," said he, "we have a surprise tonight, 'deed we do!"

The truth to the following was, he was being less subtle than practical—originally he had thought to dismember Emma. But that would have involved the wearisome task of reassembling her—and besides, it would have been the third time around for dismembering.

He unscrewed the lid of the mason jar and checked its contents. Which at first looked like nothing so much as tiny noodles or white seedlings from flowers, but upon closer inspection proved otherwise.

Neither tiny noodles nor the white seedlings of flowers move.

"Hee, hee," tittered Mr. Sprool, upending the jar over Emma's head. The creatures came loose in a welter of movement and fell like wedding rice.

Mr. Sprool then posted himself at the other end of the room and drew back the good 30-weight Indian bow. "Don't worry, sweetheart," he whispered, "I'll get them." And with this, there came a *twaang* and one of the arrows whisked across the space and *phlunked* into the figure.

Then other arrows followed, and soon Mr. Sprool was becoming quite proficient as an archer. "There," he would call, quietly, "I got one! There, I got another!"

And so it went, until the quiver was empty and the figure of Emma Sprool now resembled an outsize pincushion rather more than a human being.

Yawning, chuckling, Mr. Sprool decided he would not straighten things tonight. Doubtless it was getting late.

So he trudged upstairs, yawning two to the dozen, and got into bed and was very nearly asleep before he discovered his wife was not in bed with him.

In fact, was nowhere in the room.

✦ ✦ ✦

HE HAD searched most of the other rooms when a melancholy thought came to him.

He started downstairs. En route, he suddenly felt that he must have been *exceptionally* tired when he'd constructed this evening's Emma, because he couldn't remember placing her hand over her heart that way, not at all, when he came to think about it.

He went into the den, this time with a fresh approach.

"Emma?" he said. "Emma?" There was no response.

With a shrug he started back when something caught his eye.

Down behind the campaign chair wherein sat the arrow ridden figure of wax and other materials, huddled grotesquely in the corner as though flung there in a pique—was Emma.

Mr. Sprool began to perspire.

He bent down and made a cursory examination. He listened for the heartbeat: there was none. For a pulse: no trace.

"Darling," Mr. Sprool wailed, in an unaccountable seizure of concern.

Then he noted something fairly unusual. The hand he'd held, the one he'd checked for pulsebeat, was still in his own, though he had risen to a standing posture!

And the hand was, though cunningly, shrewdly contrived, still a thing undeniably of clay and wax and plastic.

Mr. Sprool looked at the figure in the chair, studied the expression on the face, and then rubbed off a little red wetness similar to the diluted ketchup he used. He looked back at the crumpled thing on the floor. A singular picture jumped to his mind.

The locks—they'd been open! And Emma had come down at last to look at his stamps. And then—

Mr. Sprool left the house and, without ado or adieu, commenced traveling and did not stop traveling until he had reached Rio de Oro, where he took up with a charming native girl of Spanish extraction. She posed for many a fine sculpture, and from all outward appearances would have continued doing so indefinitely, had not her husband returned one night bearing a long machete and ill-feeling for Diggory Sprool, whose career ceased abruptly then and there.

MOURNING SONG

(1963)

He had a raven on his shoulder and two empty holes where his eyes used to be, if he ever had eyes, and he carried a guitar. I saw him first when the snow was walking over the hills, turning them to white velvet. I felt good, I felt young, and, in the dead of winter, the spring wind was in my blood. It was a long time ago.

I remember I was out back helping my daddy chop up firewood. He had the ax up in the air, about to bring it down on the piece of soft bark I was holding on the block, when he stopped, with the ax in the air, and looked off in the direction of Hunter's Hill. I let go of the bark and looked off that way, too. And that's when I saw Solomon for the first time. But it wasn't the way he looked that scared me, he was too far away to see anything except that it was somebody walking in the snow. It was the way my daddy looked. My daddy was a good big man, as big as any I ever met or saw, and I hadn't ever seen him look afraid, but he looked afraid now. He put the ax down and stood there, not moving or saying anything, only standing there breathing out little puffs of cold and looking afraid.

Then, after a while, the man walking in the snow walked up to the road by our house, and I saw him close. Maybe I wouldn't have been scared if it hadn't been for the way my daddy was acting, but probably I would have been. I was little then and I hadn't ever in my whole life seen anybody without eyes in his head.

My daddy waited until he saw that the blind man wasn't coming to our house, then he grabbed me off the ground and hugged me so hard it hurt my chest. I asked him what the matter was, but he didn't answer. He started off down the road after the blind man. I went along with him, waiting for him to tell me to get on home, but he didn't. We walked for over two miles, and every time we came to somebody's house, the people who lived there would stand out in the yard or inside at the window, watching, the way my daddy did, and when we passed, they'd come out and join the parade.

Pretty soon there was us and Jake Overton and his wife and Peter Briley and old man Jaspers and the whole Randall family, and more I can't remember, trailing down along the road together, following the blind man.

I thought sure, somebody said.

So did I, my daddy said.

Who you suppose it's going to be? Mr Briley said.

My daddy shook his head. Nobody knows, he said. Except him.

We walked another mile and a half, cutting across the Pritchetts' field where the snow was up to my knees, and nobody said anything more. I knew the only places there was in this direction, but it didn't mean anything to me because nobody had ever told me anything about Solomon. I know I wondered as we walked how you could see where you were going if you didn't have eyes, and I couldn't see how you could, but that old man knew just exactly where he was going. You knew that by looking at him and watching how he went around stumps and logs on the ground.

Once I thought he was going to walk into the plow the Pritchetts left out to rust when they got their new one, but he didn't. He walked right around it, and I kept wondering how a thing like that could be. I closed my eyes and tried it but I couldn't keep them closed more than a couple of seconds. When I opened them, I saw that my daddy and all the rest of the people had stopped walking. All except the old blind man.

We were out by the Schreiber place. It looked warm and nice inside with all the lamps burning and gray smoke climbing straight up out of the chimney. Probably the Schreibers were having their breakfast.

Which one, I wonder, my daddy said to Mr Randall.

The old one, Mr Randall said. He's going on eighty.

My daddy nodded his head and watched as the old blind man walked through the snow to the big pine tree that sat in the Schreibers' yard and lifted the guitar strap over his head.

Going on eighty, Mr Randall said again.

Yes.

It's the old man, all right.

Everybody quieted down then. Everybody stood still in the snow, waiting, what for I didn't know. I wanted to pee. More than anything in the world I wanted to pee, right there in the snow, and watch it melt and steam in the air. But I couldn't any more than I could at church. In a way, this was like church.

Up ahead the old blind man leaned his face next to the guitar and touched the strings. I don't know how he thought he was going to play anything in this cold. It was cold enough to make your ears hurt. But he kept touching the strings, and the sound they made was just like the sound any guitar makes when you're trying to get it tuned, except maybe louder. I tried to look at his face, but I couldn't because of those holes where his eyes should have been. They made me sick. I wondered if they went all the way up into his head. And if they didn't where did they stop?

He began to play the Mourning Song then. I didn't know that was the name of it, or what it meant, or anything, but I knew I didn't like it. It made me think of sad things, like when I went hunting by myself one time and this doe I shot fell down and got up again and started running around in circles and finally died right in front of me, looking at me. Or when I caught a bunch of catfish at the slew without bait. I carried them home and everything was fine until I saw that two of them were still alive. So I did what my daddy said was a crazy thing. I put those catfish in a pail of water and carried them back to the slew and dumped them in. I thought I'd see them swim away happy, but they didn't. They sank just like rocks.

That song made me think of things like that, and that was why I didn't like it then, even before I knew anything about it.

The old blind man started singing. You wouldn't expect anything but a croak to come out of that toothless old mouth, but if you could take away what he was singing, and the way he looked, you would have to admit he could really sing. He had a high, sweet voice, almost like a woman's, and you could understand every word.

Long valley, dark valley...hear the wind cry!...in darkness we're born and in darkness we die...all alone, alone, to the end of our days...to the end of our days, all alone...

Mr Schreiber came outside in his shirt sleeves. He looked even more afraid than my daddy had looked. His face was white and you could see, even from where I stood, that he was shaking. His wife came out after a minute and started crying, then his father, old man Schreiber, and his boy Carl who was my age.

The old blind man went on singing for a long time, then he stopped and put the guitar back over his head and walked away. The Schreibers went back into their house. My daddy and I went back to our own house, not following the blind man this time but taking the long way.

We didn't talk about it till late that night. Then my daddy came into my room and sat down on my bed. He told me that the blind man's name was Solomon, at least that was what people called him because he was so old. Nobody knew how he lost his eyes or how he got around without them, but there were lots of things that Solomon could do that nobody understood.

Like what? I asked.

He scratched his cheek and waited a while before answering. He can smell death, he said, finally. He can smell it coming a hundred miles off. I don't know how. But he can.

I said I didn't believe it. My daddy just shrugged his shoulders and told me I was young. When I got older I'd see how Solomon was never wrong. Whenever Solomon walked up to you, he said, and unslung that guitar and started to sing Mourning Song, you might as well tell them to dig deep.

That was why he had looked so scared that morning. He thought Solomon was coming to our house.

But didn't nothing happen to the Schreibers, I said.

You wait, my daddy said. He'll keep on going there and then one day he'll quit.

I did wait, almost a week, but nothing happened, and I began to wonder if my daddy wasn't getting a little feeble, talking about people smelling death and all. Then on the eighth day, Mr Randall came over.

The old man? my daddy asked.

Mr Randall shook his head. Alex, he said, meaning Mr Schreiber. Took sick last night.

My daddy turned to me and said, You believe it now?

And I said, No, I don't. I said I believed that an old blind man walked up to the Schreibers' house and sang a song and I believed that Mr Alex Schreiber died a little over a week later but I didn't believe any man could know it was going to happen. Only God could know such a thing, I said.

Maybe Solomon is God, said my daddy.

That dirty old man without any eyes in his head?

Maybe. You know what God looks like?

No, but I know He ain't blind, I know He don't walk around with a bird on His shoulder, I know He don't sing songs.

How do you know that?

I just do.

Well and good, but take heed—if you see him coming, if you just happen to see him coming down from Hunter's Hill some morning, and he passes near you, don't you let him hear you talking like that.

What'll he do?

I don't know. If he can do what he can do, what can't he do?

He can't scare me, that's what—and he can't make me believe in him! You're crazy! I said to my daddy, and he hit me, but I went on saying it at the top of my voice until I fell asleep.

I saw Solomon again about six months later, or maybe a year, I don't remember.

Looking the same, walking the same, and half the valley after him. I didn't go along.

My daddy did, but I didn't. They all went to the Briley house that time. And Mrs Briley died four days afterward. But I said I didn't believe it.

When Mr Randall himself came running over one night saying he'd had a call from Solomon and him and my daddy got drunk on wine, and Mr Randall died the next day, even then I didn't believe it.

How much proof you got to have, boy? my daddy said.

I couldn't make it clear then what it was that was tormenting me. I couldn't ask the right questions, because they weren't really questions, then, just feelings. Like, this ain't the world here, this place. People die all over the world, millions of people, every day, every minute. You mean you think that old bastard is carting off all over the world? You think he goes to China in that outfit and plays the guitar? And what about the bird? Birds don't live long. What's he got, a dozen of 'em? And, I wanted to know, *why* does he do what he does? What the hell's the point of telling somebody they're going to die if they can't *do* something about it?

I couldn't believe in Solomon because I couldn't understand him. I did say that, and my daddy said, If you could understand him, he wouldn't be Solomon.

What's that mean?

Means he's mysterious.

So's fire, I said. But I wouldn't believe in it if it couldn't put out heat or burn anything.

You're young.

I was, too. Eleven.

By the time I was grown, I had the questions, and I had the answers. But I couldn't tell my daddy. On my eighteenth birthday, we were whooping it up, drinking liquor and singing, when somebody looked out the window. Everything stopped then. My daddy didn't even bother to go look.

Could be for anybody here, somebody said.

No. I feel it. It's for me.

You don't know.

I know. Lonnie's a man now, it's time for me to move on.

I went to the window. Some of the people we hadn't invited were behind Solomon, gazing at our house. He had the guitar unslung, and he was strumming it.

The people finished up their drinking quietly and looked at my daddy and went back out. But they didn't go home, not until Solomon did.

I was drunk, and this made me drunker. I remember I laughed, but my daddy, he didn't, and in a little while he went on up to bed. I never saw him look so tired, so worn out, never, and I saw him work in the field eighteen hours a day for months.

Nothing happened the first week. Nor the second. But he didn't get out of bed that whole time, and he didn't talk. He just waited.

The third week, it came. He started coughing. Next day he called for my mother, dead those eighteen years. Doc Garson came and looked him over. Pneumonia, he said.

That morning my daddy was still and cold.

I hated Solomon then, for the first time, and I hated the people in the valley. But I couldn't do anything about it. We didn't have any money, and nobody would ever want to buy the place. So I settled in, alone, and worked and tried to forget about the old blind man. He came to me at night, in my sleep, and I'd wake up, mad, sometimes, but I knew a dream couldn't hurt you, unless you let it. And I didn't plan to let it.

Etilla said I was right, and I think that's when I first saw her. I'd seen her every Sunday at church, with her ma, when my daddy and I went there together, but she was only a little thing then. I didn't even know who she was when I started buying grain from her at the store, and when she told me her name, I just couldn't believe it. I don't think there's been many prettier girls in the world. Her hair wasn't golden, it was kind of brown, her figure wasn't skinny like the pictures, but full and lush, and she had freckles, but I knew, in a hurry, that she was the woman I wanted. I hadn't ever felt the way she made me feel. Excited and nervous and hot.

It's love, Bundy Matthews said. He was my best friend. You're in love.

How do you know?

I just do.

But what if she ain't in love with me?

You're a fool.

How can I find out?

You can't, not if you don't do anything except stand there and buy grain off of her.

It was the hardest thing I've ever done, asking her to walk with me, but I did it, and she said yes, and that's when I found out that Bundy was right. All the nervousness went away, but the excitement and heat, they stayed. I felt wonderful. Every time I touched her it made my whole life up to then nothing but getting ready, just twenty-four years of getting ready to touch Etilla.

Nothing she wouldn't talk about, that girl. Even Solomon, who never was talked about, ever, by anybody else, except when he was traveling.

Wonder where he lives, I'd say.

Oh, probably in some cave somewhere, she'd say.

Wonder *how* he lives.

I don't know what you mean.

I mean, where does he find anything to eat.

I never thought about it.

Stray dogs, probably.

And we'd laugh and then talk about something else. Then, after we'd courted six months, I asked Etilla to be my bride, and she said yes.

We set the date for the first of June, and I mean to tell you, I worked from dawn to dusk, every day, just to keep from thinking about it. I wanted so much to hold her in my arms and wake up to find her there beside me in the bed that it hurt, all over. It wasn't like any other hurt. It didn't go away, or ease. It just stayed inside me, growing, till I honestly thought I'd break open.

I was thinking about that one day, out in the field, when I heard the music. I let go of the plow and turned around, and there he was, maybe a hundred yards away. I hadn't laid eyes on him in six years, but he didn't look any different. Neither did the holes where his eyes used to be, or the raven. Or the people behind him.

Long valley, dark valley...hear the wind cry!...in darkness we're born and in darkness we die...all alone, alone, to the end of our days...to the end of our days, all alone...

I felt the old hate come up then, because seeing him made me see my daddy again, and the look on my daddy's face when he held the ax in the air that first time and when he died.

But the hate didn't last long, because there wasn't any part of me that was afraid, and that made me feel good. I waited for him to finish and when he did, I clapped applause for him, laughed, and turned back to my plowing. I didn't even bother to see when they all left.

Next night I went over to Etilla's, the way I did every Thursday night. Her mother opened the door, and looked at me and said, You can't come in, Lonnie.

Why not?

Why not? You know why not.

No, I don't. Is it about me and Etilla?

You might say. I'm sorry, boy.

What'd I do?

No answer.

I didn't do anything. I haven't done what you think. We said we'd wait. She just looked at me.

You hear me? I promised we'd wait, and that's what we're going to do. Now let me in.

I could see Etilla standing back in the room, looking at me. She was crying. But her mother wouldn't open the door any farther.

Tell me!

He called on you, boy. Don't you know that?

Who?

Solomon.

So what? I don't believe in all that stuff, and neither does Etilla. It's a lot of lies. He's just a crazy old blind man. Isn't that right, Etilla!

I got mad then, when she didn't answer, and I pushed the door open and went in. Etilla started to run. I grabbed her. It's lies, I said. We agreed on that!

I didn't think he'd call on you, Lonnie, she said.

Her mother came up. He never fails, she said. He's never been wrong in forty years.

I know, and I know why, too! I told her. Because everybody *believes* in him. They never ask questions, they never think, they just believe, and *that's* why he never fails! Well, I want you to know I don't believe and neither does Etilla and that's why this is *one* time he's going to fail!

I could have been talking to cordwood.

Etilla, tell your mother I'm right! Tell her we're going to be married, just like we planned, and we aren't going to let an old man with a guitar spoil our life.

I won't let her marry you, the old woman said. Not now. I like you, Lonnie Younger, you're a good, strong, hardworking boy, and you'd have made my girl a fine husband, but you're going to die soon and I don't want Etilla to be a widow. Do you?

No, you know I don't, but I keep trying to tell you, I'm *not* going to die. I'm healthy, and if you don't believe it, you go ask Doc Garson.

It wouldn't matter. Your daddy was healthy, remember, and so was Ed Kimball and Mrs Jackson and little Petey Griffin, and it didn't matter. Solomon knows. He smells it.

The way Etilla looked at me, I could have been dead already.

I went home then and tried to get drunk, but it didn't work. Nothing worked. I kept thinking about that old man and how he took the one thing I had left, the one good, beautiful thing in my whole life, and tore it away from me.

He came every day, like always, followed by the people, and I kept trying to see Etilla. But I felt like a ghost. Her mother wouldn't even come to the door.

I'm alive! I'd scream at them. Look at me. I'm alive.

But the door stayed barred.

Finally, one day, her mother yelled at me, Lonnie! You come here getting my Etilla upset one more time and I'll shoot you and then see how alive you'll be!

I drank a quart of wine that night, sitting by the window. The moon was bright. You could see like it was day, almost. For hours the field was empty, then they came, Solomon at their head.

His voice might not have been different, but it seemed that way, I don't know how. Softer, maybe, or higher. I sat there and listened and looked at them all, but when he sang those words, *All alone*, I threw the bottle down and ran outside.

I ran right up to him, closer then anyone ever had got, I guess, close enough to touch him.

God damn you, I said.

He went on singing.

Stop it!

He acted like I wasn't there.

You may be blind, you crazy old son of a bitch, but you're not deaf! I'm telling you—and all the rest of you—to get off my property, now! You hear me?

He didn't move. I don't know what happened inside me, then, except that all the hate and mad and sorrow I'd been feeling came back and bubbled over. I reached out first and grabbed that bird on his shoulder. I held it in my hands and squeezed it and kept on squeezing it till it stopped screaming. Then I threw it away.

The people started murmuring then, like they'd seen a dam burst, or an earthquake, but they didn't move.

Get out of here! I yelled. Go sing to somebody else, somebody who believes in you. I don't. Hear me? I don't!

I pulled his hands away from the strings. He put them back. I pulled them away again.

You got them all fooled, I said. But I know you can't smell death, or anything else, because you stink so bad yourself! I turned to the people. Come and take a sniff! I told them. Take a sniff of an old man who hasn't been near a cake of soap in all his life—see what it is you been afraid of!

They didn't move.

He's only a man! I yelled. Only a man!

I saw they didn't believe me, so I knew I had to show them, and I think it came to me that maybe this would be the way to get Etilla back. I should have thought of it before! If I could prove he wasn't anything but a man, they'd all have to see they were wrong, and that would save them because then they wouldn't just lie down and die, like dogs, whenever they looked out and saw Solomon and heard that damn song. Because they wouldn't *see* Solomon. He'd be gone.

I had my hands around his throat. It felt like wet leather. I pressed as hard as I could, and kept on pressing, with my thumbs digging into his gullet, deeper and deeper, and then I let him drop. He didn't move.

Look at him, I yelled holding up my hands. He's dead! Solomon is dead! God is dead! The man is dead! I killed him!

The people backed away.

Look at him! Touch him! You want to smell death, too? Go ahead, do it!

I laughed till I cried, then I ran all the way to Etilla's house. Her mother shot at me, just the way she said she would, but I knew she'd miss. It was an old gun, she was an old woman. I kicked the door open. I grabbed them both and practically dragged them back to my place. They had to see it with their own eyes. They had to see the old man sprawled out dead on the ground.

He was right where I dropped him.

Look at him, I said, and it was close to dawn now so they could see him even better. His face was blue and his tongue was sticking out of his mouth like a fat black snake.

I took loose the guitar while they were looking and stomped it to pieces.

They looked up at me, then, and started running.

I didn't bother to go after them, because it didn't matter anymore.

It didn't matter, either, when Sheriff Crowder came to see me the next day.

You did murder, Lonnie, he said. Thirty people saw you.

I didn't argue.

He took me to the jail and told me I was in bad trouble, but I shouldn't worry too much, considering the facts. He never thought Solomon was anything but a lunatic, and he didn't think the judge would be too hard on me. Of course it could turn out either way and he wasn't promising anything, but probably it would go all right.

I *didn't* worry, either. Not until last night. I was lying on my cot, sleeping, when I had a dream. It had to be, because I heard Solomon. His voice was clear and high, and sadder than it had ever been. And I saw him, too, when I went to the window and looked out. It was him and no question, standing across the street under a big old elm tree, singing.

Long valley, dark valley...hear the wind cry!...in darkness we're born and in darkness we die...all alone, alone, to the end of our days...to the end of our days, all alone...

It scared me, all right, that dream, but I don't think it will scare me much longer. I mean I really don't.

Tomorrow's the trial. And when it's over, I'm going to take me a long trip. I am.

SOMETHING IN THE EARTH

(1963)

The old man came into the room and sat down on the edge of the bed and put his hands together. He sat there without moving for several minutes while his wife waited patiently or impatiently: her expression was always the same. Then the old man said, "They're going to kill us."

His wife reached out and touched his wrists. "I'm sorry, dear," she said.

"Kill us every one until we're all gone; rip us up and cut off our legs and our arms, burn us to little black cinders…then, forget we ever existed."

"Hateful people!"

"Yes. Tomorrow we'll be dead and gone and that'll be the end of us."

His wife raised herself in the bed and stroked his forehead with damp fingers. "That's a shame," she said.

The old man got up and walked slowly to a window. "I can't understand it," he said slowly.

His wife settled back onto her pillows. "Well, you know, if you'll think back, dear—it *has* been a long time since anybody has come to see us."

The old man said nothing.

"Over a year, I'll bet. Aunt Jeaness was the last, and she came only because I wrote and asked her."

"You—asked her?"

"You looked so sad, dear. Couldn't stand to see you that way."

The old man remembered how he had taken the fat woman out into the forest and showed her every tree, and had her stand quietly so she

241

could hear the insects and the birds. It had been almost like the beautiful days, when the children came from the cities, from miles away, to feel grass and small wet leaves.

The old man tried not to think of these times. He looked at his wife.

"What I mean, dear, is—well, isn't it just possible that they might have their reasons?"

"Of course, yes! They explained very carefully; with graphs and charts and great whole books all bloated with statistics. I told them, 'Why not go and build your houses on Mars, build them on the moon, anywhere!' Impossible: no choice. They must build here; and we must die."

The wife clenched her fists.

"Stop saying 'we'! I'm tired of it. Not you, not me! Just—trees."

The old man's eyes widened.

"Do you mean that?"

"I mean it. For a hundred years and more I've lived with you in this place and never a complaint from me, never. Now we've got to leave and I'm glad and—"

"The mountains!" the old man cried. "You didn't care when they took away the mountains! When we watched them dry up the rivers and level the fields and put their cities over all the Earth—you've lied!"

"I love you."

"And when the world was turned to stone, all but this little corner, you weren't really glad…"

The old man turned and rushed from the room. He ran down the hall of the house and out into the night. He ran until each breath was a sharp pain inside him. Then he stumbled and sat down and tried to think, but he could only cough.

When he breathed again, finally, the thoughts came. They came, and his hands moved across the soft grass, feeling the dying leaves, tracing their slender veins with his fingers.

He rose and walked to where the forest grew thick with tall trees. He walked past the trees, putting out his hands and touching the rough bark surfaces, running his palms along the hardened syrup, caressing the small twigs but taking care not to injure them.

The ground was soft beneath his feet with the softness of damp tufted grass and fallen leaves.

He walked.

They will *meunière* us, he thought. Eat us with tin teeth and spit us out into flames and we will die, slowly. When we're gone, they will lay over our grave a tomb of steel and stone. And then *they* will live here, and in all the world there will not be a blade of grass nor a single tree. And children will be born and raised who will never know the robin's song, whose hands will know only the feel of cold metal.

He walked and tried to disregard his head which throbbed with pain; from time to time he stopped while the smaller creatures flew out of the dark to draw the blood from his neck and arms. And when he stopped he listened, too, for the gentle rustle of other creatures, running away or—the braver ones—edging cautiously closer. From the corners of his eyes he caught the tentative movements. But he made no sign.

They will kill you too, he thought. Once they kept big parks where you might go; the parks are gone, so they will kill you.

Once the old man stooped and picked up a twig not yet saturated with damp, still brittle: he turned the twig over and over in his hands, remembering.

Now he talked aloud to the trees in the forest. And his voice was soft in the wind that came through the thousand high branches.

The trees seemed to listen—and the voices of all the forest creatures ceased; now there was only the sound of the old man's soft voice.

"Once in the earth," the old man said, "we were everywhere. We stretched across the mountains: clear to the deserts and to the very edges of the great waters. And only our friends moved among us, those who loved us because we were their shelter and their food and their life. You—" the old man paused and thumped the bole of a giant sequoia "—*you* remember. When the vines hung from your arms and the animals ate from you!" He walked to another tree, not a sapling, but one young in the years of trees. "You don't remember. But you've been told! Small boys once climbed upon you, anyway, and swung from those arms!"

The horned moon became visible at last to the old man's eyes.

He stared at the cool light.

"Idiot!" he whispered. "You'll be next. You don't believe me? When *we're* gone and their buildings fill the ground, do you think they'll stop? See, look at what they're doing to Mars—poor, tired, dried-up planet. They've just started there: it won't take long before the sands disappear and the red is turned to iron. Wait! You'll see!"

He continued through the wood, tapping the wrinkled twig against his palm. He thought of his wife, and sighed.

I mustn't hate her, he thought. How could I expect a woman from the cities to understand? How could I have hoped? But—I did think she loved us, just a little... When I used to take her out in the mornings, before she grew ill, and be careful to say nothing so she could watch the sun—our sun—come up slowly through us, so she could feel us come to life—I thought... Then, in all this world, I am the only one! The only one!

The smaller limbs and branches high above moved in a slow sad dance to the night breezes that soughed over them. Leaves fluttered softly, then, turning over and over, caught by the wind.

The old man stopped a while to rest, for his heart had begun to pound.

She was right. I knew she was. No one has come to us as they used to. Not even the old ones who lived when we were everywhere, who watched us die...

The old man looked at his hands, which had once been young and had turned to parchment and were then made young again by the cities' men and were now beyond the help of their shining tools and glass ribbons. The hands would never be young again; they would only grow older and more wrinkled.

His heart regained its normal beat, and he walked to the edge of the forest, to where the great stone wall rose, then he turned around and started to walk back, another way.

A terrible thought came to him: *and if* I *had not been born here, where my father lived, perhaps there would be no one*—No. No, there had to be one.

My father kept us alive. Twice they wanted to kill us—he told me—and twice he stopped them.

But he was not alone...

What difference? It would have been the same, if he were.

Still—one man against the world... I've asked them. I've told them, showed them, hundreds of times, since I first suspected, said, "You took your machines and stamped the mountains flat for your cities. You drained the rivers and the seas and set your people to live on the dry beds. And when you made food from the air, you ruined the fields, and the cities grew where the grass and the wheat and the corn had grown! And you made your water and spread canals under the earth so the deserts could keep your buildings!"

I told them. "You took even the great forests. The birds and animals, not the ones raised with you who think with you, but the *free* ones— these you slaughtered. Your cities are everywhere; the world is nothing but a vast city. Can't you let alone the one last corner that was not made by your hands! Let the trees go on growing and remembering, let the animals run unafraid—give the air itself a last piece of room, where it can run or rest. It's all that's left!"

But they brought out their books of numbers for me to see.

And tomorrow they come for us, with their tractors and their saws and their explosions, to kill us. And there's nothing I can do.

Something happened to the wind.

It came rushing, all of a sudden, down from the sky, straight down, through the branches and upon the old man, chilling him. It caught up the flying creatures, the dark ones and those who were excited points of fire in the night always, and sent them whirling with the dead grass and leaves. The wind came into the old man's ears, into his head.

He listened.

Then, he stopped looking old. His back straightened, and his head ached no longer: it was clear now, clearer than it had ever been.

The old man looked about him, while the wind quieted itself and went away. Then, when he had found what he was looking for, he ran as fast as he could.

It was the tallest tree in the forest. And ancient, hardened long since from wood to marble. But the hard crystal shreds of bark were strong and easily supported the old man as he began to climb.

He climbed quickly, not feeling tired or worried. The heavy thoughts were all gone from him; they left when the wind had whistled; so he climbed with the lightness of a young boy, from handhold to handhold, up finally to the first fat branch, over this; and the rest was not work at all. It made his thoughts rush back over two hundred years, when he was truly young.

After a little while, the old man had reached the topmost branch.

He looked out across the glowing cities which stretched beyond the end of his vision, in all directions.

Then he laughed, and was proud to see that the twig he had found was still unbroken.

He waited.

"They'll be at us like flies! They'll write ugly letters and scream and put up petitions!" the Undersecretary had said, but he was wrong. He read books.

The President, who lived in the here and now and did not read books, had said, "Ridiculous nonsense!" He was right.

There were a few letters, of course, but all quite insincere, from the older colleges. The strongest of these read:

We of the faculty and student body urge the president to weigh this matter with his usual discretion and knowhow before he makes any definite move.

The others were inconsequential.

"You see, Herman," the President said, "nobody cares. Nobody gives a damn. Do you give a damn, Herman?"

The Undersecretary admitted he didn't. "There's Markeson though," he said.

"The custodian? Of course. The man was born there. Why shouldn't he want to stay? Human nature. He doesn't realize that every school in the world has a whole building full of the finest reproductions of every tree that ever existed. *Permanent* reproductions, you couldn't tell from the original. Bugs, too. All kinds."

"You explained this to him?"

"I imagine. I told Jerred to, or somebody. What's the difference? We'll find him another spot. Plenty of work around. APU, WVP, UNF."

"Yes."

The President started to explain that the group planned for the new site would include a subsidiary of U.S. Rockets, but lights flashed and his presence was requested someplace else.

The Undersecretary read his instructions and called up the crews and told them to go out and destroy the last forest on Earth.

Some time later the chief engineer of the crew asked for an audience with the Undersecretary. He was handsome and looked confused.

"I beg your pardon, sir," the chief engineer said, "but something peculiar has happened."

"Yes?" the Undersecretary said.

"About the new site for U.S., sir?"

"Yes, yes?"

"Well, we've run into difficulties."

"Difficulties? What do you mean by difficulties?"

"The trees, sir. They won't saw."

"Of course they won't. They're petrified, old. You knew that."

"Not all of them. The wooden ones won't saw. We tried drills, and they—didn't work."

"You are a man with sixty years of training. You are telling me you failed to cut down a bunch of trees? What about explosives?"

The chief engineer flushed. "We tried all of our equipment, all morning. Planted V03 under one tree and blew it, and it didn't hurt a leaf. I'm scared."

The Undersecretary said something under his voice, and called upon the President.

"Ridiculous!" the President snorted. The Undersecretary transmitted the message and went to other work.

The chief engineer returned later on, looking worse.

"Well?"

"V05, Blue Test, Red Test, everything."

"And you failed?"

"May I suggest," the chief engineer said, "that the Undersecretary and the President go back with me and see for themselves?"

They all went to the forest.

The crew of workers were huddled in a group on the other side of the wall, smoking and talking in low frightened tones.

"Now, see here," the President said loudly. "The job has got to be done by tonight. By *tonight!* I've got other crews waiting to put up the buildings, lay the foundations, fill the inkwells. What have you accomplished?" The President looked around. "Good heavens," he cried angrily. "Here, give me that!" He snatched an ax from the limp hand of a pale man and went over to a small poplar. "Must the President of United World do his own work?" He swung the new ax in a wide arc. The sharp heavy edge smashed against the tree trunk and then ricocheted back, upsetting the President's unsteady balance.

"I see," he said. "Well, it must be something in the earth. The F-Bomb—that's it. Polluted the earth or something last war. Wait, I'll go talk to the custodian."

The President slapped his hands together and commenced to walk, with other men, for the small cottage hidden in back of round bushes and slender eucalyptus shoots.

He knocked, and the door was opened by an old woman who looked sick. She clutched a bedsheet to her.

"Madam, I wish to speak with your husband, Mr Markeson."

"Gerald isn't here. I don't know where he is," the old woman said sadly. "He went away last night and he never came back. All I said was I loved him!" Her eyes were wide with astonishment.

"Yes, yes. Well, where is he? Oh, you don't know. I see. Didn't the men evacuate you before they started?"

"I've never seen him angry before. Will you look for him, please, and bring him back to me? Tell him I want to understand. Tell him I'll try, very hard."

The President paused a moment, then gave instructions that the old woman be taken to a safe place; then he walked back across the leaves and grass, quickly, to where the men were.

They stood silently. "Ahh—he's gone. Someone look for Markeson all of you—now." The men scattered, unhastily. Presently, one of them returned.

"I found him, sir."

"Well, bring him here!"

"I can't, sir. He's up a tree."

"You said, up a tree?"

"Sitting on a branch, sir. He said he didn't want to come down. He wants to talk with you."

They went to the tree.

The old man called down from the dizzy heights. "Go away. Leave us alone!" he called.

"Now, now," called the President.

"You might just as well pack up and leave. Nothing you can do. Nothing in the world."

"What do you mean?"

"There had to be a stop, that's all. You can't kill us."

The President conferred with his friends. Then he shouted: "Listen to reason!"

"Reason! That's what's wrong with you. You're all stuffed full till there's nothing else. If you'd listened to something else you'd have stopped long ago. Then there would be rivers and oceans and mountains!"

"Oh, come down from there. You look foolish, a man your age. We've got work to do and you might get hurt."

The old man laughed long and hard. "Go ahead. Do your work. Try. Try to kill us!"

Three men were dispatched to climb the tree, but they didn't know how or couldn't. No one could climb the tree.

The President said, "We're going to have to blast it all out, Mr Markeson. Come down or you'll be killed."

The old man pretended to fall, then caught a limb and swung back to his position. He laughed.

An aircar was advised to pick him up, but the aircar crashed into a weeping willow, somehow, and fell to the earth. The same thing happened to others.

The President, who had sat down, took off his coat and applied a handkerchief to his forehead.

The shrill old voice carried. "Can't you see? They told me—mostly the wind did. Do what you like."

Finally the President said, "See here, Mr Markeson. We're holding up production. There's a war going on—don't you know that? This center will be essential. Either get out of that—that tree—or take the consequences."

The old man looked at the animals who waited hidden from the men; he looked at the ungrieving forest, at the expectant sky. "Goodbye!" he called.

The President shrugged, and the men walked off and did not return for several hours. They placed glass balls full of pink vapor around the bases of the trees and then left again.

Machines covered the sky. They dropped shields about the city's walls to protect the buildings. The old man watched them intently, feeling not the least bit uncomfortable, though he didn't know what they were doing.

Then, at a given command, the flying machines opened their riveted stomachs and released more glass balls, filled with vapor of yet another color. These looked light and fragile, but they dropped like great weights to the ground, where they burst open, letting the wind take up the colored mists and blow it through the trees to merge with the mist that had been left before.

The explosion took away the old man's breath. It made him close his eyes tight and hold fast to the branch. But soon the shaking and the noise passed, with the foul-smelling smoke, and when he looked, nothing had changed. The trees stood as they had stood, and he could hear the animals and the insects. He nodded, and pressed the twig to the side of his face.

Soon the men came back, blinking, shaking their heads, talking very little and in short words. The President was along, lagging in back.

"See?" shrieked the old man, bouncing.

"Something in the earth," the President mumbled, but not so softly that the old man didn't hear.

Then a new voice came up to the tree. "Gerald!"

The old man saw his wife. She was out of breath and her gown was covered with burrs and sharp rips.

"Sylvan!"

"What is happening?" she cried hysterically.

"I don't know... Something. I've prayed for it, thought about it, but I can't tell you what it is. I don't dare, because it would frighten you. Go with the others, leave me."

The pale woman put her hands to her mouth and ran away.

Soon they were all gone; and when he was alone at last, the old man put his head against the treetop and fell into a quiet sleep.

He dreamed dreams of the world before the cities had gone mad. He lay on the white sands of a lonely beach, by a river, and watched grazing sheep on the other side of the river. It ran fast and sang through golden fields and deep green forests, and broke into wild brooks and streams within the forests. And in the distance, he could see the mountains in the sun...

Then the old man woke. He shivered once and looked across the cities: then he stared with wide open eyes.

He stared at the cities as they broke and crumbled. As the air grew fat with screams of many people. As the roots of giant trees, greater than he had ever seen, came up from the stone and spread and toppled the mighty buildings over. As the water came flooding in through the steel canyons. As the mountains pulled the earth apart and rose and made room for the fields and the forests.

INSOMNIA VOBISCUM

(1964)

cannot say how it was that we fell into a discussion of so-called psychic phenomena that night at the Kings—our interest in spirits was generally limited to those found in bottles—but I suppose it is the sort of topic which must inevitably crop up among the very young, the very old, and the addled. Crenshaw, our ex-senator, was holding forth, loudly, on a trip he had taken to Haiti, and of the voodoo rites he had witnessed with his own two eyes. At the conclusion of this tale, which demonstrated either the fragility of memory or the plasticity of truth, Henderson, the retired banker, took over. In sepulchral tones he related the story of how his life had been saved by a gypsy phrenologist who, out of her fund of arcane knowledge, had warned him to stay out of single-engined aircraft. The elder of the club, Mycroft, a spry octogenarian, told of his encounter with a London spiritualist who put him in direct communication with his deceased wife. ("Thought I'd seen the last of the old termagant," commented Mycroft wryly, "but there she was, plain as pigs. Worst fright I've ever had.") Jenkins, our explorer, was cajoled into repeating his story of the Abominable Snowman, and I offered a variant of my one experience with the Great Unknown—correctly diagnosed by the group at large as a case of too much mince pie and too little regard for the facts.

We laughed, then, all but our newest member, the Scotsman, Creel—who sat, as he had done throughout the evening, absolutely still and expressionless. No one knew much about Creel, except that he was a stockbroker, single, and reportedly rich. He never said much, but from that little it was evident that he was a realist, a dweller in the here and now. It occurred to me suddenly that he must be thinking us all a hopeless bunch of nincompoops, which was true enough; still, it annoyed me, and for that reason I twisted in my chair and addressed him.

"See here. Creel, surely you've a contribution to make."

He seemed to rouse from a deep reverie. "Contribution?"

"Yes." I winked at the others. "You must have bumped up against the unknown a few times in your life, seen a phantom or two." The vacancy of his stare drove me on. "Come on, Creel. As a King, it's your duty to give us a ghost story."

"Nonsense," he said. "Such talk is pointless."

"I can't agree. The unknown surrounds us."

I expected a snort. Instead, Creel continued to stare.

"Well?"

"I've never seen a ghost," he said. "And I don't think anyone else has, either. But an odd thing did happen to me, once, a number of years ago…"

There was a quick hush in the room, as though a curtain had fallen. Creel had never before made such a long speech.

"I was visiting an acquaintance in the country," he continued, more to himself than to us. "It was a big house. There was a party. We ate a good meal and then, about ten o'clock, I decided to retire. I got into bed and tried to sleep, but I couldn't." He lit his pipe, thoughtfully. "Too much noise from downstairs. Yelling and screaming and dancing and cursing. Right below me. I never heard such noise. All night it lasted."

We waited. Finally, someone said, "Well? Go on."

"That's all," said Creel.

"You were visiting someone, and you couldn't sleep because people were having a party downstairs and that's the whole story?"

"Aye," said Creel. "That's my brush with the unknown." He sucked at his pipe until he'd got it going, then he looked up at our astonished faces. "Oh," he said, "I forgot one part. There was no downstairs at this house. My bedroom was on the ground floor."

MY GRANDMOTHER'S JAPONICAS

(1984)

I've lost track now of the number of people who died in my grandmother's rooming house in Everett, Washington—but when I was going on sixteen the count stood at an even dozen—eight men and four women. They were mostly old folks: pensioned-off railroad workers, lonely widowed ladies of the town, a few from the heart of the family itself—my uncle Double-G, cousin Elmina—but some were not so old. Joe Alvarez, for instance, was only thirty-something when he breathed out his last. And there was a pretty young girl about whom I remember just that her face was very white and she had once taught school.

Death came to the house approximately once a year. Not unpresaged: you could smell it coming. For this was when Baba's—my grandmother's—garden broke into rich bloom and the roses grew where they could be seen from any window of any room. Other preparations were made, too: the house underwent a thorough cleaning, as if in anticipation of the arrival of rich relatives; the cemetery—some two or three miles out of town—came aswarm with aunts, all bearing new flowers and vases. They clipped the tall weeds from around the headstones, they polished the marble with soft rags, they berated the caretaker for his slothful inattention. I once watched Aunt Nellie spend over an hour rubbing the grime out of the wings of a white stone cherub that marked the resting place of somebody's stillborn infant, no one knew exactly whose. You could tell Death was coming by all these signs.

The doctor, whom I thought of as the house physician, was so frequent a visitor to our place that we all considered him a part of the family. He was a tremendously fat man: his face was continually flushed and he panted a lot, which was to him an unmistakable symptom of coronary thrombosis. Each year, for as many years as I can remember, he would prognosticate with the authority of the practicing physician that he couldn't possibly last another six months. We always believed him. "I only wish one thing," Dr. Cleveland used to say. "When I go, I want to go here." That is he wanted to die at our place. As things happened, he was one of the few in town who never did. We were located second from the railroad tracks. A restaurant, a cannery, a hobo jungle and the town depot were on the immediate perimeter and they were all so disreputable that Baba's, with its fiercely shining coat of white paint, refinished each year, looked exceptionally genteel. It was an unusual house in that it was as perfectly square as a house can be: not one sliver of ornamentation, no balconies, no pillars, no filigree. It had two floors: four bedroom upstairs, three below, plus an immense kitchen with a pantry as large as a bathroom. It was all kept fanatically clean.

The furniture looked antique, and could very well have been, except that antiques cost money and no one in my family had much of that and no one was quite old enough to have acquired antiques first hand. It was a mellow hodgepodge of styles.

The pictures on the walls were generally of large dogs. My grandmother had no fondness for dogs, however, and would never allow one in the house.

When my mother and I moved there from Chicago, where I was born, I was installed in one of the unrented upstairs bedrooms. This was about the time I had discovered Edgar Allan Poe, and it was therefore not much of an encouragement when Baba let it slip that a gentleman had only two weeks previously passed on "in this very bed." Like most of the others—at least one person had died in each room—the former occupant had been elderly; but, also like the others, he did not go quickly.

No one went quickly at Baba's. They all suffered from a fascinating variety of ills, usually of a lingering and particularly scabrous nature. "My" gentlemen, a retired lumberman, had contracted some sort of a disease of the kidneys or intestines and, as Aunt Pearl reminisced, it had taken him several months "in the dying."

Heart trouble was the most frequent complaint, though. It seemed to me for a while that everybody in the house was going about clutching and reeling, catching at chairs, easing into bed, being careful not to laugh too hard.

Nothing could shake my aunts' firm belief that every disease, no matter what it might be, was contagious. When poor Mrs. Schillings was groaning out her last from advanced arthritis, movement had all but disappeared from our house. We creaked out of bed, we walked stiffly when we felt able walk at all, and it was only after the funeral that the usual bustle was resumed. At the arrival of Mr. Spiker, who had come from his bachelor quarters across the way to die at Baba's, conditions reached a low point. Mr. Spiker suffered from, among other things, what my grandmother called The Dance: the old man shook and quivered horribly. It was, of course, not long before we had all begun to tremble in a similar fashion. I used to spend many agonizing moments with my hands outstretched, trying to keep the fingers steady. Aunt Pearl, better than the rest of us at this sort of thing, fell completely apart this time. She took to her bed and stayed there for several weeks, shuddering in giant spasms which even Mr. Spiker couldn't match: he occasionally trembled his way over to comfort her. Later he died of an infected liver, a common sequel of drinking too much straight whiskey.

And yet, with Death as much a part of life as it was then, Baba's was certainly the most cheerful parlor in town. We would gather around the fire for hours every night and tell stories generally in soft voices, so as not to disturb whoever might be dying elsewhere in the house.

The subjects of conversation seldom veered from Sickness, Death and the Hereafter. Baba would spend forty-five minutes to an hour telling how her husband died as a result of an accident in the sawmill where he worked: Aunt Pearl—as with all my aunts, a widow—would describe the manner in which *her* husband departed this Earth ("Pooched out like a balloon and then bust!"); that would lead to someone's recollecting an article they'd read somewhere on how hypnosis was supposed to help cure cancer, and the next thing it would be time for bed. I don't recall a completely easy moment I ever spent in the rooms they assigned me. Most often there was a peculiar smell, relative to the disease that carried off the former occupant; the sort of smell, like ether, that you can never quite get rid of. You can get it out of the air, but it stays in the bedsprings, in the furniture, in your head.

My least favorite room was the one next to Baba's. The walls here were a green stagnant-pool color and the bed was one of those iron things that are always making noise. Railroad calendars, picturing numerous incredibly aged Indian chiefs, hung lopsided on strings, and on the door, above the towel rack, there was a huge portrait of the Savior. This was painted in the same style as old circus posters, showing Him smiling and plucking from His chest cavity—realistically rendered with painstaking care and immense skill—a heart approximately five time the size of a normal one, encircled by thorns and dripping great drops of cherry-red blood.

Now what with *The Murders in the Rue Morgue* or *The Tell-Tale Heart*, the Indians on the wall and the portrait on the door, not to mention the atmosphere of disquiet, it seems odd that I should have decided just then to paint on the green iron flowered knob of the bed's head-pieces—with India ink—a series of horrible faces. That is what I did, nonetheless, and as there were twelve such knobs, I soon had twelve unblinking masks staring at me.

At any rate, I was in no condition this night—a few nights after completing the heads—for one of Baba's pranks. She was a great lover of practical jokes, my grandmother, and her sense of humor ran to the macabre.

To give you an idea of what I mean, there was the time the lunatic escaped from Sedro-Wooley (this is where the insane asylum is). He'd been put there by reason of having cut off his wife's head with an ax one night, along with his mother's and some other relatives'. Now he was loose, and no matter how hard they looked for him, he simply wasn't to be found. The countryside was thrown into a delicious panic; I wish I had a dollar for every time my aunts looked under the beds. Baba, then aged seventy-five, took this as a springboard for one of her most famous jokes. Here's what happened:

She went over to Mr. Howe's shack—he was a bachelor and there was gossip about him and her—and borrowed some of his old clothes. Then she put these clothes on, covering up her hair with a cap and dirtying her face, and got the short-handle hatchet from the wood-house. She waited a little while—it was quite late, but we were all light sleepers: the drop of a pin would have made Aunt Myrtle and especially Aunt Dora sit bolt upright—then she crept into the house and stationed herself inside the closet of Aunt Myrtle's room.

Now Aunt Myrtle frequently got frightened and would literally leap at the sight of her own reflection in a mirror, so you can understand why she was chosen. It isn't hard for me to see Baba now standing there in the dark, clutching the ax, grinning widely...

She waited a minute, and then, from the closet, came a series of moans and shufflings that could easily have roused the adjoining township.

Frankly, it's a wonder they didn't empty the family shotgun into Baba, because when someone finally got up the nerve to open that door—I believe it was my Uncle Double-G—there were Goddy-screeches that would have terrified any real lunatic. "Goddy!" they yelled, "Goddy! Goddy!"

It all gave my grandmother immense satisfaction, however, and she never tired of telling the story.

There was also another favorite little prank of hers. It was the day I accidentally broke off the blade of the bread knife. We managed to make it stand up on her chest so that the knife appeared to be imbedded almost to the hilt in her. Then I was commanded to rip her clothes a bit and empty a whole bottle of ketchup over her and the linoleum. Then she lay down and I ran screaming, "Somebody come quick! Somebody come quick!" It was gratifying that Aunt Dora fainted away completely, though the others saw through the joke at once.

Baba was an extremely good woman by and large, I've decided. I never heard a cross word out of her. I never saw a beggar come to the door but that he went away with a full meal and frequently more—with the single exception of one old man who happened to have a dog with him. He wouldn't leave the dog outside and Baba wouldn't let it track up the house. She fretted for days about the man.

But there was still that sense of humor.

Observing my reading material at the time, she would say to me: "Now sonny, I'm old and one of these days I'll be dead and gone. I'm just telling you so that when you feel a cold clammy hand on your forehead some night, just reach out and take it: it'll be your old Baba, come to visit." That put me in a sweat: I still can't stand, to this day, wet rags on my brow.

The oddest, most unsettling experience of my life took place a few nights after I'd finished painting the horrible head on the bed.

I had been reading *The Facts in the Case of M. Valdemar* and the concluding bit about the mound of putrescence in the bed lingered long after the light had been put out. I kept trying to *imagine* it. The whole upper floor was deserted at this time, aside from myself and Baba's room, Mr. Seay having been plucked from this mortal sphere two days earlier owing to sugar diabetes and his fondness for candy bars. The window was open. I was just dozing, thinking about putrescence, when there was this soft *thud-thud* as of someone advancing very slowly up the stairs. The tread was so slow, however, that I recognized it as Baba's— she was going on eighty now. I waited, knowing what to expect. And I was partially correct. The footsteps got closer, I could hear my bedroom door opening; the *thud-thud* came across the room and someone sat

down on the bed. I braced myself. It was Baba, of course, in a puck-
ish mood. Shortly she would let out a blood-curdling scream or cackle
like a witch, or worse. But—nothing happened. Tentatively I nudged the
weight on the bed with my foot: as nearly as this sort of test can tell, it
was Baba all right. Minutes passed. And more minutes, the breathing
regular as ever. Still nothing. No movement, no sign; only, the breathing
got heavier and I could hear a kind of thumping, like a small animal
hurling itself at a dead-skin drum.

My mother came in and calmed me down. Questioned suspiciously,
my grandmother denied having put a toe in my room all night.

Now I realize what had happened. I'd no way of knowing then, however, and for years I told the story of the midnight ghost that sat on my bed.

What had happened was, Baba had come to scare me and just plain
worked herself into a heart attack from sheer excitement. No one must
know about this, so she'd sat there waiting for the pain to pass.

We all thought of Baba as several evolution-phases beyond being a
mere human. Uncomplainingly and resolutely she had for years tended
to the sick and dying of the house, but never once had she succumbed,
actually, to a single germ. The rest of us might go about clutching our
hearts or trembling or duplicating the health-agonies of whatever
tenant: not Baba. And it finally got so that we believed she was immortal
and George Bernard Shaw. We thought of the world with everybody in
it dead but with my grandmother and George Bernard Shaw, and them
walking hand-in-hand among the littered corpses, seeing to proper
burials and trying to make things nice for the departed. I don't know
what Mr. Shaw would have thought about that.

There was a particular reason why I was unhappiest in the room
right next to Baba's. It was because she never let anyone, not even her
own daughters, enter this room and I was continually overwhelmed
with curiosity. Yes, I knew I must never violate the rule, for I had more
than a suspicion it would make Baba sad—and most of us would have
jumped in front of a locomotive before seeing that happen. Also, who

knew? The room might have contained mementoes of past indiscretions, or she might have been hiding a mad sister there—for myself, I inclined to the latter view.

Neither was correct, however, as it evolved.

The truth was, Baba had a heart condition. And this was where she went whenever she felt an attack coming... In a way she sensed it was only her apparent immunity to Death and illness that allowed us to take the horror and the fear away, as we did. If we had seen her sick even once, we were sure things would change; it would have become merely a big house where a lot of people died.

Things did change when she had her stroke.

Fortunately, no one else was dying at the time. Mr. Vaughn, the former town stationmaster, was bedridden, but this was more due to laziness than anything else: his groans, which had been filling the air, ceased abruptly when the news was out.

Baba had been taking tea with Mr. Hannaford, the undertaker, and red-faced Dr. Cleveland who was in the habit of stopping by in between calls. It was morning. I knew she was feeling good, because she'd put a partially asphyxiated toad in my trousers pocket—to my terror, as I despised and mortally loathed toads and like creatures. I found it on my way to school. When I got home from school no auguries were in the air, except I noticed idly that the roses were in exceptionally fine bloom— the yellow ones particularly were everywhere. And the air was full of a natural sweetsyrup fragrance, unsuggestive of the slumber room.

But things were powerfully quiet.

My first thought was that Mr. Vaughn had died. But then I saw the old man seated on the back porch, holding his battered old felt hat in his hands and revolving it slowly by turning the brim. He looked far from happy. He stared at me.

At first they would let me see Baba. But I pleaded and bawled and finally they gave in and I went into the downstairs bedroom Aunt Nell used for her patients (she was a masseuse).

I expected something hideous, judging from the way everybody was carrying on. A mound of putrescence in the bed would not have been unnerving: I was ready.

But, aside from the fact that she was in bed where I'd never seen her before, Baba looked little different—except perhaps more beautiful than ever. Her hair had been taken down and combed against the pillow and it looked silver-soft even against the spotless Irish linen slip. Her face was lightly rouged and powdered and she wore a pastel blue shawl over her gingham gown. Her eyes were closed.

I asked everyone else to please leave the room. Surprisingly, they did.

Poor Baba, I thought. The stroke had come without warning; it had knocked her to the floor and when the doctor finally arrived, there was nothing to do. Her entire left side was paralyzed, for one thing. It had hurt her brain, for another. She would suffer a short time and then die…

I looked at her, feeling as empty as I'd ever felt before; I knew I must say something, try to be of comfort in some way, difficult as it was.

I walked to the bed and, gulping, touched her folded hands, as if to make this awful dream seem somehow real.

Baba's left eye opened. "Somebody," she suddenly screamed, "come and help me! This young man is trying to feel of my bosom!"

MY GRANDMOTHER "suffered" for three years, which fact confounded medical science as represented by Dr. Cleveland and restored our faith in her immortality.

She never got out of the bed, but few people have done more traveling than Baba did after her stroke. Mostly she returned to her birthplace in North Carolina, though frequently she would chronicle personal experiences with the wild savages of Montana and Utah. She spoke several authentic Indian dialects fluently, we knew that (though not where she picked the knowledge up) and for whole days running there would not be a word of English heard from her room. It was a fact that she'd never in her life been to Utah and visited Montana only once, to see William Hart's statue—on second thought, that might have been Wyoming. Anyway, it was all a long time after the last wild savages disappeared.

Once she spent a day calling out the sights of Chicago like a tourist guide: "Now this here is the famous Art Institute; to your right you see the Shedd Aquarium; over there is the Planetarium; we are now passing old Lake Michigan." Of course, she'd never been there.

Time took precedence over space in Baba's travels: she was a different age every day. It wasn't easy to keep up.

"Get your damn hands off of me, Jess Randolph!" she yelled one night, waking the whole house. "I am entirely too young for these kinds of monkeyshines."

Another night we were startled to hear: "The Great Letty's chopped her hand off with the ax!" This referred to the time my mother inprovidentially severed the third finger of her left hand whilst cutting up some kindling wood. Baba had held the finger on so tight that when Dr. Cleveland finally arrived it was possible to effect a mend-job. It had happened fifteen years before my birth.

BABA'S APPEARANCE never got any worse, but this was the only thing that remained static in her new life. In addition to her trips around the world, back and ahead through time, she developed one day no different from any other day the notion that she was pregnant.

Nothing could dissuade her, either. Because of her heart there was nothing but to humor her, so for almost an entire year we would ask her if she felt it was "time" yet; she'd listen, poke her stomach with her good hand, and answer no, but soon, and we'd all better stick around.

Then one day I stopped in her room for a visit and, as had become customary, inquired whether she thought it would be a boy or a girl. This used to delight her.

She just looked at me.

"Gonna name it after me, are you?" I joshed.

She rolled her eyes. "Letty!" she called. "Come and get your young'n. He's gone completely crazy!"

After that the subject of grandmother's pregnancy never came up.

By this time we had stopped taking in boarders and Death and Dr. Cleveland became infrequent callers. At least, in their official capacities. And with the absence of these two, a pall slowly descended which none of us seemed able to lift. It wasn't exactly a gloomy or joyless house, but the lively spark that pulls each moment from the level of the ordinary to something a little finer, this was certainly gone. And it would never come back.

On a nicely chill September morning, with many of the roses still left in the garden, Baba called us all into her room and announced calmly that she was going to stop living. Now since she was the only one of us who had never previously issued such a statement— Aunt Dora always said "Goodbye, goodbye" and squeezed my arms even when she was only going to the movies—we were impressed. Unconvinced, but impressed.

Baba asked Pearl and Nellie to take her to the window so that she might have a last look at her flowers: she was there fully forty-five minutes and got to see them all, plus a lot no one else could see for she remarked how lovely the japonicas were and there had never been japonicas in the garden.

I remember it all very well. I was standing by Baba's side at the window and, since it was true—it was early in the morning—I commented that the hoarfrost looked like diamond-dust on the grass.

Baba jerked her head around. "Young mister," she said, "I'll thank you to remember there's ladies present!"

For some reason that made me cry. I wanted suddenly to pray, but we all changed religions so often, I could only apologize. They sent me out for an ice cream bar, then: my grandmother always had a great fondness for ice cream bars.

When I got back she was dead.

I spent that night in the room with the horrible heads. But they didn't scare me a bit.

I imagine they're still there, if the ink hasn't faded.

APPOINTMENT WITH EDDIE

(1988)

It was one of those bars that strike you blind when you walk in out of the sunlight, but I didn't need eyes, I could see him, the way deaf people can hear trumpets. It was Shecky, all right. But it also wasn't Shecky.

He was alone.

I'd known him for eight years, worked with him, traveled with him, lived with him; I'd put him to bed at night and waked him up in the morning; but never, in all that time, never once had I seen him by himself—not even in a bathtub. He was plural. A multitude of one. And now, the day after his greatest triumph, he was alone, here, in a crummy little bar on Third Avenue.

There was nothing to say, so I said it. "How are you, Sheck?"

He looked up and I could tell he was three-quarters gone. That meant he'd put away a dozen martinis, maybe more. But he wasn't drunk. "Sit down," he said, softly, and that's when I stopped worrying and started getting scared. I'd never heard Shecky talk softly before. He'd always had a voice like the busy signal. Now he was practically whispering.

"Thanks for coming." Another first: "Thanks" from Shecky King, to me. I tried to swallow but suddenly my throat was dry, so I waved to the waiter and ordered a double scotch. Of course, my first thought was, he's going to dump me. I'd been expecting it for years. Even though I'd done a good job for him, I wasn't the biggest agent in the business, and to Shecky the biggest always meant the best. But this wasn't his style.

I'd seen him dump people before and the way he did it, he made it seem like a favor.

Always with Shecky the knife was a present, and he never delivered it personally. So I went to the second thought, but that didn't make any better sense. He was never sick a day in his life. He didn't have time. A broad? No good. The trouble didn't exist that his lawyers, or I, couldn't spring him out of in ten minutes.

I decided to wait. It took most of the drink.

"George," he said, finally, "I want you to lay some candor on me." You know the way he talked. "I want you to lay it on hard and fast. No thinking. Dig?"

"Dig," I said, getting dryer in the throat.

He picked up one of the five full martini glasses in front of him and finished it in one gulp. "George," he said, "am I a success?"

The highest-paid, most acclaimed performer in show business, the man who had smashed records at every club he'd played for five years, who had sold over two million copies of every album he'd ever cut, who had won three Emmys and at least a hundred other awards, who had, in the opinion of the people *and* the critics, reached the top in a dozen fields—this man, age thirty-six, was asking me if he was a success.

"Yes," I said.

He killed another martini. "Candorsville?"

"The place." I thought I was beginning to get it. Some critic somewhere had shot him down. But would he fall in here? No. Not it. Still, it was worth a try.

"Who says you aren't?"

"Nobody. Yet."

"Then what?"

He was quiet for a full minute, I could hardly recognize him sitting there, an ordinary person, an ordinary scared human being.

Then he said, "George, I want you to do something for me."

"Anything," I said. That's what I was being paid for: anything.

"I want you to make an appointment for me."

"Where at?"

"Eddie's."

"Who's Eddie?"

He started sweating. "A barber," he said.

"What's wrong with Mario?"

"Nothing's wrong with Mario."

It wasn't any of my business. Mario Cabianca had been Shecky's personal hair stylist for ten years, he was the best in the business, but I supposed he'd nicked The King or forgotten to laugh at a joke. It wasn't important. It certainly couldn't have anything to do with the problem, whatever it was. I relaxed a little.

"When for?" I asked.

"Now," he said. "Right away."

"Well, you could use a shave."

"Eddie doesn't shave people. He cuts hair. That's all."

"You don't need a haircut."

"George," he said, so soft I could barely hear him, "I never needed anything in all my life like I need this haircut."

"Okay. What's his number?"

"He hasn't got one. You'll have to go in."

Now he was beginning to shake. I've seen a lot of people tremble, but this was the first time I'd seen anybody shake.

"Sheck, are you germed up?"

"No." The martini sloshed all over his cashmere coat. By the time it got to his mouth only the olive was left. "I'm fine. Just do this for me, George. Please. Do it now."

"Okay, take it easy. What's his address?"

"I can't remember." An ugly sound boiled out of his throat, I guess it was a laugh. "Endsburg! I can't remember. But I can take you there." He started to get up. His belly hit the edge of the table. The ashtrays and glasses tipped over. He looked at the mess, then at his hands, which were still shaking, and he said, "Come on."

"Sheck." I put a hand on his shoulder, which nobody does. "You want to tell me about it?"

"You wouldn't understand," he said.

On the way out, I dropped a twenty in front of the bartender. "Nice to have you, Mr King," he said, and it was like somebody had turned the volume up on the world. "Me and my old lady, y'know, we wouldn't miss your show for anything."

"Yeah," a guy on the last stool said. "God bless ya, buddy!"

We walked out into the sun. Shecky looked dead. His face was white and glistening with sweat. His eyes were red. And the shaking was getting worse.

"This way," he said, and we started down Third.

"You want me to grab a cab?"

"No. It isn't far."

We walked past the pawnshops and the laundries and saloons and the gyms and I found myself breathing through my mouth, out of habit. It had taken me a long time to forget these smells. They weren't just poor smells. They were kiss-it-all-goodbye, I never-had-a-chance smells. Failure smells. What the hell was I doing here, anyway? What was Shecky doing here? Shecky, who carried his Hong Kong silk sheets with him wherever he went because that was the only thing he could stand next to his skin, who kept a carnation in his lapel, who shook hands with his gloves on? I looked down at his hands. They were bare.

We walked another block. At the light I heard a sound like roller skates behind me. A bum without legs stopped at the curb. The sign across the street changed to WALK. I nudged Shecky; it was the kind of thing he appreciated. He didn't even notice. The cripple wiggled his board over the curb and, using the two wooden bricks in his hands, rolled past us. I wondered how he was going to make it back up to the sidewalk, but Shecky didn't. He was thinking of other things.

After two more blocks, deep into the armpit of New York, he slowed down. The shaking was a lot worse. Now his hands were fists.

"There," he said.

Up ahead, five or six doors, was a barbershop. It looked like every other barbershop in this section. The pole outside was cardboard, and most of the paint was gone. The window was dirty. The sign—EDDIE THE BARBER—was faded.

"I'll wait," Shecky said.

"You want a haircut now, is that right?"

"That's right," he said.

"I should give him your name?"

He nodded.

"Sheck, we've known each other a long time. Can't you tell me—"

He almost squeezed a hunk out of my arm. "Go, George," he said. "Go."

I went. Just before I got to the place, I looked back. Shecky was standing alone in front of a tattoo parlor, more alone than ever, more alone than anyone ever. His eyes were closed. And he was shaking all over. I tried to think of him the way he was ten hours ago, surrounded by people, living it up, celebrating the big award; but I couldn't. This was somebody else.

I turned around and walked into the barbershop. It was one of those non-union deals, with a big card reading HAIRCUTS—$1.00 on the wall, over the cash register. It was small and dirty. The floor was covered with hair. In the back, next to a curtain, there was a cane chair and a table with an old radio on it. The radio was turned to a ball game, but you couldn't hear it because of the static. The far wall was papered with calendars. Most of them had naked broads on them, but a few had hunting and fishing scenes. They were all coated with grease and dirt.

There wasn't anything else, except one old-fashioned barber chair and, behind it, a sink and a cracked glass cabinet.

A guy was in the chair, getting a haircut. He had a puffy face and a nose full of broken blood vessels. You could smell the cheap wine across the room.

Behind the bum was maybe the oldest guy I'd ever seen outside a hospital. He stood up straight, but his skin looked like a blanket somebody had dropped over a hat rack. It had that yellow look old skin gets. It made you think of coffins.

Neither of them noticed me, so I stood there a while, watching. The barber wasn't doing anything special. He was cutting hair, the old way, with a lot of scissors-clicking in the air. I knew a bootblack once who did the same thing. He said he was making the rag talk. But he gave it up, he said, because nobody was listening anymore. The bum in the chair wasn't listening, either, he was sound asleep, so there had to be a lot more. But you couldn't see it.

I walked over to the old man. "Are you Eddie?"

He looked up and I saw that his eyes were clear and sharp. "That's right," he said.

"I'd like to make an appointment."

His voice was like dry leaves blowing down the street. "For yourself?"

"No. A friend."

I felt nervous and embarrassed and it came to me, then, that maybe this whole thing was a gag. A practical joke. Except that it didn't have any point.

"What is his name?"

"Shecky King."

The old man went back to clipping the bum's hair. "You'll have to wait until I'm finished," he said. "Just have a seat."

I went over and sat down. I listened to the static and the clicking scissors and I tried to figure things out. No good. Shecky could buy this smelly little place with what he gave away in tips on a single night. He had the best barber in the business on salary. Yet there he was, down the street, standing in the hot sun, waiting for me to make an appointment with this feeble old man.

The clicking stopped. The bum looked at himself in the mirror, nodded and handed a crumpled dollar bill to the barber. The barber took it over to the cash register and rang it up.

"Thank you," he said.

The bum belched. "Next month, same time," he said.

"Yes, sir."

The bum walked out.

"Now then," the old man said, flickering those eyes at me. "The name again?"

He had to be putting me on. There wasn't anybody who didn't know Shecky King. He was like Coca-Cola, or sex. I even saw an autographed picture of him in an igloo, once.

"Shecky King," I said, slowly. There wasn't any reaction. The old man walked back to the cash register, punched the NO SALE button and took a dog-eared notebook out of the drawer.

"He'd like to come right away," I told him.

The old man stared at the book a long time, holding it close to his face. Then he shut it and put it back in the drawer and closed the drawer.

"I'm sorry," he said.

"What do you mean?"

"I don't have an opening."

I looked around the empty shop. "Yeah, I can see, business is booming."

He smiled.

"Seriously," I said.

He went on smiling.

"Look, I haven't got the slightest idea why Mr King wants to have his hair cut here. But he does. So let's stop horsing around. He's willing to pay for it."

I reached into my left pocket and pulled out the roll. I found a twenty. "Maybe you ought to take another look at your appointment book," I said.

The old man didn't make a move. He just stood there, smiling. For some reason—the lack of sleep, probably, the running around, the worry—I felt a chill go down my back, the kind that makes goose pimples.

"Okay," I said. "How much?"

"One dollar," he said. "After the haircut."

That made me sore. I didn't actually grab his shirt, but it would have gone with my voice. "Look," I said, "this is important. I shouldn't tell you this, but Shecky's outside right now, down the street, waiting. He's all ready. You're not doing anything. Couldn't you—"

"I'm sorry," the old man said, and the way he said it, in that dry, creaky voice, I could almost believe him.

"Well, what about later this afternoon?"

He shook his head.

"Tomorrow?"

"No."

"Then *when*, for Chrissake?"

"I'm afraid I can't say."

"What the hell do you mean, you can't say? Look in the book!"

"I already have."

Now I was mad enough to belt the old wreck. "You're trying to tell me you're booked so solid you can't work in one lousy haircut?"

"I'm not trying to tell you anything."

He was feeble-minded, he had to be. I decided to lay off the yelling and humor him. "Look, Eddie...you're a businessman, right? You run this shop for money. Right?"

"Right," he said, still smiling.

"Okay. You say you haven't got an opening. I believe you. Why should you lie? No reason. It just means you're a good barber. You've got loyalty to your customers. Good. Fine. You know what that is? That's integrity. And there isn't anything I admire more than integrity. You don't see much of it in my business. I'm an agent. But here's the thing, Eddie—I can call you Eddie, can't I?"

"That's my name."

"Here's the thing. I wouldn't have you compromise your integrity for anything in the world. But there's a way out. What time do you close?"

"Five pm."

"On the dot, right? Swell. Now listen, Eddie. If you could stay just half an hour after closing time, until five-thirty, no later, I could bring Shecky in and he could get his haircut and everybody would be happy. What do you say?"

"I never work overtime," he said.

"I don't blame you. Why *should* you, a successful businessman? Very smart, Eddie. Really. I agree with that rule a hundred percent. Never work overtime. But, hear me out, now—there's an exception that proves every rule. Am I right? If you'll stretch a point here, this one time, it'll prove the rule, see, and also put some numbers on your savings account. Eddie, if you'll do this thing, I will personally see to it that you receive one hundred dollars."

"I'm sorry," he said.

"For a half-hour's work?" A cockroach ran across the wall. Eddie watched it. "Two hundred," I said. It was still fifty bucks shy of what Shecky was paying Mario every week, whether he worked or not, but I figured what the hell.

"No."

"Five hundred!" I could see it wasn't any good, but I had to try. A soldier keeps on pulling the trigger even when he knows he's out of bullets, if he's mad enough, or scared enough.

"I don't work overtime," the old man said,

A last pull of the trigger. "One thousand dollars. Cash."

No answer.

I stared at him for a few seconds, then I turned around and walked out of the shop. Shecky was standing where I'd left him, and he was looking at me, so I put on the know-nothing face. As I walked toward him I thought, he's got to dump me. Any agent who can't get Shecky King an appointment with a crummy Third Avenue barber deserves to be dumped.

"Well?" he said.

"The guy's a nut."

"You mean he won't take me."

"I mean he's a nut. A kook. Not a soul in the place and, get this—he says he can't find an opening!"

You ever see a man melt? I never had. Now I was seeing it. Shecky King was melting in front of me, right there on the sidewalk in front of the tattoo parlor.

"You okay?"

He couldn't answer. The tears were choking him.

"Sheck? You okay?"

I saw a cab and waved it over. Shecky was trying to catch his breath, trying not to cry, but nothing worked for him. He stood there weaving and bawling and melting. Then he started beating his fists against the brick wall.

"God damn it!" he screamed, throwing his head back. "God damn it! God damn it!"

Then, suddenly, he pulled away from me, eyes wide, hands bleeding, and broke into a run toward the barbershop.

"Hey," the cabbie said, "ain't that Shecky King?"

"I don't know," I said, and ran after him.

I tried to stop him, but you don't stop a crazy man, not when you're half his size and almost twice his age. He threw the door open and charged inside.

"Eddie!" His voice sounded strangled, like a hand was around his throat, cutting off the air. Or a rope. "Eddie, what have I got to do?"

The old man didn't even look up. He was reading a newspaper.

"Tell me!" Shecky pounded the empty barber chair with his bloody fists.

"Please be careful of the leather," the old man said.

"I'm a success!" Shecky yelled. "I qualify! Tell him, George! Tell him about last night!"

"What do you care what this crummy—"

"*Tell him!*"

I walked over and pulled the newspaper out of the old man's hands. "Last night Shecky King was voted the most popular show business personality of all time," I said.

"Tell him who voted!"

"The newspaper and magazine critics," I said.

"And who else?"

"Thirty million people throughout the world."

"You hear that? Everybody. Eddie, don't you hear what he's saying? Everybody! I'm Number One!"

Shecky climbed onto the chair and sat down.

"Haircut," he said. "Easy on the sides. Just a light trim. You know." He sat there breathing hard for a couple of seconds, then he twisted around and screamed at the old man. "Eddie! For God's sake, cut my hair!"

"I'm sorry," the old man said. "I don't have an opening at the moment."

YOU KNOW what happened to Shecky King. You read about it. I knew, and I read about it, too, six months before the papers came out. In his eyes. I could see the headline there. But I thought I could keep it from coming true.

I took him home in a cab and put him to bed. He didn't talk. He didn't even cry. He just lay there, between the Hong Kong silk sheets, staring up at the ceiling, and for some crazy reason that made me think of the legless guy and the sign that said WALK. I was pretty tired.

The doctors ordered him to a hospital, but they couldn't find anything wrong, not physically anyway, so they called in the shrinks. A breakdown, the shrinks said. Nervous exhaustion. Emotional depletion. It happens.

It happens, all right, but I wasn't sold. Shecky was like a racing car, he operated best at high revs. That's the way some people are engineered. A nice long rest is a nice long death to them, because it gives them a chance to think, and for a performer that's the end. He sees what a stupid waste his life has been, working 24 hours a day so that people can laugh at him, or cry at him, running all the time—for what? Money. Praise. But he's got the money (if he didn't he wouldn't be able to afford the rest) and he's had the praise, and he hasn't really enjoyed what he's been doing for years—is it intellectual? does it contribute to the world? does it help anybody?—so he figures, why go on running? Why bother? Who cares? And he stops running. He gives it all up. And they let him out of the hospital, because now he's cured.

A lot of reasons why I didn't want this to happen to Shecky. He wasn't my friend—who can be friends with a multitude?—but he was an artist, and that meant he brought a lot of happiness to a lot of people. Of course he brought some unhappiness, too, maybe more than most, but that's the business. Talent never was enough. It is if you're a painter, or a book writer, maybe, but even there *chutzpah* counts. Shecky had it. Like the old story, he could have murdered both his parents and then thrown himself on the mercy of the court on the grounds that he was an orphan. And he could have gotten away with it.

The fact is, the truth is, he didn't have anything *except* chutzpah. His routines were written by other people. His singing was dubbed. His albums were turned out by the best conductors around. His movies and TV plays were put together like jigsaw puzzles out of a million blown takes. His books were ghosted.

But I say, anybody who can make out the way Shecky King made out, on the basis of nothing but personality and drive, that person is an artist.

Also, I was making close to a hundred grand a year off him.

What's the difference? I wanted him to pull out of it. The shrinks weren't worried. They said the barber was only "a manifestation of the problem." Not a cause. An effect. It meant that Shecky felt guilty about his success and was trying to reestablish contact with the common people.

I didn't ask them to explain why, if that was true, the barber refused to cut Shecky's hair. It would only have confused them.

Anyway, I knew they were wrong. Shecky was in the hospital because of that old son of a bitch on Third Avenue and not because of anything else.

All the next day I tried to piece it together, to make sense out of it, but I couldn't. So I started asking around. I didn't really expect an answer, and I didn't get one, until the next night. I was working on a double scotch on the rocks, thinking about the money we would be making if Shecky was at the Winter Garden right now, when a guy came in. You'd know him—a skinny Italian singer, very big. He walked over and put a hand on my neck. "I heard about Sheck," he said. "Tough break." Then, not because he gave a damn about Shecky but because I'd done him a few favors when he needed them, he asked me to join his party, and I did. Another double scotch on the rocks and I asked if he'd ever heard of Eddie the barber. It was like asking him if he'd ever heard of girls.

"Tell me about it," I said.

He did. Eddie had been around, he said, forever. He was a fair barber, no better and no worse than any other, and he smelled bad, and he was creepy; but he was The End. I shouldn't feel bad about not knowing this, because I was one of the Out people. There were In people and Out people and the In people didn't talk about Eddie. They didn't talk about a lot of things.

"Why is he The End?" I asked.

Because he only takes certain people, my friend said. Because he's selective. Because he's exclusive.

"I was in his shop. He had a lousy wino bum in the chair!"

With that lousy wino bum, I was told, three-fourths of the big names in show business would trade places. Money didn't matter to Eddie, he would never accept more than a dollar. Clothes didn't matter, or reputation, or influence.

"Then what *does* matter?"

He didn't know. Nobody knew. Eddie never said what his standards were; in fact, he never said he *had* any standards. Either he had an opening or he didn't, that was all you got.

I finished off the scotch. Then I turned to my friend. "Has he ever cut *your* hair?"

"Don't ask," he said.

I had a tough time swallowing it until I talked to a half-dozen other Names. Never mind who they were. They verified the story. A haircut from Eddie meant Success. Until you sat in that chair, no matter what else had happened to you, you were nothing. Your life was nothing. Your future was nothing.

"And you go for this jazz?" I asked all of them the same question. They all laughed and said, "Hell, no! It's those other nuts!" But their eyes said something different.

It was fantastic. Everybody who was anybody in the business knew about Eddie, and everybody was surprised that I did. As though I'd mentioned the name of the crazy uncle they kept locked in the basement, or something. A lot of them got sore, a few even broke down and cried. One of them said that if I doubted Eddie's pull I should think about the Names who had knocked themselves off at the top of their success, no reason ever given, except the standard one. I should think about those Names real hard. And I did, remembering that headline in Shecky's eyes.

It fit together, finally, when I got to a guy who used to know Shecky in the old days, when he was a 20th mail boy named Sheldon Hochstrasser. He wanted to be In more than he wanted anything else, but he didn't know where In was. So he stuck close to the actors and the directors and he heard them talking about Eddie. One of them had just got an appointment and he saw that now he could die happy because he knew he had made it. Shecky was impressed. It gave him something to work towards, something to hang onto. From that point on, his greatest ambition was to get an appointment with Eddie.

He was smart about it, though. At least he thought he was. You don't get a good table at Chasen's, or Romanoff's, he said to himself, and to his buddy, unless you're somebody. For Eddie, he went on, you've got to be more. You've got to be a *success*. So the thing to do was to succeed.

He gave himself fifteen years.

Fifteen years later, to the day I'll bet, I met him at that bar on Third Avenue. Either he'd been thinking about Eddie all that time or he hadn't thought about him at all. I don't know which.

I turned the tap up, then, because he wasn't getting any better. I found out the ones who had made it and talked to them, but they weren't any help. They didn't know why they were In or even how long they'd stay. That was the lousy part of it: you could get canceled. And putting in a word for Shecky wouldn't do any good, they said, because Eddie made his own decisions.

I still had a hard time getting it down. I'd been around for fifty-four years and I hadn't met anything like this, or even close to it. A Status Symbol makes a little sense if it's the Nobel Prize or a Rolls-Royce, but a *barber!* Insanity, even for show business people.

I started out with money and didn't make it, but that didn't mean he didn't have a price. I figured everybody could be bought. Maybe not with dollars, but with something.

I thought of the calendars on the wall. They're supposed to be for the customers, but I wondered, are they? You never knew about these old guys.

I found the wildest broad in New York and told her how she could earn two grand in one evening. She said yes.

Eddie said no.

I told him if he'd play along, I'd turn over a check for one million dollars to his favorite charity.

No.

I threatened him.

He smiled.

I begged him.

He said he was sorry.

I asked him why. Just tell me why, I said.

"I don't have an opening," he said.

Two weeks and two dozen tries later, I went back to the hospital. The Most Popular Show Business Personality of All Time was still lying in the bed, still staring at the ceiling.

"He'll give you an appointment," I said.

He shook his head.

"I'm telling you, Sheck. I just talked with him. He'll give you an appointment."

He looked at me. "When?"

"As soon as he finds an opening."

"He won't find an opening."

"Don't be stupid, Sheck. You're just nervous. The guy's busy all the time. I was there. He's got people lined up halfway down the street."

"Eddie's never busy," he said.

Christ, I had to try, didn't I? "I was there, Sheck!"

"Then you know," he said. "Eddie's kind of customer, you don't get many. Just a few. Just a few, George." He turned his head away. "I'm not one of them."

"Well, maybe not now, Sheck, but some day. You can talk to him… Ask him what he wants you to do. I mean, he's got to have a reason!"

"He's got a reason, George."

"What is it?"

"Don't you know?"

"No! You've stepped on a few heads, sure, but who hasn't? You don't get to the top by helping old ladies across the street. You've got to fight your way up there, everybody does, and when you fight, people get hurt."

"Yeah," he said, "you know," and for a second I thought I did. I sat there looking at him for a long time, then I went out and got drunker than hell.

They called me the next morning. I was in bad shape but I had my suit on so it only took fifteen minutes to get to the hospital.

It was a circus already. I pushed through the cops and the reporters and went into the room.

He was still lying on the bed, still staring up at the ceiling, looking no different from the way I'd left him. Except for the two deep slashes in his wrists, the broken glass, and the blood. There was a lot of that. It covered the Hong Kong silk sheets and the rug and even parts of the wall.

"What made him do it?" somebody said.

"Overwork," I said.

The papers played it that way. Only a few guys knew the dirt, and they were paid for, so Shecky was turned into a martyr. I forget what to. His public, I think. I have most of the clippings. "In his efforts to bring joy to the people of the world, The King went beyond the limits of his endurance; he had gone beyond ordinary human limits long before..." "He had no ambition other than to continue entertaining his fans..." "Following the old show business motto, 'Always leave 'em laughing,' Shecky King departed this world at the height of his popularity. No other performer has ever matched his success..." "He is a legend now, the man who had everything and gave everything..."

I don't think about it much anymore.

I just lie awake nights and thank God that I'm bald.

THE CARNIVAL
(1988)

The cool October rain and the wind blowing the rain. The green and yellow fields melting into gray hills, into gray sky and black clouds. And everywhere, the smell of autumn drinking the coolness, the evening coolness gathering in leaves and wheat alfalfa, running down fat brown bark, whispering through rich grass to tiny living things.

The cool rain, glistening on earth and on smooth cement.

"Come on, Lars, I'll beat you!"

"Like fun you will!"

Two boys with fresh wet faces and cold wet hands.

"Last one there is a sissy!"

Wild shouts through the stillness and a scrambling onto bicycles. A furious pedaling through sharp pinpoints of rain, one boy pulling ahead of the other, straining up the shining cement, laughing and calling.

"Just try and catch me now, just try!"

"I'll catch you all right, you wait!"

"Last one there is a sissy, last one there is a sissy!"

Faster now, flying past the crest of the hill, faster down the hill and into the blinding rain. Faster, small feet turning, wheels spinning, along the smooth level. Flying, past outdoor signs and sleeping cows, faster, past strawberry fields and haystacks, little excited blurs of barns and houses and siloes.

"Okay, I'm going to beat you, I'm going to beat you!"

A thin voice lost in the wind.

"I'll get to the trestle way before you, just watch!"

Lars Nielson pushed the pedals angrily and strained his young body forward, gripping the handlebars and singing for more speed. He felt the rain whipping through his hair and into his ears and he screamed happily.

He closed his eyes and listened to his voice, to the slashing wind and to the wheels of his bicycle turning in the wetness. Whizzing baseballs in his head, swooping chicken hawks and storm currents racing over beds of light leaves.

He did not hear the small voice crying to him, far in the distance.

"Who's the sissy, who'll be the sissy?" Lars Nielson sang to the whirling world beside him and his legs pushed harder and harder.

His eyes were closed, so he did not see the face of the frightened man. His ears were full, so he did not hear the screams and the brakes and all the other terrible sounds. The sudden, strange unfamiliar sounds that were soft and quiet as those in his mind were loud.

He pushed his young legs in the black darkness, harder, faster, faster...

THE ROOM was mostly blue. In the places where it had not chipped and cracked, the linoleum floor was a deep quiet blue. The walls, specially hand-pattered, were soft greenish blue. And the rows of dishes on high display shelves, the paint on the cane rockers, the tablecloth, Mother's dress, Father's tie—all blue.

Even the smoke from Father's pipe, creeping and slithering up into the thick air like long blue ghosts of long blue snakes.

Lars sat quietly, watching the blue.

"Henrik." Mrs Nielson stopped her rocking.

"Yes, yes?"

"It is by now nine o'clock."

Mr Nielson took a large gold watch from his vest pocket.

"It is, you are right. Lars, it is nine o'clock."

Lars nodded his head.

"So." Mr Nielson rose from his chair and stretched his arms. "It is time. Say goodnight to your mama."

"Goodnight, Mama."

"Goodnight."

"So."

Mr Nielson took the wooden bar in his big hands and pushed the chair gently past the doorway and down the hall. With his foot he pushed the door open and when they were inside the bedroom, he pulled the string which turned on the electric light.

He walked to the front of the chair.

"Lars, you feel all right now? Nothing hurts?"

"No, Papa. Nothing hurts."

Mr Nielson put his hands into his pockets and sat on the sideboard of the bed.

"Mama is worried."

"Mama shouldn't."

"She did not like for you to be mean to the dog."

"I wasn't mean."

"You did not play with it. I watched, you did not talk to the dog. Boys should like dogs and Mama is worried. Already she took it away."

Lars sat silently.

"I'm sorry, Papa."

"It isn't right, my son, that you should do nothing. For your sake I say this."

"Papa, I'm tired."

"Three years, you do nothing. See, look in the mirror, see at how pale you are getting. Sick pale, no color."

Lars looked away from the mirror.

"I tell you over and over, you must read or study or play games."

"Play games, Papa…?"

Mr Nielson began to pace about the room.

"Sure, certainly. Games. You can, you can make them up. Play them in your head. You don't have to run around and wave your arms to play games!"

Lars looked down, where the carpet lay thin and unmoving.

"But you do nothing. All day I work, and *hard* I work, lifting many pounds, and I come home tired. All day I use my arms and feet and back and I do not want to anymore, when I come home, so I don't. I sit in the chair and read. I *read*, Lars, and I smoke my pipe and I talk to Mama. I sit still, like you, but I do something!"

With Mr Nielson's agitated movement, the room started to pick at the Feeling. Lars concentrated on white.

"And it don't take my arms and legs to do it. They are tired, they are every way like yours. I am you at night, Lars. And I am old, but I don't sit with nothing. I am always playing games, *in my head*. I don't move, but I don't worry Mama who loves me. I don't move, but I don't say nothing to my Mama and Papa, ever, just sit staring!"

"I'm sorry, Papa."

"Yes, for *yourself* you are sorry! You are sixteen years old and should be thinking about how to live, how to get along when Papa is no more here to take care of you and there is no money."

"Yes, Papa."

"Then begin to think, Lars. When I come home at night, let me see you talking to Mama, planning things with your brain. The big men are big because of their brains, my son, not their arms and legs. Nothing is wrong with your brain, you didn't hurt it. You have time to learn, to learn anything!"

"I will begin to think, Papa."

Mr Nielson rubbed his hands together. They made a rough grating sound.

"All right. Tomorrow you tell Mama you are sorry and want to play with the dog. She will get it back for you, and you should smile and thank her and talk to the dog."

"I—I can go to bed now?"

"Yes."

Mr Nielson leaned forward and slid one arm behind Lars's back, another beneath his legs.

"We are not like others," he said slowly. "When I am gone, there will be nothing, no money. Don't you see why you got to—are you ready?"

Mr Nielson lifted Lars from the wheelchair and laid him on the bed. He sucked on his pipe as he removed shirt, trousers, stocking, shoes, and underwear; grunted slightly as he pulled a faded tan nightgown over heavy lengths of steel and rubber.

Then he smiled, broadly.

"You should say big prayers tonight, my son. You have worried Mama but even so, tomorrow is a surprise."

Lars tried to lift his head. Father stood near the bed, but in the corner, so the big smiling face was hidden.

"Tomorrow, Papa?"

"I tell you nothing now. But you are a young man now, nearly, and you have promised me that you will begin to think. Isn't that what you promised, Lars?"

"Yes."

"So. And I believe you. No longer coming home to see you sitting with no thoughts. I believe you and so, tomorrow you get your reward. Tomorrow you will see happiness and it will clear your head; then you will be a man!"

Lars stopped trying to move his head. He closed his eyes so that he would not have to stare at the electric lightbulb.

"Hah, but I don't tell you. Say *big* prayers, my son. It is going to be good for you from now on."

"I will say my prayers tonight, Papa."

"Goodnight, now. You sleep."

"Tell Mama—that I'm sorry."

Mr Nielson pulled the greasy string and the room became black but for the coals in his pipe.

Lars waited for the door to close and Father's footsteps to stop. Then he moved his lips, rapidly, quietly, fashioning the prayers he had invented. To a still, unmoving God, that he could stay forever in the motionless room, to fight the Feeling. That he could think of colors and nothing and keep the Feeling—the feet across meadows, the arms trembling with heavy pitchforks full of hay, all the parts of life—in a small corner in a far side of his mind.

Lars prayed, as Father had suggested. His head did not move when sleep came at last.

"YOU DID not tell him, Henrik?" Mrs Nielson rocked back and forth in the blue cane chair, breaking green beans into small pieces and throwing the pieces into an enamel washbasin.

"No."

"He never was to one—there never was one in Mt Sinai since I can remember."

"Once when I worked for the fruit company it came here but we were very busy and I could not go."

"Henrik, do you think, will it *really* be good for him?"

"Good? Mama, you do not know. When I went to that one in Snohomish I did not have a job to work or money. I just went to look and I didn't spend anything. But there was all the people, everybody in the town, and all laughing. Everybody, laughing. And so much to see!" Mr Nielson began to chuckle. "Shows and machines and good livestock like you never saw. And funny, crazy people in a tent. Oh Mama, when I went home I was happy too. I didn't worry. Right after, I got a job and met you!"

Mr Nielson slapped his knees.

"How many? Twenty years ago, but see, see how I remember! Lars will be no more like this when he sees all the laughing. He will come home like I did. But I didn't tell him. He don't know."

A cat scratched at the screen and Mrs Nielson rose to open the door. She sniffed the air.

"Raining."

Mr Nielson took up his newspaper.

"Henrik, he can't go on the rides."

"So? I went on no rides."

"What can he do?"

"Do? He can see all the people laughing. And he can see the shows and play with the dice—"

"No!"

"Mama, he is sixteen, almost a man. He will play with the dice, he will say, and I will throw them. And he will see the frogs jump. And I will take him to the tent with the funny people. The brain, Mama, the *brain!* That is what enjoys the carnival, not arms and legs. That is what will make Lars understand."

"Yes, Henrik. We must cheer him up. Maybe after, we can bring him the dog and he will play with it."

"Sure, certainly, he will. He will be happy, not alone in this house, feeling sorry for himself."

"Yes."

"It will start him to think. He will think about how to make for himself a living, like anybody else. And he will read books then, you'll see, and find out what he wants to do. With his brain!"

Mrs Nielson paused before speaking.

"Henrik."

"Yes?"

"What *can* he do, like you say, with his brain, without arms and legs?"

"He has arms and legs!"

"As well not, as well no back, no body."

"Hilda! He *must* do something, something. Look at that blind woman who can't hear, like we read in the magazine—she did something. Can't you see, Mama, can you not understand? I would take care of Lars, even if it is wrong. But you know the railroad will give only enough for you when I die, and I am not young. We married late, Mama, very late. If Lars does nothing, how will he live? Is it an institution for our boy, a home for cripples where he sees only cripples all day long, no sunshine, no happiness? For Lars? No! At the carnival tomorrow he will see and begin to think. Maybe to write, or teach or—something!"

"But he has not been from the house, since—"

"More reason, more!"

Mrs Nielson broke beans loudly. Kindling crackled in the big cast-iron stove.

"This blind woman you say about, Henrik. She has feet to walk."

"Lars has eyes to see."

"This woman has hands to use."

"Lars has ears to hear, a brain to think, a tongue to talk!"

The cat scratched sharp sounds from the linoleum.

Mrs Nielson rocked back and forth.

"This woman has money and friends. She never saw or heard, she cannot remember."

Mr Nielson went to the sink and drew water from the faucet, into a glass. He drank the water quickly.

"So, then Lars has a heavier cross and a greater reward."

"Yes, Henrik."

"You will see, Mama, you will see. After the carnival, he will know what he wants to do. He will begin to think."

Mrs Nielson rose and dusted the bean fragments from her lap, into the washbasin. She picked up the cat and went outside onto the porch. Then she returned and snapped the lock on the door.

"Maybe you are right, Henrik. Maybe anyway he will like little dogs and talk to me. I hope so, I hope so."

Mr Nielson wiped his hands on the sides of the chair and listened to the rain.

LARS FELT his body pushed by strong invisible hands, felt himself toppling over like a woolen teddy bear onto Father's shoulder. He bit his lip and closed his eyes.

Mr Nielson laughed, applying the brake.

"There now, the turn too sharp, eh Lars? I will be more careful."

The car began to move again, more slowly, jerking, rattling. Lars looked out the windshield at the fields and empty green meadows.

"Papa, is it far?"

"Hah, you are anxious! No, it is not far. Maybe five miles, right over the bridge."

"Will we have to stay long?"

Mr Nielson frowned.

"I told Mama we would be back before dark. Don't you want to go, after what I told you, after what you said?"

Two children playing in a yard went by slowly.

"Don't you want to go, Lars?"

"Yes, Papa. I want to."

"Good. You don't know, you never saw anything like a carnival, never."

Lars closed his mouth and thought of colors. The children touched his mind and he thought of the blue dishes in his home. He opened his eyes, saw the pale road and thought of black nothing. Wind came through the open windows, tossing his brown hair and clawing gently at his face and he thought of the liquid green in a cat's eyes.

Mr Nielson hummed notes from an old song, increasing pressure on the accelerator cautiously. Soon the road became a white highway and other cars went whistling by. Signboards appeared, houses, roadside cafes, gasoline stations, and little wooden stands full of ripe fruit.

And then, people. People walking and leaning and playing ball and some merely sitting. Everything, whirling by now in tiny glimpses.

Lars tried to force his eyes shut, but could not. He looked. He looked at everything and pressed his tongue against his teeth so the Feeling would stay small in his mind. But the meadows were yards now, and they were no longer quiet. They moved like everything in them moved.

And the people in the automobiles, laughing and honking and resting their elbows out the windows.

When he saw the girl on the bicycle, Lars managed to pull his eyelids down.

"Oh, such a beautiful day, Lars! Everyone is going to the carnival. See them!"

"Yes, Papa."

The car turned a corner.

"Different than all alone in a cold room, eh my son? But, see—there, there it is! Oh, it's big, like when I went. Look, Lars, this you have never seen!"

Lars looked when his eyes had stopped burning.

First, there were cars. Thousands and millions of cars parked in lots and on the sides of the highway and wherever there was room, in yards, gasoline stations, the airfield. And then there were the people. So many people, more than there could be in the world! Like ants on a hill, scrambling, walking, moving. Everywhere, cars and people.

And beyond, the tents.

"Oh, Mama should have come, she should have come. Such a sight!"

The old car moved like a giant lobster, poking in holes that were too small for it, pulling out from the holes, seeking others. Finally, beneath a big tree in a yard, stopping.

Mr Nielson smiled, opened the back door and pulled the wheelchair from the half seat. He lifted Lars and put him in the chair and stood for a moment breathing the air and tasting the sounds.

"Just like before, only even better! You will enjoy yourself!"

Lars tried to feel every rock beneath the wheels and every blade of grass. He turned his eyes down as far as he could, to see the earth, but he saw his body. The sounds grew louder and as he glided on the smoothness he began to see beyond the crawling, moving people. It all grew louder and Father's voice faster so Lars cut off the Feeling and returned to the bottom of the ocean.

The hard-rubber wheels turned softly on nothingness...

HEYHEYHEYHEY HOW about you, Mr? Try your luck, test your skill, only ten cents for three balls... Now I'll count to five, ladies and gentlemen, and if one of you picks the right shell, you win a Kewpie Doll... All right, sir, your weight is one-fifty-three, am I right?... Right this way, folks, see the wonders of the Deep, the dangerous shark and Lulu the Octopus... The Whirlagig, guaranteed to scare the yell out of you... Fun, Thrills, and Excitement, only twenty-five cents on the Flying Saucer... Fresh cotton candy... Spooktown, Spooktown, ghosts and dragons and lots of fun, ten cents for adults, a nickel for the kiddies... How about you, Mr?...

Lars kept his eyes still, but the Feeling was there. It was small at first and he could think yet of colors and beds that did not move. But it was growing, in the shape of baseballs and bicycles and gigantic leaps, it was growing.

Mr Nielson took his eyes from the iron machine and turned the crank until it clicked. The sign read Secrets of the Harem and Mr Nielson sighed.

He put the huge ball of pink vapor to Lars's mouth and Lars put his tongue about the gritty sweet.

"Ah ah ah, you are happy, I can see, already! What shall we do now? The fish, we will look at the fish!"

Peculiar grey creatures swimming in dirty water in a big glass tank.

"Now you wait here for Papa."

Father stuffed into a small box and the box falling fast down a thin track, then up and later down again. Screams and laughter and movement. Movement.

"Watch, you see. I'll break the balloon!"

Pop! And a plaster doll covered with silver dust and blue paint.

Inside for the thrill of the century, ladies and gentlemen, see Parmo the Strong Man lift ten times his own weight...

A man with a large stomach and moving muscles, pulling a bar with a black ball at either end, hoisting the bar, holding it above his head. Laughs and cheers.

Yahyahyahyah! See her now, folks, the most gorgeous, the most beautiful, the most (ahem!) shapely little lass this side of Broadway. Egyptian Nellie, she's got curves on her yahyahyahyah...

"Lars, you wait—no, you don't. It wouldn't be right."

The candy and the peanuts and the little dirty faces. The rides and the planes and the exhibits and the penny arcades. The stale, excited odors and the screaming voices. And the movement, the jerking, zooming, swooping, leaning, pushing, running movement.

Last one there is a sissy, last one there is a sissy...

"Good, good, good. Mama should be here! But now we must eat!"

An open arena, with fluffballs of red and yellow and green hanging from the ceiling. On the floor, popcorn and peanut shells and wadded dirt.

"It's all right, Lars, it's good meat. Maybe not like Mama makes, huh? So. Open your mouth."

The people's eyes, staring, pitying, a million eyes, and hums of voices in the colored restaurant. Then a kind of quiet, like sharp prongs in the Feeling. In the little Feeling, coming awake.

"Now, so? You are finished. No, the milk, the milk to make you strong."

Off out of the arena, back into the movement.

And out into the very heart of the shining motion.

Lars stopped fighting. He let his eyes see and his mind fill.

Last one there is a sissy and Father seated in a small car, bumping the car into others and howling. First one to the trestle and the slow circling ferris wheel with the squealing dots.

Just try and catch me, just try...

"Come now, Lars, we rest."

The horror in the washroom and out again, feeding the Feeling, sending it along the spiral. The music bellowing and even in the little car in the blackness of the Fun House—movement there. Sudden lights on painted monsters, cotton bats squeaking along invisible wires.

And then—

Here we go, folks, the experience of a lifetime. Yah yah hear! See 'em all—the Frog Man, Queenie the Fat Girl (three hundred pounds of feminine loveliness!), Marco the Flame-Eater, yah, yah, all inside, all inside...

"Come, Lars, after this we will go. But if it is like last time—you never saw anything like it. Funny-looking crazy people. It's good, good."

And as a special attraction, ladies and gents, we have Jackie the Basket-Case. No arms, no legs, but he writes and plays cards and shaves, right before your very eyes. Science gave him up as lost, but you'll see him now. Jackie, the Basket-Case. And the headless girl, who defies doctors throughout the universe! Nurses in attendance! Heah heah heah! Only ten cents, the tenth part of a dollar.

Square canvas flags with strange pictures on them. A man with a sword in his mouth, a woman with an orange beard, a ferocious black man with feathers. And in front, high on the platform, a man with a striped shirt and a cane, hitting a pan.

"So, we go in."

Lars said nothing. He listened to all the sounds and how they seemed like the swift rush of cold wind and rain across his face. His heart beat and his blood pounded against his temples.

I'll beat you, Lars…

Lars felt his chair being pushed forward. Out of the sunlight and quickly into the dimly lighted interior, he could see nothing at first. Only what he had been seeing for hours.

There was the sudden quiet, for one thing. Nothing to see yet, but like dropping from a close, hot hayloft to freshly watered earth. Damp and cool, like perhaps a grave.

The Feeling stopped growing for a moment as Lars focused his eyes. He wondered where all the people had gone, what had happened, if he were back in the silent unmoving room. The cold stillness and then the soft muttering of voices, strange and out of place.

"Here, Lars, don't you see?"

Mr Nielson ran his hand though Lars's hair and touched his shoulder. The chair moved over plowed ground.

"Papa, what—"

Mr Nielson giggled no louder than the other people in the tent.

"Ha ha! Look, boy, look at the woman!"

Lars saw the object that Father had called a woman. The product of mutant glands, a huge sitting thing with mountains of flesh. Flowering from the neck down the arms and looping over the elbows, dividing like a baby's skin at the hands; the thighs, cascading flesh and fat over the legs down to the feet. And over all this, a metallic costume with purple sequins attached and short black hair, cut like a boy's.

"Have you ever seen anything so big, Lars!"

Lars looked from his wheelchair into the eyes of the fat lady and then quickly away from them.

Over the ground. Stopping.

The sign reading The Frog Man, and four people staring.

"Look! Ohhh!"

Shriveled limbs with life sticking to them. Shriveled, dried-up, twisted legs, bent grotesquely. And the young man with the pimples on his face crouching on these legs, leering. Every few moments, the legs moving and the small body hopping upwards.

Lars tried to shake his head. The Feeling started from where it had left off, but it traveled elsewhere now. It traveled from his mind to his eyes and from his eyes outward.

"Come, it will be late. We must see everything. Oh, look, have you ever seen such a crazy thing!"

Lars leaned his head forward painfully and looked.

The face of a very old man, but smooth along the creases and over the wrinkles. Wrinkled hands, thin hair. An old man standing three feet from the ground. But not merely small. Everything dwarfed. The false beard and the gnome's cap and the stretched-gauze wings.

The Feeling went into the eyes of the midget.

"There, over there! There was no such last time!"

Over the ground slowly, past the man with the pictures on his skin, the black creeping thing, the boy with the breasts, slowly past these, slowly so the Feeling could be fed and gathered.

And now, the Feeling reaching across the tent to the other side, reaching into the woman with seventeen toes, the boy with the ugly face, the alligator girl, the human chicken, reaching and bringing back, nursing, feeding, identifying. Identifying.

Then ceasing.

"Lars, look. Never was there such a thing."

Mr Nielson's voice was low and full of deep wonder as he craned his head over the people's shoulders.

Lars tried one last time to see the blue of the linoleum, the gray of his room, all the quiet things his mind had made so carefully. But his eyes moved.

I**T WAS** large, made of wicker, padded and made to look like an egg basket on the outside. There was in front of it a square card with writing, which gave dates and facts, but the card was dirty and difficult to read. The thing in the basket lay still.

A knitted garment covered the midsection and lower part. Above, the pale flesh stretched over irregular bumps and lines, past the smooth arm sockets on up to the finely combed black hair, newly barbered.

The face was handsome and young, clean-shaven and delicate.

When it lifted, Mr Nielson and the other staring people gasped.

In the mouth was a pencil and with this pencil, the thing in the basket began to write upon a special pad of paper. The lead was soft so that those nearby could make out the words, which were "My name is Jack Rennie. I am very happy."

Lars saw his father's hands about his side, lifting and pushing.

"Look, see what it does!"

Lars's body trembled, suspended above the basket, held in air. Everything trembled and shook, as teeth held a moving pencil and the pencil made words. The limbless man thought, it—he—*thought...*

The automobile came straight at Lars, and he saw it now. Saw it speeding over the trestle for him, bellowing its warning. The brakes screeched in his head and he saw the car swerve and career in the wet road. And then floating down the trestle, below it, onto sharp hard things.

Lars looked from his wheelchair at the armless, legless man in the cheap basket and in one explosion, the thoughts sprang from the Feeling and scattered through his brain, moving, dancing, swinging arms, jumping on legs, moving, moving with all the ecstasy of a dead child brought suddenly to life.

"It shaves, sees, talks, it writes!"

Lars rode his bicycle in the sunlight down through the fields near the river and never stopped, for he was never tired. He rode past laughing people and waved his arms at children blurring in the distance. He pushed his young legs on the pedals and flew past all the things of the country and then of the world, all the things best seen from the eyes of a young boy on a bicycle.

The thing in the wicker basket ceased to exist. The grinning gasping people ceased to exist and Father was someone sitting in a chair, smoking his pipe.

Lars had reached the crest of Strawberry Hill and he lifted his feet, drifting and floating downward, letting the wind and rain and sunlight whirl past.

Mr Nielson gently pulled Lars back in the wheelchair and rolled silently from the darkened tent into the afternoon.

The people were sparse. They straggled by hoarse vendors and still rides, yawning and shuffling.

Mr Nielson forgot about the tent and began to talk.

"Well, we go home now. All day at the carnival, what, my son? Ah, Lars, I tell you, Mama should not have stayed home. Now you feel good, you will be a fine man and think, eh Lars?"

Mr Nielson picked leaves from overhanging branches as he walked, feeling good and pleased.

When he got into the car, he looked at his son's eyes.

"Lars, there is nothing wrong? You don't look like you feel so good."

Lars was going too fast to hear Father, the wind was shrieking too wildly. The green hills turning golden, the leaves from orange to white, and all the boys and girls riding behind him, chasing, trying to catch him.

He turned, laughing. *"Who's the sissy now, who's the sissy now!"*

Mr Nielson scowled.

"You'll never catch me, you'll never catch me!"

"What, what is that you say?"

Lars sang into the wind as the children's voices grew faint. He waved his arms and pedaled with his legs and saw the beautiful hill stretching beneath him.

"You just watch, you just watch!"

The beautiful hill sloping gracefully downward and without an end.

THE CRIME OF WILLIE WASHINGTON

(1988)

The second after Willie Washington put his knife in George Manassan's stomach, he knew he'd done a bad thing. But all the demons in Hades put together couldn't have made Willie run or lose his head, so he stood around very quiet, waiting to see what would happen. He figured deep inside his head that he'd done an evil deed, although he wasn't exactly sorry. George had told tales about Cleota, and as far as Willie knew, there wasn't a man alive who'd stand for another man telling tales about his wife. He wasn't sorry and he wasn't glad and there was a sharp thing eating at his insides, sharper than the knife that had cut George.

Willie waited for a considerable time, but George only groaned and wheezed. And since the blood didn't stop oozing out over the rug, Willie finally decided that he must do something. He put on his hat and walked quickly down the street until he came to an apartment like his own.

He knocked hard on the door, several times.

The old woman who opened the door was very withered and dried up with the years, but when she heard the news she moved faster than she had for quite a while. She flew about the rooms, gathering all the clean rags she could find and muttering under her breath and Willie had to trot to keep up with her when she hobbled out the door and back up the street.

When they got to the room, however, there was no sign of George Manassan except for the blood left on the rug and floor.

The old woman looked around and when she was convinced that George had left, the fear in her face disappeared.

"You cut him deep, boy?" she asked.

"No'm, Aunt Lucy, I didn't. I don't think he got hurt too bad," Willie answered.

Then Willie went to the sink and wet a large cloth. He bore down and managed to get the blood off the floor, but it wouldn't come out of the rug.

"You send that to the cleaners, boy. You never get that out alone."

The old woman sat down and breathed heavily. Her face and arms were shiny with perspiration.

Cleota got off work at the bakery at eleven-thirty and when she got home Willie told her everything that had happened. She said she was sorry and that she thought Willie had done right.

Aunt Lucy later learned that Doctor Smith was the one who fixed up George. She was more relieved than she let on, to hear that the wound had been a minor one; and she sermoned to Willie and to Cleota for months afterwards when she was positive that George had left town.

Now this was the only bad thing Willie ever did in his entire life, up to the time the policemen came to put him in jail for something else, so he didn't forget it right away. He didn't miss a day on his job and he didn't spoil his record by doing poor work, but most of the fellows on the line noticed that Willie Washington was not quite himself again until almost a half year had passed. It was then that he forgot about cutting George Manassan and that Cleota once more took up smiling at men in the bakery.

It was a great surprise to Willie when they shook him out of bed and carried him off to jail.

THE NIGHT was sticky and hot but the pillow hadn't turned damp yet. It was soft and cool and he sank into it gratefully. Cleota was already asleep, silent, as always, like a cat. Willie had never slept with anyone else so he had the impression that only men snored. It struck him as a very masculine thing.

He finished his prayers to the Lord and fell into a pleasant languor that soon turned into sleep.

The sound of voices outside in the hall was not disturbing because there were frequently voices in the hall. Willie had gotten used to lovers' good nights and sleepless women's babble as a soldier gets used to sleeping amid gunfire. He didn't even hear the door tried and opened.

What did awaken Willie finally was a rough hand on his shoulder, pressing hard and shaking. He heard the voice halfway through consciousness.

"Come on, you're not kidding anybody. Get the hell out of that bed."

And when he came to completely he saw three men in his room, two of them with flashlights and the third with a gun in his hand. He did not understand.

The men were all white. They were very energetic looking men, with sharp chins and unblinking eyes. There was no hesitation.

The one with the gun pulled Willie to his feet.

"Okay, let's go, fella."

Cleota awakened with a nasal little cry. She clutched the sheets to her breasts and said nothing.

"Go where?" Willie's mind was not clear.

The man with the gun looked over his shoulder and laughed.

Willie looked angry. He didn't understand, but he knew he didn't like these men. He hated to be called a nigger in Cleota's presence.

The man with the gun grabbed Willie's undershirt and twisted it in his hand. He turned his head towards the door and took out a police credential.

Willie started to move, but the gun was pushed into his stomach. The two other men edged closer.

So Willie turned his eyes to Cleota and got dressed quickly. The men kept their flashlights on even though Cleota had switched on the lamp.

In a short time Willie was shoved into the waiting police car and taken to the city jail. He was then put into a moderately crowded cell.

No one told him exactly what he was supposed to have done, but through constant questioning he learned that he was being held for the rape and murder of a white girl. He didn't know why they had thought of him, but he did know what the charges meant. He thought and thought and could provide no good proof of where he actually had been at the time of the crime.

He had been home, reading, but of course no one would believe that.

Cleota came to see him whenever she could and so did Aunt Lucy. They both made him feel good, though it was actually Aunt Lucy who gave him hope.

During the long days before the trial she would say to him, "Willie, it's bad trouble but they won't hurt you. We both know you ain't done nothin' wrong, an' when you don't do nothin' wrong the law can't hurt you. You gonna be all right, boy. You gonna get out of this all right."

And Willie would smile until one day he stopped being afraid. He was offered a lawyer but he said he didn't want one. He ate well and looked forward to the day of the trial, because he felt sure that would be the day they would let him go.

All this time he made prayers to the Lord that he'd get his job back and that he would be forgiven for hating the people around him and the people who came to ask him deep questions he couldn't figure out. Then he stopped worrying about his job and didn't hate.

And whenever he would get confused, Aunt Lucy would come by and say, "Now rest easy, boy. Everything gonna be all right. You a innocent boy and the law ain't gonna hurt you," and he'd smile and feel good again.

When the day of the trial came at last, Willie sat in the courtroom without a fear or a doubt. He thought of the stories he'd be able to tell the gang on the Line when he went back to work, so he didn't hear much of the proceedings.

They asked him where he was on the night of the crime and he told the truth. "I was at home, readin' a magazine, your Honor," he said. They asked him other questions and the tall man in the gray suit talked so fast and so loud Willie couldn't hear him clearly. Only the words "society" and "justice" sounded so that he could hear.

And after a time, the people in the brown stall filed back to their seats. Willie folded his hands and craned his head to hear what would be said.

"...do you find the defendant: guilty or not guilty?"

Willie wasn't nervous. He kept grinning, wondering whether or not to look back at Cleota.

"We find the defendant guilty, your Honor."

The words were spoken slowly and clearly, but with some emotion. The thin man with the furrowed face who spoke the words looked directly at the judge and then sat down.

Willie wanted to scream but then something pierced his stomach and held his insides tight. He couldn't move or say a word. Confusion swam in his head, in great hot waves. He rose with difficulty when commanded.

"...sentence you, Willie George Washington, to the supreme penalty prescribed by law..."

These words were a haze out of which only one came clearly. *Dead*.

"...to be hanged by the neck until you are dead..."

Willie struggled and pulled out the thing in his heart. He screamed.

"No, your Honor, you don' understand! I didn't kill nobody! I didn't do nothin' wrong! I'm innocent, your Honor!"

And two men had to hold Willie's arms and pull him back to his cell.

No one paid much attention to the old Negro woman who cried "No, Lord!" or the young one who smiled strangely.

IT WASN'T easy for Willie, but he had plenty of time to think and so after a while he started to smile again. Aunt Lucy was able to see him upon occasion during the months and Cleota came by a respectable number of times. They both said that everything would be all right.

And since Willie had been conceived of the strongest hope there is—a woman's hope—it took only the merest spark to ignite his courage. He told himself that he had not for a moment lost his faith in the ultimate rightness of things, not even in the courtroom that day he was told solemnly he must die for a crime he did not commit.

And so the days passed and Willie grew stronger instead of weaker, all the while certain that the Lord would not permit him to be wrongfully punished.

So it was that on the morning designated as the time of execution Willie spoke lightly with the somber-looking man in the black frock coat who wore such a long face.

"Reverend," Willie said, "I knows your intentions is good, but they ain't really much sense in your being here."

And the Reverend shook his head and opened his book.

"No sir, Reverend, they ain't nothin' gonna happen to me. It say so right here in the Good Book—here, let me show you the place where it say—"

And Willie took the book and thumbed quickly through the pages.

"Y'see, Reverend, the Lord say it: 'As ye sow, so shall ye reap.' It put different in your book, but it mean the same thing."

The man in the frock coat sighed.

"But my son, you have been proven guilty of the sin of murder."

Willie grinned.

"Yes, sir, but they got that wrong. It wasn't me what did that to that little girl. You gots to be honest bad 'fore you can do a thing like that! And Aunt Lucy can tell you—I ain't honest bad, Reverend. I studied hard all I could, when I was a kid, and I been workin' for the railroad since I was thirteen. Never missed a day—up to this, I mean. Never missed a Sunday at church, neither. An' I got me a good woman too. No sir, I jus' never did this thing, Reverend, and you knows the Lord ain't gonna cast me down for somethin' I never did."

The man in the frock coat looked perplexed as he studied Willie's face. The prayers he said were not the ones he had previously considered, nor could Willie hear them.

Not too long afterward other men came and walked with Willie down a long hall and into a small yard. The sun was shining but the yard was dark with shadows. The cement was clean and smelled of soap and water.

The men led Willie up some steps and to a small door out onto the planks. Directly above dangled a rope, the end of which had been formed into a noose. The rope was sturdy and strong; the fibers were close and smooth.

They asked Willie if he had anything to say and he told them yes, he did.

"You folks is really wastin' your time," Willie said. "I told you, I never did nothin' wrong and the Lord ain't gonna let you hurt me."

Then a man walked up and fitted a black cloth bag over Willie's head. After that he pulled down the rope and put the noose about Willie's neck. The noose was tightened somewhat.

No one could see, but Willie was still smiling. He couldn't think clearly about anything except what Aunt Lucy had told him. Her words roared in his ears and he knew that they couldn't be wrong.

Willie waited. He didn't know what he waited for, but he waited. A long time he stood, with the handcuffs heavy on his wrists, but nothing happened.

All was silent and then, as suddenly as if it had always been, loud with the hum of voices. Words Willie couldn't hear, words that pierced the air, words that were filled with fear and awe.

After a long while the bag was taken off and Willie was led back to his cell. Later he learned what had happened, why everyone had looked so strange. The lever that controlled the trapdoor had been pulled but the trapdoor had remained fixed. It did not fall away, allowing the body that stood upon it to sink into the yielding air. It did not suddenly become the mouth of death, which was its function. The trapdoor simply had not worked. And this was strange because it had been tested according to routine a few minutes before the actual time of execution, and stranger still because it operated with the greatest efficiency a few moments after Willie was taken from the platform.

Willie thanked the Lord and thought they would set him free, but he was wrong. Someone told him that they would try to hang him again, and Willie shrugged and said that it was very foolish.

It was Aunt Lucy who told him the laws of the state, which required a man condemned to death to be subjected to three attempts at execution before he be freed. The old woman whose face looked older and more withered than ever Willie had known it to be, still spoke confidently and Willie believed her. The Lord would not desert him now.

When he asked about Cleota he received answers he somehow didn't like, although they meant nothing in themselves. He put it aside and continued to write her letters. The answers were cheerful and evasive and so Willie was not disturbed.

He spent his time praying, in between executions.

And when it came time for them to try to hang Willie again, the same somber man in the frock coat dropped into the cell to mumble; the same walk and the same tiny yard. The same dark shadows, but a different rope and a more thoroughly oiled trapdoor mechanism.

Willie got up to the scaffold unhesitatingly. He was stood to one side as the trapdoor was tested for good measure. He watched it drop swiftly and saw the blackness below, without relaxing his smile. Then the hood was fastened securely.

A man started to say, "Any last words," but he stopped. The man nodded to the executioner.

And when the lever was pulled all the way back, a great murmur went through the crowd. The trapdoor had not moved.

Some time later, Willie read in the newspaper about how he was fooling death but, of course, he knew that was wrong. They didn't understand. They didn't understand that the Lord protects his own and that an innocent man can't die for something he didn't do.

Time passed slowly after this. And when he realized that he had been a prisoner for over a year, Willie became bored and restless. His prayers became routine and he wished mightily that they would hurry up with whatever they were going to do, so he could get back to his job and wife. Aunt Lucy told him he looked tired these days and he agreed with her.

Cleota wrote more frequently and visited more frequently now that they had tried to hang Willie twice already. It scared her, but only this far. She found it remarkably easy to lie to Willie now, so the sacrifice was not a great one. She had fallen in love with a number of people since her husband was first put in jail. A man named Frank Jones wanted her to go to Detroit with him. She was considering it.

Time crept, the boredom of the minutes filling Willie with a grow-ing urge to leave the prison and have it all done with. The game had lost its amusement; it was like waiting interminable hours on a street corner for someone you know will show up, eventually.

So he finally stopped praying and thanking the Lord and began to pace restlessly in his cell. Even the newspaper reports had lost their inter-est. Everything had lost its interest, except getting out. Willie thought and the more he thought the more he wanted to have this foolishness over.

Sometimes he thought about his job; relived pleasant hours when work was not so hard. He'd had the job for seventeen years, and although he'd never risen in rank, neither had he ever been docked or rolled.

And he thought about stories of poor Negroes constantly out of work and how nobody would hire you if you were black. He didn't believe it. He was black and he had a job. He was black and he had a wife. What else, he wondered, could there be in life?

Time dragged, stood still, waited, inched, stopped.

Then the day arrived, the day Willie so longed for: his last execution.

The attendant delicacies were hurried this time and somewhat embarrassed. The man in the frock coat had refused to come and so another man like him came instead. Willie listened politely to the Last Prayers, but he was feeling too good to really hear them. Aunt Lucy had seen him the afternoon before and he hadn't noticed the fear in her eyes. He had only heard the kind, happy words that came from the friendly face. He knew them by heart now, every word and every nuance.

"You gonna be home little while, boy. They gonna let you go and you gonna be home. The Lord has taken care of his young lamb."

The yard was filled with many people this time. It was a special occasion; rules were relaxed. Many had notebooks open and pencils in their hands. Some looked afraid—those faces he recognized, they looked afraid. Others looked interested or expectant.

There was a slight breeze, so the rope swung gently backward and forward from the scaffold. Its shadow on the wall was many times enlarged and grotesque.

When Willie came in, everyone stopped whispering. There was absolute quiet, the quiet that is born of a beating heart. Willie grinned widely and tried to wave his hands so they could see.

He knew the way by now. He knew how many steps it was from the door to the platform of the scaffold. He knew the moment the hood would be lowered. Willie smiled at the blackness as the trapdoor was dropped five times. He smiled at the executioner, but the executioner didn't smile back.

Then the long wait. Through the coarse black cloth over his head, Willie heard the frightened gasps and the sharp little cries. He heard someone say:

"My God, it didn't work! It didn't work!"

He was carefully led from the platform back to his cell. He remembered to thank the Lord and then he went back to sleep.

The following week Willie was told exactly when he would be released, and until that time he found many interesting things to read in the newspapers.

AUNT LUCY and the men from the newspapers were waiting for Willie the day he walked out of prison a free man. Many pictures were taken of him and many questions asked and Willie was polite to everyone. But when he would ask Aunt Lucy where Cleota was, Aunt Lucy would turn her head and someone else would say something. After a time, Willie got worried and told the people he would talk with them tomorrow.

When he got home, Willie learned that his wife had left him. He didn't grasp it at first. Cleota had run off with a man named Frank Jones. She had left him.

Aunt Lucy remarked that she never did care much for Cleota and had told Willie so the day he married her. She reminded him of George Manassan and asked him why he had never blamed Cleota. But whenever Aunt Lucy would say anything bad about Cleota, Willie would tell her to be quiet. He wanted to think.

Alone in his room, he lay on the bed and wept. He understood why he had felt strange about those letters and why he had put the feeling aside. Cleota would never sleep with him again; she would never come back.

He fought the tears until his eyes hurt and then he slept.

The next morning he rose early, put on the clothes that had hung in the closet for almost a year and a half and took a bus to his work terminal.

The sight of the huge ornate building restored Willie's spirits. He forgot about Cleota. This was the other of the two important things in his life; he proposed to marry himself completely to his job now.

The foreman shook his head at Willie.

"Sorry, fella, but the Line's full up now. Union tightening up…letting off help…sorry."

The foreman had to talk a long time to convince Willie that he had no job. The big man, with his black arm-sleeves and green head shield, was puzzled that anyone could have the nerve to ask for a job after an absence of a year and a half. That a murderer could expect to have his job back.

Willie walked out of the building slowly, trying to put things together in his head. He asked the Lord what had happened, but the answer was indistinct. He boarded the bus and got off before it started. He walked the three miles to Aunt Lucy's apartment.

The old woman was crying.

"Boy, I don't know 'zactly what could he'p you now. You got no job and you got no wife. But you got to live, 'cause that's what the Lord say you got to."

And Willie knew she was right. He had to live.

He went home and put on his suit. It was wrinkled where it had draped across a wire hanger, but it still had class. Willie had never worn it much, but he always felt good in it. He put on his flamingo tie and polished his shoes with an old shirt. He sat down to decide what to do.

He walked down Government Street and entered an S.P. ticket office. He asked for a job and was quickly refused.

He went to every ticket office, steamship, railroad, and freight line in the city. He didn't pause to eat. At nightfall, when he returned home, there were smiling newspapermen waiting for him. He admitted them and talked politely.

"...you got to live, boy..."

The next day he went to garages, filling stations, and miscellaneous stores. He went through the factories and warehouses, to the Civil Service building and to the employment agencies. He was not even asked to fill out forms.

"...there isn't a thing for you..."

"No use to fret, Willie Washington, you had it good most of your life. The Lord took good care of you. You just got to scrounge a little now..." was what Willie said to himself.

He went to large office buildings, printing shops, frame makers, construction companies, the city hall, grocery stores.

Some grimaced at him, most recognized him from the pictures in the paper. But no one gave Willie a job.

He went to Aunt Lucy and she just told him to keep looking.

He put an ad in the paper, he answered all the ads. He went to janitors and street cleaners, to airports and railroad stations.

He walked until his feet hurt and turned numb to pain. And when he looked at his money he started to become a little frightened. But he didn't stop walking and he didn't stop talking.

And then one day, when the newspapermen had had enough of Willie's story and he was left entirely alone, Willie sat in his room a whole day, thinking. He asked the Lord numerous questions and waited for the answers that did not come. He looked in his pockets and saw that his money was nearly gone.

He remembered the looks of hate on people's faces when they saw him, how they whispered when he left. He had done nothing, and had proven it, but he began to see that there was no one who believed him. No one but Aunt Lucy.

Everyone thought that he had actually killed that little girl. Didn't they realize that he would have been hanged, that his neck would have been broken and that he would have died, if he'd been guilty?

Or did they care...?

For the first time in his life, Willie Washington really hated. He hated the people who hated him; he hated everything around him. He had forgiven them and their wrong, but they would not forgive him his innocence! Hate surged and churned in his heart. It did not have time to mature. It was now and it was full-grown.

Aunt Lucy was afraid. She sensed in her old heart what had happened, so she got out of bed and went over to Willie's room.

She said, "Boy, you got to get that look out of your eyes. It ain't good."

And Willie said, "But they won't give me work an' I'm runnin' out of money."

They sat.

Then the old woman looked very deep inside Willie's heart and she left in fear. It had dried up in her but she recognized the budding shoot. She remembered it and how it had conquered her. But she had been a woman, and Willie a man, and that is why she was afraid.

Willie didn't say very much to anyone the next day. He'd ask for a job and he'd be refused and he'd walk out, looking so grim and confused people would stare.

The black flower began to press his throat and his breast, so that he shook when he asked the question, defeatedly, under his breath.

"Lord, it ain't right what you're doing to me. I been good and look at me! I got no money, no job, no wife... And it wouldn't none of it a happened if you hadn't put me in that jail. Why'd you let it happen, O Lord!"

Willie had a mind full of confusion, a mind full of angry hornets.

When he heard the white woman say, "There's the murdering nigger they couldn't hang," hot vomitous acid rose in his throat and eyes and he went back home.

He spoke directly to the Lord.

"It ain't been right, you *know* it ain't been right! My money's all gone, Lord, an' I can't get anymore! What am I gonna do? Tell me, Lord, 'cause Willie Washington, he's slippin'."

He waited, hunched and silent, for an answer that did not come.

He waited for sleep, but that didn't come either.

He thought of the little murdered girl, who lay in the rain with a cruel cross carved in her stomach.

"What about the man what did that, Lord? Is you punishing *him*? Why do you gots to punish me—what did I do? Lord, tell me, tell me, WHY! If I knew that then it'd be all right, but I don't know! I don't know why!"

Willie raised his voice and called into Heaven.

"Why, Lord God?"

Then he tore at his shirt and rolled on the dirty bed, sobbing and moaning. The night went and the day came, but Willie did not sleep. He was hungry and tired.

He walked out the door, feeling dirty.

People stared at him, whispered at him and around him.

"Aunt Lucy! What am I gonna do? I got no money! You got money?"

"No, boy, you know that. I got twenty-seven cents. Here, take that. And let me fix you a little food. Boy, you look poorly!"

Willie fell in a chair and put the cereal to his mouth.

"Aunt Lucy, what do the Lord say to you?"

"He been kinda quiet lately, boy."

"The Lord ain't with me, Aunt Lucy. He against me!"

"Hush now! Don't you let me hear you talk like that. That's you daddy's blood talkin'! The Lord works in wonderful ways, boy, don't you know that?"

"He wouldn't get me a job."

"He kept 'em from hangin' you, didn't He?"

Willie put his head on the old woman's breast.

"Now don't that mean somethin', Willie boy?"

Willie cried.

"No, it don't! It don't mean nothin'!"

Willie straightened and went out of the room quickly. The old woman called for him to come back, then she fell on her knees and cried to the Lord.

Willie almost ran to his room. He looked through two dresser drawers and got his small pocketknife. He looked at it for only a few moments, remembering how he had cut a human being and why he had cut a human being.

The black flower covered him. He was full: his stomach and his heart and his soul were full.

He put it in his pocket and went into the street.

"Lord, remember. You left me. You did it. Wasn't me left you!"

Willie walked all the way to the railroad tracks without knowing why. He sat in a small clearing until it got dark, thinking. About the faces and the mouths and breathing hot that the Lord had left him.

Then he walked on down the tracks, hating. He walked for miles, walked till his legs refused to move. He took out the knife, opened it, and looked at the blade.

He walked back into town and hid behind a warehouse. He held the knife tightly and perspiration coursed down the handle.

Willie waited and he was afraid he knew what he waited for, this time. The whole world started to pound in his ears and his body shook.

And then the tears came. They fell from his eyes as if they would never stop, and he turned his back to the street, weeping onto the wooden slats of the warehouse. The knife dropped to the ground and as it struck, Willie knelt with both knees on the cement.

"Lord, Lord God, I'm sorry. I'm sorry. I'm sorry! I'll not leave you again, not ever again!"

Willie walked back to Aunt Lucy's. And when the old woman saw his face, she smiled broadly. The vise around her neck relaxed and she felt young again.

"Well, boy, you get the hate cut out of you!"

"Yes'm."

"You ain't no different from any of us, boy. It jus' come to you late, that's all. You never saw what you was, boy, that was your trouble."

Willie looked up and smiled.

Aunt Lucy hurried to fix coffee.

"You know, Willie boy, we mus' be the Lord's favorites, 'cause we got the biggest cross of all to carry. You know what I'm talkin' about, boy?"

"Do you suppose the Lord'll forgive me, Aunt Lucy?"

"I kinda think He will. He's a mighty understandin' person."

Then Willie began to laugh and the old woman laughed with him.

They laughed for a long time.

THE MAN WITH THE CROOKED NOSE
(1988)

He was very small. And, he was invisible. Or almost: there and not there, existing and not existing—like a shadow just before the lights come on, or a face you see in the window of a speeding train, or birds at midnight. He lived in the corner of your eye. Turn around, quick! and stare and—he's gone, he's somewhere else.

After a while I stopped trying to find him. It made things easier. In at nine: "Good morning, Mr Gershenson!" (a quick silent grin from the little man); out at six: "Good night!" (the same) and repeat. A few requests: bring that set of Dickens up front, please; don't forget to dust the A secton, will you?—Nothing more.

And it seemed to work all right. Actually, it didn't. Because he was there and we worked together, eight hours a day, and it isn't very pleasant, ever, to give orders to a man who is twice your age and then watch him jump and run like a monkey set on fire. Yet so quietly.

He was always running. Even when he swept up, as though his life depended on it—Switch! Switch! with the broom down the aisles, getting the dirt off the floor. Switch! billowing it over all the books, and then off, fast, to another chore. I never saw a man work with such speed. Or so hard. Or do such a poor job—poor Martin, and he had the world's easiest. An idiot could have done it better.

The others got a big kick out of him. They called him "Pop"— although he wasn't very old: maybe fifty, maybe sixty, no older—and they pulled fancy gags, thought out days in advance, planned in secret conclave. Once Berman called from New Books downstairs and asked for Martin and double-talked until he had the little man shaking. They laughed at him all day long.

It wasn't easy not to laugh, I suppose. He was pretty funny; right from the first, from the day Steinberg hired him. In a lot of ways: the quick-padding Mandarin's walk he had, feet barely touching the floor; the outsized mixed-up clothes he wore; and all those boxes and phials and bottles of medicine! It seemed that every time you looked, he was popping a pill into his mouth or swigging cough syrup. Which is funny to watch, although I didn't feel much like laughing, somehow. He was always so intense about it. As if he thought, if I don't take all this medicine, I'll die, almost certainly. I'll catch a horrible disease and die.

And that made you wonder—well? Why should he want to stay alive to the point of fighting death every five minutes? An old man with most of his years behind him, and what is he now? A stock boy in a bookstore, without a hope of anything better.

But he didn't frown any oftener than he smiled. He just worked. Gently and quickly and poorly and quietly—always quietly: I never heard him speak a word, then. It gave rise to the rumor that he was a mute, but I don't think anyone actually believed that.

Maybe it was his eyes that kept me wondering. It probably was, at first, because there wasn't anything else. They were so bright beneath those black-clumped John L. Lewis brows, so bright and full. While he fumbled about like the wrong machine for the wrong job, I watched his eyes, and sometimes they seemed about to fly loose from their sockets and sometimes they rested there like milk-glass marbles, looking beyond the shelves and beyond the walls.

Of course, after a few weeks the newness wore off. We all got used to Martin's quick little movements and his silence. Business picked up over the holidays, so there wasn't much time for finding him. Gradually, pieces floated in. Not many, not enough to make a picture—but some.

For one thing—and we should certainly have guessed it—Martin had been in America only a few months. The reason he never talked was that he hadn't learned English; he could understand it, but not speak it. And the fact that he was a foreigner explained, for almost everybody, the other peculiarities.

The "Pop" label stuck. As the days passed, he melted into a fixture, like the rest of us, as if he'd always been with the store, ever since it was built. I covered his mistakes and didn't push and he smiled good morning and good night and that was that. We had a funny little foreigner working in Used Books. He was quiet. He took medicine. He put in his hours. That's all we knew, that's all we needed to know.

But I was the one who worked with him. I was the one who saw his eyes. And "that" couldn't be exactly that, with me.

I went back on the hook when I first heard his music. It was near closing time and we were alone. He was pulling books from the F section, I was pricing some Americana. I could see his short little monkey's body scrambling up and down the ladder, and in the dusty murk between aisles, the whiteness of his skin was like white wax. Especially then, climbing, he reminded me of a newsreel I'd once seen of some man who had lived in a cave for a year, without any of the civilized comforts, and who had then been brought before the cameras, shaved and bathed, hair combed but not yet cut, cheeks scrubbed—nervous and unnatural, a little terrified and colorless as a slug.

It was very quiet and still that afternoon.

Then, suddenly, Martin began to hum. It surprised me, I don't know why exactly, but it was as if he had just ripped off his shirt and turned around and showed me his wings; or an extra pair of arms. I was careful not to look up: I knew there wasn't anybody else upstairs.

The melody swam through the heat and dust. But it wasn't ordinary humming, not at all. Each note was hit accurately and the piece was continued from its beginning to its end. When the notes got too high, or too low, he simply switched octaves. And it sent a shiver through me, because what he hummed was Beethoven's *Sonata Pathétique.* Right straight through, transposed beautifully.

After a pause it began again, this time the fugue from Bloch's *Concerto Grosso.* And then some Bach I couldn't recognize.

This little man, who couldn't even put a book on a shelf right, who ran around like a half-killed chicken, like a scared mouse, singing to himself now, his eyes lost completely—they couldn't *actually* belong to the sad bundle of wet sticks and white skin!—this little man, singing and humming, so powerfully, so lovingly, that you forgot about him and you heard the music as it was written, the pianos, the violins, the flutes; and you heard every note, every note.

I never let him know that I heard, of course. I just listened, and whenever there were no customers, he would start. Today, "In the Hall of the Mountain King"; tomorrow, "Adoramus te Christe"; the next day, "Liebestod." Giant music and small music, Beethoven and Chopin, Mussorgsky and Janequin and Mozart and Mendelssohn.

Finally, I couldn't take it any longer. I wormed a lunch out of Steinberg, the boss, and I pumped him, discreetly. It was disappointing, in a way… I'd hoped for more. In another way, it was not so disappointing.

Steinberg told me about how Martin Gershenson had once been the leading music critic for a newspaper in Germany.

About how he had once been married and how, one day, he and his family had been carried from their home and put into different concentration camps; and how Martin had escaped and learned, much later, that his wife and his two children had been executed.

How he had wandered the cities of the Earth, afterwards…

From music critic to stock boy. I began trying to find him again, and once I tried whistling, something by Rachmaninoff. I got halfway through. He didn't pause for a moment. But he stopped singing.

Dust carefully, Martin! Go unload that shipment of Rand McNally's, please, Martin! Don't forget to turn out the lights!

A smile, a jump, a running.

And a little reproachful look in those eyes, asking me why, why did I have to take his music away from him?

Gently and quietly—maybe once or twice a murmured, "Schnell? Oh, ja ja!" Gently and quietly, as quaint and funny as Geppetto, a funny character out of the comic pages, always rushing, taking the jokes of others, and smiling only at the children who came up with their mothers.

When he learned a little English, we tried him on a few customers. But he got red and frightened and nervous, and the cash register terrified him—he wouldn't touch it—so we had to take him off the job. He didn't complain.

And I kept wondering, why? With eyes like those, why was he so beaten and so frightened, so willing to fit any mold like hot lead?

"Don't *worry*," they used to say to me. "Forget it—he's happy. Leave him alone."

So I did.

Until I heard his music again. Something by Bloch, slow and full of sadness. He twisted each note and squeezed it and wrung out its sadness.

Outside, the rain washed over our thin roof like gravel. I was listening to the rain and to Martin's music, and thinking, when I heard the heavy footsteps on the stairs. At the same instant, Martin Gershenson quieted, and there was only the sound of those footsteps, slow and heavy.

The man wasn't unfamiliar to me: he'd been in a couple of times before, I remembered dimly. Now he wore a thick checkered overcoat, soggy with rain, and a wet gray hat.

"Yes, sir," I said to him. "Can we help you?"

"Perhaps," he said. There seemed to be a slight accent; that, or his English was too perfect. "I am looking for a nice set—I mean in good condition—of Eliot. George Eliot. Do you have that?"

He was a large person, thick-handed and rough-fleshed. Chinless, the neck fat drooled over his collar and swung loosely. His lips were dry and white and seemed joined by membrane when closed. But I think it was his nose that made me dislike him. Crooked, set at an angle on his face as if not quite tight on a pivot, the bridge broken and mashed against the white fat of upper cheeks. His eyes were merely eyes, soft as eggs. Perhaps a trifle small.

"I'll see," I said. Then I called, "Martin! Would you please see if we have a mint set of Eliot?" By this time the little man could understand English quite well.

"Ja—" His feet padded quickly over the floor, stopped, turned, were still.

The man was smiling. "Personally," he said, "I think the old lady is very funny, but there is a friend of mine that fancies her. A woman friend, of course. You know?"

Martin came running. Halfway across the room, he stopped. He appeared to stare, for a moment.

"We do not have this in stock," he said to me.

"No Eliot at all?" I asked.

"No," he said, paused another second, staring, and then went rushing back down the aisle into the back.

The big man was chuckling. "Well," he said, "perhaps no Eliot at all is the better present to my friend!" He thumbed through one of our special hand-tooled copies of *Tristram Shandy*.

"I'm sorry, sir," I said. "We're usually not so low in stock. But if you'd care to leave your name and address, we'll let you know when it—"

"It's all right," the man said, not lifting his eyes from the book. "I will come in again some time."

"If there's anything else we can do for you..."

"Sangorsky," he said. "Good leather." His fat hands rubbed the red morocco binding.

"Yes. As you can see, we have the book marked at a considerable reduction—"

"You don't have this Eliot that I want, do you?"

"No sir. But, I tell you what. We can order it and it would only take a few days. Why don't you let us have your name and address and we'll contact you?"

He walked about examining the books. Then he lit a cigarette.

"Pencil," he said.

I gave him a pencil and he wrote down his name—John S. Parker— and his address.

"Yes, sir, we'll let you know the minute—"

"All right. You let me know." He pulled down a large Skira volume, glanced at it, put it back. He rubbed his nose. "It is wet out," he said.

"It sure is. Not bookstore weather."

"You let me know, young man."

He turned and went down the stairs.

It was soon very quiet again, except for the rain.

Martin was padding about in the back. Slowly; not fast, like always before.

I thought about the look on his face when he had caught sight of the new customer, about the man's strangeness, his accent; I thought about concentration camps.

Then, suddenly, I knew. I knew beyond all doubt.

Martin had found what he was looking for.

Later, at home, I built the story in my mind. I dressed it up, gave it plot and structure.

I even wrote the newspaper headline:

MAN BRUTALLY SLAIN IN APARTMENT!

And the picture, not a good one, but clear enough to make out the fat face and the crooked nose.

I composed the story with a sick feeling, the feeling you get when you hear of the death of someone you know—not necessarily a friend— just anyone you've ever seen or spoken with.

A man identified as John S. Parker was found dead in his apartment at 734 No. Sweetzer early yesterday evening by his landlady. Parker was the victim of a brutal attack by an unknown assailant. According to the police report, he was hacked fifty-three times with an ax about the face, neck, and chest. There were evidences of other atrocities: cigarette burns about the legs and armpits, deep bruises in the abdominal region. No motive for the crime known...

Later reports—it was Sunday: I had plenty of time to construct the drama—revealed further information. The murdered man's name was not John Parker. It was Carl Haber. And he was in America illegally. Hiding. Because he had once been Colonel Carl Haber, and he had once run the show at one of the smaller concentration camps in Germany—one of the missing cogs in that well-oiled machine, the Third Reich. Missing until now.

The papers had the full story for their evening editions.

Haber, né Parker, had slipped into the country by the kind offices of a friend in Venezuela. He had some money. He loved books. He had taken an apartment, a small bachelor's, and lived the quiet life of a retired businessman, a widower, perhaps.

And this man with the crooked nose and the fat neck had waited for the world to forget about the millions of human beings he had helped consign to the lime kilns and the brick ovens and the shower rooms with hot-and-cold running carbon monoxide.

But somebody hadn't forgotten.

One of the city's sensational sheets got ahold of a picture of Haber's body. You couldn't look at it for long.

It was impossible to believe that one man could have had the strength or the fury or the hatred to do what was done to Haber.

The blood-smeared thing in the photograph—I saw it as clearly as if I had been holding it in my hand—wasn't human. It was a pile of carrion, like a dog after a truck has run over it, or like meat that's been picked over by hawks.

And the unknown assailant... Who could tell?

I thought of nothing all day but this one thing, of Martin, little ineffectual Martin, with his musician's hands bloody, the vengeance out of him.

Next day I scrutinized the papers. They told of a disaster at sea. They spoke of senators and dogs and starlets. But they did not speak of John S. Parker.

Well, I thought, not even aware of my disappointment, well, perhaps he's biding his time. Perhaps tomorrow.

Things were the same at work. I recall that I considered that ironic—that things should be the same. Martin was there as usual, not smiling, not frowning, hurrying up and down the aisles of books with his broom, hurrying just as fast as his short legs would carry him— Switch! Switch!—and the dust clouds after him, plumed and rolling. Martin, with his clown's suit and his bushy brows and his bright ferret's eyes caught in their pasty prisons...

Outside, it was raining, the same rain that had fallen when "John S. Parker" came to buy his set of Eliot. It was a gravel-spray on the roof, a steady monotonous dripping, drumming.

"Good morning, Martin," I said.

Stop; turn; silent smile; then, quick, back to the sweeping.

Somehow, I don't think I was surprised to hear him sing—although I ought to have been surprised. He did, softly, from the back of the store. Melodies in a minor key, sad, haunting, and so full of these things that when the customers came in they stopped and looked up from their books and listened, strangely moved.

All day he sang, as he might breathe. The second movement for the *Eroica*, the Allegretto from the Seventh Symphony, Bloch and Dvorak and Tchaikovsky and Mahler, over and over, while he worked.

And I wanted to go to him and shake his hand grimly and tell him that I knew and understood, understood completely, and therefore did not blame him. I wanted to let him know that he could trust me. I would betray his secret to no one, and John S. Parker's unknown assailant would remain unknown, forever.

But, of course, I didn't say these things. I merely waited, watching the little man, listening to him, studying his face to see if it would give any hint of what lay beneath. I thought of him with the ax in his hands, swinging the ax, repaying the beefy German in full.

And the day wore on.

Next morning I got the first paper off the stand. I'd spent a sleepless night, tossing, arguing that it was better this way; that I must not call the police and spoil things.

But there was nothing in the paper. Or in any other paper.

And the next day was the same.

I decided then that Parker's body had not been discovered yet. That was the answer. It was lying crumpled where Martin had left it three days ago! So I suffered through the hours and drove straight to the address Parker had given me.

It was a small stucco apartment, neat, old, respectable.

I knocked on the door, trembling.

John Parker opened the door. "Yes?" he said, his voice heavily accented. "Yes?"

"We have a lead on those Eliots," I said. "I happened to be passing by and thought you might like to know."

"Thank you, young man. That was nice. Thank you."

I looked at him as one would at a corpse suddenly brought to life, his wounds made well, his torn flesh whole.

Then I went home and tried to laugh.

But laughing is a lonely thing when you've no one to share the joke. So I went back outside and drank whiskey until I couldn't think about the little man.

Next day Martin didn't show up for work. He called up and said he was sick.

He never came back.

But John Parker did. The big man with the crooked nose still comes up to browse through the books, every now and then. I chat with him: he even calls me Len now. But I don't like him. Not a bit.

Because he makes me think of Martin. Because he makes me wonder if I'd been so wrong, after all, if my imagination had run quite so wild.

Perhaps Martin did find what he had been looking for. And perhaps, once finding it, he had decided it was not worth having, or that he lacked the strength to keep it. And perhaps John S. Parker is something more than John S. Parker.

And perhaps not.

I'm afraid I'll never know. But I'm also afraid that I'll never forget the little man with the bright eyes and the hurrying feet and the sad face.

I hope he's still taking his medicine, wherever he is.

THE WAGES OF CYNICISM
(1999)

ou say you believe in ghosts," said Jeremy Didge, snorting. "Do you know what you're actually saying? That you believe in life after death, in the survival—ectoplasmically speaking—of the so-called human spirit. But a dismal sort of survival, isn't it, gentlemen? Having to spend eternity clanking chains and roaming through churchyards and floating about in drafty old houses." He grinned wolfishly at his two friends. "Why not believe in witches, too, while you're at it? They make as much sense. Or leprechauns. What about it, Wilson? Seen any leprechauns lately?"

"No," said Wilson, staring down glumly into his glass.

Dodge hawked loose a subaqueous laugh and pounded his thigh. "Demons!" he roared. "Poltergeists! Genies! *Fairies!* Eh, Kagan? Fairies?"

"Don't joke," said Kagan, frowning.

"Oh, but I'm not! I'm simply pointing out the absurdity of your notion. Don't you see? Open one door and you've opened them all. Admit the existence of even one ghost and you must chuck everything we've learned in all these thousands of years. Are you prepared to do that, either of you?"

Wilson looked up from his drink. "I don't know about any of that," he said. "I only know that there is a ghost in the Spring Hill cemetery."

"Oh, really, Wilson! *How* do you know? Have you seen it?"

"No. But I have it on good authority—"

"'Good authority!'" Dodge rolled his eyes. "In other words, you believe in the after-life because a friend of a friend of a friend had an uncle whose gardener claimed to have seen a spook."

"Not at all," said Wilson angrily. "My information comes directly from—"

"But it doesn't matter, my dear fellow. If all the deans of all the universities in the world were to tell me such a story, I should still regard it as nonsense."

Kagan took a sip of his drink. "And if you were to see it with your own two sober, cynical, scientific eyes, what then?"

"Then," said Dodge, calmly, "I should revise my thinking. However, it isn't very likely, now, is it?"

"That depends entirely upon your courage."

"I beg your pardon?"

"As it happens," said Kagan, "I am the good authority Wilson was about to cite. I have seen this ghost. Of course you will say that I was suffering from an hallucination, that I am so fearful of death that my mind manufactures reassurance of immortality."

Dodge shrugged.

"Nevertheless," said Kagan, "I do not believe that you have the strength of your lack of convictions. In the long run, I doubt that you'll do it."

"Do what?" demanded Dodge.

"Spend the night at Spring Hill cemetery, alone."

"Are you serious?"

"You believe in what you can see and feel and touch," said Kagan, reaching into his breast pocket. "Would a check for five hundred dollars be an adequately tangible demonstration of my seriousness?"

Dodge's eyes twinkled. "It's almost like robbery," he said. "However, perhaps it will teach you both a lesson. Tomorrow night would be convenient—or is this particular ghost to be seen on appointment only?"

JEREMY DODGE chuckled as he made his way across the weed-choked graveyard. The moon was full and so he could see the ancient tumble of headstones clearly, but this was of no more than antiquarian interest. For an hour or so he wandered about, reading the quaint epitaphs; then at ten o'clock, he settled himself on the soft bed of a grave, leaned his head against a mossy stone and lit his briar.

It was, of course, absurd. But if he had not agreed to come, Kagan and Wilson would doubtless have counted him a member of their little group of superstitious fools, all too timid and weak to face reality. Ghosts, indeed, he thought. When will the human race grow up?

He chuckled again and was about to close his eyes when a high-pitched keening sound hurried his senses to attention. A bird. I shall be hearing various noises, he told himself, and very probably things will begin to move out there in the gloom. Birds, patterns of moonlight, animals. Perhaps even Kagan and— No; however foolish they were, they wouldn't stoop to a cheap trick. But they might. Believe anything, however improbable, before you believe the impossible.

He smoked. The silence deepened. Feeling a small shudder, Dodge cast his mind back to a number of pleasant experiences and relived them. When he glanced at his watch, it was five minutes to twelve.

Witching hour, he thought, smiling. Midnight. Damn silly business, anyway, sitting on the cold ground; I'll catch the flu.

He rose from the gravedirt, brushed at his trousers and struck another match on the headstone. The flame was reassuring. Shouldn't be, though. Of what do I need to be reassured? He pulled his collar up and sighed.

Over there, he thought, nodding in a northeasterly direction: that patch of moving light on the tree: that's what Kagan saw. And he a chemist. Shocking!

But, Lord, it was quiet. And what did you expect? Still, it wouldn't hurt to hum a bit. Dodge hummed, but the noise annoyed him, and he listened again to the utter stillness of the cemetery.

There was a shriek.

Feeling a quick jab of pain at his heart and a sinking sensation, Dodge thought, furiously, "Steady, dammit!" He made out the form of a small, scruffy dog. Ye Gods! Well, it proves one thing, he mused. There's a bit of the fool in the best of us. Being frightened of a dog!

"Shoo!"

The animal barked again and vanished.

Dodge smiled, thought of the pleasure it would be to take Kagan's check, turned, and froze.

By a mossy headstone, not twenty feet distant, was a figure. Very plainly that. A thin, white figure, with large, white, pupilless eyes.

Hallucination, thought Dodge blinking. Hallucination.

He advanced, expecting the figure to vanish. It did not vanish. It lay there, hideous, somehow—familiar?

Latent imagination plus ideal circumstance equals hallucination.

Dodge reached out. His hand passed through the figure's foot. He blinked again. He reached out again. Again his hand passed through the figure's foot.

Dodge screamed. He ran the length of the weed-choked churchyard, out onto the dark path and toward his car.

There he saw Kagan and Wilson. Unhesitatingly he vauled over to them and cried, "It's true! There is a ghost! I've seen it!"

"I tell you," said Kagan, "I heard a cry."

"I didn't, but perhaps we ought to take a look," said Wilson.

"It's horrible!" cried Dodge. "Thin and pale and—"

"I think it's gone a bit far," said Kagan. "He'll be properly chastened by now."

"Come on," said Wilson. And together they walked through Jeremy Dodge, who suddenly remembered the face of the figure in the moonlight. If he had had hackles, they would have risen on his neck, if he had had a neck.

THE CHILD
(2013)

 rs Samuelson felt the sudden quietness of the room, the strained and expectant quietness that she had caused. She looked at the little lingering rays of sunlight passing through the shabby lace curtains, and at the shadows in the women's faces. And she thought about how the room had taken her words and held them suspended in the air: the words she had kept waiting for the right moment.

"I saw Pearl Jacobean today."

Old Mrs Tweedy put her hands on the rug she was hooking and sneezed loudly. There were shufflings.

Mrs Schillings said, "When did you see her?"

Mrs Randolph said, "There hasn't anyone seen Pearl for over a year."

Mrs Vaughn said, "At least not since what happened."

Mrs Samuelson said, "I know. But there she was, walking down the street. And smiling! She was smiling."

Mrs Schillings said, "Well, now, ain't that queer. Maybe she's got over it by now—you suppose?"

Old Mrs Tweedy snorted, "Hmmph! And high time, at that. The very idea, not lettin' anyone see her and not talkin' to nobody for a whole year! Just livin' in that old house and actin' a disgrace to Tom Jacobean."

All the words loosened. The room and the words came back to life. Mrs Samuelson said, "If she had only let us help her! But Pearl was always so—odd. Even when she was coming to the club."

Mrs Randolph said, "Maybe you would be too, Mae, if you went through what Pearl did."

Old Mrs Tweedy snorted, "Fiddlesticks! Pearl Jacobean ain't the only one to lose children. My Johnny died before he was a week old but that didn't make me spite my friends."

Fingers held on to needles now and sent them through heavy cloth, sent them in and out, pulling dirty scraps of wool into dreary patterns. Gray houses, purple roses, big orange scrolls with mottos on them.

Old Mrs Tweedy started to hum "Beyond the Sunset."

Mrs Schillings said, "Losing one isn't the same as three, Elmina. And besides, Pearl always seemed to want children so bad."

"'...and remember, dear, if I go first...' Hmmph, don't matter none. Don't mean she has to go around uppity-up at her friends. Bet you Tom's thought more than once he got a handful for himself when he married that young lady."

Mrs Samuelson said, "Well, she's our friend even if she isn't yours, Elmina."

"Now I never said any such thing!"

Mrs Vaughn said quickly, "Where was Pearl headed, Mae? Oskana's a little town and I don't know anybody who's set eyes on her since her last one died. Did she tell you?"

Mrs Samuelson said, "Yes, and that's what worries me. She just smiled and said she was going to Dr Baker's office."

The fingers stopped the needles.

"What for?"

"Is she sick?"

"What do you suppose is wrong?"

Mrs Samuelson shook her head. "I don't know. She didn't look badly, except pale and thin. But she just smiled and asked about everybody at the club and said she was going to Dr Baker's office."

The sun left and the room turned gray. The rugs and the needles and the piles of wool and the women all turned gray. Mrs Randolph said, "You don't suppose..."

Mrs Schillings said, "Oh, do you think it might be?"

Mrs Samuelson felt for her handkerchief and knotted it around her hands.

"No," she said, "we shouldn't even think that. Don't you remember what happened last time? The doctor said Pearl couldn't ever have any more children. It must be something else. It could be a million things."

Old Mrs Tweedy snorted, "If you ask me, she's just a' feelin' her way so's she can get back with us. Silliest thing I ever heard of in all my life— not seein' anybody, not goin' nowhere, not even answerin' the telephone for a whole year, just 'cause she didn't born a young'n. It's mighty easy for that little lady to forget her real friends when they could help her and then come pussyfootin' around when everything's all right again. Hmmph!"

Mrs Samuelson swallowed and said, "Well, whatever it is, I don't think we've done just right by Pearl. If she's sick, I want to help her."

Mrs Randolph said, "Let's call Tom at his office tomorrow, Mae, and maybe he'll tell us."

Old Mrs Tweedy sent the needle in and out of the biblical scroll she was working on. She reached up and switched on a lamp so hard it nearly upset.

Mrs Schillings folded her rug carefully and said, "What are friends for if it isn't to help?"

Mrs Randolph said, "Oh, do let's call Tom tomorrow. If anything's wrong, I'm sure he'll tell us now, even if he wouldn't before."

Mrs Samuelson touched the woolen flower before her and said nothing.

Old Mrs Tweedy stopped humming and there was quiet once again. Soon needles were put in purses and unfinished rugs in baskets and when the little dead words were finished, the room was left alone.

DOCTOR BAKER put a nickel in the cigar box, withdrew a newspaper, and chose his usual place at the counter. He folded the newspaper on page two, after depositing his bag beneath the cash register stand, and took a number of toothpicks from a drinking glass. He tried to concentrate.

"Well, hiya, Doc. How'd it go today—take off any legs?"

Doctor Baker smiled automatically at the young man and moved his paper so that the silverware and paper napkins could be placed before him.

"What'll it be this time, Doc? The special?"

"Hmm? Oh, yes, the special by all means. What is the special, Frankie?"

The waiter laughed at the little joke he and the doctor played every night. "Same as every other day, Doc. Gumbo."

"Then gumbo it is, Frankie."

"Special! Float it in fish!"

Doctor Baker smiled once again, according to the ritual, and tried to read his paper. However, his eyes danced from beginning sentence to beginning word and when eventually the steaming bowl was set before him he had not finished one whole paragraph. He was not even aware that all the other customers had left or that the young waiter had drawn himself a cup of coffee and taken the next stool.

"Hey, what's up, Doc, ya sick? Ain't the gumbo any good?"

"What—oh, I'm sorry, Frankie. I was thinking. Sorry—no, the gumbo is very excellent."

"Then dig in, man, dig in!"

Doctor Baker took his eyes away from the dreamy motion of the big dusty overhead fan and grinned into his mustache. The waiter stirred his coffee. The lunchroom was so quiet both men were afraid to swallow.

"Yes, Frankie?"

"What's the scoop on the scoop?"

"The what on the—I don't think I follow."

"You know, what everyone's talking about tonight. All the women, anyway. Georgia's been calling trying to get me to ask you when you came in."

"Frankie, my lad, I haven't the least notion of what you're—"

"Come off it, Doc. You know what I mean. What's with Tom Jacobean's wife?"

"Really, Frankie, you should have sense enough to know that I wouldn't tell you that even if I wanted to. A doctor is sworn never to tell his patients' secrets."

"Secrets, secrets. Why secrets? A gal everybody thinks is dead suddenly pops up happy as a lark trotting off to your office. You got to admit, that's funny. I live right next door to her, and even I ain't seen her around."

Doctor Baker said nothing. Most of an oyster slid down his throat.

"Come on, come on. I won't tell anybody but Georgia. She's dying to know."

"That's enough, now. You're wasting your time."

"Is it so awful?"

"Don't be ridiculous."

"Well then, what—"

"I said, that's enough. If you're so inquisitive, go over to Merchant Forwarders and ask Tom."

The young man snapped his fingers and smiled. "Aw, no! No! You don't mean she's gonna have a—why that's wonderful!"

The spoon dropped from Dr Baker's fingers and disappeared beneath a layer of sea creatures and powdered sassafras root.

"Look here, lad, I haven't said a single thing to lead you to that conclusion. Stop putting words into my mouth."

The young man jumped up annoyedly to sell a package of cigarettes to a man who had just entered. The man counted his change and went out.

"Besides," said Doctor Baker, "there's nothing definite as yet."

The waiter cooled down his coffee and drank a mouthful.

"Y'know, Doc, by God, it'd be terrible for those folks if the same thing happened what did the last three times."

Doctor Baker sighed and said nothing.

"I kind of hope it isn't—you know. Last time you told them they couldn't ever have no more, didn't you?"

"Yes, Frankie, I did. I thought it was impossible. It will probably turn out to be something else entirely."

Then Doctor Baker took out his wallet and paid for his meal. He folded his newspaper into his coat pocket.

"Well, good night Frankie. Remember—anything that was said tonight was said by you."

"Oh, sure thing, Doc. You know me. But let us know, won't you?"

"One way or another, everybody in Oskana will know. Good night."

"Good night, Doc."

The young man cleaned about the counter until Doctor Baker had gone out the door, then he went into the kitchen and picked up the telephone. While the number was being rung, he said to the cook, "Hey, Fred, guess what! Tom Jacobean's wife's gonna have another baby."

The cook nodded and went back to sleep.

DOCTOR BAKER looked at the big ruddy man before him, watched how the massive ink-stained hands held onto the sides of the chair and how very straight and erect he sat.

"Well, Tom, did you come alone?"

"I had to, Doctor. Pearl wouldn't have come at all, she's that sure."

"She's not interested in the results of the test?"

"Not a bit, Doctor. It scares me. It scares me. She claims she's surer of having this child than she ever was before. Claims there's no doubt in her mind and that God took all the doubt away this time."

Doctor Baker folded his hands.

"I told her, I said, you've got to remember what the doctor said the last time about things being dried up, but she doesn't even hear me. Ever since she came to you she's been happy and singing and—God, God, I haven't seen her do that for years, not since she lost the first one."

The big man paused. He rose from his chair. "Doctor Baker, first you've got to tell me. What do those tests show?"

"Tom—"

"Because, Doc, I don't know what it would do to Pearl. When she didn't have the boy last year, ever since she's sat all alone in that room, just sitting, just sitting and never saying anything. What would it do to her—what? I'm scared. I'm afraid. What is it, Doctor?"

Doctor Baker looked deep into the man's eyes and remembered. He remembered a dark, happy young woman who had first come to his office four years before, and he could see it happening as if his words had been the cause—how the happiness had withered and fallen in those years. He remembered the eager, wanting, willing hunger and the death and how it seemed in a way that he was responsible for the death. He remembered thinking through hazes of alcohol, afterwards, in the sanity of his own room, thinking that he had taken the happiness and crushed it.

As he sat slowly taking the report from the desk, he remembered too the last time he had seen Pearl Jacobean. The automatic movements, the helpless submission, the awful emptiness of the eyes. And how he had sworn that he would do anything to restore a little of the happiness he had been given no choice but to destroy.

"And what about you, Tom? Do you want this child?"

"Want it? Sure, yes, I want it. But I want my Pearl more. Tell me, for God's sake, tell me, read me the report."

Doctor Baker thought only once briefly of what he had seen and remembered, cleared his throat and said quickly. "The tests are positive, Tom. Beyond that I can't say, but from all evidence, it looks like you and Pearl are going to have a baby."

The big ruddy man put his jaws hard close together. "Even if the same thing happens, it'll be nine months away and she'll have that little bit anyway. She'll have that little piece of happiness and it wouldn't be no worse than my coming home and telling her that now—thank God!"

Doctor Baker smiled and closed the desk drawer. He said, "Yes, she'll have that little piece of happiness."

Then Doctor Baker wrote down a set of appointments and went to the doorway with the man.

"Try to show encouragement, Tom. I know all this goes against what I said, but sometimes those things happen. You might have a healthy child, after all. So whatever you do, don't let Pearl suspect you have any doubts. Tell her everything will be all right this time. Otherwise—well, I think we both know what might happen."

"I know, Doctor. I know. And thank you."

When the door closed, Doctor Baker took his report from the desk and read it over. He took a letter opener and scratched at the words "negative" and "false pregnancy" until the blade cut into the heavy blotter. He lit a match and held it under the paper and he crushed the flaming fragments in his hands.

Then Doctor Baker told his nurse that he would receive no other calls.

He walked eight blocks to his apartment and took a dusty bottle from the hall closet shelf.

DAWN WAS slow in coming and only the faintest fingers of light touched the great high colored windows, so that the church was as dark and solemn as a deserted theater.

Mrs Hugo Schwartz and Mrs Ira Carlson sat comfortably in their accustomed pew, while their heads nodded and their lips moved and they attempted in every way not to intrude upon the gloom. They were dressed almost entirely in black and wore small black hats.

Mrs Carlson nudged her friend at the moment the rustling sound began. For a time they watched the young woman, watched in silence interrupted by slight jabs and pushes, watched as the young woman kneeled at the altar, watched the young woman and heard her half-audible prayers and then waited impatiently until they were alone once more.

Mrs Carlson whispered, "It isn't long for her now, Emma."

Mrs Schwartz whispered, "Eight months it is and in another it will be."

Mrs Carlson whispered, "Isn't it the grandest thing, dear little Pearl just won't give up, will she."

The two ladies shook their heads. They sat respectfully for three minutes and then left the Church.

Mrs Carlson said, "I never did see anyone want a baby as much as Pearl Jacobean. Why, just look at the change in the woman! Did you see how she was smiling when she went out? Didn't even see us, but if she had, the way she is nowadays, she'd a'said hello."

Mrs Schwartz shrugged her shoulders. She said, "Well, let's just hope it is good this time and not like before. She never had one, really, not really."

Mrs Carlson said, "And see how big she is. She wasn't the other times. So small you couldn't hardly notice and I knew then, I said, there's something going to happen there. And it did, all three times. She's big now and healthy looking. Everyone has given her presents. Baby clothes and dolls and simply everything. And Doctor Baker says he has no doubt that Pearl will get through it fine."

Mrs Schwartz said, "It is for my special intention, Pearl. She is such a nice girl and they made her so sick, all over."

Mrs Carlson said, "It's my special intention too. Oh, Emma, everyone in Oskana's just holding her breath."

Mrs Schwartz nodded, and said, "It is only one month now. We will soon know, won't we?"

THE TWO ladies returned to their beds.

Doctor Baker hunched in the dark hallway, pulling his pajamas about his waist. He held the receiver close to his ear and breathed heavily.

"Doctor Baker! Can you hear me? Can you?"

"Yes, Tom, I hear you. What is it?"

"It's Pearl, Doctor—the baby's coming. It's coming any minute, she says. She's in labor pains right this second. You ought to get over here the minute you can."

Doctor Baker gripped the telephone cord. "You must be mistaken."

"I tell you, there isn't even time to go to Putnam. She won't allow it. Hospital or none, it's on the way! Doctor Baker!"

"Yes, yes, boy. Calm yourself. You're simply excited. You must be wrong."

The voice was silent for a moment. Then it said, "I know what I'm talking about, Doctor. I've been through this before, you know. Nobody's mistaken. Pearl's in labor and you've got to come."

"Yes, Tom. I understand. I'll be there in a few minutes. And we'll see what the trouble is."

There was a sharp noise and Doctor Baker stood looking at the telephone. Then he flicked on lights and began to dress, slowly. Veins protruded from his bald head and his hands trembled.

When he was fully clothed he walked into another room and poured something from an amber bottle, poured a glass full and threw it against a wall.

Doctor Baker thought of what he had seen in the past nine months, of the reports he had made and burned. He thought of the hopeful, sure, honest voice he had just heard. Of medical impossibilities and oaths and duties and a tall thin woman.

He got his jacket and began to put things into a small bag. Then he straightened and walked toward the door, trying very hard to keep the tears from his eyes and the thoughts from his head.

OLD MRS Tweedy tore an angry hole in the cloth she was working and made a loud noise with her mouth.

She said, "Well, maybe you all can figure it out, but it goes right past me, it does. You can take it kindly, but you bet your boots ElminaTweedy don't, no sir!"

Mrs Samuelson inserted a hose fragment into a scroll and said, "Now, now, you know what Pearl says."

"Hmmph, and all I care! She can say till doomsday and not make it up to me. The very idea, why, it makes me boil."

Mrs Schillings said, "Well now, it does seem kind of strange. You'd a'thought she'd invite us over one at a time or something like that."

"Hah! Her? No sir, she's got nothing to do with us, and that's fine! And she's got Tommy acting just the same way, going around not speaking to nobody."

"Oh, Pearl isn't that way now and you know it, Elmina. She says hello to everybody. She called me up just yesterday."

Mrs Randolph said, "Elmina's just talking. Soon as it gets a little older, Pearl says she'll have everybody in town over to see it."

"Hmmph! And how many times have you heard Tom say that? None, that's how many. Got no use for friends now that things is running smooth."

Mrs Samuelson said, "Why, I'd do the same thing if I were in Pearl's shoes. She says Doctor Baker told her that it shouldn't ever be exposed to drafts or people. And after all, it does weigh only four pounds."

Old Mrs Tweedy worked furiously with her needles.

"Uppity-up, uppity-up, that's all it is and no else. You can't tell me that liftin' up a blanket and lettin' somebody get just one little peek is going to hurt any baby! And just think—calling it Wanda. Who ever heard of such a fool name?"

Mrs Vaughn said, "I think Wanda is a pretty name."

Needles went through cloth and the room was thick with thoughts.

"And what about Doctor Baker? Never a'thought he was so spine-less. Gettin' up and leavin' town just 'cause he was wrong about Pearl havin' a young'n. Shame and a disgrace."

"Dr Baker got a better job, that's all. Elmina you're getting to talk just like an old woman."

"Well, muck, fire, and eggshells, anyway! What's everybody so touchy for? Think you don't feel just as disappointed as me, an' you know blame well you do, every one of you. Just imagine, havin' a baby and almost a month now and not lettin' a single body see it!"

Mrs Randolph said, "Yes, it does seem—Barbara Fischer says she's seen it and that it looks healthy as it can be."

"Barbara Fischer. That little snip would lie to the Savior if she thought it'd make an impression. She never saw no baby of Pearl Jacobean's."

"She says she did."

"She said she was married to Saul Barzor too, didn't she?"

Mrs Randolph worried scraps of wool with her hands.

"Well anyway, it sounds healthy. Never heard a baby cry so loud before, have you?"

"No, I ain't. Passed Pearl Jacobean on the street and there she was, wheelin' that buggy grand as you please. 'Hello there, Mrs Tweedy,' she says, 'and how are you today? Thank you for the gifts and presents,' she says. And under all them blankets, like as not smotherin' half to its death, there's that—well, it just makes me mad as old Nick. I went to pull off the blanket and take a peek, just a little peek since I give it all those presents—paid twelve dollar for them, I did—and Miss Proud-as-you-can says, 'Oh no, you mustn't disturb her' and takes my wrist bent to break it if I didn't stop. Now, there's gratitude for you. And that little thing crying and taking on like you never heard. Inhuman, it is!"

Mrs Samuelson stopped her needles. She said, "You don't suppose there's something wrong with it, do you? Something she wouldn't want anyone to see?"

Mrs Schillings said, "Oh no. Pearl said on the phone it was a perfect little child. That's what she said, 'a perfect little child.'"

Old Mrs Tweedy snorted, "There. You see!"

"And besides, what doctor does she go to now? King hasn't seen her and young Cleveland ain't licensed yet, and says she hasn't been in anyway. If the baby's so all-fired sickly, then why ain't Pearl Jacobean seein' about it to a doctor?"

Old Mrs Tweedy pricked the tip of her finger and shrieked.

Mrs Schillings said, "Well, I guess Pearl is going to tell us when she thinks it's good for the baby. There's some good reason to her."

Old Mrs Tweedy said, "Not if Tom Jacobean has anything to do with it. You ask me, there's something peculiar. He don't mention that baby once ever, not never does he talk about it. It's going around that Mr Hokinson at Merchant Forwarders is going to fire Tommy, 'cause he ain't doing his work. Acts half off. Drinking like a fish. Oh, I'll tell you right enough, there's something peculiar. But it ain't with the baby or poor Tom, I'll wager."

Mrs Samuelson said sharply, "Now that's all. If you thought enough to give Pearl all those booties and dolls and diapers and everything else along with the rest of us, then you won't talk that way about her. She's a wonderful woman just trying to protect the one child she did get. When it gets old enough we'll see it, never you fear."

Old Mrs Tweedy rocked in her chair and sang "Beyond the Sunset." Then she said, "I'm just worried about Pearl, that's all. Don't understand nothing I say, want to twist it."

MRS CARLSON crossed herself hurriedly and pulled Mrs Schwartz up the aisle of the church. In the sunlight she patted her hands together and blew out her cheeks.

"Well now, Emma, I call that carrying it too far. Somebody ought to tell Pearl Jacobean, somebody ought to tell her."

Mrs Schwartz panted and said, "Yes, someone should. Who could say prayers with that baby and the noise it made! Always crying, all the time, crying!"

Mrs Carlson said, "And keeping the poor little thing wrapped up in all those blankets and on a day like this. Why, even Father Toomey was perspiring. I could see him."

Mrs Schwartz said, "And why can't we never look? Is it crippled or something? It isn't right. Everybody not paying attention to the sermon and trying to see the baby. Mrs Randolph told me for eight months, nobody has seen it."

Mrs Carlson said, "Oh, somebody has, I'm sure."

Mrs Schwartz said, "But all the time! Every Sunday, only her, not the husband. Every Sunday with that baby and always crying. But she always says hello so nice and she's a nice woman."

Mrs Carlson said, "I'll bet you anything the baby is blind and she won't let anyone know. I'll bet she won't let the doctors tell."

✤ ✤ ✤

FRANKIE LOMBARDI pulled a dirty dishcloth languidly over the spatterings of a cheese soufflé. He held a toothpick in his mouth and spoke through it to Harry Schillings.

"Beats me how the guy keeps his job. I never saw such a wingding! Came in here not twenty minutes ago higher than a kite. You should'a heard him! Now frankly, I'm not along with the crowd here. If those people want to keep their kid to themselves, then I figure that's their business. And if Tom Jacobean wants to take a flier, that's his business too. You know me. But honest to God, he was soused to the gills. Said he wanted a coffee to put him back in shape."

Harry Schillings looked at his watch and turned the page of his newspaper.

"Beats me how it could happen to a swell guy like that. Here his old lady finally came through with a kid, he's got a good job, he's got more than I've got, but he goes on a wingding. Can you figure it, Harry?"

Harry Schillings looked up and said, "No. I don't know Jacobean very well. Those things come up, you know."

"The kid's supposed to be first class, too. Georgia says she hears it every day, getting healthier and stronger. Hears it cry all the way over to our shack. So what happens? After losing three the poor dame wants to keep it strictly to herself and this crazy town goes nuts. I've heard it around that the Jacobean kid has fifteen toes and it's a nigger and wobbles and a million other things. Georgia says she can tell from the way it cries, never was a healthier kid. And that's what Mrs J. tells folks. All she says is that the kid's not old enough to lug around. So what, I ask you, so what?"

Frankie Lombardi pulled a stack of checks from beneath the cash register drawer and began to add them up on a large sheet of paper.

Harry Schillings turned to the sports page and lit another cigarette.

"Hell, I seen enough myself to tell that. Couldn't be happier, that woman. Never saw so many smiles on a person. And brother! You should have seen her before. The couple times she did come out, she looked like death warmed over. So now she's happy. And her husband decides now's the time to throw in his chips on a boozer."

The big overhead fan distributed the hot night air over the lunchroom. Outside it flew in dry hot currents, crisping and blowing.

"Oh, I'm telling you, Harry, you should'a been here tonight. Brother, it was the clincher. He talked like old Doc Baker used to. Gloomy about this, gloomy about that. I asked him, I said, 'Look, Tom, what the hell, can't you tell me? Is there really something with your kid?' And he gets sore first, then he laughs like a fool and he goes out the door cussin'. Absolutely owl-eyed. Can you figure it?"

Harry Schillings reached in his pocket for some change, said that he could not figure it, and went back to his overtime at the office. Frankie

Lombardi shrugged and locked the front door to the lunchroom. He tasted the hot dry night and almost forgot to wake the cook.

The beer and the night and the thoughts pushed him up the steps of his house, up the steps and into the kitchen and down the hall. And finally to the door, the plain cream-colored door, the door where he had stood and thought so many times for so many months. The thoughts alone held him there, waiting and breathing and frightened.

He put his big hand gently about the knob and turned it. He looked into the room. He looked at the woman lying in the bed and at the small thing covered in the blanket and in her arms. He closed the door and went into the kitchen.

He felt the heavy dryness and the heat. He felt the hot breezes floating through the cracks and the holes, passing over his face and over his hair.

He sat in the green cane chair and took from his shirt pocket a cigarette. He dropped it, picked it up and put it between his lips, and felt in his pockets again.

He pulled a splinter from a stick of kindling and put this into the flame of the water heater. He lit his cigarette and opened the door and tried to breathe the hot air.

Then he stooped to pick up the cigarette again and he chased it as the wind blew it across the floor. The beer and the night and the thoughts filled his mind. The tiny thing in the blanket, the tiny crying thing next to his wife, filled his mind.

He lay on the floor and watched the little white sliver roll out of sight.

HARRY SCHILLINGS was sipping a mug of tepid bitter tea and staring at a sheaf of papers with numbers on them when the phone rang. He shook the calculations and the sleep from his head and walked quickly past the rows of empty desks in the big dark office. He lifted the receiver to his ear and removed his green eye shade.

"*Oskana Eagle.* Circulation. Schillings speaking."

"Hello, Harry, is that you, Harry?"

Harry Schillings recognized the high-pitched excited voice.

"Yes, Frankie. What is it?"

"You gotta drop everything quick, Harry. All hell bustin' loose! Call Fred and Jorgenson and the rest quick."

"All right, calm down, calm down. What is it? Now talk slowly."

The voice squeaked over the wire, squeaked and jumped and shrilled.

"What is it, he says. I just seen it and it's goin' to beat hell!"

"What is, what is? Calm down, damn it!"

"I just seen it. I just got home from the restaurant, see, and I was tired, so I said to Georgia, come on honey, let's go to bed. And then I look out the window, happen to glance, and, jeez, the place is up in smoke and fire's spurtin' out the windows. I can see it now, Harry, and it's gettin' worse—"

"Frankie, for God's sake, whose place? Somebody's place is on fire?"

"Yeah, yeah, what do you want, a written report? The Jacobean house. It's blazin' like a rocket! Get on over here quick, I mean quick!"

Harry Schillings looked at his watch and began to snatch off his sleeve guards.

"All right. I've got it, Frankie. You call up Frederickson and Schwartz and Carlson, I'll get Jorgenson and we'll get out the truck. Go over quick and see about the people, too."

"Oh my God! I'll bet Tom's still soused. Maybe he don't know what's goin' on—and, God, Harry, it's going to burn like a wad of cotton!"

"Do what you can about the Jacobeans. I'll make all the calls and be over there as soon as I possibly can."

"Okay, Harry. Maybe now that son of a bitch Granger will get a fire dep—"

Harry Schillings tossed the phone back into its cradle, huffed the length of the office and put on his jacket and hat. Then he cursed and ran back to the phone. He made four calls, cursing and pounding the bar for speed. The hot dry wind pushed at him as he raced his automobile toward the ugly red barn seven blocks away.

MRS SCHWARTZ and Mrs Carlson and Mrs Samuelson and Mrs Randolph stood with their husbands, overcoats pulled over their night-clothes. Mrs Schillings paced and mumbled. Old Mrs Tweedy stood holding to a fence, her face white with excitement. Other women and men filled the street and the yard. Some watched the old red truck and the men pumping water from it. Some watched the men bringing the water, speeding down the sidewalks and the streets, trying to open pipes, trying to do something.

They all watched the little streams of water shooting from the little lengths of hose, shooting and falling into the crumbling, crackling, billowing blossoms of fire. The receding and the advancing fire, the tiny born flames from the wet dead places, burning the air and the sky, fighting the water. They heard the wood snap and fall and screamed when they heard. They felt the searing heat flirt with their skins, play with their clothes. They screamed and bellowed and hopped and stayed to watch.

Mrs Samuelson ran across the brown lawn, pushing people and staggering. She ran until she found her husband and clung to him.

"Ralph, what about the baby? Are they all right? Where are they?"

Mrs Samuelson's husband said, "Damn it, Mae, we're doing everything we can. If they're all in the bedroom we think maybe we can get to them, but it's going to take time. Frankie tried but he got too excited, that's all. We've got to get that piece out. So let me alone, Mae. We're doing everything we can!"

Mrs Samuelson pulled at her husband's sleeve. She said, "They're not going to die? You're not all going to let them die, are you? Why wasn't that the first thing somebody did? Why?"

Her husband said, "For Christ's sake, Mae, what do you want me to do? Maybe they're not even in there. Maybe they're away at somebody's house, maybe—"

"They are, they are in there!"

Mrs Samuelson ran back to the spot of lawn nearest the bedroom of the flaming house. She stood very still and then she screamed until her throat hurt.

"Listen!"

The people turned to look at Mrs Samuelson, and as they did so, they fell into silence. Only the flames were not silent. The frenzied furied flames and one other sound.

"Listen!"

Old Mrs Tweedy caught at her breast.

"Listen!"

Mrs Schillings clenched her fists. Mrs Randolph held very tightly to her husband's arm.

"Listen!"

The sound could be heard, faintly but piercingly. A thin staccato sound, from the center of the leaping redness.

Frankie Lombardi looked up from the pipe he had been trying to repair. He strained to hear.

The little sharp whimpering sound hurtled from the house and caught on the air.

Somebody cried, "It's the baby! They're in the bedroom!"

Frankie Lombardi began to wave his arms.

"Here, you, Harry, Mr Randolph, all of you, get all those hoses on the bedroom. Get around to the other window. Quick!"

He twisted the nozzle of a hose and turned it toward himself.

"Somebody gimme an overcoat!"

Mrs Samuelson ran from one person to another.

She cried, "Why, why? Why did you wait so long?!"

And then everyone was silent once more as they watched Frankie Lombardi walk in line with the streams of water. They held their breath as the young man broke a window and pulled himself through it into the smoke and flames.

Harry Schillings pulled the hose with him toward the house until he could feel the heat sear across his face. He directed the stream through the window. There was no sound but the flames and the falling timber and the thin little whimper that roared and thundered.

And then after a while Frankie Lombardi came out of the house.

He stood wet and hot and sick with the blackened bundle still in his arms. He did not seem to know he held anything.

"I saw her, I saw her but I couldn't do nothin'. I saw her layin' there with the smoke all around her face and I couldn't help her. All I could do was grab the kid out of her arms and run..."

Mr Randolph said, "It's getting better now. I'm going in after Pearl and Tom. We may be able to save 'em if they're still alive."

Mr Schwartz said, "I'll go with you."

Frankie Lombardi sat on the ground. From the covered blanket there were the little staccato sounds, the little whimpers.

Mrs Carlson came from her group and said, "Well thank God, Frankie, you saved the baby. Listen to it, it don't seem hurt none."

They looked at the soiled, scorched wool cover and listened to the sounds inside.

Mrs Carlson said, "Well, we've got to see if it's all right. Pull off that dirty old blanket so we can see to the child!"

Mrs Samuelson stepped forward and stopped. Frankie Lombardi said nothing and clutched the bundle closer to his body.

The sounds seemed to grow stronger, louder, sadder. Whimpers of pain and of loss. Little gurgling terrible baby sounds.

"Pull off that blanket, boy. The poor little thing'll suffocate!"

Old Mrs Tweedy pushed from the group. She walked quickly and took a crisp, crumbling corner of the wool with her hands.

She said, "Come on, come on. Tom's got out. They've got Pearl and there ain't much left to the fire. Come on, you want that little sprite to die for want of air? Listen to it beller!"

Frankie Lombardi took his hands from the bundle and watched. The women watched and the men that were near came to watch as old Mrs Tweedy pulled off the blanket.

For a while no one said anything. For a while they all looked at the crumpled, melting thing that Frankie Lombardi was holding in his arms. Where the little pink dress and the soiled diapers had been burned, those near enough could see the metal plate with the words upon it, "Wanda the Wonda Doll. She cries. She wets. She coos. She's almost real."

THE LIFE OF THE PARTY

(2013)

can't tell you how pleased I am," said Mr Hulbush, smiling shyly at his companion. "Of course, I'd always meant to invite you, but somehow I could never find the courage. I suppose I was afraid of being turned down." He laughed. "I agree! It *is* silly. But that's what comes of being an only child. You'll meet my mother and then you'll understand completely. Not that I blame her. She behaved like any normal mother, I suppose. Under the circumstances. I mean, with the first three dying and all, and my father running away. It was natural that she should want to protect me, coddle me, keep me out of harm's way. Don't you agree?"

The white-haired man beside him said nothing.

"Still, it wasn't the best start in the world. And my appearance didn't help much, either. From the age of twelve I was plagued with acne, you see. What with that, my crooked ears, and my bulbous nose, I did not present a very attractive appearance. But of course Mother always told me I was a lovely child, and I believed her. Until I started school. And you can imagine what happened then. The children mocked me. They told me my face looked like a relief map of the Adirondacks. I remember that one. I didn't know exactly what Aiderondacks were, but I got the point, nonetheless. And it crushed me. Mother said the children were simply jealous of me because I lived in a big house and got high marks, but I wasn't sure. I thought perhaps it was simply that I was ugly. So I went to the doctor for shots and sent away for ointments and salves and gave up sweets altogether, but nothing did any good. Every night I would stand before the mirror, touching the great tender sores and weeping. Do I bore you?"

The white-haired man did not reply.

"Well," continued Mr Hulbush, "I heard of a dance coming up about that time. I had seen a girl in class and, though she and I had never exchanged a word, I found that I was dreaming about her. I would go to sleep and dream about her smooth tan skin, the little tiny hairs on her legs shining gold in the sunlight, the heavy ring dangling from a chain between her breasts. And I determined that I would go to the dance and see her. For hours I worked at preparing myself. First I squeezed all the pimples and boils. Then I applied a special salve. Then I covered it all up with a white powder, which I patted just so. Then came the combing of the hair, again just so, and the donning of my best, and only, suit. Mother warned me that I was making a terrible mistake, but I wouldn't listen to her. I was *determined*." Mr Hulbush laughed sadly. "Did I go through with it? Yes. I went alone, long after the festivities had begun. It was at Barker Hall, which at that time stood in the midst of a dark field. I walked across the field and presently I could hear the sounds of music and laughter. Barker Hall was blazing in the night like a beacon, I thought, or a lighthouse. With every step my fear grew. My palms were hot and wet. My heart was hammering. But the fear forced me on. Much as I wanted to turn and run, I could not. So I stood for a moment at the door, wiping my hands on my trousers, and then I went in. It was bedlam. Thousands of young people—or anyway it seemed like thousands—were dancing and laughing and drinking. The air was full of smoke and the smell of alcohol. There were all the children I saw at school, only now, in their dark suits and tight gowns, they didn't look like children, but young Apollos and Dianas. No one noticed me, of course. I continued to stand by the door, trying to swallow. Then I saw her. If she was lovely seated at her desk with the sun on her legs, she was incredible now. The gown she wore was black velvet. It hugged her. God! She was so beautiful, and I wanted her so much, then, so very much…"

Mr Hulbush turned off the main highway onto a rutted, unpaved road walled on either side by thick dark trees. Then he glanced at his passenger, Professor Brady. "Remember, though we were classmates, we'd never spoken to one another. Less than a foot away from her every day for two years, I'd worshipped her from afar. Now she was pressing her body close to a young man and laughing. I admit that I thought terrible, unwholesome things then. I will tell you because we are friends now. I thought of her flesh beneath the dress, and of the young man's flesh, and of how close each was to the other now. Their naked flesh separated by less than a fraction of an inch! And what I would have given then to exchange places with that fellow, I cannot tell you. Consummation enough, only that, and far more than I ever dreamed possible for me. The music stopped after a moment. The young people uncoupled, and the boy walked away from the girl with the golden legs, leaving her standing there, alone. I rushed forward, pushed from behind by the desperate fear of fifteen agonized years. She turned her head. She saw me. Recognition flickered. I said, 'Hello.' And she answered me. Do you know what she said, that Diana with the golden legs, that object of my dreams and hopes? She said: 'Who let *you* in?'"

Mr Hulbush drove in silence for several minutes. Then he smiled at Professor Brady. "That was a long time ago. And there's a happy ending. When she left her husband last year, we became friends, you see—as you and I have—and one thing led to another and now she's Mrs Hulbush! In fact, you'll meet her tonight!" He chuckled and reached into his breast pocket. "Cigarette?"

The white-haired man did not reply.

"Admirable," said Mr Hulbush, drawing fire into his cigarette and hacking out a gray cloud. "However, 'Better one major vice than a host of minor ones.' D'you know who said that? *You*, Professor Brady. *The Quintessence of Morality*. Chapter Seven. And besides, 'It ain't the cough that carries you off, it's the coffin they carries you off in!'" He laughed heartily, then lapsed once again into silence. "I suppose you find that a crude joke, considering my occupation. Well, let me tell you, if I didn't make a joke once in a while, I'd go mad. Being what I am isn't easy." He dragged on the cigarette, then turned his head quickly toward his companion. "No, of *course* I didn't choose it. One's life is determined from the moment one is born. That's what I've been try-ing to say. It was my father's occupation and so—naturally—it had to be mine. We can thank my mother for it, too, and the Adirondacks. But what's wrong with it, anyway? Somebody has to do the job, isn't that so?" He stuffed the cigarette into an ashtray and tapped on the car's high beams. The road ahead snaked through a veritable forest. "People couldn't understand, for a long time. Even after my pimples disappeared, they shunned me. Mother and I lived alone. Sometimes I would go to a film, but always it was by myself. I would sit in the darkness, alone, looking at the bright pictures, and wonder if I would ever have a friend." He shook his head. "Though it seems so far away now, I remember that people wouldn't even shake my hand in those days. When I would enter a restaurant, they would shrink away from me, as though I were diseased, as though I were some sort of strange beast that didn't belong in society. Never once was I invited to anyone's house. Never once would anyone accept an invitation of mine. And my mother kept saying, 'They're jealous of you' but I knew that it went much deeper. They hated me because I reminded them of something they didn't choose to think about, and because every town needs at least one person to shrink away from, to despise, to hate."

The beams of the car suddenly illuminated a large two-story house. The limbs of dead trees scraped against its unpainted boards. No light shone from its shuttered windows. Mr Hulbush turned off the car.

"I'm trying to explain," he said, "why I never asked you over before. If I sound self-pitying, it's because I haven't told you the conclusion. I gave up hope, of course, when I realized that a man in my position—or, at any rate, myself in my position—could never enjoy what is called a normal life. But at that moment, at the moment I decided to adjust to a lifetime of loneliness, everything changed." Mr Hulbush grinned at his companion. "Suddenly I began to make friends. People began accepting my invitations. The very best people in town, too! The ones who wouldn't have spit on me before, who turned their backs, who laughed at me, who called me 'that strange little man.' Now, suddenly, they were my friends. Not all, of course. You couldn't expect that. But little by little they've been coming around. In fact, my at-homes are threatening to become the social event of Hilldale!"

Mr Hulbush got out of the car, extracted a wooden device from the back seat and folded it into a chair.

"*I can't* account for it," Mr Hullbush said, easing the chair up the steps of the house to the front door. "Perhaps it was the change in my attitude. Or perhaps they realized that my line of work is no less respectable than any other. Who can say?"

He inserted a key in the lock and turned it. They entered a dark hall, hung with paintings of Indian maidens in canoes and mountains. "My mother's," Mr Hulbush said, "but don't be embarrassed. I don't like them, either."

He rolled the chair down the hall, past many doors.

"It's wonderful, having you," he said to the white-haired man. "Somehow I knew we'd hit it off, but—well, I've told you all about that. I suppose it's just that I can't accept the fact that I'm popular, after all these years. I can't *accept* it. Isn't that silly?"

Mr Hulbush removed another key from his pocket and inserted it into another lock. He pulled open a heavy door.

"I see they've started without us," he whispered, smiling.

A number of persons stood and sat about a large living room. Some were old, some young. All were dressed formally. Mr Hulbush entered the room with his companion. After closing the door securely, he turned and waved his hand.

"Excuse me. Folks, excuse me! I'd like to introduce Professor Edward Brady. Some of you know him already, but to those who don't, I'd like to say that Professor Brady is one of the outstanding citizens of Hilldale. In addition to coming from one of our oldest families, he is an educator of the first rank. His books on psychology are considered indispensable in universities throughout the world. He is listed in Who's Who, the Social Register, and Celebrity Index. In high school, they voted him the most popular boy on campus. Throughout his life he has won the respect and admiration of all who have known him. He is one of my best friends."

So saying, Mr Hulbush guided his companion slowly through the room to a couch whereupon sat an old woman in a violet dress. "Professor Brady, my mother, Edna Hulbush." In a low voice, he said to the white-haired man, "She has been dying to meet you for years."

They moved on toward a woman in a black velvet gown. She appeared to be in her late forties. "Isn't she lovely?" Mr Hulbush said, softly. "But of course you've guessed who she is. Marianne, the girl with the golden legs. How long I waited for her! But somehow I think I knew, even as I stood burning with shame and praying that the ground would swallow me up, even then I think I knew that we would be together some day." He placed the chair next to the woman, who stood looking off in the direction of a window. "You two get acquainted, while I find us a drink," he said.

Mr Hulbush greeted his guests as he walked to a bar in the corner. He mixed two martinis and returned to the white-haired man, who had not moved. He placed a glass in the man's hand and then, holding his own drink at arm's length, said: "To good companions, to acts of kindness, to pleasant conversations, and to hell with everything else!" He drank the martini in one long swallow and hurled the empty glass at a fireplace.

"Careful," he said to the white-haired man, "or she'll ask who let *you* in!" He laughed and wheeled the chair around. His progress through the room was slow as he halted by each guest.

"Miss Tatum, chairman of the ladies' league, she owns the oldest house in Hilldale. Built in 1787. The house I mean!"

"Mr Pedderson, of O'Brian, Ingley and Pedderson, our leading law firm. He was the boy who held my Marianne in his arms that night, though I doubt he remembers it."

"Peter Grant, student body president. You remember that witty description of my face? It came from Pete. Now we're inseparable."

"Mrs Crandall, here, once lost her appetite because of me. They'd served her a fine meal and she was about to eat it when she looked over and saw that I was in the restaurant. She left the table. And look at her now, enjoying my hospitality!"

After each person in the room had been approached, Mr Hulbush turned on a radio, selected a program of music, and went to the woman in the black velvet gown.

He lifted her slightly off the floor and, holding her closely, danced until dawn.

Then he went out looking for new friends.

THE BEAST OF THE GLACIER

(2022)

The Elgart Research Laboratory is a vast, sprawling empire. Within its maze of buildings, hiding behind deceptively ivied walls, work goes on quietly twenty-four hours a day—work that might, in the near future, benefit the entire human race. For the problem at hand at Elgart Laboratory is cancer. Stubborn, pernicious, deadly cancer. In the game of "catch me if you can," cancer has had an all-too-uncomfortable lead for far too long. Many of the other man-killing diseases have been wrestled to the floor, some have been defeated, some have fought to a draw, but cancer has ruled with fear and loathing since it arrived on the scene and travelled its fatal way throughout the Ages. There has been progress, to be sure; treatment by radiation, Roentgen exposure, surgery, diet: but the killer Cancer is still the greatest foe of medical science, and the most fearful disease known.

At Elgart, the work is being done by doctors and scientists and, for this reason, it is a slow, tedious business; for a fact is not a fact to a scientist until it has been checked, re-checked, and then checked again. Aware that radiation treatment can go just so far, that it is effective only in the early stages, the heads of the Research Department have decided to experiment with other methods.

Among these treatment methods is a promising, but untried approach called Frozen Therapy.

Doctor John Preston, a relatively young but intensely focused man, is Director of this operation. It was he who first convinced Edmund Elgart, chief of the lab, that the method was worth investigating, and he who kept the experimentation going even in the face of strong resistance by opposing factions.

John Preston is a good doctor and, by all appearances, an intelligent and reasonable person; but he lacks one quality—patience. His experimental trials have been in effect for over a year, yet they have not progressed beyond the initial stage of using laboratory animals. White mice, kittens, guinea pigs; again and again and again, in a series of controlled experiments. He sees that the theory is feasible—it is working in a high percentage of cases—but Edmund Elgart and the staff in charge absolutely will not hear of trying the method on living human beings.

"That is not the scientific way, John, and you know it," Elgart tells him. "We must go slowly, carefully, cover the same ground a hundred times, and only then can we move on. The greatest discoveries, which seem like overnight sensations, are merely the result of such procedure. A wrong move now and the project—as well as Elgart Laboratories' reputation—in short, everything we've worked for—would be ruined."

John Preston hears the words and he understands their value. But they leave him unsatisfied. Call it ambition; call it the restlessness of every person who has ever ignored the call to "take it slow." Aren't they the ones who succeed in the face of crushing odds? Aren't they the ones who take the words "reckless" and "headstrong" and forge them into "determined" and "steadfast"...and "successful?"

John's moment of reflection is interrupted by the sound of a woman's voice. "Hello, stranger." The voice belongs to Linda Carmody, a research physicist and, more importantly, the one person in the world whom John trusts. She loves John, and she understands his impatience. But she also understands how badly—some would say recklessly—he wants to succeed at any cost, and so she does her best to steer him in the right direction, away from his instincts to forget the rules and race full speed where his instincts tell him to go. She's made it her job to urge John to wait, to pace himself and hold his stronger impulses in check. This is what she wants for John; this is how she thinks he will best reach his goal. But lately she's been worried.

Linda is no stranger to ambition. She grew up with it. Her father was a driven man, determined to scrape his way to the top of the business world, no matter what it took. And he succeeded beyond his wildest dreams. Rich, admired and, most of all, feared. Feared by everyone he worked with; feared even more by his wife and children who tried to love him but failed. In the end, he died alone with an empty bottle of very expensive Scotch as his only friend. Maybe that's why Linda is so drawn to John. She understands him. And while she couldn't save her father from himself, she's determined—and well equipped—to help John avoid that sad fate.

But it's not going to be easy work. John is furious with the slow pace of progress at Elgart Laboratories. "While people are dying!" he rages. "While thousands suffer—*they* stand still! Well, I'm not going to be one of them. I can't. Now is the time for work, he says, for some *real* work."

Unknown to his associates or even to Linda, John has proposed his treatment to an old man named Fitzsimmons who is riddled with cancer of the stomach. Fitzsimmons has no more than six months to live in any case, and he agrees of his own accord to participate. "I'm gonna kick off anyway, ain't I?"

After much soul-searching and deliberation, John decides to go ahead with his plan. Working alone in his home, referring to a thin volume which seems to be his Bible in this procedure, Preston begins the treatment.

He freezes the old man, according to a rigid formula, and then thaws him out in exactly the manner in which the animals had been thawed—by training a pencil-thin ray of warm light on the patient's heart, warming it first; then stopping; then by degrees thawing the rest of the body.

It is at this delicate moment that Linda shows up unannounced. She knows John, she knows his rhythms, and she was sure that something was going on with him and his work. Now she knows her instincts were right. She takes one look at the old man, Fitzsimmons, and she knows that he's dead.

"That isn't quite correct," John tells her. "Wait," he says. "Wait and watch what happens!"

Soon, unfrozen, the temperature slowly brought back to normal, the old man begins to breathe again. After a minute or so, he is actually able to sit up. When John asks him how he feels, Fitzsimmons smiles and answers "Hell, I feel fine. How'd you do that?!" John can't hide his excitement and even Linda gives in to this moment of amazement.

But they both know it's only the first step. John makes Linda promise not to divulge what she's seen. The last thing he needs now is interference from Elgart and his cohorts… He works furiously, repeating the process six more times on Fitzsimmons—just as his Bible instructs him to do—and each time John makes the necessary changes in the formula, strengthening it for maximum effect.

At last the job is finished. Examinations show that the diseased cells in the old man's body have been killed or rendered dormant, whereas the healthy tissue remains undamaged. Six times the old man had "died" and six times he has returned to life, stronger each and every time. And now, to all evidence, he is cured. From a man doomed to death within six months, he is now a healthy and spry old gentleman. And did this miracle occur due to John's adherence to a "take it slow" approach to the problem? It most definitely did not!

Sure that his method is the answer to the world-wide problem of cancer, Dr. John Preston calls up the laboratory and advises Edmund Elgart, his staff of ten physicists, as well as doctors and scientists, to come over at once. He has something rather remarkable to show them.

They arrive and Preston tells them the story. He shows them slides proving the old man's previous condition, additional slides to demonstrate the gradual improvement; and finally he asks Doctor Frederic Curzon to make a personal examination of Fitzsimmons who has graciously consented to join them.

The examination proves definitively that the patient is now completely free of cancer. He is sound and healthy. There can be only one word for it: remarkable!

But Edmund Elgart remains his usual dour, cautious self. He wants time to consider all the science involved in what he's seen. It's not enough that the process seems to have worked. Elgart wants to know *why* it worked.

The last thing Elgart wants at this point is publicity, but that's exactly what he gets.

Someone has leaked the news and soon the press gets ahold of it. Headlines blast across the newspapers:

CANCER CURE FOUND AT LAST!

ELGART DOCTOR CONQUERS CANCER!

NO MORE CANCER!!!

Dr. Elgart is not pleased. To his strictly scientific mind, Preston acted in haste and without wisdom regardless of the significance of this discovery. And so we witness his deep annoyance with the methods John used to achieve his "miracle." And then, at the height of the publicity, a ghastly thing happens.

Fitzsimmons dies. Suddenly, violently, and for no apparent reason.

The press goes up in arms. Preston is asked to explain what has happened, but—he can't. He has no idea what has happened. Obviously, the formula was incorrect somehow; but, he can't be sure what's gone so terribly wrong. But even in his shock, he insists that he's on the right path, that, given time…

But the headlines continue to shout him down:

DR. PRESTON'S CURE BACKFIRES!

FITZSIMMONS DIES!

PRESTON UNABLE TO EXPLAIN TRAGEDY!

ELGART DOCTOR ACCUSED OF MANSLAUGHTER!

ACTED IN HASTE!

On and on it goes, hammering away.

A consoling Linda is present at John's house when he gets a visit from Edmund Elgart. His message is crystal clear; this tragic death is on Preston's hands. Worse still, the freezing experiments have been set back for God knows how long. It might be years—decades before the public will forget about his fiasco.

"It might have worked, John," Elgart says, "If you'd given it time. But no, you were in a hurry. You're always in a hurry. And now, as a result of one mistake, and all the publicity that has come with that one mistake, the world must wait twice as long for the cure. You didn't only kill that old man, Dr. Preston—you killed hundreds of thousands of innocent people who might have been saved if we'd perfected the freezing technique. But now..."

Deeply moved, John Preston asks to be allowed to resign from the lab. But Elgart's shakes his head. "No, John, I won't make it that easy for you. You're a brilliant and valuable man, and brilliant and valuable men are extremely difficult to find. No, I won't accept your resignation. You got us into this mess, and I'm going to give you the chance to get us out."

John accepts Elgar's decision without a word.

"But whatever I think about your methods, I know that you've been working extremely hard and your nerves have to be very raw just now. What I want you to do—instead of quitting—is take some time off. Go on a vacation of some kind. Take a couple of months, let things cool down. Then come back. I think... I hope you've learned you lesson."

"I have, sir," John replies.

"Good. And say, why don't you take Miss Carmody along with you... it occurs to me that she hasn't had a vacation in several years either. How does that sound, John?"

"That sounds...excellent, sir. Thank you." John nods and holds his silence, but when Elgart leaves he slams his fist down hard upon the desk.

"John!" Linda exclaims, suddenly alarmed. "What are you doing?"

"You heard him, didn't you? I've robbed thousands of people of a chance to be cured of cancer. Do you think I can live with that knowledge, Linda? Do you!"

"But, darling, it wasn't your fault. You were trying to—"

John stares intensely for a long beat before crossing to his desk and unlocking one of the drawers. He removes an old book, the markings of which indicate that it is a book on medicine.

"I need to show you something," he tells her. "I've never shared this with anyone; I've never trusted anyone enough."

He holds the book up for her to see.

"It's called *Frozen Therapy*; printed more than fifteen years ago. It was written by one of the greatest—and most neglected minds in the medical profession. His name was—or *is* Dr. Rudolph Moray and he—"

There's obviously more to the story, but John stops there. The silence hangs heavily in air between them.

"Do you believe in me?" he asks Linda.

"You know the answer to that question, John. I believe in you completely" she answers. Her hand reaches out to lovingly touch his shoulder.

John goes on to explain to her that Doctor Moray is the author of the book. He was one of the first to recognize the possibilities of frozen therapy as a cure for cancer, as well as other similar diseases; killers like leukemia, Bright's Disease, on and on. "He was a real pioneer, but—" But Doctor Moray, just like John Preston, was not content to sit still while the gears of science ground slowly into action. He experimented and was forced to withdraw from the University at which he was a full professor; a "panel of his peers" made it clear they didn't appreciate the way he worked. They ordered him to stick with protocol or else. Nobody knows what happened after that, what research Dr. Moray pursued. The only thing that was known was that he exiled himself to an island somewhere in Canada, where he published *Frozen Therapy* at his own expense. It was condemned at the time as the work of a crackpot, a charlatan. After that, there were reports that Doctor Moray had died—or, at any rate, disappeared. No one ever saw him again.

"And I'm absolutely convinced that science lost a very great man, Linda! A very great man!"

Linda Carmody studies the face of the man she loves. And then she says; "There's more to this, isn't there, John? There's something on your mind. Tell me what it is."

The words are aching to come out, but John hesitates.

"I can't help you if you won't tell me," she gently asks.

John exhales and tells Linda that his faith in the frozen therapy method is as strong as ever. Whatever happened with the old man, he still believes in the science of the method. Somehow he made a mistake in his preparations; somehow there was something he's left out. Now, if he could visit Doctor Moray's former home—it was also his laboratory—perhaps he could find some notes or papers that would show him how he'd gone wrong. After all, he'd gotten the idea from Moray in the first place, hadn't he? It seems like the least he could do; to not give up now; not after what has happened.

John insists that he do this alone. It wouldn't be safe for Linda to accompany him, for it would involve considerable travelling, some very long hours and perhaps even some danger. Too many unknowns. Linda says she understands and agrees to stay behind.

But the next day, as John boards the train to Banff, Canada, Linda appears in his Pullman car roomette, bearing a smile and a ticket. "I used to be a nurse," she says, "and I have the feeling that you just might need one around."

The train ride to Banff provides them with something neither is used to; time with each other; time for the chemistry between them to create the passion that exists between them. But even now, John seems preoccupied with what lies ahead. What will they find? Will they find anything? Everything? Linda is also excited by the possibilities of unlocking the code to this amazing cure. But she's also worried about the man she loves. Ever since Elgart's lecture about lives lost because of John's mistake, he seems driven—like a man possessed.

When they arrive at Silver Rock Lake—the tiny one-time resort area that had been Doctor's Moray's last home and laboratory, they rent a boat from a lakeside resident named Barney Collins. He is reluctant to turn the craft over to them when they mention that Doctor Moray's home is their destination. "Stay offa the island, I tell ya," he snorts, pointing to the tiny knob of land in the middle of the cold blue water. "Ain't sayin' why. Just sayin'. Stay off."

John presses a twenty-dollar bill in the oldster's hand and asks for details. But the old guy can only give him disconnected, rather wild snatches of the story. Even so, it is certainly a fantastic one. Rudolph Moray is described as an eccentric, half-mad professor, without soul or heart. "Brilliant, mebbe; but not a good man. Nah, not a bit of it."

Barney Collins parts with his boat at John's insistence as well as the incentive of another twenty dollar bill in his weathered palm. "I'm a doctor, too," John tells him, "and I thought Miss Carmody and I might find some notes we could put to good use at the hospital. Surely you wouldn't want to interfere with work like that, would you?"

They set off in the boat. "Well," Linda says, shuddering slightly at the sight of the crumbling, two-storey house set squarely in the middle of the island, "it's certainly a weird yarn. I wonder what all the equipment is that Moray was supposed to have brought on to the island—and for heaven's sake, what use would large animals be to him?"

"I'm not sure." According to Collins, the boat keeper, Doctor Moray had made constant trips back and forth across the lake, lugging heavy electronic equipment; and equally heavy cages, with things in them that were alive... "Then one night he just up and disappeart. Just like that, I tell ya! Moray's skiff's still moored at the island, if it ain't sunk yet—nobody goes messing around over there. Nobody! We didn't hear from the Doc for a month after he took the gorilla—yep, that's what it was, I'm tellin' ya: a regular zoo gorilla!—and we knew his supplies couldn't of lasted that long—so we went to have a peek, way back then. Place was deserted. Not a soul on the whole island... Man nor beast. Searched it good, too. And there weren't anything. Or anybody."

"How do you figure it? John asked.

"There ain't no figuring it, that's the whole trouble. Unless you believe that that gorilla tossed the Doc into the lake and then jumped in after him... An' even if that had a happened, the body woulda come up to the surface. But I want you to know, we dragged that area good and proper. There ain't no bodies in this here lake, Doctor Preston. An' none o' that electronic equipment ever showed up neither. So looky here, why don't you just stay away now and don't mess around with it? There's big trouble over on that chunk a mud there. Don't know what kind exactly, but trouble sure enough..."

John and Linda tie up at the island and they walk down a little stone path that leads to the house. It is a monstrous structure, in a gross state of disrepair. It's obvious that it has stood against the weather alone and unaided for at least a decade. The windows are dark and forbidding, and the wooden slats are stained with wind and time.

John looks somewhat embarrassed; clearly he had not expected this Mad Doctor routine. His hero, his mentor, this brilliant mind tilting against the windmills of lesser talents; here referred to as "mad"—and without soul and heart.

Sensing his discomfort, Linda finds a way to inject a touch of humor into the moment. "Face it, Johnny, if you were all alone out here in the middle of nowhere, you'd probably have a joint just like this one. Don't blame the professor—we all know that scientists are notorious for their lack of taste!"

John laughs uneasily and they enter the house.

The furniture is gray-white with thick layers of dust, the floors are creaky and warped, and the walls are stained; no one has been here for years, that much is certain.

He goes through the living room to what appears to be the library. He sees a desk and goes through it, but, aside from a curiously antique set of keys—which he pockets—- he can find nothing of value.

In his investigation, however, he does find that the window sill crumbles in his hand. It is dry rot, which means that probably the entire house is unstable. Then, suddenly, as if to validate this observation, he is startled by a shrill scream and whips his head around to catch a glimpse of Linda as she falls through the rotted floorboards. He dashes over and stares into the murk. "Linda! Linda, are you all right?"

"I—think so."

He shines a pocket flash and spots Linda, crumpled on the floor, nursing a sore ankle.

John lets himself down, and they find themselves in a sort of a basement. One which does not seem to coincide with the overall scheme of the house.

They walk to a large door; it opens with difficulty. Below is a twisting flight of crude stone steps, leading to blackness.

John suggests that Linda stay behind while he investigates.

"Stay here by myself?" she protests. "No, thank you. I'm coming along."

Together they walk down the circular stairs, and encounter yet another door. This one is of heavy iron. And it is locked.

John tries it a few times with no success. He is about to walk away when he remembers the keys he picked up in the library. He tries one of the keys; it doesn't work; tries another—it fits perfectly. He turns it. There is a rusty sound.

The door opens. And John and Linda are faced with a sight which causes them both to gasp.

It is a room of ice. Blue and white and crystalline glacial ice! A strange interior palace, refrigerator-cold, and coruscating with a million lights.

Linda cries out. "John—look!" John's eyes follow her horrified gaze and he sees—imbedded, imprisoned in the ice—two figures. One is an ancient man with a deadly look of peace to him; and the other—an immense, and strangely grotesque gorilla.

"That man—it must be Doctor Moray," says Linda.

"No," John tells her. "I've seen photographs of Moray. That isn't him."

They build a fire and begin to chip at the ice. Soon they have the two bodies removed. The first, the man, is most certainly dead. But the other, the gorilla, is still breathing. He's alive!

They leave the simian on a table and rush upstairs for equipment.

But when they return, the gorilla is gone.

They are about to bolt, in fear, when they are stopped by a voice. "You will pardon the condition of my laboratory. I don't often have visitors, you see..."

"Doctor Moray!"

It is indeed Doctor Rudolph Moray. He tells John and Linda a fantastic story—how he has lived here, underground, for the last ten years, working alone—without success. "As for the gorilla, it revived," he tells them, "and seems to have stumbled into the central shaft over there. It's a drop of several hundred feet, I'm afraid. No question that it is dead."

"But how long had it been frozen?"

"Not long," replies Moray. "By the way, I've become such a recluse... would you mind telling me what year it is?"

"1956."

Moray, a hawk-faced, gray-haired man with intense eyes, starts slightly at the information; then relaxes. "Of course."

Moray goes on to tell John that he's had to abandon his experiments, owing to lack of equipment. He now knows that radiation absorption is a necessary step before freezing; and he hints that if man were possessed of certain animal characteristics...perhaps it would be possible to cure every known disease by frozen therapy. Before his funding ran out, Moray was working on that very thing. For instance, with the gorilla's strength and resistance, certain of its glandular characteristics might enable a human being to make better use of the freezing therapy, if only...

Excited by what he's hearing, possibilities swimming in his imagination, Doctor Preston makes Moray a proposition. "See here, doctor, the day of the lone-wolf scientist is past. It's a lesson I learned only through a terrible experience. But if we are to accomplish anything, I see now that it must be done in a strictly scientific manner. Together, as a team. You've proved it, and so have I—recently."

Linda can't help but smile hearing these words come from John. They are the words of reason and maturity. They signify something that rarely happens in humans, whether they are of the brilliant type or not. They signify growth.

"The idea you have originated is excellent," John continues. "It can work. So—why don't you come back to the city with me, join the staff at Elgart. I know they would be happy to have you. Then the two of us could work together, with all of the lab's vast resources at our disposal..."

Moray thinks it over and agrees. He'll give the scientific world another chance.

But it's late and he is extremely tired. He suggests they spend the night and all leave first thing in the morning.

That night turns out to be filled with the bizarre and fantastic; how much of it is real and how much imagined or dreamed is not exactly clear.

Doctor Moray, wide awake in his room, is staring at the list of names of the men who forced his withdrawal from the medical profession and from the university. Slowly, strangely, he begins to *change*. His body grows large and simian in appearance, and shortly he has become the monster we saw earlier trapped in the ice.

The monster prowls the halls of the house, stopping at Linda's room. He enters and is about to—God knows what! But John awakens when he hears Linda's screams and comes rushing to her aid. The beast bursts away and disappears down the hall...

John goes to Moray's room and finds the man asleep. Moray professes to know nothing of the beast. "You must have been dreaming..." he says. "Gorillas on the brain, I suppose." Given the strangeness of the day, and of the place, it's quite possible. And so John and Linda choose to return to sleep.

The next morning, Moray joins John and Linda and they all go to New York. To John's irritated surprise, Elgart is not at all happy about the idea of hiring Moray. In fact, he refuses to do so. He remembers all too well how difficult Moray can be and he wants no part of that. Especially not after all the bad publicity the Laboratory received after the death of Fitzsimmons.

"It doesn't matter," Moray says to John once they are alone. "We'll work together, you and me. With the resources of the lab… And don't worry. I'll find us plenty of suitable subjects."

Moray persuades John to break into the lab and together they put the mighty radiation machines to work.

Moray begins to show up with what he calls "derelicts" as subjects for their ongoing experiments. They work at a furious pace and, once again, Linda grows worried for John. That gleam of ambition, that tunnel vision that led to the tragedy of Fitzsimmons. It's back. And Linda fears for him.

Moray, and only Moray knows that his so-called "derelicts" are actually the men who were responsible for his expulsion from the university. These were the men who destroyed his work before, and now they are going to pay in the most horrible way.

Also known only to Moray is that once every twemty-four hours he is transformed into the beast we saw back on the island. It *was* him that Linda saw back in the house. But now this transformation helps to keep Moray off any list of suspects that the police might have as they investigate the sudden disappearance of some of the more prominent scientists and professors in the city. There were eyewitnesses who swore they saw a gorilla committing these heinous acts, but nobody reports the sighting of an old, bespectacled scientist.

Whether by accident or by Moray's secret plan, John is horrified to see that all of their experiments have failed. Maybe it's the balance between radiation and dosage. Whatever it is, all the subjects die.

Doctor Moray's transformations are becoming more and more frequent, more and more unpredictable. The "antidote" that he takes to change himself back into a human is becoming weaker and weaker. He does everything he can to control the cycle, but he's losing his ability to do so. He is quickly going mad and it isn't long before John realizes what has happened. John witnesses the change and he begins to realize just who these "subjects" are. And now it's John's life that is in grave danger. There is no reasoning with Moray. His need for revenge is too great. His fury at these men who thwarted his dreams of success is too strong. And if John dares to stand in his way...

When Moray realizes that John is going to turn him in, he resolves to make John his next victim.

But this time when the "transformation" occurs, there is no going back. John has found and hidden the antidote. A call to the police and the location of their killer—a beast that science created—becomes much easier.

It all ends in a hail of bullets. The gorilla-beast is killed; by the police? By his own ambition...? Surely both played a part in this ending. It is only in death that the creature resumes the form of a brilliant but terribly flawed old man, at peace at last.

And now the conversation between John and Linda takes on new meaning. It is the wisdom of her words, her repeated warnings that finally ring true for him.

With hat in hand, Doctor John Preston begs forgiveness from Edmund Elgart; his lessons hard learned.

COPYRIGHT INFORMATION